PAID IN GOLD AND BLOOD

By

Lazette Gifford

Copyright 2014 Lazette Gifford

An ACOA Publication

www.aconspiracyofauthors.com

Katashan left behind his past; all the good and the bad, including his belief that the gods would help him in a time of need. Moving to a new land, he has every intention of starting a new life. What he finds, though, is the body of a woman sacrificed at the foot of a statue to a benevolent Goddess. Katashan is soon caught up in a mix of magical and political troubles -- and drawing far too much attention from the gods he no longer serves.

Paid in Gold and Blood
A Conspiracy of Authors Publication
www.aconspiracyofauthors.com
Copyright 2015, Lazette Gifford
ISBN: 978-1-936507-55-9
Cover Art Copyright 2015, Lazette Gifford

First Print Edition, July 2015

This novel is dedicated to all the wonderful authors who have captivated me with their tales and made me hope that someday I could do the same.

CHAPTER ONE

At Silver Pass the snow still stood knee deep except where others had trudged through and flattened the dirty white to mud and ice. A frigid wind swept over the white-capped mountains and felt like the cold hand of death itself against any uncovered skin. Katashan pulled his heavy cloak closer and tried not to notice the bone-aching chill. Emista himself, the old God of Ice, could still rule in a place like this where summer probably never reached.

In a few more steps he topped the crest of the high mountain pass and stopped to stare at the distant golden shore and sapphire sea far below. He waited for a feeling elation at seeing the end of his five month journey and the new future the distant view promised.

Unfortunately, he'd already wearied of too many new beginnings in his life. He couldn't look at the sparkling sea and the land of Cyrenia and believe they promised him any better life than what he'd already given up: the good and the bad, and all of it lost to him now. At best, this was simply somewhere different and not haunted by old memories.

The windswept silence suddenly filled with the bray of donkeys and the inharmonious yell of the caravan master. The rest of Katashan's traveling companions would soon make their way up the trail to this final pass along the Old Iron Road. Tyren, the shaggy, unkempt caravan master, urged the others on. He had a voice that could wake the dead, but as far as Katashan could tell it had no influence whatsoever on either the thirty donkeys or the half dozen workers in his employ.

Tyren had been an odd companion for someone like Katashan who had spent a few years serving in the temples of home. The caravan master believed in every omen and superstition, while at the same time he cursed gods and men alike. It had made a very long, and loud, journey.

Tyren did have his virtues, though. The man knew every trail, village and ford between Taris and Cyrenia. He also had no problem taking hire from a northerner, even though Katashan might be unpopular where they traveled. The war between Cyrenia and Taris had ended only three short years before and trouble still erupted along the border now and then.

Katashan had hurried ahead of the caravan to do more than gawk at the welcoming sight of the Inner Sea. Stone-carved Verina Guardians -- waist high images of the kneeling Goddess -- stood sentinel at every important locality along the ancient Iron Road. The statues represented an old religion now in abeyance in the south since the old Taris Empire had long since fallen into smaller, often warring, kingdoms.

Katashan hadn't realized he could feel any affection for the Gods who had turned their backs on him when he had needed them most. Yet the first time he had seen the kneeling statue of Verina, protector of travelers, he'd felt an odd stirring in his heart. During the long journey he'd stopped at every Verina statue and made a token offering of food or drink. He had served in her temple for a few years when he was younger and the memory came back as calm and pleasant -- one of the few he did not mind remembering. Those days seemed so long ago now, that it might have been another person who had prayed at the altars and wished all travelers in the world peace and safety.

A shame those prayers had never been saved for himself.

At first Tyren and his men had scoffed at the superstitious northerner, but as the journey progressed with few problems, he saw the caravan master eyeing the old Goddess with some consideration. It amused Kastashan to think he may have helped to reintroduce a piece of the old religion to counter the apostasy of the south, where the Cyrenian monarchy had immediately introduced new gods as soon as they broke allegiance with Taris.

"Up! Up ye' damned beasts!" Tyren bellowed and the donkeys answered in much the same tone. Soon the pack would catch up with him. After so many months on the trail, Katashan knew better than to waste the few precious moments he had to himself.

However, even knowing where to look, he still had trouble finding the Verina Guardian for this pass. He had started to believe --being this close to the Cyrenian heartland -- that it had been thrown down during the wars.

Then he spotted the very top of the statue's head showing through a snowdrift off to the right, farther from the trail than he had expected. By then he could also hear the plodding step of the lead donkeys and knew he didn't have much time if he wanted a moment to say his thanks in private for having had such a trouble free journey.

Getting to the statue wasn't easy this time. He tried not to curse as he forced his way through the ice-crusted snowdrifts. Katashan had always believed the Gods listened at the worst of times, and he had already dared their ire too often in the past to take a chance with careless words now. He even bit back a curse when his foot caught on a snow-covered limb that sent him sprawling at the feet of the Guardian.

Katashan stood and quickly brushed snow from his pants and cloak. Tyren had almost topped the rise, all but dragging the lead donkey with him. Katashan took the last step and reached out, brushing snow from the covered statue --

The stone felt uncommonly warm and should have melted the snow for several feet around the shrine if this had been true heat. What he felt was magic and that could not be good.

"There you be," Tyren said from behind him. "Why'd ya not take the cleared path to your Guardian? Never struck me as a snow lover."

Path? Katashan turned and could clearly see the stone-lined trail a few steps to his left. He could not possibly have missed the path before, except that the Goddess intended him to trample through the snow.

And even fall as he had.

She would not have done so on a whim. The Gods had never shown a taste for burlesque before, though irony and farce seemed common enough. So why send --

"Damn," he whispered, despite himself.

Katashan quickly retraced the three steps back to where he had fallen. He knelt, ignoring the cold, and brushed snow away from the limb . . . and found frozen cloth beneath and then fingers, blue as the ocean below.

"What norther ritual is it this time?" Tyren demanded as the rest of the caravan began to move past, his men anxiously herding the laden donkeys onward.

"Tether the animals and bring a blanket," Katashan ordered. He looked up into Tyren's scowling face. "I've found a body."

CHAPTER TWO

Tyren stood close by shaking his head, his matted hair bouncing from side-to-side. He snarled curses barely loud enough to be heard as Katashan carefully brushed snow from the body, uncovering an arm, a shoulder . . . a woman. Tyren would do nothing to help. Neither would his men, of course, though they all gathered at the trail to watch and mumble about bad omens.

Katashan didn't feel better about the discovery than they did. However he knew matters would be far worse if he walked away from something the Goddess had so obviously indicated she wanted him to handle.

As he uncovered her -- a young woman, her golden hair shimmering with ice crystals -- he noted her ankles and wrists had been tied with a silken rope. The frozen blue silk of her expensive dress showed no rips and he saw no bruises on her ice pale skin. The woman had come here without a battle, either willingly or drugged.

The blade that had killed her still rested hilt deep in her breast where it had pushed through blue silk cloth and pierced her heart. There wasn't much blood staining the dress, so she had died quickly and had not been left to freeze to death. He couldn't guess how long ago this had happened since the body showed no signs of decay. It wouldn't in this winter land, but he still felt as though this had not been done more than a few months before.

The knife was no ordinary weapon; gemstones formed a spiral pattern on the long jade hilt and he could see the edge of a design etched into the silver of the blade itself. This looked like a very easy weapon to trace and he mistrusted its presence for that very reason. No one would purposely leave such a clue behind.

"What do ye plan to do with it?" Tyren demanded.

"Her," Katashan corrected as he stood. He pushed his half frozen fingers up under his arms and looked at the trail where even the donkeys appeared anxious to go on. Contrary creatures. "I suppose we ought to take her back to the fort at the upper pass --"

"Ah, no." Tyren said with a shake of his shaggy head as he glanced over his shoulder. "Took us a full day ta' hike down ta' here. It would take two, maybe three goin' back up. Times bad enough, but supplies are low."

"Excellent point," Katashan said. "Is there some place closer?"

"Chances be she came from the mountain village there along the trail," he said, pointing to where a path traced along the summit and leading into the trees. "Half a day. No way to take the caravan, but you could get her there --"

"I don't think she's from the mountains," Katashan reluctantly said. "She's not dressed for the cold. I think she must have come from one of the shore villages. Are there many close by?"

"Two days ta' the closest," he said, and looked even more unhappy. "What would she be doin' up here, so far from the shore?"

Katashan could see no way around the truth though he dreaded making the situation worse. They would have to know before they moved the body, though.

"Someone brought her here, bound in chains, and

murdered her."

Silence greeted those words. Tyren held his place but the rest of his men had backed up a few steps, wrists crossed and palms held outward in a sign to ward against evil -- and they were right because this had been *evil*. The woman had been murdered at the foot of a benevolent Goddess, who wished harm to no one. The act had perverted the place.

"Want nothin' ta' do with this," Tyren said. "This can't be good."

"No, this isn't good," Katashan agreed. He tried to warm his fingers again. "But we cannot leave her here unless you wish to risk the wrath of the Goddess."

Tyren glanced nervously at the statue and frowned in annoyance. However, having spent so long with Tyren, Katashan knew the caravan master would not ignore such a possibility. He was a superstitious, though not truly religious, man. Katashan hated to use the ploy against him, but he would need help.

Just as he expected, Tyren muttered a curse or a prayer, and stomped his way across the snow pack. He stopped over the body, glaring though his look softened a moment later.

"Young," he said shaking his head. "Not her fault. Damned fancy blade that killed her and she be a shore dweller, it's true. It wouldn't be right to take her elsewhere and we can't leave her here to upset your Goddess. We'll take her down wrapped in blankets and packed in snow. I'll make a travois."

"Thank you." Katashan knelt and began to carefully brush more of the snow away from around her. "Someone is bound to ask how we found her. I'm going to make certain there are no clues nearby. I'll move her when you're ready to leave."

Tyren looked relieved to find that Katashan would handle the body. He nodded and went back to his men, shouting orders and brooking no disagreement this time. Katashan did see him cast one plaintive look toward the distant shore though; this close to the end of the journey and they had to find trouble!

Katashan waited until everyone had gone out of sight where they gathered wood and blankets for the travois. Then, his fingers tingling, he began to carefully brush the snow away from the area around her body.

He found the first glyph to the left of her shoulder, almost even with the blade in her heart. The pattern had been carved into the dirt and filled with sand and the sand and then fused to glass with the power of the spell. This had been a sacrifice, not just a murder, but he had known that already. What he hadn't known for certain until he saw the first glyph was if the person who had worked the spell had known what he was doing.

Unfortunately, he looked as though he had known far too well.

"Goddess guide me," Katashan whispered. He swept his hand over the rest of the glyphs to the left of the first and quickly dislodging the snow. One glyph curled into another: life, bondage, death.

He heard the tinkle of ice and the body twitched.

Katashan covered the glyphs over again, his heart thumping and his hands almost aching with the cold and the power mixing in the touch. The body went still but he could already feel other forces beginning to stir and gather nearby.

For a brief moment he considered leaving her and reporting the find to the first authorities they found. He didn't want to be involved in anything like this, not in a place so far from his home and with no personal prestige to back him up if he ran into trouble. However, Verina had obviously brought him here for a reason. Unlike any other hapless traveler, he could read the glyphs and feel the magic all around him, calling to the magic in his own blood.

Verina wanted this work undone and the taint removed from her shrine. He could do the work, though not all today with people so close by. The first step would be to take the body away from the powerful glyphs. He slowly stood, turned his back to where the others still searched for suitable wood, and crossed to the statue.

After another glance to make certain no one stood too near, he withdrew the small black-handled knife he kept on a chain and always close to his heart. The blessed silver blade held magic of its own and was a dangerous relic of his past, but one he dared not part with since it would be far more dangerous in the hands of anyone else. He whispered the ritual, trusting the Goddess would not fault him for being discreet.

His hand didn't tremble as he made a small slit in his left wrist, even though he had not done this act in many long years. The blood flowed quickly into her upheld hands, forming a small puddle in the palms, bright red against the white of the marble. He watched, silently praying and hoping -- and starting to feel light headed --

The blood seeped into the stone and disappeared. *Accepted.* With a feeling of relief mixed with dread -- he didn't want to be involved with the Gods again -- he laid the silver blade against the wound and quickly whispered words that seared the cut shut with a sharp, hot pain.

He stumbled back to the body, almost grateful when he could kneel once more in the snow, even though he now had a new awareness of the delicate magic all around the area. The power tingled and stung like fire ants moving up his arms and he'd never felt anything like it before.

Katashan could hear Tyren and his men coming back up the incline from their foray into the woods. Katashan had no time for subtlety or to reacquaint himself with magic he hadn't used in far too many years. He wrapped both hands around the fancy blade that had killed the young woman and whispered a quick incantation, dispelling as much of the ritual's power as he could as he pulled the knife up and out.

Power fled from the blade in a flash of blue light and a

surge of power. He dropped the blade to the side of the body and took his own ritual blade from around his neck -- still red with a little of his own blood -- and cut at the glyphs. The magic dispelled so quickly it called a wind in the void and snow blew up from the ground and flew around him, sending a chill through the world.

He looked up and saw an outline in the veil of white: a human shape, reaching for him.

"Away!" He held up his left hand, power flashing bright from his fingers as he ordered the specter back.

The shape fled with a howl of wind and the sudden storm disappeared as quickly as it had arisen. He could hear shouts of surprise and dismay from Tyren and his men who likely felt the dark power in that wind even if they didn't understand the implications.

However the danger had gone, though he couldn't say for how long. The magic here had lessened and he needed to move quickly because it hadn't gone far. He strung the ritual blade back over his neck and under his shirt, then put the blade that had killed her in his pack.

Katashan picked up the body and carried her to the trail, anxious to be away from this place, even though he took part of the trouble with him and feared more would follow.

CHAPTER THREE

They left Silver Pass, the donkeys picking up speed on the downward slope and men trotting along at a good pace. Katashan could have wished them to travel with less fervor towards the distant shores, however warm and inviting they looked. The magic had left him weak though he dared not show it and risk the others asking questions. Instead, he trudged along at the end of the caravan, keeping pace with the travois carrying the body. They'd attached it to the last, and most placid, donkey. He kept his arm on the donkey's rump, grateful for even that much aid to keep to his feet.

Katashan often glanced down at the snow-shrouded form. She bothered him in ways the others wouldn't understand. Power clung to her long after they left the mountain top, and he couldn't shake the feeling that whatever had tried to grab him back at the site still followed behind, malevolent and unhappy at his tampering.

Tyren stopped at the snowline and silently helped Katashan pack more snow in around the body even while his men mumbled and glared. The day had moved to late afternoon, the growing shadows ominous and uninviting. Once they started downward he couldn't always see the ocean, except occasionally when the view cleared of trees and rock. Closer, each time, though still too far away. And what safety would there be in the lowlands anyway?

"We be movin' faster now," Tyren warned as he stood, brushing his hands against his dirty cloak though Katashan could tell it wasn't the snow he tried so desperately to wipe away. "I want to reach the caravansary before dark."

Katashan nodded empathically. He wanted inside walls tonight, behind the safety of wood and stone, where he could surreptitiously set a quick ward. This was not a night to make an open camp. After Tyren left him, he paused only long enough to make certain they had the body secured for rougher travel. He stood and swatted the donkey before Tyren had a chance to complain about another delay. They began jogging down the gentle slope, and then up again over a foothill. No one paused and he heard few comments over the next few miles as they climbed and descended again at turns. They made a steady pace and by evening he could clearly catch the scent of the sea on the breeze.

Over the next hill they reached a slope filled with the decimated stumps of trees, probably cut away by the lowlanders, which meant they were closer to civilization. A fog began to build near the ground, wrapping the stumps and twisted saplings in ghostly white arms. As the sun sank lower in the sky the shapes changed colors, taking on a hint of red and blood.

His fingers began to tingle; not a good sign. Katashan dared a quick glance over his shoulder and found the fog following him in thin tendrils and closing in. He still felt the whisper of magic from the body as well, and he feared that it drew *something* towards them.

From the way the others began to pick up speed again, he thought they sensed something wrong as well. The donkeys spooked at a sudden gust of wind and even the men had trouble keeping up with them as they hurled themselves onward. Katashan purposely fell behind, placing himself between the body and whatever followed them.

He didn't dare use any magic openly. The southerners

banned the art and occasionally had a habit of rising up and killing anyone they suspected of having the ability, at least during the war. Magic was associated with the hated Taris northerners. Katashan had known about their distrust before he headed for Cyrenia, but since he'd intended to leave all the trappings of his former life behind, it hadn't mattered to him. And now, barely a day into the new land, and he'd already broken his vow. Somehow that didn't seem like a good omen.

Katashan briefly considered abandoning the body, but leaving a receptacle of power discarded on the road, and within reach of something that obviously wanted it, didn't sound like a good idea.

They pushed on over the rolling hillside and down towards the base of the mountain, breathless now and even the donkeys panting as they topped another small hill. The fog had gathered in the ravine behind them and there he could see shapes forming and shifting in the near darkness. If there had been even the least bit of breeze he could have pretended it was normal.

Tyren gave an inarticulate yell that startled everyone, but a moment later Katashan could see the light from a building somewhere not far ahead. The others, seeing shelter so close and the night nearly upon them, did not look back. Katashan slowed, and stopped at the top of the final incline. He spun, pulling the knife from beneath his tunic once more. The blade flashed in the dark, magic drawing magic out.

He hadn't a chance for any subtlety this time. He quickly stabbed at his finger, slicing it open, and spattering the ground as he cast a hastily whispered spell. The magic brightened for a moment drawing a line between him and the oncoming enemy. The misty almost-human shapes drew back. They would have to abandon the path to reach him and the body. Traveling over unbroken ground would slow these unformed creatures. Paths gave access to more than mundane traffic. In fact, some magical apparitions couldn't find their way at all, except by the paths traveled and clearly marked.

"Hey, you fool norther," Tyren yelled from somewhere far down the path. "Get ye'r ass moving or ye'll spend the night outside with the fog!"

That sounded like a particularly bad idea. Katashan shoved the little blade back into place beneath his tunic and turned around, holding his hand clinched closed as he jogged toward the building set back from the cliff side. He could hear the ocean not far away, but he couldn't see it in the growing dark and fog.

The path curved slightly at the base of the hill, and there Katashan found a single, low building of some length and an open-sided stable to the right. High walls surrounded the complex, and Tyren's men already had the first donkeys through a gate and into a yard. By the time Katashan arrived the animals had gathered, still fully laden, by the water trough and hay. Several of the caravan workers had gone in after them and began stripping away the bags from the creatures' backs, ferrying them from one man to another and into a shed that they closed and a local locked up for them. The men didn't go near the donkey pulling the travois and once they reached the gate Katashan hurried to turn the poor creature loose. The animal had done a good job with little complaint and he plodded on inside the walls to join the others.

The rest of the people avoided him when he stepped inside, leaving the body outside the gate for a moment while he got a feel for this place. He saw crossed-wrists when they saw him and distrust in their eyes. Word had already spread to the main building, and he saw a group of strangers arrive at the doorway, scowl, and go back in.

He could hear horses in the stables beyond the yard where the donkeys had been tuned loose, and the sounds of contentious men inside the building. The scent of food, laden with strange spices, filled the air. He would have rushed to that food on another night, but right now the scent almost made him ill.

He started to take the body inside the gate and to the stables. Then he realized the horses would not brook a dead body near them, especially one so laden with magic. The members of the caravan would not be happy with a dead body in their sleeping quarters either.

He didn't intend to sit outside the walls in the cold with it, though. Not on a night like this.

"Tyren is there another building?" he asked. "I'll take her and stay there for the night."

"You'll stay with the body? Why not just leave her out there?" Tyren said with a flick of his fingers towards the gate.

"Because it would not be wise to leave her to fate and wolves tonight, would it?" he said, still trying to keep his calm. Fog rolled in around the building and he couldn't tell if it came naturally or with a purpose. "We have, you know, taken her from the place where she was murdered --"

"Sacrificed," Tyren said. He spat on the ground, and growled an inarticulate curse as he realized the implications at last. His eyes looked up the road and then darted to the fog tendrils moving restlessly around the walls. "Damn you, norther!"

"Once the Goddess directed us to her, what could we do?" Katashan asked, trying to remain calm. "In a choice between making enemies of Verina, or someone who must seek power, I will side with the Goddess every time."

"You bastard. You knew what you were getting us into, didn't you?"

Tyren's men had gathered, glaring and unfriendly. Katashan didn't want a confrontation, especially since he couldn't expect to find allies here.

"We should have left the body," Tyren insisted. "You've

brought unnatural trouble down on us!"

"You know that's not --"

Tyren reached for him, and Katashan barely danced back out of the way. He saw a flash of fire in Tyren's eyes and suddenly suspected there might be other magic at work here, magnifying the darker emotions of the men who, wisely, wanted nothing to do with trouble of this kind. Katashan felt an uncommon urge to throw himself into the fight as well, but he lifted his hand and when Tyren swung, he blocked the blow and left a small smear of blood on the man's tawdry cloak.

Katashan stepped back and muttered a quick spell, hoping the words sounded like a curse in his own language. He knew Tyren spoke some Tarisian, but he hoped the caravan master's rage precluded his understanding very well just then.

Tyren swung again, hitting Katashan in the shoulder and sending him sprawling against the trough and startling the donkeys. However, the fight seemed to go out of the man with that blow, though not his anger. Katashan suspected, under the circumstances, that part might be real. He could not even blame Tyren for it.

Katashan got back to his feet, shaking his hand and spattering a few more drops of blood on the ground as he *cursed* under his breath again. He hoped he had managed enough magic to hold back the darker forces until he could ward the compound.

"Is there another building where I can stay with her for the night?" he asked once more, keeping his voice calm, even in the face of Tyren's rage.

"There be a hay shed," Tyren said, nodding curtly beyond the stable area. "Take her there, and mind that you don't upset the horses or we'll have hell to pay with the others here. We'll talk in the morning about what more is to be done."

Katashan started to mention contracts and breach of faith but that would only inflame the situation tonight. Instead, he gave a single, polite nod. Tyren herded his men and the strangers up the stairs and through to the door that led into the building. Katashan could see tables, bedding and a fire in the corner. He would have welcomed that warmth at another time.

As the caravan master reached the door, the others in ahead of him, he turned glared back at Katashan one more time.

"I'm bolting this closed," Tyren said, patting the weather-worn oak door. "Don't try to get in with us."

Katashan gave a regal bow of his head which annoyed the man. No matter. He didn't want to spend tonight with them and the journey was all but over anyway. He could find his way to the city from here, if he had to.

The door slammed shut and he heard the bang of a wooden latch shoved into place. The windows had already been shuttered, but he could clearly hear the muttering and curses of those inside.

Katashan went to examine his shelter for the night. The building looked small, but the roof was intact and the door sturdy enough to close against the chill night. Katashan peered within, his eyes narrowed against the darkness and saw nothing but hay.

Night had fully arrived and a single flickering torch by the larger building's door gave him his only light. Covered stalls stood to the right, all but three of them filled with horses. The animals watched with worried glares and looking far too much like the humans.

Tyren appeared briefly at the door, dropped a leather pouch on the step outside and pulled the door shut again with loud bang, startling all the creatures. The leather bag contained his personal supplies, so at least he wouldn't go cold and completely hungry tonight.

Time to get his companion put away so he could finish warding the building and settle in for the night. He stepped outside the gate grabbed the ropes of the travois, but as soon as he started pulling it inside, all the horses turned, their ears folded back, and looking far fiercer than he horses ought to look.

Taking a body imbued with magic past already half-panicked animals did not seem wise. He would have to get the horses settled first which meant magic and more time. He could see the tendrils of fog had moved closer to the walls and lingered at the half-open gate. Time to get that closed, at least --

As Katashan reached the gate, he unexpectedly heard the clap of horse hooves on the stone of the road. The sound echoed eerily through the night and he couldn't guess which direction the animal traveled from, though it seemed unlikely there would have been anyone this close behind them.

A moment later the sound centered on the trail to the right and within a heartbeat a ghostly figure of horse and man came into view. The rider sat wrapped in a black hooded cloak, the same color as the horse he rode, so that they looked like a single piece of the night taking shape in the mist-filled darkness. Katashan took a step back, ready to slam the gate shut.

"Ah, I made it!" the stranger said as he threw back is hood to show dark hair and a pale face. The man vaulted off his remarkably calm horse and looked around, his eyes settling on the travois and the ice-packed blankets.

"She's dead," Katashan said.

"I would certainly hope so at this point."

Someone, at least, with a sense of humor. Young, too, but he didn't seem to have the bravado of most young men Katashan had known at home.

"They're not going to let you in the building, I'm afraid," Katashan said, waving a hand towards the door. Raucous laughter and shouts erupted from the inside, and a sound that might have been a body hitting the floor. Maybe he shouldn't feel annoyed about being left out. "They're spooked by the fog and the body."

"Ah. I see." The stranger looked out at the fog and made a little dismissive gesture. "They're not from around here, then. We have such fogs quite often. But then, from your accent, you aren't from here, either. Are you a Northerner? Tarisian?"

"Yes. You are a local?"

"Mostly," he said, and flashed a smile. "I have traveled quite a bit in the service of my lady. Shall we go inside? There are bandits in the area and the weather is cool besides. I think there is a shed we can share? Providing, of course, there is room for the three of us."

"This does not bother you?" Katashan said, indicating the body.

The smile left his face. He looked older. "It bothers me a great deal. But I don't want to stand out here in the night and invite the sort of people these walls were made to protect us from. Shall we go in?"

Katashan nodded and moved aside, letting the stranger and his horse inside the wall. He started to pick up the rope to the travois again, wondering how to get the stranger away so that he could ward the walls.

"The horses are spooked. I think if I get them food and water, they'll settle."

"I'll stay here and watch," He said, and drew back his cloak. A long-bladed knife showed in a sheath. "You get to handle the horses."

Katashan glanced back out at the gate, where fog was slipping a little inside -- normal looking, but still sinister. He pushed the gate closed in haste and dropped the bar into place, though he still hadn't warded, not with someone standing this close.

"Your horse is well behaved. Do you think he can be left outside a stall tonight?"

"Night will be quite content with a little hay," he said. "And, since we are spending the night in close quarters, we should introduce ourselves. I am Peralin."

"Katashan," he said, started to bow and then offered his hand instead, the custom in the south. They clasped each other's wrist. Peralin had warm, soft skin, and had not been traveling long from the state of his clothing. Katashan, after months on the trail, and few places to bathe, felt as though he would never be clean again. "Can you take her back toward the shed? The sooner we get her out of the area with the animals, the better. I'll feed the horses and get the donkeys settled for the night."

The torch on the building wall had started to flicker fitfully already, casting out more smoke than light now. Peralin frowned as he glanced around the area, but he didn't slow to pick up the rope to the travois. He whistled to his horse and started toward the back of the enclosure, the horse following close behind.

The horse wasn't bothered by the scent of death or even magic, which made him a soldier's mount. Katashan silently thanked the Goddess for the presence of someone willing to help and not as omen-bound and skittish as his other companions.

Katashan kept an eye on Peralin until the man had slipped into the shed. Then he hurried to the gate, pulling out his blade and slicing his finger once more. He made quick dabs of blood on the bottom of the bar, out of notice, and whispered an incantation of power that ran from the gate to the wall. Fingers of fog had started to work their way through the crevices and over the top of the wall but they retreated even before he finished.

When he looked back, Peralin stood at the doorway to the shed. Katashan unobtrusively pushed the blade away and started herding the donkey's into a fenced corner of the enclosure. The black horse -- Night -- stood like a guard outside the shed. Anyone would be leery of going up against such a formidable animal.

He fed and settled the horses and donkeys and then

grabbed his pack from by the door and approached the shed. Peralin looked past towards the wall with a frown and for a moment Katashan thought he might know about the magic. If so, he said nothing.

"The night is going to be cold," Peralin said as he stepped aside. "Let's get settled, share a little dinner perhaps?"

"I have very little left in food."

"And I'm over-stocked for the short journey I'm going to make."

"You are very kind."

"And glad for the company," he said as Katashan came to the shed. Peralin had already set a little candle in place, dispelling some of the darkness. It didn't seem like such a bad place. He had even put the body at the far side with some hay packed in around her. "All in all, I thought at best I would be spending the night alone, since I had no intention of sleeping with a group of snoring, bad-tempered men. You seem the far better choice."

"And my companion?" Katashan said, nodding to the body that was settled against the wall.

"I doubt she snores."

Katashan looked back at him and weighed many things, but mostly he thought about the danger he might be putting this man in.

"Perhaps you should know something more before you make a final decision about staying here," he said and leaned against the wall as he sat down, exhausted. "I found her, bound in ropes and chains, and with a knife through her heart, at the base of a Verina Guardian. I believe she had been sacrificed and I can't guarantee that she is such safe company as she appears."

The man's dark eyes didn't flicker, though he remained still for a half dozen heartbeats. Then he shrugged. "I'm glad you told me. This makes things much easier. Here, have some wine. I think you need it."

He reached within his cloak and pulled out a decanter and two crystal goblets.

He could not have been carrying them there.

Katashan would have sensed magic had he used it. He knew of no spell strong enough to hide such power from him. This stranger had no magic. But he did have power and there was only one other way --

"Gods protect me," Katashan said, lucky he had his back to the wall. Peralin stood in the doorway and he had no chance to escape the shed and the stables before . . . whatever this was caught him.

"We shall share wine," Peralin said, putting the goblets on a ledge by the door. He poured the liquid and it sparkled as it fell, glittering in the candle light. A scent, rich and heady, filled the tiny area and left Katashan half dizzy. When Peralin held a goblet out, Katashan shook his head and pressed harder against the wall, his hand reaching for his blade.

"Don't," Peralin warned and stilled Katashan in his movement. "Take the wine."

"Who -- what are you?"

"A guard," he said with a deceptive little shrug. "You need one tonight, don't you?"

"I might need one from you," Katashan said.

"Not everything of the dark and the night is your enemy."

That, most certainly, was the truth. And this *person* didn't need to have gone to this much trouble if he'd intended harm. Katashan finally took the offered goblet, though he didn't drink. He felt his arm start to tremble.

"Drink your wine. You need it."

He sipped. Why not? If Peralin was an enemy, he was already within the walls and past the wards. Katashan knew he had little defense against something with enough power to pull wine (and very fine wine, at that) from somewhere else. Even a tiny sip filled with him strength and left him giddy for a whole new reason. The liquid held the very taste of life and power, but it didn't help to clear his head.

"Where did you come from?" Katashan finally asked.

"I used to be from the north, like Verina," he said and smiled. He settled on the floor beside the door, stretching out and looking more comfortable than he ought to be in such squalor. "But I have traveled far since then. Just not often in this . . . form. However, Verina asked me to watch over you tonight. She does not ask such favors often."

He believed in the Goddess, of course, though not in such a way that made this so personal. She asked another being to watch over him?

"What have I gotten myself into?"

"Now *there* is the question. And I fear I cannot fully answer it. Whoever made that sacrifice on the mountain top did so by pulling power from the Verina Shrine but we do not know what you are dealing with, Katashan. We believe this might be the work of a new power, young and anxious to gain ground in the world. Or a mage of some power could do it. Or else it is something very, very old and just awakening again. Any of those possibilities can be extremely dangerous."

"What about her?" Katashan asked, waving a hand toward the body.

Peralin sipped his wine and frowned which was a not a reassuring sight. "Be careful of her. Whatever happened, the power clings to her. She is a magnet for trouble, my friend."

"I'd already guessed that much."

"You were wise to ward the wall," Peralin added and sipped again. Katashan didn't think he dared if he wanted to ask anything coherent. "You've awakened things out there tonight, and we can't tell if they come at the heed of some power or if it's just backlash from breaking the spell."

"But I have made an enemy, haven't I?

"Didn't that occur to you when you took her from that

place, knowing someone would not want her gone?"

"I hadn't thought about it," he admitted.

"Because you only knew it was wrong and needed righting," Peralin said with a nod. He reached back within the cloak that still rested around his shoulders and began pulling out a few more items. "Bread and cheese?" he asked, sitting them on silver plates between them. The bread held a scent of the oven still and he didn't doubt it was still warm and fresh. "Perhaps some orange slices, still warm from the sun of . . . somewhere else."

Katashan's mouth watered at the sight of the fruit. He hadn't had oranges in years.

He glanced from one companion to the other, briefly wondering which of them was the more dangerous.

"Why the hell not?" he finally said.

"Why not, indeed. Feel free," Peralin said, waving towards the repast.

Katashan dared to eat the soft, fresh bread, creamy cheese and a piece of orange. The last tasted as though it had come straight from a tree in some paradise. He'd never tasted something so perfect. Then he picked up his goblet of wine and sipped again. The liquid tasted like life in a liquid form: sunlight, spring, honey, ambrosia. He leaned back, shoulders relaxing.

"Rest well," Peralin said. "The Gods alone know what might come tomorrow."

"Really?" Katashan said, meeting his companion's look this time. "Do you know?"

Peralin smiled brightly. "No, not always, at least not at my level. If we did know what would happen, I would not be here tonight to protect you, would I? I would be out dealing with the trouble before it got this far. And besides life -- well, existence, at least -- would be terrible dull, don't you think, if everything were easily handled, everything known and nothing up to chance or choice?"

Katashan shrugged, certain he was not up to discussing such things with a god tonight. He sipped more of his wine and then curled up in his blanket and slept, confident, at least, that his guard could handle any trouble that came their way.

CHAPTER FOUR

"Wake up. It's very nearly dawn."

Katashan turned over and stretched. He hadn't slept so well in months. He was rather startled to find himself in a hay shed stretched out on the cold, hard floor.

Peralin stood by the shed door, which he had pushed partly open. The world looked inky black outside, and a cold damp breeze blew in. Somewhere nearby a bird made a startled chirp, as though the idea of the coming of morning came as a surprise.

With a start, Katashan rolled over and looked at the wall. The body still rested there, shrouded in cloth, with snow still packed around her. He felt chill, knowing today he would be taking the body of this woman to some authority.

"Are you awake?" Peralin asked, sounding anxious. Katashan grunted a reply and nodded as he sat up. "Good. You need to open the gate."

"Why?" Katashan asked, stretching his shoulders and slowly standing.

"Because," he said with a little wave of his hand out into the dark, "you sealed it last night with a spell, and I cannot open it without a bit more show than I think either of us wants to make. And I need to be away before the dawn and before your companions find me here. I don't think you really want them to know I was around, now do you?"

"No, I suppose not." Katashan brushed at his rumpled clothing, dusting off bits of dirt and hay. He still felt remarkably good, although his hand hurt when he moved it. The finger he had sliced open looked swollen and the wrist inflamed as well. He hadn't taken much care last night, so worried about other things. He didn't want a fever settling in and started to reach for his travel bag to see what healing herbs he might still have.

"Give me your hand," Peralin said. He reached, touching warm fingers to the cool back of Katashan's hand. He didn't pull away as Peralin wrapped both his fingers around Katashan's wrist.

For a moment he felt dizzy, wild, elated. When Peralin drew his hands away, Katashan had to brace himself back against the wall, trying desperately to focus on the world again.

"You should have prepared me for that," he said, gasping.

"Really? How?"

"Well, warned me at least." His vision finally came back into focus and his breath came with less of a gasp. He looked down at his hand and spread his fingers a few times. Nothing hurt. In fact, old scars had disappeared, and even the slight pull in his knee seemed to have faded. "Thank you."

"I didn't want anyone noticing the recent wounds," Peralin said. "The less notice others take of you, the better. Right now we suspect the powers involved in the sacrifice were caught by surprise when you broke the spell and the mage is having trouble finding her again."

"But we've barely gone a few miles!"

"I think that, in fact, is what has confused them. You broke the bonds of a major spell. I suspect they don't realize they are looking for a mortal. Few in this part of the world have possessed magical power for more than a century."

"Surely someone must still know the magic."

"What would make you think such a thing?" He nudged Katashan out the door and towards the gate. Night came out of the darkness and followed them, far too well-behaved for a real horse.

"They must know magic," Katashan insisted with a shake of his head. He lifted the bar and settled it to the side, away from gate and brushed aside the ward. "We had our mages on the front lines. They were powerful men and women. How else could the southerners have won the war?"

"The locals don't have that kind of power. A few hedge wizards and others in hiding, have some power but they were not with the army. The priests have some power, but they don't go to war either. Look to other reasons for their win." He swept up into the saddle, dark cloak and dark horse almost lost in the black night. Katashan could only see the face now, still deceptively young and human. "We will meet again, I suspect. You've many long nights ahead of you. I will be of what aid I can, but you know that our abilities to work within the real world are limited."

"I know."

"Take care, Katashan."

Peralin rode out of the gate and into the night. The hint of fog retreated and disappeared as he passed and the sound of the horse disappeared long before he could have ridden far, at least on trails that mortals took. Katashan watched for a long while as the sun rose, turning the gray and black world to a green paradise of bright trees and sea blown grass. He could smell the ocean on a soft breeze.

The door to the main building snapped open behind him, spilling out the scent of wood smoke and the mumbled curses of men awakening to a new day. Tyren stumbled out, shading his eyes against the bright morning light. He took a couple limping steps forward shrugging and scratching, as he looked around.

"Damned flea-bitten building," he mumbled, then noticed Katashan. "Trouble?"

"No. This looks like a much better morning than I had expected."

"Ah. Good." He went to the well and pulled up a bucket of water, watching Katashan who headed back towards the shed. "Hey. About last night --"

"We were tired after a day filled with difficulties. Today will be better. How far to the next village?"

"Should be there about sunset," Tyren said, obviously willing to let the matter go. "This is the half-way point between the last stop and the town."

"Not very many villages along this trail? I would have thought the shoreline would be littered with them."

"No. The people cluster at the bays, but the rest of the countryside is wild. Too craggy and temperamental for farming this close to the shore." He splashed water over his face and scratched under his arm again. Then he scowled. "Don't know how they'll greet us with the dead we bring."

"I know. But this needs to be done. I will handle the matter as best I can."

Tyren frowned, and then nodded. "We'll leave soon. Be ready."

Katashan went back to the shed, checking the body. The ice had held up well, no doubt with Peralin's help. He packed up his scant supplies, thankful for the meal he'd shared with Peralin last night and for the chance to sleep. He hadn't expected to rest well, if at all.

He pulled the travois out, found the good-tempered donkey from the night before, and tied her to him again. In fact, he was ready long before Tyren could roust the rest of his men and get the donkeys packed. The four strangers with whom they had shared quarters last night acted equally surly in the morning light. Katashan watched in some relief as they headed in the opposite direction, up towards the mountains. He wouldn't have wanted to travel far with them. Tyren looked pleased as well.

As they finally moved away from the building, Katashan found himself looking over his shoulder. Worries over what had happened the night before, both before and after they reached shelter, haunted him for the first mile.

After that he gave in to the lovely morning with a bright and cloudless sky and a soft sea breeze blowing in off the ocean. They'd left the wintry mountains for the spring of this narrow coastland, and here crabapple trees, laden with bright flowers, filled the air with a wonderful perfume. Tyren, who sneezed almost constantly, didn't seem to appreciate it though.

The others soon began to pick up speed, the promise of the next stop in the journey luring them on. From the bits of conversation he heard, Salbay was a real town, and not just another cluster of ill-kept buildings at the crossroads of a trail.

Katashan kept his place at the back of the caravan, most often walking behind the body. The trail wound along the edge of seaside cliffs, and opened often to a wide vista of the white-capped sea. Gulls floated on the air currents, dipping now and then to the shore or skimming the water. Dolphins leapt and played. Sometimes he saw small rocky islands jutting from the water where sunbathing seals and pelicans gathered in languid harmony. Once he spotted a ship farther out from the shore, too far to make out more than a colorful sail bobbing along with the wind.

At midday the trail began to climb again, but only by small increments, with wide even stretches between. On one of those stretches he saw a half dozen wrecks on the rocky shore below them, the bare bones of the ships gutted by fire and now a haven for noisy birds and fat seals.

Tyren had called a halt for a meal and short rest. He crossed to where Katashan sat, his legs dangling over the cliff as he watched the animals below. The caravan master handed him some stale bread and a small bit of cheese.

"Thank you. Do you know what battle was fought here?" he asked, waving down to the shore.

Tyren obviously didn't like standing so near the edge. He backed up several steps in haste before he answered. "Don't know the name. Happened about six years ago. Most of these be the enemy ships, run aground in a storm and fog. Nasty fogs here and not a place for sailors who don't know the waters."

Katashan nodded. He had sailed, unwillingly, in enemy waters on stormy nights and paid the price for it, though not with his life as doubtless many had in this battle. His three years in slavery had hardened him to many things . . . though not, he found, to the sight of ruined ships. He wondered what had happened to the crews. All dead? Slaves? Ransomed back to their people as he should have been?

Tyren looked over the edge again and grunted before he turned back to the others, already chiding them for being lazy, and to get moving again. Katashan, knowing full well how long that would take, remained sitting as he ate his food.

He remembered his own time at sea, and worse, he remembered being pulled from the frozen sea, half dead, and dragged to the village by people who had rushed to the shore to collect what they could from the wreck in riches and slaves.

He banished those old thoughts by looking back at the blanket-shrouded body. That took away any memories of the past and replaced them with worries of what would happen next. He knew there would be trouble taking her to the town, and more so if she happened to be from there. The ice had begun melting and he could see a trickle of water gathering around her. Short of an obvious display of magic, Katashan could do nothing more than pack some leaves in around the body, hoping another layer of insulation would help slow the melt. They would reach the town at about sunset and long before a body that had spent the winter in snow would become a problem.

The donkeys complained as Tyren bellowed his orders, and the men were little better. Some scowled at Katashan, as though he was somehow responsible for the fact they had to go somewhere. The journey had been overlong and this stress at the end did not help.

Eventually Tyren got the line of men and animals moving. They made another short climb up the path, which brought them to the summit, and a wide -- though windy -- view to the north and south. Katashan stopped to take in the breathtaking scene from the bare cliff top that overlooked a rocky, wave-racked shore below. Along a curve to the north he saw the tip of a bay filled with a dozen colorful sails, and a moment later he found the village. A few buildings sat along the shore, but more nestled into the tiers of stone up the cliff side. Colorful roofs vied with what looked like gardens hacked out of the stone itself. He could see movement along the paths, and people traversing stone stairs. Surprised, he stared for a long time, while the others moved on without him.

This was *not* home. The bayside villages of Taris were sprawling affairs, with shacks and tents along the tide line, and walls shielding the true city from the poor who lived in those ramshackle tenements. He traced a stairway path to the tree-shaded roofs of even more buildings on the very top of the cliff. One very large building, looking like a giant boulder, stood in their midst. Everything appeared so strange and exotic that Katashan had to tear himself away from the view and jog to catch up with the others.

Tyren spun at the sound of running feet, his hand on his belt knife. He frowned, grunted, and turned back away. The others kept going without apparent notice now that they had their destination in view.

The trail wound up and down the cliff side for a few more miles, and the sun had nearly slipped behind the curtain of the sea by the time they reached the cliff top buildings. Here he found a solidly built fortress protecting the path down to the village. A half dozen inns and taverns of varying degrees of respectability stood close by the fortress, as well as stables and pens.

People watched as they passed the first few buildings. Some knew Tyren, the man's name called from a couple doorways. For the moment, at least, people hadn't noticed the body, and they made no special notice of Katashan, who probably looked as shabby as one of the regular caravan workers.

"This be Salbay," Tyren said, waving a hand towards the buildings. He sent his men to quarter the donkeys with instructions to meet again at some place they all seemed to know. Tyren stayed with Katashan and the last donkey as they headed straight for the gate to the fort. The travois, so obviously holding a body, drew the attention of those on the mud-packed path. Katashan saw crossed wrists and heard muttered comments as they passed. Although he spoke the language well enough, Katashan still had trouble following the guttural slang of the locals.

They were not saying anything good.

Katashan had second thoughts about coming to this far land for the first time. He had nothing in common with these people, who dressed in strange styles, the men with their hair cut short, the women in bright dresses, their hair hanging down their backs. Now, as he reached the end of his journey, he wanted to turn back --

But he could never return to the life that had already been ripped from him, and lost forever before he decided to come south. So he kept his place behind the travois, watching warily as Tyren finally stopped by the fortress gate and presented his travel papers.

The guard, who looked like he must have been on duty for most of the day from the amount of dust on his chain mail, boots and gray cloak, glanced at the seal of the pouch and handed it back to Tyren.

Then he looked towards the body and shook his head. "Looks like you're bringing in more than spices and cloth, Tyren."

"Found her, up in the mountains," Tyren said. He looked to Katashan with a glare.

"She had been murdered," Katashan said, speaking calmly so that he was easily understood, despite his accent. "I found her near the Verina Guardian at the Silver Pass, buried in the snow. She was not dressed for the mountains, and this being the closest lowland village, I thought it best to bring her here."

"He's not one of your workers, is he?" the guard asked, frowning even more.

"He's come from the north to set up a shop," Tyren said, glaring again.

"We have rules for foreigner merchants." The guard looked Katashan over from head to foot as though gauging if he was worthy enough to do business here. Katashan almost protested that he hadn't decided on this town, but then the guard shrugged. "But that's not my business. And neither is she. You better go in to see Captain Serrano."

"This be his business," Tyren said, waving a hand towards Katashan. "Me and me men are going down to the Crate and Ale for the night. If you have questions, you can find us there."

"Tyren --" the guard began to protest, but stopped when the caravan master glared at him as well. He looked at Katashan. "Are you going to argue?"

"No."

Tyren flashed a yellow-toothed smile, nearly lost in the bush of his unkempt beard. He quickly undid the travois and began leading the donkey away.

"You have several items that belong to me, along with the merchandise I paid to ship with this caravan. I shall be by to collect them when I'm done."

Tyren started to mumble something doubtlessly rude, but he stopped, looked down at the travois, and back at Katashan, realizing he could have easily been detained. He nodded. "I'll have your items put under guard."

Katashan bowed his head in a polite thank you and said no more as he picked up the two poles to the travois. The guard called another to the gate and the man looked out, listened to some whispered comments, and muttered a curse of his own. The gate slowly opened, swinging inward to a dark tunnel.

Katashan went inside feeling like a sacrifice willingly prancing right up to the altar.

CHAPTER FIVE

The second guard walked ahead of him through a long passage beneath a stone-lined archway. Small, dark windows looked down from the close-fit stones of the gray walls, and Katashan knew bowmen would stand guard there in times of trouble. They had the same sort of entryways at home.

Should he have stayed home? Should he have learned to live with the pain of loss, perhaps gone back to the temple? So many choices he might have made that would have precluded pulling the body of a dead woman into this courtyard.

Or maybe not. The Goddess had obviously directed him here.

He banished those thoughts and concentrated on what he must do. He could hear whispers echoing eerily around him and the sounds of footsteps in the passages behind those windows. He kept his head bowed and concentrated on what to say. How much of the truth?

He dared say nothing of the magic. If he hadn't been drawn into this trouble, he never would have used his ritual blade, and he had no intention of using it again -- except, feeling the weight of the body he pulled behind him and the brush of magic that came from her, Katashan knew that likely a promise to himself he would not keep.

Still, as far as the locals were concerned, he wanted to be

nothing more than merchant moving south in hopes of starting a new business. They need never learn more about him. If he settled in a small town like Salbay and stayed clear of the capital, it was unlikely he'd ever even see another countryman.

However, if Peralin was right -- and why wouldn't he be? -- Katashan knew his troubles were just beginning. If he were wise, he would probably hand over the body, make a wild display of magic, and scare everyone into letting him leave.

And do what? Live in the hills like a wild animal as he had after he escaped slavery? He'd had enough of that in Sidien.

The guard took him through another metal gate and onto a hard-packed dirt yard. Horse stables stood to the left, close enough that a few of the horses started at the arrival of a body cloaked in magic and their protests brought the stable boys at a run. Beside the stables an array of tack sheds gave way to a smithy filled with smoke and the clang of iron.

People moved everywhere and he found far more of the gray cloaked soldiers within than he had expected. A guard stopped and searched him, surprised to find he carried no weapon. As usual his little ritual blade went undetected. It really wasn't much of a weapon as soldiers would see it, anyway.

They also made a quick search of the travois, only lifting a corner of the blanket, though the soldier patted the rest down with an obvious show of distaste. Others gathered, words whispered in a rush, making it impossible for Katashan to follow anything except the feel that no one was happy.

A tall man arrived, dressed in what appeared to be well-made servant's clothing. He looked at the travois and shook his head with disbelief. "Captain Serrano will see him right away." He waved towards the main building. "This way."

Katashan took a quick look around, hoping the fog had not already started building up for the night. There was a problem he had not considered. He might have to ward the body in some way to keep these others safe.

They crossed to the inner bailey of a square, stone building that looked as though it had been carved out of stone rather than built from it. A man came out through the wide, wood doors, brushing back a strand of dark hair that had blown into his face by the evening wind. The others nearby came to attention. The guard who had silently escorted him this far saluted. This man, with a silver crescent on the shoulder of his black tunic, was obviously a person of power.

Katashan gave him a proper bow, but he looked back up to meet the man's glance, refusing to be too subservient in this encounter. He knew he would already be counted lower by virtue of being an outsider. He needed to hold to his dignity in order to face down what could be a serious problem, if the locals decided to make it so.

"Tell me about this," the man said as he came close enough to nudge the travois with his clean, black boot.

Katashan knelt by the body and began uncovering her while he told an abbreviated (and very boring) tale of how he had found her body at the base of the Verina Shrine where he had gone to pray. Being from the north, and a follower of the old religion, they didn't seem to think that unusual, at least.

He'd gathered quite a group before he pulled away the last blocks of melting ice from around the dead woman's face. That first -- he hoped he didn't have to uncover the knife in this much company. That seemed something better left to a more private group.

Uncovering the face drew reaction enough.

"*Oh Gods curse all,*" Captain Serrano said softly. He dropped down on his heels beside Katashan and ran both hands through his hair. Until that moment he had seemed aloof and unconcerned. Now he looked worried. "This is Lord Arpan's daughter, Sherina, who has been missing since last fall."

"Just before the first snowfall in the pass, I imagine," Katashan said.

The Captain nodded and then frowned. "You've brought us quite a problem."

"I didn't feel it right to leave her there."

"That's true enough." He ran his hand through his hair again. Katashan saw a hint of grey, though he didn't look very old. This was plainly a stressful job and he had made it worse. "It's just not the kind of problem I like to have dumped at my door step."

"I understand," he said. He nudged the man's hand, drawing his attention and carefully folded back the edge of the blanket so that only he could see the knife.

"Damn," the Captain said softly again. He nodded and Katashan let the blanket fold down. Captain Serrano stood and looked around the group. "We better take her inside. I'll need to send a rider to the estate and someone else needs to go down to the city to bring back Pater Matish. I want this handled properly. Gorton to the estate and say only that she was found dead. Briggs to the city and tell the priest only that I want to see him. Go."

Two men took off at a jog. The others took that as a dismissal and quickly disappeared, obviously hoping the Captain wouldn't find something for them to do as well. For a long moment Serrano stayed there on his heels, his head bowed. Katashan wished he knew what the man thought. The Captain's head came up and he stood.

"Bring her inside."

Katashan started to bristle at the order -- he was not one of the man's soldiers -- but he swallowed back the ire and pulled the blankets around the body once more. He reminded himself he had to get used to being subservient to the locals. The captain looked back at the door and then signaled one of the other men to help carry the bundle up the steps.

They slipped into the cool, dark interior of the building. Captain Serrano spoke quietly to a shadowed man to the left, who hurried away on his own errand. Then he moved in front to lead the way through a narrow hall and into a bright courtyard, past a fountain carved into the shape of flowing waves and dancing seagulls, and into the kitchen. The scent of food won a growl from Katashan's stomach as they passed startled and frightened servants.

Serrano looked around and waved Katashan and the other soldier towards another door. "We'll put the body there for now."

"Body?" a woman said, backing up as though she hadn't noticed the bundle they carried.

"Finish up here. Quickly. You are all dismissed for the night," Serrano said. "I'll take cold supper later or eat in the mess. Go."

The cook cleared away whatever she had been working on and fled with the others, all of them white-faced and whispering. The Captain opened a door to a cold closet, already packed with ice, and began moving some things around. In a moment they were able to slip the body off the travois and lay it on the floor. The captain shook his head, and pushed the door closed.

"You will guard this door, Epas."

"Sir," the man said, saluting. He eyed Katashan with suspicion, but said nothing.

"Come to my office," Serrano said. Then he stopped and shook his head. "Please, come to my office where we can speak in private."

"I would appreciate learning something of what I have gotten myself into."

"Yes, I'm sure you would. Damn mess, northerner."

"Yes sir. I realized that as soon as I tripped over her."

"Huh."

Katashan and Serrano walked back through the courtyard and up some stairs into the main part of the building. They passed what was clearly the main hall with a chair raised at the end, tables and benches elsewhere. Servants were clearing away the signs of a meal, and Katashan's stomach growled again at the thought of food he'd missed.

They went up a floor and into an area of smaller rooms, narrow halls and more stairs. The place seemed more a home than a fortress with tapestries hung on the walls, and rugs covering the floors. As his eyes adjusted, Katashan could see well-appointed rooms and a few clerks working. Servants came and went, bowing and stepping aside for Captain Serrano and his guest.

Captain Serrano led him past the maze of rooms to yet another long narrow set of stairs. Katashan plodded upward, feeling tired, dusty, and long since ready for a real bed, and perhaps even a dip in the sea to clean the long months of trail dirt from him. He had oils and scents in the trade goods he had brought south. If he could get to them, he would spare a little for himself.

Servants and soldiers mingled in the halls, some saluting and others bowing as the Captain went past. He was equally polite to all, but he didn't stop to talk to anyone.

Just when Katashan thought they might never stop climbing stairs and walking down halls, the captain pushed open a door and ushered Katashan into a suite with an office and a bedroom glimpsed through a door to the left. The servants had banked a fire in the hearth on the far wall.

A window stood open to the view of a magnificent sunset over the bay. Katashan walked to it without even a 'by your leave' and stared for a long moment before he caught himself and looked back.

"Your pardon, sir. The view is magnificent."

"It is." Serrano settled behind a desk and waved towards a chair by the fire. "You look as though you could use the rest."

"Thank you." He took the chair and tried not to feel nervous under the man's stare. "Is there a problem?"

"Oh yes. Many of them, but then you know that much. How far from the north do you come, Katashan?"

"As far north on the Iron Trail as you can get," he answered. "I came from Kirin, the capital of Taris."

The man winced. "I feared as much. Why did you come here? Hostilities are still fresh in people's minds."

"I'm not sure why I came, except that I didn't want to stay in Taris. I came here on a whim. And on a whim I might sail farther south."

The captain looked at him for a long moment, but didn't ask the obvious question about why he left Taris. Good. He didn't want to start by lying or hedging his answers.

A servant knocked softly on the door and came in with a message, handing it over to Serrano. He gave a quick look to the foreigner before retreating back out of the room. Katashan caught the sight of a younger woman, lingering at the door to get a glimpse of him. He hoped he hadn't disappointed them.

Serrano read the note and put the paper aside. "You realize the trouble you have brought down from the mountains?"

"I knew this was trouble the moment I saw the knife. I did not know she was nobility, but I'm not surprised." He leaned back in the chair, worn and worried. "I would rather not have been part of this, sir."

"No doubt. You'd be a fool to have courted this purposely. And I'm not entirely certain you aren't a fool since you came in here alone with a body you knew would draw considerable trouble. Why did you send the trader and his men away?"

"Because, in order to keep calm the last day and half on the trail, I told them that I would take care of this part of the matter. I keep my word."

"Do you? Do you indeed?" Serrano sat back and stared again. "I'm not sure what will transpire from this business. I am going to insist you stay here, as my guest, until I have some feel for the trouble you might stir up."

"Guest."

"Yes, my guest, to be housed in one of the rooms, not the cells. I wouldn't have marched you all the way up here to my quarters if I intended to lock you away. I assume you won't mind if the servants take care of you for a few days?"

He frowned. But --

"Is there, perhaps, a bath to be had as well?"

"I can arrange it," Serrano said and smiled. "And a meal, some wine. I wouldn't mind a dinner conversation with someone who is not going to quote lists of supplies or discuss horse mange. I trust that won't be too trying?"

He gave a little laugh this time, feeling some of the dread easing from his body. He could feel comfortable here. The Captain seemed an amiable man.

"Tyren has my belongings, including the items I brought south to start a shop."

"Tyren? Ah, the caravan master. Interesting man, Tyren, who travels from the south to the north and back again, trading for the last few years, even when hostilities were still fresh in the minds of people on both sides."

"I wouldn't know. A merchant recommended him as honest."

Serrano gave a quick nod and asked no more, but Katashan had the feeling of a conversation only delayed, not forgotten. "I will have your belongings brought here for the time being."

"And searched."

"Yes."

"I trust your people to be careful. There are vials of expensive oils in the trade items, and some personal mementos that are irreplaceable in my own belongings."

"I shall be careful and discreet. And you are not just a merchant. Your speech betrays you. You are far too well educated."

Katashan winced, even though he'd known the question

would arise sooner or later. He would have rather it had been later and not under these circumstances, however.

He thought about saying nothing, but Captain Serrano stared at him, obviously awaiting an answer.

"My father had a post in government. I had a good education," he said, and shrugged. "But I was also in the army during the Sidien invasion and spent a few years as a slave. I came back to find my home destroyed and my wife and children dead. So . . . I came south."

Serrano blinked. Perhaps he hadn't expected so much truth. Katashan couldn't even say why he gave the story, except there seemed no reason to draw this out in long, painful discussions.

He looked down at his hands, taking a few deep breaths.

"I'm sorry," Serrano said.

Katashan looked up and spread the hands in a gesture meant to convey . . . something. He wasn't certain what, but the Captain nodded. They were saved from any further soul-searching conversation by another discreet knock at the door.

"Enter."

A soldier stepped inside, saluted and cast one wary glance at Katashan. He began to wonder if they got many foreigners here at all, though that would be odd for a port town.

"Yes?" Captain Serrano asked.

"Sir," the man said, looking back at his Captain. "Pater Matish is nearly to the outer gate. Do you want him brought to your office?"

Serrano appeared to consider it for a moment. "No, he'll need to see the body. We'll meet him in the courtyard."

"Yes sir." Another salute, a last discreet look, and then he left.

"I probably shouldn't have brought you here after all, but I wanted some little privacy to ask my questions," Serrano said. He shrugged. "Would you like a quick glass of wine? We have time."

"You are kind, but I don't think it wise. My last meal was sometime yesterday, and I think you shall want me coherent when the priest arrives?"

"Ah." He pushed papers around on his desk, and then stood with a shake of his head, as though he knew he would never get to the work. "As soon as we're finished with this business, I'll have a cold dinner brought up and we'll talk about other things."

"As you wish." He dreaded the thought of standing again, of walking back down to deal once more with this body. Katashan, remembering what Peralin had said about the priests and power, wondered if this man might have a sense of the magic involved. His head pounded at the thought, and he regretted having come straight to the city with the body. A night, resting in the woods, didn't seem like such a bad idea now.

Except he would likely have faced another fog and the gods knew (or apparently didn't) what else might have come after him.

By the time Captain Serrano stood from behind the desk, the world had turned dark outside the window. He closed the shutters on his way out, tying them with a leather thong though they rattled in the breeze. Katashan reluctantly stood and followed the man to the door. The pause in the madness had been too brief.

Captain Serrano only said a few passing words on the way back down to the lower levels. He had the look of a man who had fallen into a pit and wondered if the shifting of dirt he heard came from friend or foe. He didn't rush, and they reached the lower hall just as the guard escorted a gaunt man into the courtyard. Obviously Serrano knew how to time the journey. Katashan half held his breath as he waited to see if he would face an enemy or not. He had not intended to search out any of the local priests when he arrived. So far there had been far too many things he hadn't intended but had already managed to do.

The tall, lank man stood covered in a long dark cloak, though he pushed back the hood to show an angular face of indeterminate age. He seemed very calm. Beneath the cloak he wore an equally dark, long robe, tied with a white rope, which indicated the man held a high position in the temple.

Oh, and a hint of power. Katashan felt the magic and wondered if the priest could feel the same from him. He saw no indication in the man's attitude.

"Captain," Pater Matish said with a polite nod of his head. He looked to Katashan, his face emotionless.

"This is Katashan. He brought a body in today and I sent for you."

Pater Matish nodded and said nothing, but Katashan could see a hint of worry in around the dark brown eyes. Had he picked up the hint of magic from Katashan, just as he had from the priest? Or did the man worry about the body? Either, or both, might be likely.

Serrano abruptly turned away and started out of the hall, as though he purposely avoided any questions by the priest. Pater Matish again bowed his head and indicated that Katashan should go first. Having the man at his back made him uncomfortable as he listened to the quiet shuffle of bare feet on the floor. The man was either a true believer who followed the dictate that one must always be in touch with the world, or else he was very good at the show.

Or maybe he just didn't like shoes and sandals.

The Captain sent the guard at the cold storage out into the hall and pulled open the door. Katashan stepped to the side as Serrano began to unfold the blanket from the face.

"Ah --" the priest said as he came forward. He looked toward the doorway and lowered his voice. "Sherina. This is not good."

"There is worse," Serrano said just as quietly. He drew back the blanket all the way to the waist. "We found your missing ritual blade."

"Oh." The priest went down to his knees and the move had the look of something he had not planned to do.

Katashan stepped back, surprised to find out where the knife had come from since a ritual blade, devoted to a god and purified by a priest, could be more trouble. Or not? He hadn't felt anything particularly holy about the blade. And they did things differently here in the south.

Captain Serrano put a hand on the priest's shoulder. "No one but the three of us knows about the blade. I wanted you to see it first. I've sent for Lord Arpan, but he's not likely to arrive before sometime tomorrow."

"Yes. You found her?" Pater Matish asked, looking up. The priest had turned very pale.

"I did. Silver Pass, at the foot of the Verina Guardian."

The priest's eyes grew a little wider. The man did know that probably meant further complications. And then, before Katashan could react at all, the priest did what Katashan had feared most.

He whispered a spell to detect magic.

Matish slowly ran his hand over the body, the little glitter of magic settling like a frost on the form, brightening where magic lay concentrated in the head and the area around the knife. Katashan couldn't tell how powerful the priest might be or if he could sense Katashan's magic so nearby as well. He held his breath and began to compose his thoughts in Cyrenian, hoping if he explained well enough this man might understand.

However, instead of turning to him and demanding an answer, Pater Matish drew his hand back, frowned, and looked at the Captain without even a glance at Katashan.

"This is not good, Captain. There has been considerable magic involved in her death. The use of a ritual blade from the temple is very troubling."

"I feared as much," Serrano said with another sigh. "What do we do now?"

"The magic is done," he said. "I think, for the sake of the others, that we remove the evidence of a crime worse than murder. The people will be frightened if they learn there is dark magic afoot again."

"Again?" Katashan asked, despite himself.

They both looked up, frowning as they turned to him. Katashan almost cursed aloud for having drawn their attention. In fact, it would have been wiser to act as though he didn't understand the language nearly as well as he did, though far too late to make any such change now.

Serrano finally shrugged. "It's not as though we've kept it a secret. We had a dark mage in the area about two years ago and had to get help from the temple in the capital to finally kill him. The scars the mage left behind are barely healed."

Katashan clamped his mouth shut before he asked more, especially concerning magic. Salbay, he quickly decided, was not the place where he wanted to settle. The sooner he got away, the better.

"I can cover the signs of what happened with her," Matish said. He examined the blade, and the rope that bound her. "At least for the moment, no one else need know that we might have a problem with magic again. Given Lord Arpan's attitude, we don't want to add magic into the pot when we tell him about his daughter's murder."

"Huh," the Captain said, less happy with that comment. "I am in service to Lord Arpan. I don't think keeping information from him --"

"What do you think will happen if we tell him that his missing daughter died in a magic ritual? Do you really want to be part of what happens next? Because you will be, since you are under his command and he's going to order you to do . . . things again."

"Damn. Your pardon, Pater -- but damn nonetheless."

"I am asking that we be discreet," he said. "We need not mention magic right away. I will take the responsibility for the matter later, if need be, but I wish first to deal with the magical aspects quietly. We can leave it as a matter of the temple, and even Lord Arpan cannot entirely argue with the decision."

"I can agree to that much," he said. "And while I do serve Lord Arpan, my first obligation is to keep the King's Peace. Getting Arpan worked up over magic would not help. So I'll go along with this. We'll not mention the magic."

The priest looked up at Katashan. "And what about you?"

"Me?" he said, and barely kept his hand from the ritual blade at his chest.

"You have heard what we've said, including the part about keeping information from the Lord of this area. You could cause us considerable trouble."

"Not me," he said with a shake of his head as he leaned against the wall. "I am a foreigner. I hope to perhaps start a shop in some other village along the shore. I do not think making enemies of the local captain and the head of the temple would be a good start. Nor do I particularly want to be a stranger in a town where people are looking for an enemy."

"Wiser and wiser," Serrano said as he stood. "Katashan will be spending a few days with me. Which reminds me: I must see that your belongings are brought to the fortress."

"Tyren likely knows there was magic involved. Is there a way to ensure that he'll be quiet about it as well? I suspect it might already be too late."

"He's not a local, and he's been known for spreading wild tales about his travels before, so people will take what he and his men say with a grain of salt. I will, however, have some words with him and suggest that he moves on immediately. I'll send a guard to get your belongings and him."

"I heard him say that he will be staying at the Crate and

Ale."

"Thank you." He quickly left the room. Katashan heard quiet voices in the hall, but he and the priest remained silent. He did see the priest give him a surreptitious glance, but there seemed nothing more than curiosity in the look.

Katashan didn't mind having to stay at the fortress for a while, though he hated the thought of being held here against his will. Still, he had spent time in worst places. So he bowed to the priest and followed the Captain at the man's signal, heading out into the halls again and away from the body and the trouble it was sure to still cause him.

CHAPTER SIX

A couple nervous clerks pulled the Captain aside before they got back through the first floor. He gave Katashan a look of apology and called a guard over who took him up through a series of stairs and halls. There he found the servants had already prepared a room, and brought in a tub filled with steaming water.

The room looked well-appointed; the sort of room one would give to a visiting dignitary. A fire had already been laid against the cool night, and the bedding newly cleaned.

"The privy is there to the left," the guard said with a wave of his hand toward a door. "Captain Serrano would like to see you after he's done with other work. He said you will have time for a leisurely bath and he will make allowances if you are not quite ready when he calls for you."

"Thank you," Katashan said with an automatic bow of his head which was politeness in his own lands.

The soldier saluted as he turned to leave, which made Katashan wonder what sort of rank they supposed him to have. The guard went back out of the door and closed it. Katashan listened. The man did not leave the hallway outside.

This neither surprised nor angered Katashan. In fact, he found it reassuring in some ways. He didn't want to think Captain Serrano the type of fool who brought a stranger (for whom he already had some doubts) into his stronghold and then turned him loose. And besides, Katashan didn't really give a damn what was outside that door. He had hot water in a huge tub by the fire and scented soap as well.

Rather nice looking plain black pants and tunic sat on the bed as well. Clean clothes. Katashan began to strip off the clothing he had been wearing for days, grimacing as he did so, until only the ritual blade remained. He thought about tossing the clothing into the fire to burn, but it would only make the room stink. He considered throwing them out the window, but then realized he might need them later. After all, the only other clothing was borrowed.

Katashan rolled them into a ball and dipped them in the water to catch some of the scent of the soap in hopes it would help dampen the stench. Then he tossed them on the floor in the far corner of the room.

A moment later he slipped down into the steaming water. *Paradise.* He had found his way to paradise after all.

Later, a quick tap on the door woke him. The water had cooled but still felt wonderful.

"Sir? The Captain says he's ready to see you at your leisure."

He wanted to tell the man to go away and tell the Captain to do the same, but he had been raised to be a better guest.

"I'll be there shortly," he said and began to pull himself out of the tub.

"Yes sir."

He found a cloth to dry with, grateful the fire that had been set to keep off the chill. He even found a brush on the table. Damn good host for a military man.

Ah. High rank probably meant he came from nobility of some sort since things worked that way in Cyrenia. This made sense of the man's manners and attitude and Katashan could feel comfortable with this person. That meant a lot on a night like this, with all else in such a flux.

He dressed in the provided clothing and carefully dropped

the ritual blade back under the tunic, adjusting the thin chain beneath the collar so it didn't show. The body of Sherina rested inside this building and it might take more than guards with good weapons to keep out the kind of trouble she could draw. Besides, leaving the blade behind for the servants to find would be very unwise.

He didn't bother to braid his hair back, and after a last brush over the tunic to make certain the blade didn't show, he went to the door. He paused there reluctant to leave the nice room, but he had no choice.

Katashan bowed politely to the waiting guard and followed him back down through the maze of halls. A longer rest -- a night of sleep -- would have been very nice. He felt lethargic and out of sorts, and worked hard to curb his own bad temper tonight.

The scent of food, even just cheese, breads and fruit, proved surprisingly invigorating as he came through the door into Serrano's suite. Candles brightened the table at the center of the room. The Captain put aside a stack of papers with a nod of greeting and a wave dismissing the guard, at least to the far side of the door.

"Captain," Katashan said with a little bow.

"Katashan." A wave toward a chair across the table from him. "My apologies for the poor repast --"

"I've been living for weeks on journey bread and a few scrounged winter berries the deer missed. This looks like quite a feast to me. It's kind of you to invite me."

Serrano laughed. "Ah yes. Having been out on campaign far too often, I know the feeling."

"Campaign," Katashan repeated, slipping into the chair across from the man. He looked up to find the Captain starring across at him again. "Ah. You were in campaign during the last war with Taris."

"Yes. I was an officer in the King's Own, and we held the

Tatalin Pass to the northeast against the main brunt of your forces."

"And won convincingly, I might add," Katashan said as he settled into the chair.

"It doesn't appear to bother you."

"I was not in that war, Captain. I was a slave elsewhere at the time. No, it does not bother me -- the king was unwise to try to retake the south, hoping to win glory for his name. Though, do you mind if I ask a question?"

"I'll let you know after I hear it. Have some food."

"Thank you." He carefully placed some bread and cheese on his own plate and thought about Peralin again. "On the journey I spent a night at one of the many Inns, and had a discussion about the war. Someone told me you did not win because you had superior magic."

"Ah."

"You need not answer. I am only curious. I had always just assumed --" He stopped and shrugged. "But people rarely talked to me about the war when I returned to Kirin, so I assumed -- never mind."

"We were outnumbered three to one," Serrano said. He sat the food on his plate and stared at the wall for a moment, before he shook his head and looked back at Katashan. "It's no secret how we won. We had far better weapons and armor. Your people depended too much on the magic, and your mages could not be everywhere. Once they were removed, the Tarisians had nothing strong to fall back on."

"I see. Yes, that would make sense. In a way, that's what happened to those of us in the fleet as well -- in a different war." He picked up the little knife and sliced the bread and cheese, and purposely turned the conversation elsewhere. "I hope to settle somewhere along the coast and open a shop for scents and spices. I have connections back in Taris for such things, if I can show a profit. Do you think I'll be allowed to do such work here?"

"I can't say," Serrano answered. He looked relieved to have left discussion of the war behind. "I can't say this is a good time to approach business as an outsider in this area. Let's find out what happens in the next couple days."

For the remainder of the meal, they would not, Katashan knew, talk about anything more serious than the price of grain in the market. He didn't mind. They had a pleasant meal. He had the distinct impression Serrano wanted to ask him about things as well, but having already set the limits on his side, didn't feel it fair to press for what he would not give himself. They discussed travel, far lands, cheese and wine. Neither magic nor murder worked their way into the conversation, nor did any more discussion about old wars.

Far later than he expected, a guard came at Serrano's call and took Katashan back to his room. He appreciated the guide. The halls were darker with only a few torches flickering at the intersections. The numerous stairwells all looked alike to him. He would be glad for the bed and blankets, even though he had slept remarkably well the night before --

He didn't want to think about that part just now.

"I don't think I would ever find my way through these halls," he said aloud, startling the guard.

"No, sir, I imagine not. It's quite a maze until you're used to it. Built in pieces, the building was. It fits like a puzzle, sir."

"I can tell." Katashan found it disconcerting and wondered if perhaps the guards took him through different halls each time. He almost asked, but stopped himself. There could be a reason why they would want to keep a stranger uncertain of his way inside their fortress.

He wondered about the history of the place, though. Some of the walls seemed worked stone and others brick, and sometimes He thought they were inside a cave rather than a building -- but then they would go up a level and walk past room with open windows to night sky.

They reached his door and the guard pushed it open, looked inside and gave a little nod before he stepped aside. "Sleep well, sir. We'll change guards about midnight. I hope we don't wake you."

"I suspect I shall sleep undisturbed. Thank you."

Katashan stepped inside to find the fire banked, a single candle on the table by the bed, and the blankets turned down. Gods, it looked like this room held one paradise after another. He slipped off his sandals, his shirt, and decided that was enough. He barely had enough sense left to blow out the candle as he slipped beneath the blankets.

CHAPTER SEVEN

atashan dreamt about his wife.

Maybe it was the bed. He had not slept in a real bed in years -- in fact, not since that last night with her. He hadn't thought of her so clearly since the day he came back to find their home destroyed, and she and the girls dead. He had stopped dreaming about a lot of things that day.

Katashan had spent only a day with his parents, but they'd already had a strained relationship, and his father's suggestion that he remarry -- almost an order -- had led to words that probably should never have been said.

He spent the next days sleeping (though not often) wherever he happened to find himself when he was unable to go on. He somehow arranged to join the caravan, selling a few jewels to buy items to start a new life. He left ten days later. He would not go back.

But it wasn't his father's coldness that he dreamt about this time. Tonight, he saw Ava before him, laughing and bright. She had fastened her dark hair up with golden rods and lined her eyes in dark, royal blue. She laughed when he reached for her hand, and pulled away with a playful smile. She paused again, and lifted her hand out to him.

But he knew, even in the dream, that he would never touch her again. And yet he still reached, as though he might find a way past the barrier of death. He wanted to have her back again, with an ache that made his heart pound. Wanted --

She took his hand.

Cold. Ice cold.

Katashan awoke with a cry of surprise and found a woman holding his hand. He recognized her: Sherina, who was long since dead at that high pass. She floated on a soft breeze from the open window, her body and arms unnaturally long and nearly transparent. Her golden hair, still glittered with ice, looked hardly brighter than the pale, snow-white skin. Clouds of mist hung around her, but she wore no other covering.

He tried to yank his hand back, but her fingers, though they looked no more substantial than clouds, grabbed hold and felt like the clutch of winter around his wrist.

"Be gone!" he shouted, his voice harsh and too loud. She reached for his other wrist, but he moved faster, grabbing at the blade still hanging by the chain around his neck. Thank the Gods he had the sense enough not to remove it when he went to bed.

She snarled, her thin blue lips pulling back to show pearl white teeth and a frozen black tongue. When he started to pull free again, she slapped at him with her free hand and the icy touch nearly numbed his arm. Only the ritual blade in his hand saved him. He clenched his fingers around it and drew blood which sent her scuttling back, keening loudly.

He started to stand, shaking his hand to try and clear the ache of cold from the skin and bones. Seeing him show a sign of weakness, she swept forward again, but he lifted his bleeding fingers and almost spattered her this time. She drew back in haste with a yowl of anger.

The door snapped open, spilling torchlight from the hall into the room. The guard stepped in and stopped, his breath catching as he choked on whatever words he had meant to say.

"Get back!" Katashan warned.

"Gods -- Gods!" he finally cried out.

"Close the door!" Katashan leapt from the bed, drawing Sherina's brief attention from the guard, who looked petrified, poor boy. Not the one who had brought him here, so it was past midnight. "Get out and close the door! Now!"

He was a good soldier, at least; he stepped back to obey the order, though never taking his eyes from the enemy. Sherina spun in the air, a gauze of light and almost substance, and then swept down on the soldier, settling around him like a fine mist.

The guard slumped against the door and slid down, a glaze of white over his form, a film through which he gasped, his eyes rolling up as she drew power from him.

As she drew the life from him.

"No!"

Katashan threw himself at the two, his bloody hand held up while he chanted and focused the magic into his fingers. Until he felt the warmth growing in his hand he hadn't realized he'd instinctively called fire. She had become a being of ice, a demon of the cold and she drew away from the flame he held out towards her as a high bred lady shied away from a mud puddle.

The guard had turned pale white and his lips blue. However, his chest moved, though erratically. Katashan had paused only long enough to be certain he still lived and then spun back to the malevolent spirit drifting in the center of the room, red-tinged eyes glaring at him.

He lifted his hand, calling up more fire to rest upon his palm. She backed away, mouth drawn back with a sound like a hissing wind.

"Be gone, Sherina --" He lifted his hand prepared to throw the flame into her icy heart.

Before he could finish the spell, she screamed and retreated out through the window. Wind shook the room and rain poured in, some of it turning to ice in her wake. Lightening rent the sky as the gale hit, blowing through the room with a new sweep of torrential rain. He heard the sound of people and animals suddenly awake everywhere and regretted seeing the bed almost immediately soaked.

Katashan grabbed his tunic and quickly pulled it on, hiding the ritual blade. He could hear people shouting in the halls not far away and knew he had little time before others arrived. He crossed back to the guard and knelt, placing his still bleeding fingers against the young man's forehead. He hadn't time for subtlety and whispered a quick and powerful spell that nearly sent him unconscious against the fallen boy. He pulled back, gasping, but glad to see some color return to the guard's face and the breathing come easier as well.

Hell. He didn't want to lose his secret now. And he might not have to. With a little more power he swept as much of the recent memory of Sherina from the boy's thoughts as he could, though he feared the whisper of memory might prove troubling for the soldier. Gods, what a mess!

Guards and Serrano arrived, the door bursting open and slamming against the wall.

"Are you all right, Katashan? What happened?"

"I'm not sure," Katashan said. "The storm . . . I thought I heard something. He must have slipped on the water and the rain when he came in."

Serrano looked, his lips pursed, and nodded. "It's an unexpected storm. Is Dartil all right, Kennit?"

"Seems so, sir," another guard said as he knelt. "A little cold. Must have really hit his head when he slipped."

"Yes," Serrano said.

Katashan saw distrust in the man's face. Did Serrano think him responsible for this accident or had he somehow given himself away? His head pounded and when the wind blew again, he feared he saw her at the shutters. He stood, perhaps too suddenly because he swayed. Serrano grabbed his arm, giving him unexpected and needed support. He nodded his thanks and crossed the room grabbing at the shutters to pull them closed.

Serrano helped.

"You've cut your hand," Serrano said.

Damn. He looked blankly at the bleeding fingers, wondering how to explain. Perhaps the look only conveyed confusion because Serrano seemed a bit less hostile afterwards. Someone brought him cloth and Serrano went off with the wounded guard. A few minutes later the servants arrived and took him to new quarters.

Just as well he hadn't healed his hand, Katashan realized. He would have had to cut it again to set the new ward. Once everyone had gone, he set seals on the shutters and the door. Nothing unnatural would come through this time, though when he sat on the bed, something rattled the window.

He did not sleep nearly as well through the rest of the night.

CHAPTER EIGHT

Afftter such a horrendous night, Katashan wasn't ready to face Lord Arpan the next morning. Unfortunately, a servant came barely after the dawn to say that the Lord had already arrived, the guard having found him on the trail and closer to Salbay than expected. The servant said Serrano would send for him soon and more than hinted he would be wise to be ready.

The nervous servant had spoken quietly and that marked a definite change since the arrival of the local lord, and nothing for the better. Given the conversation he'd heard between Serrano and Pater Matish, he wasn't particularly surprised that the arrival of this man upset others.

At midmorning, the guard knocked softly on the door and said he would escort him to the hall. He had been watching out the window where he could see down into the courtyard. Many people had moved along there and none of them looked very happy.

Katashan quickly straightened his clothing and stepped out of the room, giving the guard a nod. He recognized the young man as the same guard who had brought him from the late meal the night before, but even he seemed more reserved today. Katashan regretted the loss of ease he'd felt since he first arrived.

As they walked down the long, silent halls, Katashan

realized he had never felt so far from home as he did at this moment. Even when he had been a slave he had felt some tie back to the place he'd lost. Perhaps that had only been because he had believed, back then, that he could go back home and return to what he had been.

Katashan heard Lord Arpan before he reached the main hall on the lower level of the building. Unlike Serrano, Lord Arpan did not hold meetings in his suite and he obviously enjoyed the show. His voice boomed through the outer room before Katashan and his guard arrived. He winced a little at the loudness and saw the guard give him a look of commiseration.

Then they entered the larger room and all emotions left the guard's face. Captain Serrano and some of his men stood to the right. A large man, swathed in red and furs, sat on a slightly raised stage, like a king before his subjects. No one sat in this man's presence.

"This is the Northerner?" he growled before Katashan was fully into the room.

"Yes, My Lord," Serrano said, and gave Katashan a very discreet look of warning.

Lord Arpan leaned forward in his chair, his eyes narrowed and his mouth a thin line behind his shabby beard. "Come here, Northerner."

Katashan crossed to the man without comment, bowed well, and did his best to look as though he didn't resent Lord Arpan's glare.

"Do you speak the language?" Arpan asked with his voice still very loud. "Do you understand me, boy?"

"Yes, my Lord, I do," Katashan said without raising his own voice. Perhaps he should have played with a little pidgin. He doubted the man appreciated anyone who spoke well and likely had a better education than his own. Katashan had met many boorish people in his life, and he knew the look and sound of them by now.

"You found my poor daughter."

"Yes, sir."

"How did you *happen* upon her?"

The tone of the question came close to hinting at an accusation. Katashan suspected the man wanted someone to blame someone for the death. Yet, at the same time, he got the distinct feeling the death of his daughter would not cause the man an inordinate amount of grief. There was no loss in the man's face, but anger lurked there, looking for an outlet.

"I only found her by accident, sir. I tripped, in the snow. She must have been there most of the winter, I fear."

"And where were you this winter?"

"In Taris," he replied evenly. No use lying since he'd have the answer from Tyren or any of the other workers in the caravan. Katashan carefully bowed his head, trying to make his home not sound like the land of the enemy. He heard whispers from his men. "I joined the caravan. It took us several months to get here."

A subtle way, he hoped, of pointing out he wouldn't have had time to come here, kill the girl, go back to Taris before showing up again. The little hint did not help; Katashan saw Lord Arpan's mouth clamp shut and his eyes go harder.

"The captain tells me you are a merchant." Apparently, from the tone, being a merchant was no better than northerner.

"Yes, my Lord."

"I don't approve of foreigners taking money out of my land."

"I understand, sir. I had come looking to take ship farther, if I found no place to settle on this shore."

Silence. Katashan held his place, his head slightly bowed as he carefully listened to the sounds of Arpan's grunting breath. He knew this type. Lord Arpan preyed on the weak and that made him wonder where the father had been when the daughter died.

"We've had trouble with outsiders before. I won't tolerate it. I don't trust you, not bringing a body in. If you expected to be paid --"

"I did not, sir," he said and could not keep the indignation out of his voice. He looked up and met the man's piggish stare. Subservient wouldn't work with a man. Nothing would, so he might as well speak the truth and stand his place. "In my land, we would not leave a body if we might return it to the appropriate people and the priests who would see the person to a proper grave and rest."

He heard mutters behind him, but this more favorable, he thought. People who fought in the war would know the Tarisians always returned the dead to the enemy, along with all their belongings intact. They were not thieves and they were not scavengers.

Lord Arpan sat forward, his small eyes angry behind a fall of dirty gray hair. Katashan knew he couldn't win in this situation, not with a man who found him to be a convenient enemy. Saying nothing would damn him for being secretive and hiding something. Saying anything in his defense would make him too bold and a troublemaker.

"I will not brook insolence -- not from anyone in my land, and especially not from a foreigner whom I already have reason to mistrust."

"Yes, sir." But he did not look down.

Lord Arpan suddenly surged to his feet and backhanded Katashan hard enough to send him sprawling. Others scrambled out of the way and out of the man's reach. The piggy eyes protruded and the vein in his neck pulsed. "That is how I deal with people whom I dislike and distrust! That and worse. Remember it, especially if you have any urge to lie to me. The Captain will deal with you for now. I have other business."

"Yes, sir."

Serrano made a little gesture. The same guard came back,

but did not offer a hand to help him up. Katashan stood and gave a polite bow of his head, refusing to give way to the man's bad manners, but glad to be leaving so quickly, and with nothing worse than a bruise.

"If I find that you've lied about anything, you'll pay for it."

Katashan nodded, still holding to his manners, even in the face of this bore. Arpan had already stumbled back to his chair and waved his hand. A servant rushed forward and handed him a flagon of something that plainly wasn't water. He swigged it, and drops ran down to his chest.

He shoved the flagon back and glared at Katashan. "Go."

He left with the guard, getting only one quick glance of relief from the Captain. However, before he left the room Lord Arpan started again. "I don't trust foreigners. They bring trouble."

"Yes, sir. However, so far he has done what is proper. He could have pretended he never saw the body. We wouldn't know."

"Why didn't he? What's he hope to gain? I won't pay the bastard."

The guard gave a quick glance down the hall when they reached the stairs and appeared relieved to find no one following. He shook his head in disgust, but said nothing at all.

"What now?" Katashan dared ask when they reached the second floor. He rubbed fingers against the side of his face, feeling a small bump and the start of a bruise. At least the man hadn't broken his nose. Katashan wasn't certain what he would have done if things had gone worse.

"I'm not certain, sir," the guard said softly with another glance behind. "His lordship might be here for a day or two. He will be making the day-to-day decisions during that time."

This, if he read the tone properly, wouldn't make anyone particularly happy. Katashan imagined the man was chaotic. Chaotic and despotic wouldn't be a good combination.

Everyone would have trouble dealing with such a leader, especially if the men were used to working with Captain Serrano.

They'd climbed two flights of stairs and gone down three halls before the guard seemed comfortable enough to speak again. "Your belongings were brought from town last night, and they've been put in the room you first had. I was instructed to take you there if that's not a problem for you."

He thought about the ward on the shuttered window in the second room, but it wasn't likely to be a problem unless Matish found it. And if so, he'd deal with the consequences. And a shield anywhere in this building during this madness had to be some help.

"No problem at all. I rather liked the room before the storm."

"Yes, Captain Serrano thought you might since the view looks out over the sea. He said to tell you the sunsets should be lovely."

"Did he?" Katashan said and smiled. Perhaps there was no breach between the two of them and Captain Serrano only played his part with Lord Arpan around. "Thank you."

The guard gave him an odd look. "You don't seem upset by his Lordship's behavior."

"I don't like it, but I am in his lands. One must be prepared to accept such encounters when one wanders so far from home. I think settling here would be difficult with such a man in charge, so I will move on as soon as possible after this business is settled."

"It's not so bad here, really, sir. His lordship lives at Prina, his estate in the north near the capital. He doesn't spend much time in Salbay. We're a small port, really. It's the salt pans, the wood from the foothills, and the shipments of snow that makes us important."

"Shipments of snow?" Katashan asked, startled.

"Yes, sir. In the heat of summer we pack snow down from the heights and ships sail here from Atshila, the capital, and load up with snow in their holds to take back. They sell it on the streets there as an antidote to the heat."

"What a strange business."

"You never been in the heat, have you, sir?"

"Katashan," he said. They had started up the third set of stairs, and he felt a little winded. They slowed. "I admit I haven't been to the warmer climes. In the north, even the edges of the salt bays freeze in winter, and the rivers aren't navigable. Snow is something you curse, and no one makes a profit from it."

"The rivers freeze? Like in the mountains?" The guard looked at him, startled. "How do people live through the winter, then? How do you get food?"

"Stockpile foods that will last in the autumn. However, a long winter and a miscalculation can mean starvation for the outlanders on their farms if they get snowed in for too long. People generally do all right in town where they can share and where the government stockpiles more food -- unless the winter is too long. Then it's twice as dangerous to be in the city where you might be murdered for a loaf of bread."

"We get snow down here for only a few days in winter, but the weather can be fierce in the mountains behind us. We get rain and floods in the spring, though. Those can be trouble enough." He stopped at the next hall and held out his hand. "I'm Cork, sir."

"Cork." Katashan shook hands and smiled, despite the slight sting in the side of his face. "It's nice to have a name. I appreciate it."

"Don't blame none of the others if they hold back, sir. It might not be. . . ."

"It might not be wise or safe to be my friend. I understand. And I'll be discreet about knowing your name, Cork."

"Thank you, sir." He started out again, shaking his head

now at whatever thoughts he had. "It'll be all right in a few days, once his Lordship goes home. Wish you hadn't brought the body here, sir, but really you had no choice. And we'd have had it fall to us soon as the melt comes, anyway."

"Did you know the young woman, Cork?" he asked as they neared the room.

"Yes, sir. She stayed here quite often." He looked around, and his voice dropped again. "She was too much like her father. They couldn't stay in the same building without trouble erupting. And then her husbands had died within a few months of each other. It looked bad. So she -- traveled a lot. I can't say I cared for her much, but I wouldn't have wanted this to happen to her."

"Her father has other heirs?"

"Yes, sir." Cork stopped by a door and carefully pushed it open. He looked inside and then nodded back to Katashan. "Fordel is the last of his children. He keeps the troops at Atshila. A good man. The room looks fine, sir. I suggest you stay here and rest for the afternoon. If his Lordship goes out for a while, I'll let you know."

"You can be blunt, Cork. It's best if I stay out of sight as much as possible. I agree. Besides, I've had a long, tiring journey with a troubled ending. I can stand to rest for a day or two."

Cork nodded and looked relieved to find his charge still so reasonable.

"I'll see to it the kitchen staff remembers you are a guest here," Cork said. He smiled as he stepped aside. "Thank you, sir. It makes this easier if you cooperate."

Katashan bowed and went into the room, which had been cleaned, well turned out, and a fire set and ready to light at nightfall. Cork pulled the door closed, but he could tell the man stood guard on the other side.

Beside the bed sat several bags and boxes of his personal belongings and trade items with which he hoped to start a new life. Katashan went to the window and opened it up to the fresh sea air, and then settled on the edge of the bed, pulling up the first box. The small bottles inside had been examined, but carefully replaced in the cloth wrappings. Captain Serrano had been true to his word, but he hadn't expected less from the man.

Katashan entertained himself through most of the morning by sorting through his belongings. He still had no idea what might sell in these southern lands. The perfumes and spices of the north seemed exotic and out of place.

In the early afternoon, he abandoned the work and went to the window. He pulled a chair over, and watched sails along the hazy horizon and wondering where the ships came from and where they went.

Did he want to settle here at Salbay? It did meet many points of his personal criteria: not too large, not a governmental center, and friendly people as long as he didn't count Lord Arpan. And he could watch the sea from this town, which despite his horrendous experience as a sailor, he still loved.

He spent most of the afternoon watching the ships and trying to make decisions about his future. It proved a very quiet, restful day despite the annoying start. He hadn't minded staying here at all, and suspected he could stand even one or two more days of such peaceful rest. The journey had been hard enough, but the use of so much magic after he found Sherina had been worse. He'd been badly out of practice, and was -- thinking about it now -- amazed the ability had come back so easily.

A discreet knock at the door drew him away from the window and the view, and the darker thoughts that had haunted him.

"Enter," he said.

Cork came in, balancing a tray covered with a cloth. "Sent up from the hall, sir. They're feasting tonight and Captain Serrano didn't see why you shouldn't share in the excellent food."

Cork place the tray on the table and uncovered the array of bread, venison, various vegetables and what looked like sweet cakes. Katashan hadn't been particularly hungry until the moment he smelled the food.

"My compliments to the Captain and the chef. Is there some reason you cannot join me?"

"Me, sir? Join you?" He looked at the food he had just put on the side table as he pulled a small decanter of wine from inside his vest, startling Katashan with thoughts of Peralin.

"There is obviously plenty to share, Cork. Is there a reason you must stand outside the door, rather than sit inside?"

"I, a --"

"You are not guarding against people getting in, Captain. You are making sure I don't go wandering out. I understand. I'm a stranger here and arrived under troubling circumstances. The Captain would be a fool not to have me watched."

Cork looked at him and finally gave a small, half embarrassed shrug. "The Captain would like me to get to know you better."

"Would he?" Katashan said and grinned, grateful for the honesty. "Well, here's your chance."

"Yes sir, I suppose so. And the food smells damn -- ummm, very good."

Katashan cleared his supplies from the rest of the table and they moved it over by the window. He sat on the bed, Cork taking the chair, and unobtrusively making certain he stayed between Katashan and the door. He couldn't be certain Cork did it to keep danger from charging in past him or from keeping Katashan from charging out. He really didn't care.

They had a companionable meal with a witty, amusing conversation. Cork had left the door open and Katashan occasionally saw curious servants wander past. Many of them slowed to look in. Cork did not drink any of the (very fine) wine, but they shared everything else.

The conversation stayed well away from anything dangerous, including discussions of the army, Lord Arpan, or anything else that might be considered delicate.

"This seems like a pleasant location," Katashan said, waving toward the dark window. "I look forward to visiting the rest of the city. Can you tell me about it?"

Cork smiled and pushed aside the remains of the food, and his fingers traced invisible lines on the table top as he spoke. "The fortress is here atop of the bluff, along with a few trailside inns what cater to those traveling the trail towards the capital. The Old City is on the cliff below us. You can't see it from here because of the curve of the cliff, but it's pretty damned impressive. The buildings are carved right out of the stone. Then there's the fishing village down on the shore. It's new, but mostly because it tends to get wiped out every fifteen years or so by either nature or invasion."

"A hard life down there on the shore."

"Yes, it is. That's where I grew up but I didn't want to live and die on the sea, and that left only one other place for a man of my background. Happens that I got lucky because Captain Serrano took over the year after I joined. Things have been better since then."

Katashan nodded and didn't ask about the previous commander or what problems there had been. He also didn't ask if war had come here. Better to let that go without comment.

As the night drew later, Cork lighted the fire and then banked it a little later. They spoke for a while about the fishing fleet and the few days Cork had sailed with his uncle and brothers. From the look he gave, he didn't like the sea nearly as much as Katashan did.

They had a pleasant evening, and Katashan found himself more unsettled than he had expected when another guard came to take Cork's place. The two men exchanged a few words at the doorway and then Cork bade him good night. The new guard closed the door and stayed outside the room.

Despite the late hour, Katashan didn't feel like sleeping, mostly for fear of repeating last night's fiasco. After Cork left and with the night dark and cold outside, he closed the shutters and sealed them with a ward. Then he went back to dusting and sorting the bottles and vials.

He knew there would be trouble here either from Sherina or from her father. He'd managed not to think much about it while Cork kept him company, and he felt grateful for that respite, but now, alone in this foreign room he felt the precariousness of his situation again.

A soft knock.

"Enter."

Captain Serrano opened the door and stepped in, looking over the bottles Katashan had lined up on the table, and the parchment and quill that he'd just sat out.

"I feared, as late as it is, that you might be sleeping," Serrano said. "I didn't expect to find you working."

"I'm not particularly tired tonight. How are you?"

"Tired enough. I just saw his Lordship to bed. He's trying to convince me that you had something to do with his daughter's murder."

"Why would he think so?"

"I didn't say he *believed* it. But you are a convenient target. And there are questions."

"About my magic."

Captain Serrano stopped beside the table, staring across at Katashan. "What made you decide to tell me?"

"I've done nothing wrong, but the longer I kept the secret, the more it would seem as though I had a reason to do so. I trust you, Captain Serrano. I assume you realize that something dark tried to get into this room last night."

He glanced at the tightly closed shutter and nodded. "Yes,

I'd figured that part out. Why did it happen?"

"Because Sherina wasn't just murdered: She was killed in a powerful ritual and I broke some of the links when I took her body away from the site. We had trouble following us on the way down from the hills on the first night and I kept that from my companions as best I could. I couldn't hide last night's trouble as well, though."

Serrano glanced towards the door. They had not spoken loudly. "With Lord Arpan here, you do not want to be blatant about the magic."

"I thought as much."

"Did you tell Cork?"

"No, although not for lack of trust. I felt you should be informed first."

"Thank you. Can you tell me more about the death of Sherina?"

"I cannot tell you by whom or why it was done." He carefully pushed aside the bottles and put both his hands on the table, considered telling him about the Godling, and decided against it. This was complicated enough. "She had been tied to the spell with very powerful glyphs. The blade that killed her belonged to Pater Matish and likely held power as well so it became a power perverted, which gives it special abilities. I suspect you already knew about the involvement of magic. Matish knew when he checked the body. Did he know about me?"

"Yes."

"I thought as much. Forgive my deception of silence. I found myself already far more involved in a dark and dangerous situation than I wanted to be. I didn't want to open myself to trouble I might have been able to avoid."

"You could have avoided all trouble by leaving Sherina where you found her."

"The Goddess directed me to the body. I did not even see

the open trail, only a few steps away. Instead, I trudged through knee deep snow and fell over her. I do not take such signs lightly."

Serrano stared, looking as though he would like to disagree, and knowing better. Katashan felt sorry for the captain, imaging what it must feel like to realize be had become involved in something far more serious than he might have expected.

"What do you know about the ritual? What kind of danger are we in?"

"I only know for certain it was very powerful. The runes were of life, death and bondage which are not a good combination."

The Captain finally settled on the chair where Cork had been and waved a hand towards the table and the bottles. "I had Matish go over your belongings. He found no sign of magic in anything you brought along. That surprised him."

"I'm not here to sell magical potions or my services as a mage. I had renounced magic long before I left Taris. I did not come here looking for a use for it."

"And yet you have."

Katashan stared at his hands, spreading the fingers and looking at the small cuts. Most of the old scars had disappeared at Peralin's touch, but in some ways he could still feel them there . . . like the other wounds that had never really healed for him.

"Katashan?"

He looked up again. "My magic betrayed me when I could have used it to save what I loved most. It betrayed me when I fell into the hands of those who enslaved me as well. They tell me it is a gods-given gift, but if so, the gods could have been considerate of the pain they caused me. I had intended never to use magic again. An unwise resolution: My life has never gone the way I planned."

Captain Serrano looked at him for a long, silent moment,

weighing many things that Katashan could only guess at from his look. At last the man sighed and shook his head. "You present a damn lot of problems, Katashan."

"Your pardon. It was not my intention in coming here. I had hoped to find peace."

"Which you could not find at home?"

"Not after I had lost so much."

Serrano nodded, and then stood, looking towards the window and frowning. "Damn mess. We don't need this, not after the last time."

Katashan asked nothing, although it would have been helpful to have known something of the history of the last encounter with magic, if only so he could find out how they fought and won. But he did not ask, and the Captain seemed relieved.

"I would like to assign Cork as a permanent guard and servant. That will keep the others from having more than minimal contact with you and whatever trouble you encounter. I'm not certain how many of the servants or guards would deal directly with Lord Arpan. He's a stickler for protocol in most cases, and would normally be appalled at the thought of someone talking to him out of turn. However, if he thought he could use a servant to make you into the enemy he wants --"

"I would be very happy to have Cork as my companion and guide."

"Excellent."

"And you do trust him."

"Oh yes. He's a good fisherman's son, a local. He'll do what's right, not what's politic. Tell him as much as you think might be important."

"That works best for both of us."

The captain gave another curt nod, but he already looked distracted as he turned back to the door. Katashan watched him go, trying to decide if he had given the right answers or if he'd only created more problems.

Serrano paused at the closed door and glanced at the window. The breeze shook the shutter. "Will there be problems again tonight?"

"There might. However, expecting it this time, I can take precautions. The room should not be drenched nor should any guard be put in danger."

"Yes, about that part. Matish said you saved Dartil's life."

"Did he?" Katashan asked, wondering how far he could trust the local priest.

"Be careful, Katashan," Serrano warned softly, a hand on the door handle. "I am not in a position to offer you more than words of wisdom. Don't provoke Lord Arpan."

"I intend to avoid him completely," Katashan said.

"This may not be your choice."

"I know."

The captain nodded and appeared relieved that Katashan understood the situation. Katashan wondered if Cork would start his new duties tonight or in the morning. No matter. He trusted Captain Serrano to make certain the guard who stayed at his door was someone whom he trusted. He would have someone to watch over him and protect him -- at least from anything which a weapon would stop.

Tired. He looked at the bottles arrayed on the table and thought about leaving them there . . . but no; it would be too dangerous if Sherina came for another confrontation. So he laboriously wrapped each in cloth and carefully slid them back into the boxes. Then he covered the boxes with lids and pushed them into what he hoped would be a safe corner.

When he finally moved back to the bed he barely had the strength left to strip off his borrowed tunic and left it neatly on the stand by the bed. His finger brushed along the blade, wondering if he should think ill of it, of the magic of --

Of the things which had already saved others here, because

at some point the magic would have come to fruition, unless Pater Matish somehow learned of it first and . . . No. The Goddess would not have directed him here if there had been another who could have handled the trouble.

He slid into the bed and pulled the blankets up. The banked fire gave a soft blow to the room, and though he could hear the occasional movement of a guard outside, it seemed more a relief than a distraction.

And he slept well -- at least for a while.

CHAPTER NINE

The shutters rattled with a force stronger than the breeze, waking Katashan with a start. A pale, moon-white light flickered at the window and a soft keening voice rose on the growing wind.

Katashan sat up and pulled the warm blanket up around him, frowning at the play of shadow and light across the floor. He looked to the door and wondered who stood guard tonight.

The shutter shook harder as the wood bounced against stone.

"Not this time, Sherina," he said aloud, annoyed at having another night's sleep disturbed. He lifted his hand and brought a small amount of magic to his fingers; not as strong as if he used blood, but still a noticeable glow in the dark. "Be gone."

The keening became a howl. She would wake the entire fortress again if she kept up, and that certainly wouldn't go well with her father. Katashan wondered if she would try any of the other windows if he sent her away.

No. He realized she needed a link to draw her in, and he was her key -- the person who had severed her other links to the world when he broke the ritual.

Did she come to him out of need to bond to something or a more sinister reason? He still didn't know who had performed the sacrifice and might still have enough hold on the ghost to use her against him.

He lifted his hand toward the window, whispering as he called up slight magic. He only wanted to test her out, to gently dissuade her without drawing down all the keep on them.

She wearied of rattling the shutter and left. He closed her eyes and felt out the ward and the trail of magic she left behind, but she had gone far away and would not bother anyone else in the fortress. Katashan curled back up in his blankets and slept well.

"Sir?"

He came awake. Cork stood at the door, out of his uniform, and looking not altogether comfortable. His dark hair, no longer confined by his cap, twisted in curls around his face. He'd replaced the high collar of his uniform for an open necked tunic with long, wide sleeves.

Katashan blinked, connecting the familiar voice with the new look. "Oh. I slept late. Past the dawn?"

"Yes sir. An hour or so by the bells."

"My apologies."

"No need, sir." Cork picked up a chair from outside the door which he had obviously carried up from elsewhere. Wise man. Now one of them didn't have to sit on the bed. "I just ordered breakfast, sir. You'd have missed it entirely otherwise."

"Thank you," he said, although he didn't find the idea of food particularly appealing as he sat up. He put his feet over the side of the bed and ran a hand through his long, matted hair. "Should I apologize for your change in assignment? It was not my intention --"

"Oh, no need to apologize, sir. I volunteered." He settled the chair by the window and sat down, grinning. "All in all, I'd much rather be up here jawing -- talking with you, sir, than out on the work field or down patrolling the docks. Or, gods forgive me, worse yet would be walking his Lordship up and down the halls while he rants about the Gods knows what. He was badly drunk last night. He'll pay for it this morning, and that won't put him in any better mood, either. I don't mind being here at all, sir."

"I'm glad this isn't an arduous assignment, then," he said. "Excuse me."

He went to the privy, came out and splashed some water on his face and brushed down his hair. The food arrived not long afterwards brought in by a servant boy who looked around nervously and scampered out without a word. Cork uncovered the tray, and the food smelled so good he decided it would have been a crime to miss this after all.

"Captain Serrano said to tell you his Lordship will be taking the body and going home either this afternoon or early tomorrow morning. He warns that Lord Arpan will probably want to see you again before then."

"I would guess so. Is he aware of the unusual occurrence here the night before last?"

"Yes sir," Cork said. He put aside his cup of cider. "But -- just an observation, not anything the Captain has said -- he seemed damn little interested in it."

"Really? Is magic common in his family?"

"His Lordships? No, not at all. At least not so it's common knowledge. They frown on nobility with powers at court. There's always rumors, a'course, but that's common in any noble house. We like ta' gossip about those in power, and tales grow in the telling."

"True enough." Katashan sipped at his cup and decided it would not be a good idea to pursue that line of questioning, even with Cork. "Well, we're in for a boring day, I would think. Let's talk about the town again. If there's a chance at all I'll settle here, I'd like to know more about the merchants and their shops."

Cork settled into his food, looking very pleased. "I can't tell you much about how they're run. Maylee might be a help there.

Her father owns one shop and her uncle another. She works here in the kitchens. Once his Lordship is gone, maybe we'll go down and see her."

Katashan guessed from the man's smile that he had other reasons he wanted to see the woman. They discussed Salbay and the people who made up the town. Cork turned out to be an excellent source of information about a number of business practices, including general information on the taxing of different establishments.

"And the boats hire themselves out to a person or a shop, usually for a season, sometimes for an entire year," he said later as they stood by the window, watching sails out on the bay and beyond. "You're bound by law to sell only to them, at a set rate, everything above half the catch of the day."

"And the other half?"

"One third goes to the temple, which uses it to feed the poor here and in the smaller villages and the capital. The rest goes to his Lordship's men, who have first chance to sell in market, though more often they just pack it in ice in another ship and send the catch off to Atshila where there's more money to be made. You need a special license to ship to the capital, though, and they don't give them out for free."

"Fishing is the biggest market here?"

"Yes but there there's also salt, wood and snow," he said. "Atshila has the better bay, but the city is set back from the mouth of the Black River, with no easy reach of the high passes like we have -- and they've stripped the land there about of all trees anyway. We're a little wiser here. We farm the trees, but we make sure there's plenty of second growth. We can pack wood and snow down to the bay with ease, and the city is only a day's sail away in good weather. We're lucky because the winds run true in the summer when they most want snow down in the hotter plains. And except for the bay itself, Atshila is mostly marshland along the shore -- good for hunting fowl, but they've never had a good salt pan there. So that's really our big contribution, and why we rate a garrison and fortress. You can see the outer edge of the larger salt pan, off to the left of the bay."

Katashan craned his neck out the window to see, and found the square dyke filed with a discolored stand of sea water and larger than any of the salt pans he'd seen in the north. The bright green of the salt pan looked lovely at this distance, but he knew they were hard to work.

"Salt mining is our boon and bane," Cork said as he stepped away. "This is the only defensible spot of any worth on the coast between here and the capital, so this is where the salt pans went. But that makes us a target as well. Five years ago --"

He stopped suddenly, and Katashan turned back to see the man frowning and looking embarrassed for the first time.

"Five years ago, my people were here and we were at war," Katashan said. Cork nodded trying to hide his dismay. "We need not go any farther with that discussion."

"Yes, sir," Cork said, formality returned. "Best to let it be."

"When we were up at the pass, Tyren said there was a village nearby in the highlands. Are there many such places, up in the mountains?"

"He'd have been talking about Holding, I suspect. It's one of the villages along the mountain edge. There are far more then we will ever know about," Cork said with a little frown, but he looked relieved for the change in subject. "They don't take allegiance with his Lordship and refuse to pay taxes unless they come down to the towns for some reason. We hold the coast, and they have the inland valleys and mountain peaks. We've got the better deal, truth be told. There's no good land back there -- but you've seen it."

"Yes." Katashan stepped back from the window, and thought about crossing the mountain range. "Craggy mountains, high peaks, and pines everywhere."

"That's what I hear. I've never been farther than Silver Pass on the inland trails. Most everyone follows the old Iron Road, like you did. We never know what's back there, really, off the main path. Hear tales, of course, about huge cities and temples of gold, but only fools go looking, and they never come back. There be some outlying villages up on the mountains above us, like the one Tyren spoke about, but we think there might be much more, in the valleys where we can't see."

"Really," Katashan said, sitting down at the table again. Now this was a fascinating bit of trivia. "And you've no contact with the mountain people?"

"Once a year we hold a tax-free market by the fortress and that draws some down to sell sheep and crafts. But any other time, encounters are not usually friendly. They don't like that we are cutting down the forest, going ever higher for more wood. I can't say I like it much myself. And every five years, when the king's tax is due, his lordship sends an army up to collect their share of the tithe. It's never worked as far as I can tell. And nine years ago he lost a whole squadron -- a little over a hundred men -- to the mountains."

Katashan looked up, surprised by that statement. "That's no myth; it's well within current memory."

"Yes, sir. It's real enough, those disappearances. My uncle was a corporal in the group; fool, he was, to ever leave the sea. But then, that makes me a fool, too, doesn't it?" he said with a sudden laugh and a glance at the window and the ocean beyond. He shook his head and looked back. "They went off to the mountains and never came back."

"Killed?"

"Most likely, sir. We never knew."

None came back. He thought that very odd and intriguing.

"Don't get that look, sir. People what get that look head up into the mountains and never come back as well. I'd regret that, having told you the tale."

"Ah, well. I'm just fascinated by the idea of unexplored lands and strange places. It's what brought me here, you know."

"Dangerous life to lead. Sometimes there's no going back."

"And sometimes there's no reason to go back. Maybe they found the temples of gold and the vast cities."

"Yes sir, maybe so."

"Does make me wonder why Lord Arpan keeps sending people, though, if he just loses them."

"Oh, the guards, we joke that it's to cut down on the tithe he has to pay on kept soldiers," Cork said. He grinned. "You're too easy to talk to."

"But I am discreet."

"That's probably going to save my neck."

"There's no gain for me to cause trouble to the only person who's been of help since I arrived."

"Captain Serrano likes you, sir," Cork said softly, glancing at the doorway again. It reminded Katashan that there was reason to worry. "Otherwise you'd be in a cell now rather than a room here with a warm bed and nice view. I get the feeling he thinks you did us a good turn somehow, by bringing her ladyship's body here. Odd thing to be grateful for, I think, especially since there's magic involved."

"You figure that one out on your own did you?"

Cork ran a hand through his hair, glanced at the door, and then leaned closer, his voice dropping to a near whisper.

"Wasn't hard to figure, not the way Pater Matish has been hovering around the body ever since you brought her in. And then there have been those . . . incidents at night. Rather hard to ignore, though his Lordship is doing a fine job of it."

"And you find that very odd," Katashan said just as softly.

"Yes, I do."

They said nothing more of that matter. In fact, they were discussing -- of all things -- rabbits when Captain Serrano came into the room. Well, at least the man wouldn't suspect Katashan of getting important information from Cork. He stood in the doorway for a moment while the conversation died down and both men looked at him.

"I thought you should know that His Lordship has gone to the bay to inspect the wharf and will be back by third bell. He wants to see you then, Katashan." Serrano stopped and shook his head, his mouth clamped shut.

Katashan knew the look, and he quelled the worry that almost came to his face. There was more news, and it wouldn't be good.

"And?" Katashan asked.

"I think he shall order your arrest."

"Ah. What will happen then?"

"He'll transport you back to Atshila with him to be dealt with at the Court." Serrano glanced outside the doorway, and then stepped into the room. His voice softened. "Providing that you ever reached the city for trial. I've reason to think he would rather that didn't happen at all, no matter if he could rig it or not."

"I don't understand. Why bother? Why not better to leave me here -- ah.'

Captain Serrano nodded.

"Sirs?" Cork asked. "I don't follow."

"He doesn't want word of how I found his daughter's body to be spread. One assumes it is the question of magic that worries him?"

"I think so, but I can only assume that by default," Serrano said. He didn't look any less worried. "Magic was the *one thing* he does not discuss."

"What about Tyren and his men?"

"I seem to have failed to mention that you came in with the caravan and I suggested they move on last night. They're already gone," Serrano said. He didn't look happy with any of these admissions.

"And what about Pater Matish? He knows what's happened and about the magic."

"He presents a different problem and one I'll keep watch over to make certain he remains safe. I don't think Arpan will do anything to draw the attention of the temple, though. Arpan has avoided Pater Matish as much as possible since his arrival. I think the priest is safe. That still leaves you. If --" He stopped and looked at Cork, then continued softly. "If you were to leave the fortress before next bell, I would not be able to say where you went."

He hadn't expected the Captain to make such an offer. The magnitude of it was far beyond just letting him slip away. He would have to answer to Lord Arpan afterward. "Why would you risk this for me?"

"Because I know you're not involved in the murder. Because I don't want Lord Arpan to do something irreparable. Because I believe in justice, and not just a noble's rights." He looked at Katashan, and gave a nod again. "But mostly, I think you should go because I talked to Tyren, and he says there's no way you could have missed the cleared path to the Verina Guardian. I believe the Goddess directed you to the body and that means this is something none of us should undo. I don't want to be part of another man's folly to step between you and a Goddess-given fate."

He had several good points but Katashan still felt uncertain. It put the man in a very dangerous position. "You think I should go."

"Very much so," Serrano said. "I would not be here risking my career, and my life, by making such suggestions if I didn't think this was important."

"I don't want to put you in danger," Katashan said, shaking his head. "This isn't wise. He'll know you had to --"

"He believes you have magic," Serrano said. "I can use that to my advantage if I need to, and direct his attention to magic when you can't be found. So unless you really do have magic to fly away, I suggest you clear out quickly."

Katashan cast one quick look around the room and all the supplies with which he had hoped to start a new life. Nothing had ever been that easy in his life. He pulled up his bag filled with a few pieces of clothing and dragged out his cloak, a hat, and his purse of gold coins. "How do I get out of here?"

"Cork, take him down to the cliff gate. His Lordship won't be coming back at that way, but keep an eye open for Arpan's men. Get into the hills, Katashan. His Lordship won't go that way, not himself."

"I'll do my best."

"I'll take you," Cork said. "With the Captain's permission, of course. I know some the trails near here, and I'll keep you from wandering too far, sir."

"Good man, Cork," Serrano said and dropped a hand on the soldier's shoulder before Katashan could protest. He didn't want to drag someone else into this mess. "Get down into the city and wait for nightfall before you go up to the top again. Five days, Katashan. By then his Lordship will be back in his keep. He has a notoriously short memory, especially if anything else takes his attention -- and I'll find something to do so, Katashan. Five days. Then you come back, because I damned well want answers to all of this before we're done."

Katashan hastily pulled on his cloak, and looked at Cork, shaking his head. "You don't want to go with me. I draw trouble."

"And you draw the eye of a Goddess herself," Cork reminded him as he stood. "Should I not want to be part of such a cause? Besides, I don't think it's wise to let you go wandering off into danger, sir."

"Just go, go," Serrano said, frantically waving towards the door. "I'll see to your belongings."

"Thank you."

Cork hurried to the door, looked out, and then signaled that it was clear as he started away. Katashan followed him, glancing back only once to see Serrano close the door and head in the opposite direction.

Damn and damn again. This was not right.

CHAPTER TEN

Cork knew his way through the labyrinth of servant's passages as well as he had known the maze of halls and stairs in the rest of the fortress. Katashan wanted to ask how he came by such knowledge. He wanted to ask more about the building which still fascinated him as Cork led they way farther down into the heart of the fortress. He said nothing, though, and instead followed as quickly and quietly as he could.

They descended several fights of bare, stone-walled steps where only an occasional torch at an opening to a floor lit the way. When they had to leave the stairwell, they slipped past closed doors and open archways and twice abandoned one set of stairs to scurry down a hall until they found another set. Katashan was lost beyond all hope of finding his way back. He realized they had gone down well below the ground floor, and here the walls felt damp and cold. Soon the steps grew narrower, carved from the living rock. He wondered if they were going all the way down to the sea. He could take ship, perhaps --

The first time they met up with a servant, Katashan nearly panicked at the sight of the old woman, a shawl across her shoulders and a basket of herbs hanging from her scrawny arm.

"On our way out, Elga," Cork said, patting her on the arm. "Not a word."

"None, Cork," the older woman said, slipping back to a slightly wider area so they could go past. "Go by the south wing. His Lordship's guards are harassing the servants near our quarters."

"Bless you, Elga," Cork said, and gave her a quick hug. She smiled, a crooked-tooth grin full of delight, as she nodded to Katashan, and continued to trudge up the stairs. Katashan turned back to watch her disappear.

"Don't worry. You can trust the servants -- many of them, at least. Serrano treats them fair and that wins a good deal of loyalty in this place."

"Dangerous for them, helping us like this," Katashan said, worried again.

"Not really. No one will ever know we went this way, and even if they do, they'll never know if we met a servant or not."

"Then you're the only one who's putting himself in danger."

"And you. And the Captain." He stopped on the stairs and looked back at Katashan, his head tilted to the side. "Tell me it's not worth it, sir. Tell me we don't live in dangerous times and that there's nothing more to this than a young woman's death and his Lordship's bad manners? I'll take you right back to the room if you tell me that's all there is -- and nothing to do with Gods, ghosts and magic."

"Go, go," Katashan said, waving his companion on. "Things are dangerous enough, you're right."

Cork nodded and started down the stairs again. These steps were older, the stone worn slick in spots, and grooved in the others

"How much farther do we need to go?"

"Another two levels, sir. We'll come out below the fortress and just inside the herbarium, which is all nicely walled and private. I'll scout things out a bit before we head out into town proper, just to make sure none of His Lordship's men are taking in the sights or heading for a tavern."

"Sounds wise," he said.

"Wise, I wouldn't know, sir. But it is a plan."

Katashan didn't argue. By the time they made the final flight of stairs, he felt as though disaster followed close behind them. He even glanced back when they reached the old oaken door at an otherwise dead end. Perhaps something white and diaphanous moved at the corner of his sight.

Cork shoved the door open and they stepped into a surprisingly lovely little garden, fragrant with flowering trees and herbs planted on ledges carved out of the red stone of the cliff. He looked up to see deep, blue sky high above, a spot of white cloud, and the finished stone walls of the fortress towering above them at the top of a nearly sheer cliff.

Looking down, he found worn stone beneath his feet, and the only dirt in wooden boxes where the herbs and trees had been planted. It was an ingenious little garden. They even passed a well in the midst of the garden, and servants gathered there. They waved to Cork and looked away again.

"A well within the walls," Katashan said, nodding towards it. "That's wise, but quite a surprise, considering the ground seems to be solid stone."

"Yes sir, it is," Cork said, and stomped his foot against the stone as though to prove it. "But that's an artisan well, dug in from a water table in the hills just behind the city. That's what they tell me, at any rate. Hard work it must have been, but it's a century or more old and still providing water when we need it."

Katashan looked back at the well, the wall around it, and the buckets stacked nearby. The servants didn't seem to be gathering water to take into the fortress. It was probably just a popular resting place, and water most times provided by easier access like rain gathered in cisterns.

"There's the gate into the city, sir. I'll take a look. If you would hold the gate so the bell doesn't ring twice, we'll draw less attention when we leave."

As they went past a flowering bush a couple tame chickens rushed them like dogs looking for a treat. Apparently they knew Cork well, because the guard reached into his pocket and scattered bread crumbs with such ease that it looked like a natural thing for him to do. Katashan smiled and followed behind, careful to avoid trampling the creatures.

The tall, narrow wooden gate stood at the far end of the garden. Two small towers flanked the heavy wooden door but the parapets stood empty today. No doubt anyone trying to take the fortress from this side would be in for a hell of a fight, both here and on that narrow stairwell the two had descended.

Cork pushed open a gate, the bell ringing loudly. He gave a slight smile and moved out, while Katashan held the gate slightly open, seeing nothing but more stone across a wide path.

He could hear voices outside, but there didn't seem to be too many people. Someone shouted a hello to Cork. Probably not a surprise that the local man should be recognized but it made Katashan nervous.

Cork finally came back, slipping inside the gate and gave a nod of encouragement. "Stay close beside me. We'll head to the right and past the temple. I know a tavern where we can sit for a bit and get the feel of things. We can't head for the gate until this evening, and we'll have to find out if his Lordship has already put his guards everywhere on the path."

"I'll walk nearby, but not with you," Katashan said. He met Cork's stubborn look with one of his own this time. "If they put out a description of me, this cloak isn't going to be much disguise. I'll stay close enough that I won't lose you."

"I'd feel better if you were close enough that I knew I could use my sword, if need be --"

"And that's exactly what I don't want." Katashan caught hold of Cork's arm and made certain he had the man's full attention, even with the chickens trying to get past. "If they come after me, Cork, there's no reason for you to go down as well. Remember that you are here to help me avoid trouble as best you can, but nothing more."

He frowned and finally nodded reluctant agreement before Katashan let go. Katashan couldn't be certain his companion would back away if they ran into trouble, so he determined not to find any.

Cork listened for a moment at the gate and then carefully slipped out on to the walkway. The people outside laughed when he shooed the chickens back in, but didn't seem to take any other notice.

"Now, sir. Quick, and to the right."

Katashan obeyed, bowing his head, and moving as fast as he dared though the gate and along the stone pathway. It seemed narrow, and then realized there would be no need for anything wider. No horses down here, Katashan realized. No wagons. Just people walking.

Sounds echoed oddly and he could smell fish everywhere. He walked along, close to the stone wall on the right, which he took at first to be nothing more than the smooth surface of the cliff.

Then he saw the carved relief of waves and fish.

He looked up.

The sight stopped him, even now in the midst of danger. He could do nothing but stare.

A city of red, beige and white stone rose all around him, the buildings carved out of a chasm in the cliff. To the left, buildings of only a story or two had been carved from the rock - - carved completely through in many places, because he could see to the sky and ocean through openings. To his right stood buildings so tall he had to crane his neck to see the tops. The locals had carved them into the cliff wall, and around the doorways stood pillars of multicolored stone, topped with gargoyles, eagles and dragons. Statues of men, gods and creatures seemed to grow from the building walls, carved from the world around them. He could not take it all in --

"No time for gawking, sir," Cork said, taking hold of his arm and hurrying him along.

"I have never -- I am -- words fail me."

"Yes, sir. I've heard that before. I admit, even for a local boy, it still takes the breath away -- but we haven't the time to play tourist. This way, sir."

"Get away from me."

"I don't think so," Cork answered with a bright smile. "We'll walk along like a couple old pals, heading for the tavern. You can look around to your heart's content, and I'll just steer us along."

Katashan stopped arguing because he did, truly, want to see, and with a glance around, he could tell no one seemed to pay them any attention. He ran his hand over the edge of one pediment covered in near perfect stone roses. "It's magnificent."

Cork looked at the wall, and then at the buildings to the left. He smiled. "Yes it is, sir. People in the capital say this is a city built by the gods themselves. It might be that old. There's another level further down the cliff side, a single row mostly of suites and apartments. Up here are the markets, the shops, the taverns, and the temples. City government has buildings here, as well. That building there on the right -- the one with the two hawks carved over the door frame -- that's the Hall of Justice, where the city council meets and settles disputes and gives judgments in trials. The building goes far back into the cliff, a cubbyhole of offices and they say you can get lost in there. That people never come back out."

"You live in a dangerous world where people are forever disappearing into mountains, one way or another."

He laughed. "Yes, sir, you're right. I'd say it's safer to be a ship's man than work for the government -- soldier or clerk -- but, of course, we lose ships now and again as well. I've lost more relatives to the sea than to the mountains." He looked towards the ocean, visible through the windows of the stone-carved building to the left. "That's the Salt House. Always a busy place there, so keep your head down and we'll hurry by. And the next door down, that's the Fish House. You go there if you want to arrange the hire of a ship for the sake of the catch. Always busy as well --"

"Magic," Katashan said and almost lifted his hand. He stopped before Cork did more than draw a quick, hissing breath. "There's magic everywhere."

"Of course there is, sir. How else could they keep a place like this dry and livable, so close to the sea? Do watch yourself, sir. Common people don't have magic here, so they don't take notice of it. But we have a priesthood and they keep their eyes on such things, and every generation or so a true mage comes in and renews the spells, though that's not well known either. The locals, they just wouldn't understand, since they've no magic of their own and mistrust it."

"I understand. The common people at home don't have magic either --" He stopped himself with a silent curse.

Cork gave him a look that showed no surprise, but rather a little nod as though confirming something he had obviously already considered. Katashan quickly steered the conversation away from that dangerous ground, though. He wasn't ready to answer questions about himself and why he was *not* one of those common people.

"What is that building with the dolphins carved all over it?" he asked, pointing to an area with dolphins carved around a wide opening. Two women entered, laughter echoing back out from the cavernous interior.

"That's the baths, sir."

"Baths. Really? How delightful."

"Oh yes, sir. We're very nearly civilized here. There's a hot spring inside, and cool water from the same source as the wells. It's a lovely way to spend a free afternoon."

"Do you see any sea people here, Cork?"

"Once every ten years or so. They come in to trade, mostly bringing their lovely pearl work and trading for good nets and rope. Twenty or so will come in at once, and then swim out and another twenty will come in. We're the only city on the entire coast they visit. The gods alone know why. If their visits were more often, or at least predictable, we'd be famous and rich for it."

"Is that what you want for this city? For it to be famous and rich and filled with people?"

Cork gave him another startled look. "When you put it like that -- no, I guess not. How odd. I always thought -- well never mind."

Katashan nodded. "I've lived in cities famous for one reason or another. I'm looking for somewhere less hectic now. However looking around, I would think it must be hard to get a shop here," Katashan said, deliberately turning the conversation aside again. "Limited space, yes?"

"Yes. Many shopkeepers start up on the bluffs by the fortress, and apply for a cliff shop with the council. The list is long, but shops do close here every year for one reason or another. And some businesses join forces and share a space. Usually the wait's no more than three years."

That sounded like a frighteningly long time to Katashan, although he wasn't entirely certain why. Perhaps he only wanted to fit in here -- or somewhere -- and feel as though he had found a home. Maybe he was ready for the journey to end and to find peace again. He pushed that thought away, though, with the reminder of the things going on here that didn't promise much peace in the near future.

"And there, at the branching, is the temple of Peralin, the patron god of Salbay."

Katashan looked up with a start and found the path parted before him with a narrow crevice to the right, a wider one to the left. In the center stood an ornate building that put the others to shame for the amount of detail carved into the surface. Stairs lead upward, narrow at the bottom, widening before two broad doors of silver.

Between the doors stood a statue, and not one carved of the local red and pale stone, but rather jet black: A man cloaked, sitting upon his horse with the animal's head high. Katashan felt his heart pound and his breath catch. He stopped and he stared, aware that Cork tried to urge him on. He could not, for the moment, move.

"What -- the statue --" he said, fighting for words in a language the man would understand.

"Ah, yes. No one knows how they got so large a statue down here, either. Myth says he rode in all by himself and took sentry there. And that, on the day we see him riding elsewhere we'll be in a damned lot of . . . damned . . . lot. . . . Oh hell, sir. No. Say it's not true."

"We shared a hay shed the night before I arrived. The horse is called Night."

"So it is, sir. Yes. It is. Gods all. What does it mean?"

"It means, I suppose, that we are all in a damned lot of trouble."

CHAPTER ELEVEN

C ork led him down the right side path past the temple and to an otherwise empty tavern where a single man stood behind a bar made of drift wood and more stone. Huge shells hung from nets along the walls, and a stuffed shark stood sentinel over the bar. Strange place, Katashan thought.

He wanted to go back to the temple and pray. Or maybe not. He hadn't been to a temple to pray since he put aside his robes to go to war. This was not his god. . . .

Or maybe it was.

He looked back at Cork, finally. "It's quiet here," he said, because saying anything else seemed fraught with too much else.

"It's too early for the usual crowd," Cork answered as they settled at a wooden table in the shadowy corner of the room. "This is the favorite spot for the fleet captains and their men, but they'll not be back until nearly sunset. Two ciders, if you would, Sarton."

The order won an odd look from the proprietor who must usually provide Cork with something a bit stronger. Cork had been wise though; today they both needed clear heads to face any trouble Lord Arpan might create. Katashan waited silently at the table, looking down at the surface; it had been worn and nicked in places by careless knives, and some not so careless with pictures and names. Sarton brought the drinks in plain clay mugs, took coin from Cork, and retreated back to where he had been wiping out other mugs. Katashan traced out a few crude letters with his finger as he sipped the cider.

"Sir," Cork said. Then he stopped and shook his head. He sipped more cider. Then he started to shake his head, and drank more.

"You'll never get drunk enough on this stuff, Cork," Katashan said.

"Ah, too true, sir." He put aside his already nearly empty cup, placed both hands on the table, and looked Katashan straight in the face. "I would like you to tell me that it was a joke, sir. A very bad joke."

"I'd like to think it is," Katashan said. He sipped the sweet cider.

"But it isn't. Gods all," Cork said. He picked up his empty cup and sat it down again with a frown.

"Finish mine. Then we'll have another round on me."

"Very kind of you, sir." He took the cup and sipped. Katashan could see calculation in those dark blue eyes and he wondered what the guardsman intended to do next.

"You can still walk away, Cork."

"Can I, sir? And how far do I have to walk, do you suppose, to be free of this mess?"

"From what I can guess about this trouble, and those involved. . . ." He glanced out at the street, thinking about the temple, the Gods, Sherina and magic. "I would suggest you go to Kirin, the capital of Taris. I can give you names and assure you of a good reception."

Cork started to laugh and cut himself off abruptly. "You're dead serious, aren't you sir?"

"Very much so."

"Kind of you to offer . . . but this is my home. And I have - - Maylee!"

Cork abruptly pushed himself up from the table and quickly

crossed to the doorway. A slight girl with light hair and flushed face stood there, breathless as she let Cork take hold of her. He started to pull her to the table, but she shook her head and pushed him away -- though not far.

"No -- time," she said, still gasping. "His Lordship -- he came back early. He wants the foreigner." She glanced at Katashan, and took a deeper breath before she continued. "Begging your pardon, sir. Not finding you at the fortress he ordered a full call of guards. Serrano said Cork, went to the city to get supplies for his lordship's lunch. No matter. His Lordship -- going to start flogging guardsmen until the foreigner is found. Disband the troops, strip Captain --"

"We must get back." Katashan stood and headed for the door.

"Sir, I've no idea why he wants you so badly," Cork said, his face pale in contrast to Maylee's blush. "I don't like it --"

"Neither do I, but I won't allow men to be flogged or the Captain stripped of rank onn my account. Get me back in. I'll take my chances with Arpan later. I'm not helpless. Let's go!"

"Get back before you're missed, love. We'll be there shortly. What should I bring for his bastard lordship's meal?"

"There will be supplies by the herbarium door, Cork," she said. Her hand brushed lightly against his face. "Just bring them up to the kitchen. His guards are already there, waiting for you to show up."

"I will. Go now. Take care. And thank you."

She nodded, giving Katashan one last quick look that mingled relief with worry before she left again, running back along the path. Katashan worried that others had seen her, and that it would bring her trouble and lead back to Cork still.

"Sir --"

"We go back. You get me into the fortress and as close to my rooms as you can. I'll play it from there."

"I don't like it."

"Neither do I. However, there's not been a lot about this business I have liked. Come on, man. We don't have time to waste!"

Cork no longer made any sign of arguing. He started out the door and Katashan looked back at the proprietor, worried.

"Not a problem, sir. Maylee's uncle."

Katashan nodded with relief as they hurried out into the street and rushed back towards the fortress gate. Katashan cast one worried look at the statue of Peralin and Night as they passed, wishing the god could help him -- and at the same time wishing he didn't find himself involved in something that might need a god or two to unravel.

They passed only a few people along the way, and none of them took any real interest in the two. Katashan almost thought they might have been warned to look the other way. Lord Arpan wouldn't be popular with many of his people, seeing his tyrannical ways. And Cork was a local boy and liked, which might yet save him from the trouble that followed Katashan.

They finally rushed back through the garden gate, the bell ringing to announce entry this time. The chickens ran up, got a sprinkling of crumbs from Cork even now, and disappeared again as the two men hurried through the garden. They found the herbarium empty, but true to her word, three tiny leather bags sat by the door. Cork grabbed them up, but he shook his head with sudden panic as he looked inside one.

"What's wrong?"

"I don't know what this is. What if his Lordship asks? How can I say I went for it, if I don't even know --?"

"Saffron," Katashan said, looking into the first bag, and then the others. "Cinnamon, red pepper."

"Bless you, sir."

"Let's go."

Cork swallowed nervously -- his first real sign of worry -- and opened the door. They slipped inside and started up the stairs, pausing to listen at the first landing. The silence grew oppressive and it seemed better to move upward towards the danger than to wait like mice cowering in a hole.

They passed one opening, another; hurried down a quiet hall, and up another set of stairs. At the next landing they could hear loud voices above them. Cork shook his head and pushed Katashan back downward again.

"That's not good, sir. We'll have to find you another way."

"Get me somewhere away from you, Cork. That's all we need worry about right now."

"No sir, that's not all. I'd not be happy with myself if I didn't do my best."

"Cork --"

He plainly didn't intend to listen as he started down a hall for another set of stairs. "This way, sir."

Katashan had no choice but to follow, unless he intended to go charging away on his own and straight into the hands of the enemy. That seemed neither wise nor a good way to keep Cork safe if they found his friend in the same area. So he followed the guard back down into the hall to other stairs and up another flight. Loud voices rose at the top of the next flight. They reached the opening and Cork looked out, and then back, shaking his head.

"His Lordship's guards are everywhere out there. But I think we can get past this set of the bastards and up to the next level. If we can get an old door open there, that'll take you far up into the tower, away from the paths that lead to the city. That's the best I can do, sir. I don't know where you'll come out."

"I'll take it. Let's go."

Cork pushed his hand through his curly hair and nodded, then sidled back up to the archway. He held his hand out and Katashan readied himself, grateful he'd had a moment to catch his breath.

Cork signaled with a lift of his hand and quick wave. Katashan hurried past his friend and to the next set of stairs with barely a glance at the line of dark jackets seen from the back, and the face of a couple servants who beyond a doubt saw him. In fact, he had the distinct impression they got louder to keep Lord Arpan's guards watching them and so they didn't hear the people passing behind.

Cork crossed after him and smiled brightly with relief. He patted Katashan on the shoulder, and squeezed past to lead the way once more. They'd entered an area which obviously hadn't been used very often and found no torches beyond the first turn, leaving only a dark tunnel ahead.

Cork cursed. "It's not safe to go on in the dark, sir. There are twists and turns, and a few paths that we wouldn't want to take. I'll go back a level or two and get a torch. You wait here. If they catch me I can say I was only coming up from the city."

"With a torch in hand," Katashan said, shaking his head.

"Making sure the others are lit, of course. It's custom coming up the stairs this late in the day."

"Cork --"

"Just hold here. I'll be back soon, sir."

"I could --"

"If you're thinking about using magic, may I suggest you don't? Not unless you absolutely have to, sir. Because magic draws magic, or so I've heard and I'm thinking that might be dangerous right now."

"True. And I don't need to draw attention to myself."

Cork nodded and moved back down the stairwell. Katashan waited, wondering what he'd do if his friend didn't return. Get lost, probably, and end up where he shouldn't be.

Cork returned before he could even fully formulate a plan of action. They started upwards again. Cobwebs fizzled in the fire from the torch, and a rat squealed and rushed past them, winning a curse from Katashan's guide. At the next landing

Katashan found what Cork had been talking about -- three passages, all of them equally dark and uninviting. Even Cork paused for a moment, and then turned to the left and started upward again on a narrow set of stairs. They continued upward past another three such spots and finally reached an old oak door at the end of the stairs.

"Ah, here we are, sir. This is the door we want. It's not been opened in decades, I fear."

"How the hell do you know your way around so well?"

"Ah. Never occurred to me you wouldn't know. My uncle on my mother's side was the fortress archivist, sir. He had a fascination with these halls. And the former Captain, he wanted to know every twist and turn and set my uncle to work mapping them. Didn't trust the place, not knowing where an enemy could hide. So my uncle and me mapped them out. Well, most of them. Some we just never bothered to put on the map for the good Captain Muden."

Katashan grinned, not at all surprised. Cork shoved the torch into the dusty holder on the wall and took a look at the ancient oak door. Katashan could see it had not been opened in a long time, but a slight pull on the handle got it to move. Cork looked relieved.

"Cork, go on down and get yourself inside with the others," Katashan ordered.

"Sir --"

"Go." Katashan waved his hand back towards the shadowed steps leading downward, anxious to get Cork where he needed to be. "I'll get the door open, but I'd like you to do something for me." He drew the ritual blade up over this neck and dropped the small knife and chain into Cork's hand. "Take this and put it somewhere safe. I don't want it taken. It's very important to me. If anything does happen to me, take the blade to Pater Matish. He'll know what to do with it."

"Yes, sir. I can do that," he said, looking as though he held a poisonous spider in the palm of his hand.

"Go on now."

"I --" He stopped, looked at the door, and then nodded. "Yes, sir. I'll see you inside."

"I'll see you there. Be damned careful, Cork. And remember, no matter what happens, throwing yourself in trouble with me will not help."

Cork had taken one step away and now looked stubbornly at him.

"Think of Maylee, friend. You have a future with her. Don't throw it away."

Cork frowned. The man plainly hated giving up what he considered his duty. Cork put a hand on Katashan's shoulder. "Don't antagonize him, sir. I don't know it will help either way, mind you, but I do know you can make it worse."

"I'll keep that in mind. Thank you."

Cork nodded, grabbed the torch, and hurried away, soon lost in the curve of the stairs. Katashan couldn't hear him after the first half dozen steps. He wished his friend well.

Katashan leaned against the wall and let his hand trace the edge of the door waiting until Cork had plenty of time to get away. He counted to five hundred, and then counted again before he tried to pull the door open.

It came half a hand's breadth and stuck.

Katashan had to pull and grunt until he could see inside the dusty room with shuttered windows. Mice scattered for the corners and he thought something larger flapped up near the ceiling, though he could see nothing when he looked. The room had plainly not been used in years, and he'd leave tracks. Light filtered in from cracks in the shutters, coloring dustmotes with hints of gold.

With another grunt, he pushed the door wide enough to slip inside, and then fought it back closed again. He almost sneezed at the dust raised by his entry and did his best to keep to the edges of the wall, moving past piles of old rugs and boxes of things long since forgotten. He wanted to stop and see if he could find treasures, like a child playing in a forgotten storeroom, pretending to be a pirate. He wanted to stay --

Katashan knew remaining hidden here would not help anyone, including himself. He also knew he would regret going willingly to Lord Arpan. The man was not reasonable. Hee went anyway because he had always been appalled at the idea of letting the unreasonable ones win, or letting others suffer for his sake.

Katashan slipped out of the room by another old oak door that creaked loud enough to wake the -- no, best not to even think that one.

The hall, though clean, didn't appear to be used as often as others he had traversed since his unfortunate arrival. Katashan found a stairwell at the farthest end of the silent corridor, and headed down to another hall. He saw no one there, crossed it, and headed down again, zigzagging through two more levels before three of Lord Arpan's guards stepped out of a room and almost ran into him.

Damn. He had hoped to fall into Captain Serrano's hands or at least get picked up by one of the local guards. He didn't put up any sort of disagreement when the men captured him, feigning surprise to learn anyone had been looking, but that didn't help. Katashan still arrived bruised and bloody by the time they dragged him into the main hall.

Lord Arpan sat in his chair at the end of the room, glowering over something the others were saying. Captain Serrano and Cork glanced up at the entrance, and both looked away again, anger in their eyes. Damn. He didn't want Cork here. He feared the guard had an impulsive streak that could get him into trouble. He saw Serrano give a warning shake of his head, a danger in itself, if Arpan saw but right now His Lordship's full attention had turned to the captive. Katashan wanted to remind them to be discreet and careful but he dared not even look their way.

"So you send a guard to do servants work?" Lord Arpan said to Serrano, though his eyes kept going back to Katashan with a hint of pleasure and maybe a little relief.

"Only for the very important work," Serrano said. "I wanted to make certain the items were well selected, my Lord."

"Thank you for the kind words, Captain," Cork answered, his voice quiet and tight with control, though Arpan would likely not realize the difference. "And here's the coin back that I didn't spend. The saffron was slightly less expensive than we thought, sir."

That exchange of coin seemed to do the trick. His Lordship saw Cork hand over a few coins, and lost interest in the man. Good. Now if Serrano would just dismiss Cork and get him out of the room --

By then Katashan had been dragged fully across the room and settled on his knees before Lord Arpan's chair. When Arpan finally looked down, Katashan saw anticipation in his face.

"You were not in your room, foreigner."

"No, sir, I wasn't. I stepped out for a little while. I do not like to be confined."

"Where were you?"

"Walking the halls."

A movement of his hand -- someone kicked Katashan hard in the lower back. He tumbled forward.

"Tie his hands," Arpan said, leaning back in his chair.

"Your Lordship, I must protest!" Serrano said as he came forward half a dozen steps, as though to get between the guards and Katashan. *Hell.* He'd expected something from Cork, but had hoped the Captain had better control. "As far as we know, this man has done nothing more than taken a walk from his room and he had not even been told to stay there. It is hardly a cause for this treatment."

Katashan had gotten back to his knees, silently cursing Serrano's folly, especially since he didn't think annoying the good Lord of the land would help. Lord Arpan did little more than glance at the captain, though. Katashan had all his attention. Just as well.

"Where were you?"

"I walked," Katashan said, not bothering to fight as the guards yanked his arms back and tightly bound the wrists. Afterwards, though, he fought back an unexpected surge of panic: the last time he'd been bound with his hands behind his back he had gone into slavery. Not this time. This time, if he didn't get free, he was going to his death . . . and he couldn't say that would be worse.

"Where were you?"

"Down the hall," he said. When the soldier kicked, he couldn't stop the fall this time, though he did have sense enough to turn his head so he didn't break his nose.

"Where were you? What are you involved in?" Lord Arpan demanded. He came down from the chair and caught Katashan by the hair, jerking him back up. "You will tell me," he said. "You will tell me everything I want to know."

Whether it was the truth or not, Katashan thought, though he didn't say so aloud. Ah, but it did, finally, give him a thought on how to end this part of the fiasco quickly. Looking directly into Lord Arpan's face, he showed a little worry for the first time and then lowered his eyes. The bait worked. Lord Arpan leaned closer.

"I followed a woman," he said, softly. "I thought she was a dream at first, she looked so like the poor dead woman I brought here. She came to me and asked me to go with her. She said -- she wanted me. A beautiful woman, with golden hair and bright eyes -"

"Who was she?" he said, letting go of Katashan's hair at last. He barely kept from falling again. "What was her name?"

"A lovely lady," Katashan said, letting his accent sound richer, his voice steady. He stared up at Lord Arpan as the man straightened and stepped back. "She said she was Sherina."

His Lordship's face went white and he stepped back, nearly falling. Then he growled a curse and kicked, catching Katashan in mid-chest. He feared bones cracked at the impact and he tumbled backward onto his arms, the pain excruciating.

"You will not say such a thing again. Do you understand me, bastard foreigner? You will not say it again!"

Katashan barely managed a nod. He could see fear, anger and despair in the man's face.

But there was no sign disbelief.

And he didn't ask where Katashan had been again.

CHAPTER TWELVE

Lord Arpan and his people left that afternoon with Katashan bound and gagged, and a rope tying him His Lordship's horse so he had to walk behind him. Serrano protested but Arpan still ignored him, having become so clearly fixated on Katashan that even his men looked unsettled.

Katashan appreciated Captain Serrano at least trying. They all knew that no matter what Lord Arpan said, he did not intend for the prisoner to arrive alive in the capital city. Justice had not been a word mentioned at all on either side.

They brought the body along as well, reminding Katashan of the other problem he faced. This family, living and dead, appeared to have fixed on him as the enemy, and he feared he wouldn't survive it. He may not have really seen Sherina in the halls earlier but he'd seen her often enough since her death.

He considered putting up a fight and forcing -- or encouraging -- Lord Arpan to kill him and forgo what was bound to be an unpleasant day on the trail. He had no illusions about the future and a hope for survival --

He had braced his legs and lifted his head --

"Sir, Tarin is missing," someone said. "Parino and Matili, too."

"Are they, by damn! I'll have them hanged for deserting their posts!"

"Yes sir. A servant girl said she saw the three going off with some lady --"

Breath caught. "Damn them," Arpan said more softly this time.

"We'll need replacements, sir. It's not safe to travel these trails with so few men."

"I don't trust Serrano or his men."

"Surely they're more loyal to you than to a Captain."

Odd. Very odd. Katashan had the feeling his Lordship's man tried to push him into taking others along -- and yet the glare he gave Katashan showed no hope. Lord Arpan had apparently arrived with only a handful of men, and with three missing, he wouldn't feel safe enough to leave. Lord Arpan obviously had few friends among his own people. For a moment Katashan thought he might even have a reprieve.

And a heartbeat later he felt something that sent a chill up his spine. Magic. Magic used --

He looked back over his shoulder and found Pater Matish, standing at the edge of the shadows, his hands moving, his lips forming words Katashan coudln't hear at this distance. The priest knew Katashan had looked his way and gave a little nod of his head. And then he looked toward Lord Arpan and his hand rose a little more. Katashan could feel the magic in the air, like warmth on a cold day.

"Serrano!" Arpan suddenly yelled, startling everyone including Katashan. "I want two of your men. Your best men. That one you sent to market -- you seem to be able to do without him. And another."

"Sir --"

"Don't argue with me. I've not hanged you, but I haven't left yet."

"Epas, get Cork and Ona. Tell them to grab their kits."

"Sir."

Cork. Katashan lowered his head once more, wondering how -- and why -- this had all been arranged. He would have at least one ally on this journey. He decided immediate death was not the best answer. A little hope would see him through for a while.

The two guards arrived at a run and Cork didn't look his way at all. Good. Moments later Arpan yelled and they were on their way. Katashan jogged behind Lord Arpan's horse and knew, at least, that the man would not go charging off away from his guards who were mostly on foot.

The path out of Salbay wound up through the hill country, over narrow trails and through rocky defiles, always with the sea not far to the left. In some ways the terrain helped Katashan. The horses had started out at a canter that he, bruised and bound, had a hard time holding. Before long, however, they'd left the scattered buildings behind and the trail began to twist and climb, forcing the horses to slow. Katashan limped along, his ankle already twisted and his mouth dry around the gag.

The guards traded off point duty during the long day. When his turn came, Cork went past without a sign, but later Ona glared. He didn't need another enemy in this group, but at the same time it seemed like a wise choice. If Ona showed outward hostility, then his Lordship might not look too closely at Cork.

The soldiers traded off carrying Sherina's body which now rested in a simple casket. None of them looked happy.

Even though the pace remained slow, by the time they made camp the first night Katashan had fallen a number of times. He felt bruised, scraped, battered and very nearly senseless. The guards tied him with his back to a tree, his arms still behind him, and left him there with the gag in his mouth.

His Lordship had a tent set up on the headland overlooking the sea and straight in front of Katashan. The man shouted for his food, bullied his men, and finally retreated after a final glare at Katashan.

A thick, grey fog began to roll up over the cliffs as the sun went down. Katashan watched it, vaguely aware that she would come soon. He didn't care.

He did note when the missing soldiers showed up, though.

Tarin, Parina and Matilli won shouts all around from their companions, and a roar of anger from Lord Arpan. They went into his tent and they came out sometime later, quietly and heads bowed. But he had heard Sherina's name spoken loudly by her father. He didn't know what the three told him, but Katashan suspected there had been magic involved anyway -- though from Pater Matish, rather than Sherina. He wondered if the men would survive much longer than he did.

If those three had been wise, they would have headed up into the mountains, rather than come back to Lord Arpan. However, they survived the meeting. Maybe his Lordship had few men he could trust.

The night grew quiet as the guards settled by their fires to the right and left of his Lordship's tent. The fog brought damp cold and he could hear the men muttering over their cooking pots. He ignored the scent of food. He'd learned to do that as a slave. He had even learned to ignore pain and privation during that time. He hadn't thought he'd have reason to pull those controls back again.

A guard stood at the tent entrance, and as the darkness drew in the others huddled around campfires, curling up into blankets.

Katashan wondered where they had put the body.

A hand touched his shoulder. If he hadn't been gagged he would have given a yelp of surprise.

"Calm, sir," Cork said softly from behind the tree. "Calm and quiet. I'm going to untie you now. No, don't shake your head. You'll only draw the bastard guards' attention. There. That's done."

The rope that had been wound too tightly around his chest loosened. He almost fell forward, but Cork caught his shoulder in time. No one saw, which was Lord Arpan's fault for being so cruel and leaving him without a fire on such a cold, damp night. No one could see Cork in the shadow of the tree, and the rising fog only added to their cover.

"There, now. Let me undo your arms. This is going to be hell, sir," Cork warned softly. He felt one hand slip between him and the tree while the other still held tight to his shoulder. Cork bent close to his ear, whispering words as he worked. "I could see earlier that your hands were swollen, and from the falls you've taken I wouldn't be surprised if at least one of the shoulders isn't dislocated. I'm leaving the gag in, sir, until I'm done."

Katashan took a deep breath and gave a little quick nod. He tried to prepare himself with another ragged breath. Even the little movement Cork made with his arms sent agony through his shoulders and neck. He feared he would be in no shape to escape. And worse, he couldn't stop Cork and tell him to leave. What Cork had done already would draw attention and his friend would be one of the first suspects. Katashan only feared Cork would have to carry him if he passed out and they wouldn't get far, fog and dark or not.

Magic would have helped, but he hadn't his ritual blade, and without it the ability to draw magic would be far too difficult in his current condition. So he sat still and tried only to take deep breaths, pushing down into his center, looking for the core of his power --

But the possibility of drawing on that power disappeared in a blaze of blinding pain as his arms finally came free of the rope. He moaned despite himself, and loudly enough to draw the attention of the tent guard. The man looked Katashan's way and laughed. Cork held him in place and held his breath.

The guard never came any closer, standing with the flames between him and the prisoner, effectively blinding himself at that distance.

"Okay, sir. We're almost there," Cork whispered again. He sounded shaky now as well. "I was going to leave the gag until we're away, but I think you'll need a drink of something with a little fire in it before you have the strength to go. I'm taking the gag away now."

The filthy cloth pulled free, tearing at wounds around his mouth and leaving the coppery taste of blood behind. For the first time Cork peered fully around the tree placing a small metal flask to Katashan's lips. He sipped carefully so he didn't cough or sputter.

The liquid -- he couldn't name the liquor -- burnt the cuts on his lips, inside his mouth, and then drew fire all the way down his throat, chest, and into his stomach -- but it did help a little.

"More, sir?

"No, thank you. Not if you really expect me to walk away." His voice sounded weak and Cork had to lean close to hear.

Even the movement of his lips hurt. But the liquor had cleared his head somewhat. Katashan carefully turned to take a look around the area. He saw only shadows of other trees, barely outlined in the flickering light of the campfires. The darkness and the fog, conspired to help them tonight.

"Okay, then, sir, we're about ready. We're lucky. I'm a fisherman's son, remember. I know this weather. The fog will fall in thick around us soon, and that's our best chance to get away. When it does, we'll have to move quickly lest someone gets smart enough to come close to watch over you. I thought about trying to borrow a horse or two, but where we're heading we'd just have to abandon them anyway."

"Put the gag back until we're ready to go," Katashan said, shifting his shoulders a little, but keeping his hands down to the ground. "They'll notice that missing before anything else."

"Yes, sir, that's true." He put the foul cloth back in place and then gently patted Katashan's shoulder. "Not much longer now."

Cork slid back behind the tree again and Katashan, though he kept hold of Katashan's shoulder so that he didn't fall.

Katashan spent the time carefully moving his hands and stifling the urge to moan at the pain. His legs felt stiff and sore, the knees protesting even a little shift of movement. He feared he would not be much help in this escape. He forced himself to calm and ignore the pains as best he could. Cork risked his life the moment he cut Katashan loose and he didn't want this to be on a useless gesture, aborted before he even tried.

Cork certainly did know the weather. The fog rolled in off the ocean like smoke rising up the cliff side, swallowing up the edges of the camp, and finally obscuring the tent and the guard until they seemed little more than shapes of grey in white.

Cork moved; time to go. He quickly crawled around to the front of the tree and pulled the gag down again. "Ready, sir?"

"Yes," Katashan said, which was mostly a lie, but they had no choice and they'd never have a better chance.

As Cork helped lift him, agony swept through body. Cork didn't ask any questions or wait for him to recover. He caught Katashan under the arms. . . .

CHAPTER THIRTEEN

Katashan realized he must have fainted. Cork carried him, tossed over the guard's shoulder like a bag of grain. Cork huffed slightly but otherwise made remarkably little noise as he moved across the rocky ground. They hadn't gone far, though. Katashan could still hear the horses, loud and nervous, as the fog slipped around them.

"Down," Katashan whispered, fighting the urge to be ill. "Faster if I walk."

"Only if you're able to, sir," he said, but lowered Katashan to his feet.

His legs started to buckle. Pain swept through his body like fire, and he trembled. Appalled, Katashan felt himself start to go faint again. He fought the feeling away as much out of embarrassment as desperation. The combination worked, and in the faint gray light of the fog-filled night he could see Cork looked pleased. The guard wouldn't have gotten far climbing the rocky hills with a dead weight slung across his shoulder.

Katashan, already half-breathless and unsteady, suspected they wouldn't make very good time anyway. The ground seemed to shift under his feet and everything blurred more than he could blame on the fog. His shoulder and chest ached, and his head pounded, but he moved because he would not give up after all Cork had done.

And for a few steps he thought they were actually going to

get away.

Lightning brightened the fog as though filling the world with fire. Shapes, if not features, stood out starkly for a moment.

The ghostly figure of Sherina waited, barely a yard away, her arms reaching for them. Then the night and the fog swallowed her again. Thunder rolled across the world.

Cork's breath hissed, followed by a nearly silent litany of prayers and curses. He caught hold of Katashan and changed direction, leading him off toward the right. She moved as well, a willow wisp in the wind, a faint hint of magical light slipping ahead of them, and waiting. With Sherina there, Katashan didn't even pay attention to the startled yells from the others. The camp had come awake too soon.

He and Cork changed direction again, but she moved as well --

"Gods all," Cork whispered. "She's playing games with us, sir. Letting us see her --"

Lightning illuminated the fog once more. She drifted on the breeze, closer than Katashan had thought. He barely had time to pull Cork back out of her reach.

"Damn all. What game --" Cork whispered, frantic.

"No. I don't think she brought the storm," Katashan said.

"Sir?"

"She's not happy that we keep spotting her."

The lightning flashed again, and her scream of rage rivaled the fury of the growing storm. He and Cork scrambled away, but now they had Lord Arpan and his men at their back. Those men quite obviously hadn't seen the apparition but they did realize their prisoner had escaped. It wouldn't take long for them to notice Cork had gone missing as well.

"Sir?" Cork said. He sounded worried and apologetic as he leaned Katashan against a tree and pulled his knife. "I don't think we're going to get away."

Men rushed at them through the fog. He heard swords drawn but at the same time Katashan saw the faint movement in the fog as she swept forward as well, with a scream and a laugh from hell.

"Down!" Katashan dragged his friend to the ground. She brushed over them, and he felt her touch like the hand of death upon him: cold, lifeless.

Cork whispered and prayed as the two scrambled away on hands and knees, Katashan forcing his arms to work despite the agony. He looked back, but he could see no sign of Sherina this time and it worried him where she had gone --

Cork continued to move forward, pausing only to help him over some broken terrain, and then starting forward again. Screams filled the night and he knew where Sherina had gone now -- she had found others, and for a moment at least, they had a chance to get clear.

"Go!" Katashan ordered, pushing at his companion. Cork got to his feet and pulled him up as well, and held on even when Katashan's legs refused to cooperate. He could see the trail not far away and a smaller path worn smooth up the slight incline to it. They dared not go that way where the guard would easily find them -- and Sherina too, following a path. Instead, they slipped on the damp rock along the edge, nearly crashed into trees -- but the sounds behind them drove them on. Men screamed in agony and fear. He heard her laughter, darker than the night, and it drove Katashan upward, away from her with a fear that gave him strength when his body otherwise failed.

They rushed across the trail and to the rocks. He slipped again and this time pulled Cork down with him. When Katashan lifted his head, he saw a face near the trees. And another. He gave a startled cry, and Cork stopped -- but the strangers already charged away through the woods, sounding like a herd of startled deer.

"Damn. Mountain people, sir. Gave me a start," Cork said,

half panting. "But not a problem for us, I'd say."

"Go on without me!" Katashan ordered and tried to pull away.

"No sir. I'm already damned, one way or another. His Lordship will know by now. And that being true, I might as well be damned for a good reason and see this through. I don't want it to be for nothing."

"You are a fool," Katashan gasped, nearly breathless now as Cork dragged him on.

"I thought you'd figured that out by now, sir."

"Ha."

"But even so -- I wasn't the one who walked straight into the fort with the dead body you knew had to be trouble. Sir."

"Excellent point."

They'd reached a ledge of the rocks and a flat spot where Katashan went to his knees and gasped for breath while everything in the world -- fog, screams, and worry -- dimmed. He could hear sounds of men in mortal terror behind them, and some tried to follow, but none caught up with Cork and him, even as slow as they were going.

Cork finally got him back to his feet and held him there, whispering prayers again. They took a step away, and another --

Katashan heard Lord Arpan call his daughter's name, terror in the quavering word. Katashan tried to look back, but he lost his footing. Cork took tighter hold.

"Don't look back, sir. We can't help them."

"I should have warned them," Katashan said. "I should have used my magic --"

"Would it have helped?" Cork asked.

"I don't know. But -- oh Gods. We must go back! She gets stronger when she takes the life from others. She'll be too dangerous, Cork, for us and for everyone else. I can't leave her like this --"

"Oh damn," Cork said. He stopped and looked towards the

camp, lost in the darkness and the fog.

"I'm weak," Katashan said. He thought the fog began dissipating on the wind. "I can't -- without my ritual blade --"

"Ah, yes sir. I forgot."

Cork reached into his tunic and pulled the fine chain up over his head and handed the blade to the startled Katashan. "You said to keep it safe. I figured on me was the best place, once I knew I would be traveling with you."

Katashan took the blade in trembling hands, felt the warmth of the magic and saw the surface even flicker a little. That came from his own need, he knew. He could see Sherina through the fog and glowing now with power from the lives she'd taken. Even with the knife in hand, he wasn't entirely sure he had the power to stop her.

He couldn't destroy her until he found the knowledge of what had created so powerful a death entity. She had become more than a ghost or a lost spirit. He would have to learn more, which meant he would have to find answers to things he would rather not have known about at all.

Right now he only hoped to survive. He drew back the sleeve of his torn and filthy tunic, his fingers still swollen and clumsy. Moving his arm sent agony through his body again, but he laid the blade edge along his wrist and made a good, straight cut, knowing he would need more than just a few drops of blood from a pricked finger this time.

"Gods all," Cork whispered and his fingers tightened on Katashan's shoulder. "I didn't realize -- the magic you used."

"Blood magic," he said, his voice still trembling, but a little stronger. He felt the fire where the blade had cut into skin, and the magic pulled there through his blood gave him a bit of strength -- though the power would ebb away before long. "It's the oldest and most powerful magic man holds. If you're going to be a fool and stay, then you better stand behind me and keep me to my feet."

"Yes, sir."

Sherina turned to them and began to move like a bright moon come to ground. The fog disappeared in a hiss of warmth around her, so unlike the cold of moments before. He could see dead littering the campsite and no movement anywhere except for her. She glowed a lambent yellow with the power she'd taken and she had grown more substantial. When she looked at him, Katashan could feel her intent like a blow against his face, even at this distance.

Cork began whispering fervent prayers to a number of gods. Katashan whispered one of his own -- and in his native language -- to Verina whom he tried not to think had lured him into this madness and to his death.

Sherina floated towards them, cloud-like and smiling.

"Mine," she said and the word real this time. Ah, now that was power she'd gained. "*Mine.*"

"Gods," Cork whispered, prayers forgotten, though he didn't falter as he held Katashan to his feet.

Katashan had no time for anything fancy and no strength for anything complex. He kept the ritual blade carefully hidden in his hand, the blood spreading down over the blade. He hoped she didn't realize the words he now whispered weren't a prayer this time, but a rather a conduit for power.

He waited as she came slowly closer.

He had thought she was being cautious in her approach, but when he saw her face he could see her gloating. She came slowly because she wanted to enjoy this moment and make him dread what she would do. Her smile grew when he purposely took a step backwards, as though in fear. He could use her cruelty against her. The longer she took the more certain his own spell became.

Cork had stopped praying and cursing. He didn't seem to be breathing much, either.

Two arm lengths away. Katashan held the last word,

brought the blade up and as she swept in on him, he shouted the last of his spell and threw the blade at her.

Power rose around him like a wind. Hurling the blade and the blood away from him meant tearing the spell from his body and that action came at a cost. The weapon found the target and she had become solid enough that it did not pass through, but hung there in her midst, burning --

She screamed and power slashed at the world like the knife ripped at her. Katashan and Cork tumbled backwards, with the gale that tore branches from the trees. As they landed, Cork threw himself over Katashan before hit hard enough that he felt the impact, even underneath the larger body. Cork grunted and pushed it off again, relieving Katashan of many worries. Cork immediately began to scramble out from underneath what appeared to be half a tree that had fallen. A moment later he pulled Katashan out as well. Not gently, but they had no no time for gentleness.

The downed tree gave them a little cover. Katashan looked back, a hand on his bleeding wrist, wondering what to do next. Sherina still hung in the air, wailing into the wind, though the sound seemed less piercing, and the wind grew less fierce. The fog even started to roll back up over the cliff side, though Katashan could wish for it to stay away a little longer.

"You need that bandaged," Cork said, remarkably calm under the circumstances. He tore cloth from his already ripped tunic and began to wrap it around the wrist. Katashan couldn't tell if Cork had suffered any injuries or not. "Can you heal yourself?"

"I could, with the blade," Katashan said, waving a hand towards Sherina. The weapon had dropped at her feet now, a sign she had become less substantial and lost power. However, he didn't think that made it any safer to retrieve.

"It's important to your magic?"

"Yes."

"Well, hell. We need it then, don't we?"

He wanted to say no. "I can do some magic without it," Katashan said. "Just not much, not very often -- and not very well."

"That doesn't sound like a promising combination under the circumstances, sir."

"No, it doesn't."

"If we could lure her away from the knife, sir --"

"Yes."   He looked at the bandage and nodded. It had slowed the loss of blood, but if he didn't get to the blade quickly, he'd be too weak to stay to his feet, which wouldn't help, either. They had few options and running wasn't one of them. Sherina would only follow and find them in an even worse position.

Besides, with the knife no longer within her, Sherina had begun to recover. She didn't look as strong as she had been but Katashan saw less madness and more control. Had the input of so much power so quickly driven her mad? From what little he had seen of her before, she had been evil and dark, but not insane.

"I'll draw her away," Katashan said. "You get the knife and toss it to me."

"Sir --"

"You have a better plan?"

"No."

"Crawl around the other side of the tree. Quickly. Once you're there, I'll draw her towards me. Be quick, Cork. We will not have a second chance."

"Yes, sir."

He started away but Katashan caught hold of his arm, and held tight, fear silencing him for a moment until he took a deeper breath. "Carefully, Cork. Move very carefully."

He nodded, put a hand on Katashan's arm for a moment and said nothing. Then he scrambled away, crawling on hands and knees. Katashan couldn't be certain she didn't see everything anyway. Sherina was no longer of this world and he really had little experience with such creatures.

He waited, watching Cork move around to the side of the tree and snake his way down the boulders. When Cork finally gave a little signal -- Gods all she had to see that -- Katashan took a deep breath and stood.

His body threatened to collapse. He felt the pains of misuse and the weakness of blood loss, but he also saw Sherina watching him like a cat before a mouse, and as long as he kept her attention they still had a chance of surviving.

Katashan stepped out from around the fallen tree and limped a few steps towards her, his hand raised, a whisper of magic drifting out from the fingers in slow, sinuous curves, drawing her attention. He could still call on the power he'd used to create the first wave of magic, but it wouldn't last for long.

"You are not of this world any longer, Sherina," he said aloud and surprisingly in his own language. He'd gotten used to speaking the southern tongue, training himself to do so during the long months with Tyren and his men.

She watched him as if she understood the words. Perhaps her existence went beyond the power of language. She did not, he noted with worry, leave the vicinity of the knife. He didn't look directly at his friend, but he knew Cork crawled very close, edging along the ground. Unless she moved, he could not get the knife quickly enough to throw it.

"You cannot harm me," Katashan said, but in the language they all understood this time. He didn't want Cork confused. He took another step forward. "Whatever hedge wizard created you, he was weak. How else could I have so easily severed his spell and bound you to me instead?"

"Fool," she said and moved closer to Katashan. She still held considerable power to be able to speak. He shivered at the thought of all the people she had killed and the life forces she had taken to be able to say that word.

Sherina kept moving towards him with a slow and deliberate pace. He wished his knife had taken more from her, though he considered it lucky they'd managed to slow her at all. She still glowed, though not as brightly, and the substance that made her drifted on tendrils around her head and outstretched hands.

She obviously wanted to destroy him. Not only would killing him break her tie to him, but no doubt a person with the amount of magical power he held would give her far more power. He lifted his hand, drawing on more power he could scarce afford to waste on a show like this, but it did hold her attention. Just a moment --

She sensed when Cork grabbed the knife, and spun in the air, parts of her spreading outward like a large and insubstantial sheet in the wind. Cork kept his head and his nerve. He surged to his feet and threw the knife, aiming the weapon straight through her. She screamed, but the passage hardly slowed her.

The blade clattered to the ground to his left. Katashan leapt for it as Cork scrambled for cover. Sherina pursued the guard, and before Katashan could call up a spell, he heard Cork give a cry of pain and fear as he collapsed beneath her.

Katashan rushed to help his friend, yelling out a spell that drained the power from him even as he moved. He kept going, until he and the knife were upon her, and he slashed, feeling the cold of her through his hands. She howled and pulled away from Cork who remained where he had fallen, pale and unmoving. Katashan prayed he wasn't dead. He put himself between her and the guard, willing more power into the knife even when the work sent his heart into a labored beat and he feared he would not stay to his feet. If his spell failed, they were both dead anyway.

He pushed the power out into the blade and from the conduit into the air as tendrils of blood red power encircled her in ropes of light. Sherina wavered back and forth before him, screaming, and wailing so loudly the night seemed to be filled with nothing but her as she tore at the bonds, pulling them apart. He had nothing more to throw against her, and when he went to his knees, she laughed.

The fog spread in again making a gray-on-gray world. Katashan held his head up by a force of will and held to his power for a little longer, for whatever reason humans always held out as long as they could against the inevitable.

The beat of horse hooves.

Cork stumbled to his feet -- not dead, praise the Gods! -- and ran towards the sound, shouting to warn the traveler away. Katashan lost his hold on Sherina and tried to get it back as the rider appeared --

Peralin.

Sherina screamed and swept towards Katashan intent on killing him before she lost the chance. However, Peralin and Night cut between the two, the God shouting words that held the power of life in them. Katashan felt it like warmth and spring and as though new air blew through a tainted world. Light grew, as golden and luminous as a sunny summer day. He could see Cork back on his feet, and stumbling towards Katashan, though he stayed very far away from the rider and Sherina.

"Thank the Gods you're all right," Katashan said, grabbing his friend's arm. Cork sat down right there beside him, still pale and gasping, and wide-eyed as he watched the rider.

Katashan had the blade in his hand. He dared to use a little more power and seal the wound beneath the bandage on his wrist, though not to heal it. The magic flashed bright and he gasped at the sudden fire, but the pain wasn't really much compared to all else he felt.

He went to his knees as he put a hand to Cork's shoulder. His companion shivered and Katashan couldn't decide if it was because of the cold or the sight of Peralin standing between them and the enemy.

"The world's gone mad," Cork whispered, his voice hoarse. He rubbed his hands together, like a man might do on the coldest, most bitter winter night. "I fear I'll never be warm again, sir."

He looked at Cork, blinking back exhaustion, trying not to watch Peralin and fear he would lose. "Call me Katashan. Or Kat, if you prefer. After what we've shared, I hardly think formality is proper."

"I don't know, sir. It might be the only normality I can still hold on to in the world."

Looking up at the God doing battle with the ghost of a dead woman, Katashan agreed. He had to believe Peralin would win, because he hadn't the energy even to stand, let alone fight anymore. If Peralin failed, he might as well go down with him. It would, in fact, be almost a relief to know this work -- and madness -- was over.

Sherina gradually retreated to the cliff's edge as Peralin pushed forward until it seemed horse and rider would leap and take her over the edge. She howled with the wind one last time and took to flight like a screaming banshee, flying off over the ocean. The fog and the night swallowed her and the world went silent; the quiet of the dead who lay all around them.

Cork shivered again. He looked at Katashan with his face white, and then he looked to Peralin and his horse as they came closer. Cork started to stand, but he hadn't the strength left in his legs.

"Sir," Cork said and bowed his head so deeply he nearly fell over. "My Lord."

"Peralin will do, Cork."

The fact the God knew his name didn't appear to help Cork much. He looked up with a start and shook his head, denying . . . something. Katashan kept a hand to Cork's shoulder so he didn't fall. Peralin leaned down from Night in a sweep of black, and a strange scent of spring, and pulled out the decanter and glass, pouring the golden liquid. Cork stared at the offered glass and Katashan finally took it in hand.

"Let him sip. You know how strong this is. It will be more powerful for him since he has no magic at all."

The scent alone gave Katashan strength once more. He carefully put the goblet to Cork's lips; his friend seemed nearly senseless and still very cold. Cork sipped, swayed, and sipped again. Color returned to his face, and his eyes blinked and focused once more. He looked at Peralin with his head tilted a little, and Katashan suspected he was probably half drunk already.

"Are they all dead, sir?" Cork said, waving a hand towards the camp.

"Yes, they are," Peralin said.

Cork took the goblet and sipped again. Katashan accepted another from Peralin with a nod of thanks sipped as well, grateful for the warmth, the power, the taste of life.

"Why didn't you come to save them?" Cork asked.

Katashan saw the God's face go very calm and he feared maybe Cork had stepped over the line. He took a longer drink of the damn wine. If they were about to be chastised (or worse) by a God, he decided he might as well be drunk for it.

"There was a choice I had to make," Peralin said. "If I had come to save them, then Katashan would have been lost. I saved that which is more important --"

"No!" Katashan shook his head with more force than he had intended. The wine splashed out, dripped onto the ground and grass grew up in an eye blink where it had touched.

"In this battle, Katashan, it is true," Peralin said with unexpected gentleness. "You know this already. I had to make a choice, but because I did, they go to a good reward, having died to save another even if they were not aware of the sacrifice they made. Even Lord Arpan, though he little deserves such care."

Katashan, feeling the pains in his body even after the wine, tried not to give way to relief knowing the man had died. Then he realized it left him and Cork in a rather bad position, with everyone but the two of them dead.

"Where is Sherina now?" Katashan asked, trying to figure out what they could do next.

"Gone, though not far enough," Peralin said. He glanced out at the ocean and looked annoyed as he lifted his hand, as though to feel out the trouble. "I chased her off for the moment, but being already dead, I can't kill her. And something I cannot quite grasp still ties her to the world of living."

"What will happen now?" Katashan asked, daring to look up at him again.

"Whatever you make of it."

That was the sort of answer Katashan would have expected from a priest. The sort of answer, in fact, that had always annoyed him and had been partially responsible for what drove him from the temple. Now he suspected the priests were not being purposely vague or facetious, but only following the true words of the Gods they served. He supposed that should worry him about the state of the world in general.

He realized he was trying to concentrate on anything except what he would *make of it*. The wine, at least had given him strength though not clarity of mind. He looked at Cork, still pale and trembling as he held tight to the goblet in his hands. Cold? Shock? Fear? Katashan wondered if he, too, should tremble.

He looked back at Peralin, trying to get his thoughts focused and at the same time considering drinking more wine and maybe hoping everything would go away, at least for a while. Is that what he would make of it? "We can't go back to Salbay and tell them their lord is dead, along with all this men, and only Cork and I survived."

Cork gave a little moan as he realized the implications.

"They'd be certain you had your hand in this one, sir," he said. He looked stricken now, no doubt thinking about friends and family, and the lovely and brave Maylee whom he might never see again.

"I will fight your battle, my Lord," Katashan said looking up at Peralin, who seemed confused and uncertain by the statement. "But I will ask a boon. Find a way for Cork to go home."

"No, sir!" Cork protested. The color came back along with an unexpected fire. He held the goblet tight in one hand but caught Katashan's arm with the other. "I will not abandon you in this battle, Katashan. *No.*"

Katashan pulled away, lifting a hand and stilling him from further comment. "This is not your war --"

"Like hell it isn't!" Cork all but shouted, and then gave the God, watching with a little amusement, a look of apology. "Your pardon, my Lord. I did not mean --" Cork stopped, stared up at the waiting God for a long moment, and then apparently gave that conversation up as hopeless. He turned back to Katashan, his face set with a stubbornness Katashan didn't find really surprising. "Sir, you cannot fight this war alone. We've already seen so."

"Your home is important to you," Katashan said softly, hoping he kept the feelings about his own home, and all that he had lost, from his words.

"Yes it is. Important enough that I would fight and die for it, even if I could never go back there again. But you know what that's like, don't you, sir?" That one hit home. Katashan bowed his head, and only looked up when Cork put a hand on his shoulder. "I'm sorry. But I still won't go home --"

"Would either of you care to hear my thoughts on the matter?" Peralin asked.

They both looked up, startled. Katashan wasn't certain if he should feel hope or dread, but he nodded.

"Go back to the fort at Salbay. By the time you get there the others will have spread the tale of what happened here and about the evil spirit that killed all the men."

"But you said they all died," Katashan replied and tried to quell a hint of frustration.

"I said all of *them* are dead." Peralin waved towards the camp. Katashan looked and turned away again so quickly his head pounded. He didn't want to see the dead, and wonder if he could have saved them or if he should even have tried. "However, a group of this sort is bound to draw the attention of others. There were some mountain people on the heights who thought this group might be easy to rob since the guards were so lax. But then they saw the fog roll in, and the two of you escaping just as the evil fell upon the camp. They are even going to say that the troops deserved it, having watched how they treated their prisoner."

"Will they?" Cork said, startled.

"Certainly. They have already headed back to the fort."

"Why?" Cork said. "It's not that the mountain people are apt to bring us news in the past."

"Because they believe that there will be a reward for telling the commander of the fort that his Lord has been killed. However, they are going to be disappointed since they will be the second with the news. The first will be a party of ten soldiers who had followed some ways behind, in hopes that you could get Katashan free, and they could help spirit the two of you away. Their scouts saw what Sherina did. You and Cork will be assumed dead until you get back, and the Mountain People have told their part of the story. There will be suspicion, of course but nothing will be charged against you."

"Oh." Katashan's head started to spin. He held the goblet of wine back up to Peralin with some haste. Drunk enough after all. "So, it's safe for us to go back to the fort now."

"Safe? Did I say *anything* was safe?" Peralin asked with a

shake of his head. "There is no safety, Katashan. Not until this matter is resolved. But you would be wise to head back to the fort and what allies you have in this world. And you would be wise to do so quickly. There are horses, still -- spooked, but better than walking. The dawn is coming. I cannot stay."

"Thank you for your aid," Katashan said, with sense enough to bow his head to the God, reminding himself that this was a being whom he should not take lightly, no matter how amiable and helpful he had been.

"My Lord." Cork bowed his head as well. He didn't look very sober, but that might have helped. This was not, Katashan thought, a night to be sober or sane -- not sitting here by a fallen tree with the dead all around and a God giving them suggestions on how to survive.

"Get a horse, Cork," Peralin said. He held out his hand and Cork, tentatively, took it to stand and handed back his own goblet. When he got his feet under him, Cork looked back at Katashan with worry.

"I'll be safe here."

"Yes, sir. I'll be back as soon as I can calm one of the beasts and get it saddled."

He walked away and didn't look back. Katashan grinned. He had gotten lucky to have Cork with him. The soldier kept his head, even at a time like this.

"He'll stand by you . . . but it's dangerous," Peralin said.

"Will he be killed?" Katashan asked, panicked again.

"I don't know. He might be. But then, you might be killed as well." Peralin frowned and blinked. Katashan had the feeling he looked elsewhere for a moment before he glanced back down at Katashan. "And while it is dangerous to stand with you, I cannot say it is safer to be somewhere else. Remember, these men were your enemies," he said, with a wave back towards the bodies. "It didn't save them."

Peralin made an excellent point. And, if he took the larger

view of the situation, he had to admit that he wasn't up to fighting this battle alone. He needed help and so far Cork had done an admirable job of getting things done.

He would need a guard when they got back.

"The dawn comes," Peralin said again, looking towards the horizon with a worried shake of his head. He offered a hand and Katashan stood as well, though less steady than his friend.

Then Peralin leaned down, closer to Katashan, who found himself looking into eyes of black and gold, green and blue. Not human eyes. They did not look at the world in the same way that a human would.

"Take care Katashan. Be careful. I dare not heal you this time because your very weakness is your protection just now. Your secret is still safe for the moment, but given the war that will continue until Sherina is banished to a true death, your knowledge of magic and your past cannot be hidden for much longer."

Katashan nodded. Peralin finally let go of his hand, as though he had not trusted Katashan until that moment. He felt not quite as drunk as he had before and regretted it. The power of the wine had made the night less troubling.

Cork brought a skittish horse back. Peralin nodded to him, then turned his horse and rode off into the dark and the fog. In a moment the sound of the horse disappeared, long before the man could have ridden away.

Cork stared in that direction for a little longer. "Gods," he whispered. "Gods help us."

"I think they're doing the best they can."

Cork laughed; a sound foreign to this field of death and Katashan heard a hint of hysteria in his friend's voice. He understood far too well.

Katashan looked around the area, feeling wounds again, and the loss and dread. So many dead, and he didn't know why. What did it serve, except to feed Sherina, and surely she was not the only reason all of this was happening?

He could hear the waves upon the shore, far below them. Stars shone through the canopy of the trees, and somewhere a bird cried out a warning that the day had almost come. Everything seemed too normal, until he looked down and saw the dead everywhere again.

This madness and blight would grow.

"Can you ride sir? I'll lead the horse for a ways, at least until dawn. And then we can ride together, when we can see the ground better. I don't think it wise for you to ride alone for very far. You're very weak. At least we don't have far to go back to the fort, and we'll get there quickly on horseback."

Katashan looked at him for a moment, weighed the words, which took him a moment to translate, and then nodded. He moved slowly towards the horse, every pain coming back, though still dulled a little by the wine. It took Cork two tries to get him up on the horse. The soldier led the animal, slow steps away from the madness.

But Katashan knew it would follow them.

CHAPTER FOURTEEN

The patient horse plodded along the trail, though still unsettled at any sudden sound, and ready to bolt from Cork's hold. Katashan didn't want to be on the horse if it ran, but he didn't want to be walking either.

Cork led the horse through the gray dawn and into a morning filled with bright greens and colorful flowers. Katashan wanted to stop. He wanted to rest and take the scents in, but every time he lifted his head from the horse's neck, he ran the risk of passing out and falling.

He stayed where he was, eyes closed, trying to measure the distance with each step of the horse. Closer, closer . . . and he tried not think about how far they had to go.

"Sir?" Cork said. He'd stopped, praise the gods. Katashan didn't know when or why, but he gave a grateful sigh. The horse stayed relatively still for a moment at least. "Sir, are you conscious?"

"I would rather not be," Katashan admitted softly. Even speaking hurt.

"Yes, sir," Cork said. He sounded as though he understood too well. "We can rest here, if you like."

Katashan slowly lifted his head. They had reached a spot with a long view of the ocean to the side and high cliffs behind them. The trail wound away, with clear views on either side. Nothing could easily slip up on them here.

He saw the way Cork stood with his hand on his side and his face still pale, and decided he should look beyond his own misery and consider the work Cork had done to get them here. This seemed a pleasant place, though a bit chilly. He didn't care.

Katashan started to slide down from the horse. Cork quickly put a steadying hand out and helped, though he didn't let go of the horse. The creature still looked apt to take off at a run.

Katashan sat down on a nearby boulder, head bent forward, trying to gasp in air through bruised ribs. He couldn't move his arm without sending fire through half his body.

"Be easy, sir. Just be easy. We're past the danger. I'll see what I can do for your wounds. Damn them all for doing this to you."

"Damn them? We're far past that, Cork," Katashan said and slowly looked up at the man. "Peralin took care of whatever needs be done with them."

"Gone to paradise, I guess, from all he said." Cork shook his head. A bruise stood out, dark and angry, on the side of Cork's face. "There's no justice in it."

"None at all," Katashan agreed. "But it is done."

Cork nodded. He secured the bay horse's rein by wrapping it around a large rock and then began looking through the bag he must have found with the saddles.

"How far?" Katashan asked, looking along the trail toward Salbay. "I know we came this way, Lord Arpan and I, but I don't remember it."

"Just as well, sir. It wasn't a good trip, and it came to a bad end." Cork stopped and looked to the trail and the way they would, all too soon, be going again. "We're about a quarter of the way back, sir. We don't dare stay too long."

"We need to be to the fort by dark," Katashan realized. He swallowed and tried to stand, but stopped before he got too far. He wasn't going to move on his own, and he only hoped Cork had enough energy left to get him up on the horse. "We don't want to be outside of a building tonight, when she comes looking for me again."

"Oh Gods. Hell." Cork looked out at the ocean, as though he expected Sherina to come for them even now, in full daylight. It made Katashan shiver, fearing such a thing. "You're right. We need to go."

Cork reached for him, catching Katashan under the arm and starting to pull up. Katashan moaned and Cork gasped and a moment later they both went back down again.

A woman laughed.

They both tried to get back to their feet and slipped again. Katashan could not get his arms under him to push up and Cork stood protecting him --

"It's not *her*, sir," Cork said with the sound of relief. Katashan managed to turn his head enough to see Cork looking up the cliff. Something moved up there, shadowed, but solid. Dust crumbled under the movement, and a pinecone tumbled down to land at Katashan's feet. "I think it must be a one of the mountain women, sir. Watching us."

"Praise the Gods. I feared -- if she could come out in the daylight like this --" He stopped and took several small breaths, unable to speak.

The laughter had abruptly stopped. Something softer than a pinecone hit the ground to the right and Katashan painfully turned his head to find a small leather pouch.

"My apologies," a voice said, the laughter gone. "That may help."

A little more dirt tumbled down, and then silence.

"She's gone sir," Cork said after a couple moments. He limped over to the pouch and picked it up as if he expected a viper to leap out. He untied the flap and looked inside. "This will help, sir. The plant grows up in the highlands. Tastes like sweet clover, it does, and helps to dull pain. Here, sir. Try a little."

Katashan managed to get a little of the dried, palmate leaves into his mouth. He chewed. Even that movement hurt. However, after a few moments he did feel, if not a dulling of the pain, at least lethargy of his body that allowed the pain to slip aside, as though it took a different path and didn't quite reach his mind. He welcomed the feeling.

Cork helped him back on the horse and then slid up behind him this time. "I don't think you can ride any more on your own, sir," he said as though in apology. "And we've got a fair ways to go still. We can't dawdle anymore, I fear."

"Go while we can," Katashan said and tried to brace himself.

Cork kicked the horse into movement. Katashan held on, closed his eyes, and trusted himself to Cork's care. He began to suspect he would not survive to reach the fort, though.

"Damn and damn," Cork mumbled.

Those words brought Katashan back to awareness that went beyond the haze of pain. They'd moved a long ways. Five miles? Ten? Every step had set agony in his bones, but Cork had him chew some more of plant and the pain slipped aside again for a while. Now it started to come back and he felt chill. . . .

Thunder.

He lifted his head at the unwelcome sound and looked off towards the sea.

"Yes sir," Cork said. He sounded weary and annoyed. "There's a storm rolling in. A big one from the looks of it, and moving fast."

"Of course it is," Katashan said. His voice sounded too soft. "We need to get off this trail."

"There's nowhere else to go, sir. You need a little more of the mountain grass --"

"No." He forced himself to sit up straight and look around

to gauge the trouble they were in. More trouble, as though the entire world had moved against them. "It makes me not care and I think I need a little bit of my wits left. Just go, Cork."

"We haven't a chance of outrunning the storm, sir."

"I know. I don't remember -- is there any shelter along here?"

"Not until the fort, sir." Cork gave the horse a nudge in the ribs and the animal seemed more than willing to move off at a pace that might not have been wise on the narrow ridge. The animal plainly knew they had to get off the cliff-side trail with the storm blowing in. The horse's hooves clattered against the hard rock, and thunder growled to their right. The breeze off the ocean had turned cold, but Katashan hadn't the strength left to shiver.

They hadn't gone more than a couple yards before the first strong wind broke against them, startling the horse, which nearly lost Katashan his seat on the beast. Cork grabbed at him just in time, but even that sent waves of agony through his body.

"Well, this is just hell, isn't it, horse?" Cork said.

Time had passed. Katashan knew he had been unconscious and wished he could be again. But he found it amusingly pleasant to listen to Cork talking to their mount, even in the pouring rain.

"You know, if I had wanted to be wet and cold all me life, and to die drowning, I would ha' gone to sea like every other damn fool in my family. I'll be the laughing stock, I will, if I drown on land."

The horse shied at the flash of lightning, but Cork kept the animal in hand. The day had gone ominously dark with the storm, as though night fell on them already. Katashan found himself more alert and lifted his hand to touch the air, and test the world around them. The rain fell hard, and the wind still blew around them, though he could tell they were not quite so close to a cliff edge now.

"Is there magic in the storm, sir?" Cork asked, worry in his voice.

"Not magic made, but drawn by it perhaps," Katashan said. He found the words difficult as he fought to speak in the Cyrenian language. "Magic sometimes makes a void in nature and storms develop. She used a lot of power. So did Peralin."

"Peralin," Cork said. "Gods all, to be on the first name bases with such a being, like we'd go down to the tavern for a drink or two with him. My world has gone mad, you know."

"I know. I apologize."

"I hadn't thought you brought the trouble, sir."

"But I did bring you into it."

"Not that I noticed. I made my choices. I'm not regretting those choices now, you know. I'd rather the trouble hadn't come, but I've never been one to back away from the work if it needs done. And you, sir, need a keeper. My pardon, but it's true."

Katashan laughed, painful though it felt. He didn't even think to argue, given the circumstances. "I appreciate all that you've done for me, Cork. I'll do my best to see it all right."

"I wouldn't expect any less of you, sir. In fact, I expect that you'll do your best, whether I'm with you or not."

The statement was a clear message Cork knew he might not survive. It came as a painful jab in Katashan's heart -- but he held his words for a moment and thought it through.

"Yes, you're right," Katashan said. "I'll do my best. But you give me a link to this place, Cork." He shifted a little, and shivered. "Don't do anything stupid or dangerous."

Cork laughed. And a moment later Katashan found the sound contagious. He laughed as well, there in the storm from hell with the wind trying to kill them. They'd seen hell already, after all. Maybe the storm would wash them clean. Katashan lifted his face into the rain and wind as they rode on.

"Praise the Gods," someone shouted; a stranger's voice and far too close. Katashan and Cork both shifted to look up and even the exhausted horse gave a little nervous prance that nearly unseated them both.

Soldiers rode towards them in the pale light of a storm-drenched sunset. Katashan felt his breath catch in a cry of dismay certain they were caught again. He tried to grab the reins out of Cork's hand.

"No, sir. Careful," Cork said, catching hold of him when he started to fall again. "That's Captain Serrano himself."

"Serrano," Katashan said, but the name meant nothing for a heartbeat or two. He only knew there had been soldiers, and ghosts, and he did not want to go back to that trouble again. He wanted to run, but Cork held the horse still and he knew he wouldn't get far on foot.

Cork had saved him. He would trust Cork.

His head had fallen forward again before the party rode the little distance to them.

"Cork, thank the Gods we found you. We had heard that everyone --"

Katashan lifted his head and looked at Serrano. Yes, he did know this man. Good man. He could not, for the life of him, come up with words in the local language to so much as give a greeting of welcome.

"He's had a hard time, sir," Cork said softly, as though to explain something Katashan hadn't heard. His hand tightened a little at Katashan's side, holding him up. "We need to get him to some place he can rest, Captain. Soon."

"Yes," Serrano said. "Katashan? Are you able to ride still?"

"Ride," Katashan said. "In-inside tonight."

Serrano's gaze turned to Cork again. "Can you ride, Cork? Let's get both of you paired with people who might be able to hold on a bit better."

Cork started to agree, but Katashan caught hold of his friend's arm, unaccountably panicked at the thought of riding with anyone else. He couldn't even speak the words to convey his worry, but Cork patted his arm and didn't let go.

"We'll make it like this," Cork said softly. "He's had it rough at the hands of the soldiers, sir. I don't think he'd be comfortable riding with one now, not until he's a little more himself again."

"Yes," Serrano said, looking into Katashan's face once more. Regret showed in his eyes. And worry. "I wish I could have stopped Lord Arpan -- but it's done. Sunset is upon us. We've still a ways to go back to the fort. Hold tight."

He couldn't hold any thoughts, and he let his head fall back against Cork while he watched the trees above them, spring green and lovely, haloed in bright light, the rain water dripping down.

It couldn't be very far. . . .

He could no longer see the trees. Stone walls and excited soldiers crowded around them. People yelled as they brought torches, a cacophony of voices speaking words he couldn't quite understand. The torches spread flickering light everywhere, dispelling shadows in some places and creating other in their wake. Darkness had come, and he had not been there when it fell.

Dangerous, the darkness and the things the night brought. However, they had made it to the fort. He recognized the walls, and felt oddly safe, like coming home. He lifted his head, wondering if Sherina followed close behind.

He found, instead, a ward -- not his, but good, steady magic. Pater Matish, he thought. Excellent.

"Can you hand him down Cork?" Serrano asked, standing by the horse. "Careful now."

Cork lowered him, and he was quickly lost in a haze of pain. He wondered how he'd managed to survive this far. Before he was fully in Serrano's hands he was unconscious again.

CHAPTER FIFTEEN

T he room smelled of food. Katashan wanted to taste some, though he hadn't the strength even to swallow. Light came from somewhere. Soft blankets. Safe.

"Coming around are you, sir?" Cork asked, his voice quiet and friendly. "It would help if you spoke the local language. I would know what you want."

Katashan slowly opened his eyes, the eyelids feeling bruised and battered. He could hardly breathe. Cork sat in a chair beside the bed, leaning forward to look into his face. Cork had a bandage on his neck but he looked clean and rested.

"Sir?" Cork said, still looking into his face as though searching for some hint of life.

"Cor-k," he said, somehow making the name into two syllables.

"Yes sir. Can you sit up? Maylee brought some broth up from the kitchen. I think it would do you some good and better now before it gets cold."

"Broth," Katashan said, trying to sort the word out in his mind while Cork started to sit him up.

He protested with a hiss and a whispered curse in his own language. Darkness edged in around his already blurry sight, but by the time he could have protested, Cork had placed pillows behind his back and had an arm around his shoulder, steadying him. Katashan felt a wave of embarrassment that he hadn't even the strength to sit up on his own.

"Careful now, sir," Cork said, taking no notice of his mood or his curse. "Here. I'll hold the cup to your lips. Just sip a bit."

He still wanted to protest but he could tell Cork wouldn't listen anyway. He gave up the battle as soon as the warm liquid touched his lips. He tasted something that hinted of chicken and swallowed. And again.

Half a cup later he felt as though the world had begun to settle back into place. He looked at Cork and frowned. Bruises, he noted, had started to fade on his friend's face.

"How long -- back?" he asked, still fighting for the proper words in this language.

"Five days," Cork said.

Gods. That long? The idea startled and frightened him, but he didn't doubt it given the weakness of his body. He'd been well cared for, though. He could sense magic that had been used to help heal the worst of his wounds. Pater Matish again. He would have to thank the priest.

"Ah now, you look more yourself, sir," Cork said and sounded pleased as he put aside the cup. "That's good. We've all been worried."

"Trouble?"

"Not as much as I would have expected," Cork admitted and sounded worried for that odd reason. He helped settle Katashan against the pillows and looked relieved to be able to talk to him. Cork lowered his head and whispered, "There's been no tale about your own magic, sir."

"Is this good?"

"Yes, sir. Very much so." He glanced towards the door, and then to the open window, as if he feared someone might have scaled the side of the tower and hung outside. "There's been a wild outcry over magic hereabouts. So many soldiers killed, you know, and it could have been anyone in this fort if they had gone with his Lordship. Ona -- well, he wasn't well liked, but he was one of us. There's talk of even more trouble in the Atshila and that the king himself is concerned. You don't want the king looking your way sir, not at a time like this."

"I hadn't thought --" He stopped and closed his eyes. "I'll be very careful."

"I know you will, sir. You have been until now. And I am grateful, you know, that you saved my life."

"I brought this danger," Katashan said.

"You've said the like before, but I still don't see how this could be your fault."

"I took her from the place of sacrifice, set her spirit on this path --"

"And would it have been better, sir, if you'd left her?" he asked, sitting back again. "What would have happened then?"

"I . . . don't know," he admitted, but that was only half the answer and they both knew it. "It would have been nothing good. If this is the power of a broken spell, things would have been far worse if the work had been completed and the spell set in motion."

"And it wasn't? Why not? She's been long dead."

"Some spells take time to grow," Katashan replied. His head pounded and he wished he didn't have to think about such grave matters right now. However, he could tell from Cork's worry that this had been weighing heavily on him, and likely the same was true for everyone else who knew the truth of Sherina's death. "This was no simple casting."

"How long would the rest have taken?" Cork asked and drank down the last of the broth himself.

"I don't really know, Cork. I will likely have to go back to the site to find out, though. Going there may give us the answers we need to destroy her."

"That would be good sir, though not yet. You're a long ways from well enough to travel."

He nodded without a protest. Even talking seemed to take a great deal of strength from him.

"Anything more I should know?"

"I sleep in the room here with you. Captain Serrano made it official that I will be your personal aide and servant. Maylee brings us food, and we're damned careful of everyone else. I've feared *she* would be back at the windows, but Pater Matish says we're safe. Gods help us; I didn't realize he could do magic, too. He said yesterday there's been no sign of her. I can't say that makes me feel any better."

"No, me either." If Katashan closed his eyes, he could see her clearly in his mind; a wavering shape of white and power, hovering like a malevolent cloud above the camp of the dead soldiers. Peralin had fought her away when his own magic had not been strong enough to stop her. Though, granted, he had not been in the best of shape at the time. She had not been close to destroyed, and yet she hadn't taken advantage of his weakness. That made him uneasy.

"Perhaps Peralin has been some help."

Cork's face paled a little. His voice lowered again. "I had convinced myself that had been -- madness, sir. That surely the god himself hadn't given me wine and hadn't come to our aid. I'd really rather he hadn't, sir. Things can't look good if he's involved."

"I know."

"But he is."

"Yes. I'm sorry."

"Me too, sir. But there's nothing we can do about it." He shook his head, but apparently the reality would not be persuaded to leave him this time. "I've not mentioned his appearance to anyone. The others are worried enough."

Katashan nodded though it hurt to move his head. He did finally lift his hand and saw bandages wrapped around the wrist and up over the hand.

"Seemed best, sir, not to draw attention to that cut on your wrist. The wound had started to heal, but looked too obvious to me. I did that one myself, and let the Pater Matish deal with all the rest."

"Thank you. My ritual blade?"

Cork pulled the chain out from under his own tunic. "I'll keep it a while longer, until the priest is finished and doesn't plan to come back, if you don't mind, sir."

"Katashan. Kat."

"Kat, sir," Cork said, and then laughed. He looked unexpectedly happy. "I'm glad you're awake now. I've had a world of worry, not knowing what to do next or what to do if *she* came back. Do you have any plans on how to deal with this?"

"I'd like to be awake for a little more time before I'm asked how to save the world."

Cork laughed again. Color had returned to his face. "Yes, sir. Good point. Rest now, Kat. Rest while you can."

By the next morning Katashan had already begun walking, though a slow, painful stumble seemed a more appropriate description. He moved twice from one side of the room to the other. His legs didn't want to hold him but he knew better than to take more time at ease.

Besides, he had spent far too much of the long night awake and staring out the window while wondering where Sherina had gone and why she hadn't attacked him at his weakest. He hoped he was right and Peralin kept her at bay and could continue to do so for a while longer. Anything else meant something more going on that he didn't understand, and he understood too damned little as it was.

Cork brought him clean clothing, though not from his own supplies. He looked at them with a slight frown.

"From Captain Serrano, sir, with his compliments," Cork

said, carefully laying the pants and tunic out. He finally turned back to where Katashan sat, wrapped in a huge warm robe, huddled by the fireside. Warmth did not come easy to him. "You've lost weight. I think these will fit better."

"And make me look more like a local?" Katashan said.

"Maybe, but I doubt it."

Katashan started to complain that he wanted his own things and then realized how petty that would sound. The clothing looked warm, comfortable and likely would fit better. He even let Cork help him dress since his hands still seemed uncooperative. The fingers at least moved now, though.

"That's better, sir. And just as well that you're up and moving, since his Lordship will be here this afternoon."

"Lordship?" Katashan asked, startled.

"The late Lord Arpan's son and heir, sir," Cork quickly explained.

"Oh. I thought, for a moment --"

"No sir. *He's dead.* They held the funeral two days ago in the capital, for him and all of the troops who died with him. There have been all kinds of trouble brewing in Atshila over it, too, from what we've heard this morning. Not a place for either of us to visit any time soon, sir. Some of the Salbay city council suggested that at least I go, being one of only two who survived -- but Serrano talked them out of it, pointing out that I was too good a soldier to send on a suicide journey. He seems to think the good people of the capital would be apt to kill either of us on sight."

"Excellent point," Katashan said although a little breathless just from the work of pulling on the tunic.

He limped to the chair by the window and looked out at the sea. A ship leaving with the tide skipped across the water, sail unfurled and oars adding their power with beats he could almost hear from here. He watched the craft make good time out past the breakers. Cork came to watch as well, nodding as the crew shipped oars and the wind caught full hold of the sails.

"I keep thinking I should be sailing on the next tide," Katashan said, watching still

"Would you leave us behind to deal with this madness on our own, then?"

Katashan looked back at Cork with a start, and then shrugged. He felt a sharp pain through his shoulder and sighed, as much at it as at Cork's look. "You are right, of course. I wouldn't go, at least until I have done all that I can to end this misfortune." He settled in the chair by the table, his hands on the surface. "I weary, Cork, of fighting wars that are not my own."

Cork looked at him for a moment. Then he grabbed a second chair and pulled it over by the table and sat there with his hands on his knees and looking Katashan fully in the face for a long, silent time.

"What is it?" Katashan finally asked, unsettled by the stare.

"That's what I've wondered, sir. You don't sound yourself at all with this talk about leaving and about wars that aren't your own. I know this isn't your place, but you've never acted like . . . well, like you're a foreigner. Are you homesick?"

"No," he said, but it wasn't really the truth, and he thought Cork could see some of the truth in his face. "Well, I guess I am, but not for a place so much as a time before the war. I can't go back. I can't have it again, because it's gone, Cork. I came here looking for peace since I couldn't have my own world back and staying where I had been only made the loss worse. And now I find myself fighting for others and people are dying. I didn't want this again."

Cork nodded, though Katashan wasn't sure he understood since he still looked worried. He didn't like to see his normally jovial friend upset and decided he had better pull himself out of this foul mood which didn't help either of them. He needed to find out what was going on if he intended to be of any real help.

"Tell me about the new lord. Are we likely to have the same problems from him?"

"Truth be told, I don't know for certain," Cork said with a sigh and didn't look happy about this conversation either. "There are some matters you should know, though."

"And they aren't good from the sounds of it."

"Not all, no. Fordel is -- was -- his Lordship's youngest of three children. Sherina was the middle child. She was always willful and strong-minded."

"Doesn't surprise me, having had a few encounters with her."

Cork started to speak, stopped, and nodded. "You're right, you know. She isn't much changed."

"And the other two children?"

"The older son was Bronsan. He was, I'm afraid, much like his father. But he died in the last year of the war with your people, killed in battle."

"Hell."

"Yes, I thought that was something you ought to know, sir. I've never met Fordel. I've heard he's something of scholar, and that may be a good sign, though the Gods know I've met more than a few scholars who weren't reasonable people. Some think he's just weak but I don't think a weak man would have lasted to be the only heir under his father's care."

"What of his politics?"

Cork shrugged.

"His feeling towards magic?" Katashan asked.

"I suspect in that, sir, he will follow the same as almost everyone else in the area. They don't like it much at all."

"Then best to keep that part quiet. Not that I intended to say anything right out anyway."

"Good plan, sir."

"I'm making you nervous again, aren't I?"

Cork had been looking at his hands but now he lifted his

head. The bruises on his face had nearly faded, but the skin still seemed pale, as though the man remained perpetually cold after Sherina's touch.

"It's not you what makes me nervous -- well, not *just* you at least. It's everything that's happened since you arrived with Sherina's body. Nothing's gone right since then but it's not your fault," he added hastily. Then he shook his head, looking to the window again for a moment. Maybe he thought about sailing away as well. "I don't like the unknown, sir. I'm a soldier. I like to know where I stand with the enemy. But this . . . there seems to be nothing here I can understand and face, not from the enemy all the way to the new lord. No answers. I don't like it."

"And it seems that all my life has been filled with questions and damned few answers," Katashan replied. He leaned back in the chair and let the tension ease from his aching shoulders. "I had come to Cyrenia to get away from the past and to find a place of calm. I haven't yet, but I do like it here, Cork."

"Do you? Given everything that's happened I can't say that makes me think you're really sane."

The words caught him by surprise and he tried not to laugh, though only because it would hurt. Cork got him a bit of wine from the bottle by the bed and smiled. He liked to see his companion back in good spirits and the timing turned out to be perfect since Maylee arrived a moment later with news.

"The young lord is in the hall, sir," she said, bowing to Katashan. "Captain Serrano asks if you can come down. He said to tell you he thinks the meeting might go better in a less private area if you are well enough."

"I'm well enough," Katashan said and stood. He caught at the chair. "Mostly. Can you tell the Captain that we'll be down soon?"

"Yes sir. I'll do that." She gave Cork one bright, though nervous, smile, and then hurried away.

Katashan watched her go and then slowly moved, testing

his ability to walk even to the door. He barely made it that far and Cork helped him down the long, tedious path to the main hall. Cork moved slowly and all but carried him in the stairwells.

Even so, by the time they reached the last part of the walk, Cork finally just put an arm around his waist and took most of Katashan's weight since he had begun to limp worse. Katashan started to pull away, but Cork shook his head.

"Don't argue, sir. Save your strength for dealing with Lord Fordel. I want you at your best, sir -- or at least as good as you can manage today."

Katashan didn't argue. Servants paused, some asking softly if he needed anything. He saw worry in their eyes and Katashan couldn't decide if they feared him for what had happened, or feared for him and what might happen when he and Cork went into that hall.

But he had no choice. He couldn't have escaped, even if he had the strength to run. Cork had reminded him of his duty, odd though that seemed. He couldn't walk away from these people even if he somehow had the chance. It would have put a lie to everything he told himself he would have done to help others if he'd has the chance. Besides, he thought Verina wouldn't be happy with him.

He pulled away from his friend as they neared the archway, standing straighter and preparing to walk on his own. The room sounded quieter than it had been when his Lordship -- when the last Lord -- had been to Salbay. As they stepped in, he found guards stood by the opening. They glared as the two entered, hands conspicuously on their weapons. Katashan reminded himself they had lost friends to Sherina and having him and Cork survive couldn't be any good news for them.

The guards were not, he noticed, placed near the table where Captain Serrano and another man sat. At least Fordel hadn't taken the chair where his father had sat in judgment. Katashan hoped that meant the Lord Fordel trusted the captain, or at least didn't feel the need to intimidate him. Katashan badly needed some good news as he limped across the room and even something as small as this helped his step steady.

The man sitting in the place of honor at the table looked younger, smaller, and less impressive than his father. That started to put Katashan at ease, but as he drew a few steps closer that feeling evaporated.

Magic. Lord Fordel radiated the power. Katashan, had been approaching with his head bowed, hoping he could get away with a show of meekness but now he knew that wouldn't work. Katashan looked up. Yes, Lord Fordel knew the feel of magic as well. Hell! He had to think of a way to get Cork out of this mess --

"You must be Katashan," Fordel said, his voice uncommonly steady and deceptively quiet. "I had worried about meeting you. Now I am relieved."

Katashan paused with worry still playing at his nerves and not daring to hope the reaction was more than anything but a deception, a trap.

"Captain Serrano, I'm going to make a confession," he said softly, his head bowing a little.

"Lord Fordel?" Serrano said, worried and confused.

"I know magic. I know magic very well, in fact; far better than my late, and dare I say unlamented, sister would ever know. However, she was more ambitious than I am. She sought . . . allies."

"Answers," Katashan said, despite himself. He took four quick steps forward and caught at the nearest chair, feeling the charade that had gotten him this far into the room weakening. He didn't think he could stand for much longer. "Finally, answers."

"A few, though not enough, I fear," Lord Fordel said. "Please, sit down. You are Cork?"

"Yes, sir." Cork sounded uncertain but steady as well.

"Sit with us. We have matters to discuss."

"Yes sir," Cork replied. He didn't look any happier.

Cork pulled a chair out and steadied Katashan as he moved into it, grateful to be off his feet again. Lord Fordel looked him over and the young lord's fingers moved a little, measuring power, no doubt. Katashan didn't do the same. He hadn't even that much power to waste right now.

Cork settled in the chair beside Katashan. Captain Serrano, across the table from them, looked as though he still didn't quite understand what was going on.

Lord Fordel, oddly enough, appeared at ease with his companions. Katashan decided to plunge straight into the fray without any preamble. He still, somehow, felt they didn't have time to waste.

"You are not upset that I know some magic," Katashan said, though softly. This was not a conversation to let loose among the servants and soldiers.

"No, I am not," Fordel replied, his voice just as quiet. Oh, they had secrets and more secrets here. "Not as long as I believe you and I are allies. And since you have been doing battle with Sherina, I must believe we fight on the same side. True?"

"As far as I know," Katashan said.

He looked startled for a moment and then nodded more somberly. "True. You can't really know what side I'm on, can you?"

"I can't be certain, and given my dealings with the rest of your family. . . ."

"Ah. Of course." Fordel looked contrite and spread his hands on the table, leaning forward as he spoke. His voice had dropped to a near whisper, but the words still seemed too loud in the cavernous room. "My mother dabbled in magic. She had northern blood in her. They still hold to magic there, but then you would know that, being from the north."

"True," Katashan said. "And she taught you and your

sister?"

"She taught Sherina. However, my sister proved unwilling to work in the ways my mother thought wise, safe, and helpful. So she stopped teaching her daughter. I had come of age by then and she turned her attention to me. It was, I think, a bad mistake. Sherina never forgave her."

"Your mother is dead," Katashan said.

"Yes. And while everyone else thought it was an unfortunate accident, I could feel the magic involved. By then Sherina had found another teacher."

"Any idea whom that teacher might be?"

"None."

"The person must have turned on her in the end," Katashan said. He sat back, trying to ease aches in his shoulders again. "She ended up the sacrifice. What else should I know?"

"I will give you what aid I can, but I must be circumspect in that work." Fordel looked from Katashan to Cork and then to Serrano. "I trust the three of you with my life, because if word reached the king about my ability, it would be more than my lands I would lose. As it is, this is going to be a tricky passing of the title. My father had never formally named me, believing Sherina the far better choice."

"He wanted her rather than you?" Katashan asked. "I had the impression they couldn't stand each other."

"They couldn't stand to work together. However they held very similar views. Though, I suppose, having never known her in life --"

"I have come to believe she's not much changed," Katashan offered.

Lord Fordel gave a quick nod. "That's been my impression, given the tales I've heard, and the things I've seen." He sat back, staring at Katashan in silence for a long moment. "I don't know what to make of you, but I do know that I need an ally in this battle. I don't have the power to control her."

"Neither do I, but more than that . . . I don't know where to begin to control her." He considered his choices, and while working with someone from this family worried him, he knew he had no choice either. Fordel, at least, seemed reasonable, and if this were an act, he was better at it than his father or sister had ever been. "I need to understand the magic used in her death, and perhaps the magic she dealt in as well. I suspect they were interlocked."

"I have no idea who had taken over teaching her," Lord Fordel said, sounding truly frustrated. His fingers began to tap on the table, and his dark eyes -- too much like his father's -- narrowed in anger. "I have tried to find out, believe me. When she disappeared, I feared she had gone to learn more magic and I would have to deal with her if she came back. I wanted all the answers I could find. I found none at all."

"Damn," Katashan said. "Your pardon, your lordship."

Lord Fordel smiled, though it looked nervous and uncertain. "I'm not used this position of power. I was never the chosen one. It'll be some time before I worry about things like protocol. That seems like a terrible waste of our time, given all the other problems. Any ideas of what we can do?"

"I will trust that you know magic enough to have done a good search of your home to find what you could," Katashan answered. Fordel nodded. "That means we need to search elsewhere. I think you should want to go to see the place where your sister died."

"Ah. Is there something there to find?"

"Yes, but I could not, under the circumstances, do any real study when I first found her. I did find glyphs there, Lord Fordel. Life, Bond, Death."

He looked worried and by that Katashan judged he knew his magic very well. "Did they have power?"

"Yes. I destroyed them as best I could, but I wouldn't mind going back and completing the job, especially with spring coming. They are not something to leave for the unwary to trip over."

"True. And we might be able to divine more about her death by the study."

"When shall we go?" Serrano asked, finally seeming to understand there was hope in the presence of Lord Fordel.

"As soon as possible," Katashan replied and Lord Fordel nodded. "I don't think we dare wait until she returns again."

"You aren't in condition to travel, Katashan," Serrano protested

"I can be."

"Careful, careful sir," Cork dared speak and laid a hand on Katashan's arm. He looked more worried and nervous than he had when they first came in. "You must not be obvious, not with magic -- neither of you. Wait a day or two, sir. I know it's a chance, but there are other troubles to count as well. What good would it do to bring down the wrath and the distrust of the locals? Neither of you could gain any good from such action, and I think you have enemies enough."

"Very true," Captain Serrano said. He had finally seemed to regain his color and his nerve. "Can this wait a couple days? At least give you the semblance of healing? No one knows how badly injured you were, Katashan."

They were being wise, even though he hated to wait. He still felt as though time moved against them. However, Katashan noted that Lord Fordel waited on his word, and he finally nodded agreement to the delay. He wanted to rush off to the mountain but he suddenly felt very weary.

"Good," Cork said, sounding considerably relieved.

"I am grateful for your notice of the problem," Lord Fordel said. "It would be easy to lose sight of smaller tribulations in the larger battle, but we will have to come back and face them sometime."

"Exactly," Serrano said. "And speaking of problems, I

suspect those coming for tonight's feast will be arriving soon. We must be a bit more proper at least for the Salbay Council."

"Gods, yes," Lord Fordel said with a glance around the room. "I'll meet with you again later, Katashan. Or better, yet, tomorrow. Rest tonight. We've things to do and you are essential to the work."

Katashan bowed his head in a quick nod of thanks as he prepared to leave. With Cork's help, he stood to go back to his room, though he didn't look forward to the long journey through the maze of halls and stairwells.

Cork hovered nearby as he turned to go, ready to help as best he could. Katashan knew himself lucky to have found such friends. He hoped he didn't let them down, though he'd begun to fear his own tampering with Sherina's sacrifice had already created problems which would be hard to fix.

But he'd had no choice.

Cork touched his elbow. He must have been standing there, half-insensible and lost in thought. He bowed his apology to the two at the table who looked at him with obvious worry and let Cork lead him away toward the archway again.

Before they had moved more than three steps from the table, a group of five men in long gray robes entered the room. Katashan didn't need Cork's little hiss of warning to know they were important. He bowed his head and hoped he could easily slip away while Lord Fordel made his greetings.

He saw narrowed eyes turn his way with looks of mistrust. They stepped aside as though they feared to have him too near. Katashan tried not to feel overwhelmed by their presence or to feel as though they were more enemies.

"Your Lordship," one of the men said as they neared the table. "We of the Salbay Council have come to pledge our allegiance to you as the heir to your father's holdings and to pledge our help in whatever way we may be of assistance."

After he had spoken those words, the councilor gave what

Katashan felt was a rather ominous glance in his direction. Cork must have seen something in the look as well, because he put a hand on Katashan's arm. He wanted to warn the guard back, but he knew by now that Cork would do what he felt was right and not worry about the consequences.

"I am grateful for your loyalty and your offer," Lord Fordel said with a very regal bow of his head. He did know the show. "You are dismissed, Katashan and Cork. We will discuss the matter again, at my convenience."

"Yes, Your Lordship," Katashan said and attempted a proper bow. Cork caught him in time before he landed face-first at the feet of the councilors. The show might have been dramatic enough but really wouldn't have helped.

Cork kept a hand on his arm and steered him past the others, around a few servants bringing trays of food and drink, past Lord Fordel's guards, and finally out past the archway and to the stairs.

He felt almost dizzy with the speed that Cork made in their retreat and he finally grabbed at a banister. He feared he would pass out.

"Stop, stop please." He leaned back against the bannister. "There's no reason to run, Cork."

"Sorry, sir." He stopped and leaned against the wall opposite him, where he could still watch the archway. Katashan could still see worry in his look. "Sir --"

"Yes, we can go. But move slowly, Cork. I want to get to my room and rest, but I want to be conscious enough to enjoy it."

That won a quick smile from the man. "Well, I shouldn't be in such a rush, I suppose. Here, let me help you up the stairs, sir. We'll get to the room and the servants will bring us a nice meal."

"That sounds wonderful," Katashan agreed as Cork carefully took his arm again.

"I'm just glad we weren't expected to stay and join the

feast," Cork said as they slowly started up the steps. "I think there are going to be too many strained nerves tonight, sir. No one expected Lord Fordel to take the lands. I suspect a few who may have been . . . less than polite to him in the past."

"Very unwise on their part. One never knows when a younger child will become an only child."

"Yes, sir."

"Were you one of those people, Cork?"

"No, not me, sir. Did my best to avoid them all, in fact."

"Very wise."

"For all the good it did me." He stopped at the top of the first landing, allowing Katashan another moment's rest. He could still hear the faint echo of voices in the hall below. "I seem to be under a great deal of their attention lately."

"Ah. And my vow to leave magic behind seems to have fallen by the wayside as well." Katashan gave a slight shrug, feeling the pull in his shoulder, though it didn't seem too bad, at least. "The world rarely gives us what we wish. We're lucky if we are given what we need."

"And sometimes we might be given the chance to help others with their needs," Cork added.

Katashan looked back at Cork and nodded agreement. He could have been more akin to Sherina. It would have been very easy to go that way after everything that had happened to him.

They reached the sanctuary of his room in good time. Realizing how he had tired he was just from that little sojourn proved he couldn't have gone off to the mountains, even if he could heal the worst of the injuries. The healing would take energy all its own.

Maylee brought them dinner. The food smelled heavenly.

"Thank you!" Katashan said as he settled at the chair. He saw the smile she gave Cork. Praise the Gods their relationship had survived the madness. "Can you join us?"

"Join you, sir?" she said, softly, her gray eyes gone wide.

"I don't mind and I'm certain Cork wouldn't." He waved a hand to stop whatever Cork had started to say. "I'm sure having to spend so much time with me hasn't been pleasant for either of you. So sit down, if you're free, and chat for a while."

"Oh." She looked at Cork who gave her his chair and settled on the bed by the far corner of the table. He looked in much better mood for her company. Katashan decided to try and convince Cork to go for a stroll with her later.

"What have you heard, Maylee?" Cork asked as he passed her bread and cheese. "Are they talking about us?"

"Oh, yes," she said, nodding emphatically, her hair bouncing at the top of her head. "There's much relief that you and the young lord seemed to get along so well, sir."

"Kat. Katashan. Not sir."

She frowned and glanced at Cork, as though to make certain it was all right. He gave a little shrug.

"Kat, then," she said. A bit bolder than Cork, he suspected. She nibbled the food and seemed to carefully consider what more to say. "There's talk that you brought the magic trouble here. I've heard that from the guards and some of the servants. The people in the city, though . . . they don't seem to have any opinion at all, yet. Shock that his lordship is dead, but. . . ."

"I suspect they hope Lord Fordel will be less demanding," Katashan offered as he picked up a cup of cider. The scent made his mouth water and he sipped a little before he spoke again. "Lord Arpan couldn't have been very popular."

"That's true enough, sir," she said and smiled again. "Kat."

"I think he will be a better noble for this area, for whatever worth my opinion might be," Katashan said.

She looked at him, nodded as though she had measured his worth and his words as she nibbled at a little of the food. "I can't stay long. They'll expect me back in the kitchen. What should I tell them, sir?"

He hid his smile at the title again. "Tell them that His

Lordship and I had a pleasant meeting, under the circumstances. And that I am very weary and will not be up and about much for the next couple days."

"Yes sir," she said, her eyes narrowed as she stood. He suspected he looked the part of an invalid too well, especially since his hand trembled as he lifted a piece of bread. "Rest well, sir. I'll be back later for the plates and tray."

She gave Cork a quick smile and left the room, and he could hear her skipping step out in the hall.

"Feel free to walk her down --"

"No sir," Cork said with a vehement shake of his head. "This is where I am supposed to be. As tempting as time with Maylee sounds, I'd rather not risk it."

"I'm not helpless." As much as he appreciated Cork's help, he did not want the man to feel as though he could do nothing else.

"No, you aren't helplbess," Cork agreed but there was still stubbornness in his face. "However, you are every bit as weary as you said. I am your guard. I take that position seriously and this is where I am going to stay."

"I'll know if Sherina tries to come in here."

"No doubt. Maybe it hasn't occurred to you that you could have other enemies, too." He played with a piece of bread for a moment, obviously choosing his words. "I am a native boy. Maybe I understand the area too well, and I know how some of the locals are going to think. You are a foreign stranger, and you and I are the only ones who survived what are obviously not natural deaths for the others. I'm a local boy and they know me so while I have a bit of the taint of that foul night, I'm not suspect. But you, sir . . . you brought in a body, you brought Lord Arpan down on us, and you were part of his death. You guard against the magic. I'll watch out for the men."

"Fair enough," Katashan said, knowing Cork was right. They made a good team. He thought they might both even survive it, if they remained very careful.

"Stop staring at the plate and finish your food. *Sir*."

He grinned and ate a little more.

CHAPTER SIXTEEN

T hree days later they began the journey to Silver Pass. The morning felt cool and damp; the wind came brisk off the ocean, and gulls screamed as they took off from the cliff side as the horses moved past

Katashan rode wrapped tight in a cloak, the wool already damp from the fading fog but warm. For most of the first day he watched the ocean off to their right where gray clouds scuttled across the sky and white waves crashed against the rocky shore below. He remembered standing at the summit of Silver Pass and thinking how warm it looked below. He wondered if he would ever be warm again.

The horses made a steady climb upward along the trail, following the cliff that overlooked the sea, far below. He hadn't had much of a chance to enjoy this trail on the way toward Salbay, when he had been watching over the body of Sherina and wondering what trouble he'd fallen into. He enjoyed it as much as possible this time, despite knowing he headed toward trouble again.

Lord Fordel rode ahead of him with five of his own men, keeping up appearances very well for the sake of the people they passed. They'd had a couple late night meetings in Katashan's room to discuss matters, but they knew they could do nothing until they learned more at the site. Sherina had not returned, but neither was convinced that meant she had been destroyed.

Katashan traveled with Cork at his side. Lord Fordel's, men seemed to take guarding their new Lord far more seriously than Katashan thought necessary from two men, one of whom needed help up on the horse after each stop. Then again, there was the matter of Lord Arpan's death which the two of them alone survived. He thought maybe they were being wise in their care of Lord Fordel, after all.

He and Fordel hadn't spoken since they left the fort, which proved annoying. His men kept him close, bundling him off every time it seemed Katashan or Cork got too close. Katashan wondered how they could work together if these men were so bothered just by his presence on this trip.

There were other problems as well, and one in particular that worried Katashan. Fordel had told him last night that a company of Lord Arpan's men still hadn't turned up. Mercenaries, some of them, and well paid. Fordel had no intention of keeping them on, but he couldn't dismiss them if they didn't show themselves. Both he and Cork feared the men might think they had reason to attack the two who survived when they're benefactor didn't, and perhaps even kill the new Lord who didn't want to keep their hire.

As the morning drew on, he let go of the annoyance and worries and watched the ocean, letting the waves soothe him. He thought there should be an escape across the sea, traveling off to lands he could not see. Would it be better?

"Katashan."

He looked up with a start to find Fordel had pulled back to ride beside him. He glanced around and found the guards had spread out this time.

"It's all right. We're no longer being watched and my men will let us know if anyone tries to come close again."

"Oh," Katashan said. He felt dull-witted. "I hadn't thought of someone watching us. I had started to despair of the work we needed to do if your men didn't trust me."

"They don't trust you," Fordel said with an unexpectedly bright grin. "But they are *my men*, not my father's, and they understand about the work we must do. They're coached in magic as well."

"Cork is not," Katashan said, glancing around at the men, realizing how careless he had been not to notice.

"I know. I really think we have far more than enough people working magic already, don't you?"

"Ah. Yes." He pulled himself up straighter in the saddle. "Who was watching us?"

"Mountain people, mostly." He glanced over his shoulder towards the rocky headlands. "They keep eyes on the trail, making certain we're not mounting an attack against the villages. But there were others. Bullis has a feel for that sort of thing. He thinks there might have been a spy from the capital who probably followed us out of Salbay."

"And gave up?" Katashan asked with new worry.

"Not exactly gave up. Just became discouraged and fell back." He shrugged. "A little subtle magic that might not have worked if he hadn't run into the mountain people. They'll entertain each other for a while. Probably for a couple days, in fact. The mountain people are often very curious about people sneaking around and spying on others."

"Will they kill him?"

"It doesn't seem likely. And under the circumstances, we can't complain if they do. If they don't stop him, we must. This business is far too important to risk because of one spy. I dare not let my own abilities be known, Katashan. And I trust you don't wish to be any more open than I am. If others learn, we might be stopped from doing our work."

"Quite true. My apologies, Lord Fordel. I know this business is serious, and people have died already. I just keep hoping for better answers than to get others killed."

"And this is why you and I are allies, Katashan. You are not careless of lives, the way my father and Sherina had always been. Let us hope we find those answers at the place where Sherina died," he said and sounded worried again. "I think it little more than luck that she hasn't struck again."

"Luck," Katashan said and looked over at Cork. He gave a slight nod, not lost on Fordel. "More than luck. We've had some help."

"Pater Matish, yes --"

"Oh yes, him too," Katashan said, and had Fordel's attention. The man looked both curious and worried. "But there is a reason why Cork and I survived the encounter with Sherina."

"I thought you --"

"I couldn't even stand, let alone cast enough magic to save us. No, it was not me, not entirely," he said. He looked into Fordel's face. "Peralin came to our aid, as he had the first night after I took Sherina from the pass."

"Per --" Fordel said, frowning first and then looking startled. "Peralin. The God."

Katashan nodded.

"Surely you are mistaken," he said, his voice raising enough to draw attention from his men. He waved their worry away while he took several deep breaths. "You must be --"

"He rides on Night himself, my lord," Cork said. "And I've seen him as well. And drank of his wine."

"Gods, gods -- I don't like this at all. Peralin has a reputation for being involved in matters that are . . . well, *dire*. And he's not always won his wars."

"I suspected as much," Katashan said. He brushed long hair from his face, his hand not quite as steady as he would have liked. "But he's been of aid so far. I thought you should know, though I hadn't wanted to worry others. Are we stopping at the caravansary tonight?"

"Yes." Fordel shook his head, as though trying to dismiss

what he'd been told. "We'll leave early tomorrow since it's a long climb to the pass. It takes far more time to go up than to go down. We might camp in the open most of the way to the summit and then go the rest of the way at first light. Does that sound reasonable?"

"Oh yes. I wouldn't want to be up there in the dark, and especially not with the work we need to do, though camping in the open is going to be dangerous, you know."

"*Everything* is dangerous." He tilted his head, looking at Katashan as though he hadn't really done so before. "May I ask why you haven't gone on, dismissed our troubles from your mind, and left this place that isn't your home?"

"Even supposing Sherina isn't tied to me in some way -- which I fear she is -- and would follow wherever I went, I wouldn't leave without this matter settled. We both know there are wars that go beyond nationality. This is a war between the living and the dead and by that I choose my side."

"Ah. Yes." He looked a little startled at first, and then smiled. "You've seen the bigger picture. I am a noble in this place. I probably think too much in terms of territory, even now. You look worn already, Katashan. We're not far from the caravansary."

"Good. I'm tired. A good night's rest will help."

Lord Fordel still looked worried. Katashan felt sorry for the man who had stepped into this magical mess at a time when he also had to take over the reins of leadership as well. They both knew the trouble would get worse.

The ride went without incident and they reached the building well before sunset. However, much to Katashan's dismay, they found it already occupied by what appeared to be an entire clan of people. Even Fordel pulled back as they neared and shook his head with some dismay.

"Damn. They're early this year," he said.

"They?" Katashan asked, wishing only that he could get off

the horse and rest.

"The spring field workers, sir. Mountain people who come down for the growing season," Cork explained with a shake of his head. "Starlings, we call them. They arrive in the spring and leave in the fall, going back to the mountains. They work the lowland fields, mostly in his Lordship's lands."

Cork glanced at Fordel, probably only now remembering that the young man was *His Lordship* now.

"This does indicate we'll have a long planting season, so that's not all bad," Fordel said, obviously trying to find some good in the situation. "They've never been wrong about the weather. But hell, I'm not ready to meet them as the new lord, and especially not during this journey."

"I suggest we ride on and camp on open ground tonight," one of his guards said.

"No," Katashan replied with a quick shake of his head. "We don't want to be out in the open tonight. I don't care to spend another night like I did with your father, Fordel."

"And you think we'll be safer inside?" the guard asked.

"I can ward buildings. I cannot ward the air itself."

"Ah. Good point," Fordel said. "And we'll have to rig something up for tomorrow night. No use wasting that much power tonight, though. We'll need it later."

The others nodded, none of them looking happy, but then there would be little on this trip to inspire a man to smile.

"Then we join the starlings." Fordel started his horse forward and stopped again, barely a yard closer. He looked back at the others again. "Though perhaps there's no reason they need know who I am? I fear it will only slow the journey if I am held here by duty."

"And that's a good point as well," Katashan conceded. He looked around at the little group. "Will the rest of you have any trouble with a charade to hide Lord Fordel?"

"No sir," Cork said and the others nodded. "But, if I can

suggest . . . ?"

"By all means, Cork," Lord Fordel said, looking relieved to have anyone offer a suggestion.

"Take off the jewels. They're noticeable. And we'll go in as Katashan's guards, so they'll look at him rather than the rest of us, including you. He's exotic enough to draw most of the attention anyway."

Cork had a good point, though Katashan didn't like the idea of having the attention, though he would have had it anyway. They might as well make use of it. Lord Fordel nodded and carefully pulled off rings and his jeweled cloak clasp. He looked trail worn and dusty enough that the fine weave of the clothing should go unnoticed as dusk sat in, as long as he didn't draw any attention to himself.

The people at the caravansary had noticed them by now and appeared worried that the group had stopped a ways off. Katashan didn't want them to wonder what kind of trouble approached. The starling men were already reaching for weapons and that didn't look like a good way to start the evening.

"Shall I deal with this, sir?" Cork asked with one glance at Fordel but then his attention turned to Katashan. "I've had some contact with the mountain people before."

"Yes, please," Katashan said, hoping for rest soon.

As they arrived at the gate to the shelter, he quickly learned why the locals called these people starlings and it wasn't just for their migratory predilections. They came pouring out of the building, most dressed in black with bits of silver and gold dangling everywhere. And they twittered. They seemed to fairly fly around Katashan and the others, the small ones coming too close to horses until Katashan's guards leapt down and shooed everyone away.

He could not imagine how they were going to get any rest in this cacophony of sound. He looked at Fordel who appeared equally dismayed. The young lord had gotten down and had hold of the halter to Katashan's horse, waving the children away again and keeping the mount somewhat in control. Katashan would have thought the starlings knew about horses, since he could see they had mounts of their own in the stables.

Then he remembered how his own children had never believed anything would hurt them. . . .

The thought felt like an old, dull knife digging into his heart. He fought the pain of the loss back with anger, but that wouldn't help now, to glare at those happy children because they were not *his* children, and they were alive when his were dead. It was not their fault. His fault, yes; he had believed, childlike, that nothing would hurt the ones he loved.

"Damn," he whispered, and closed his eyes, though the ghosts stood clearer there in his mind.

"Sir?" Cork said, a hand resting gently on his leg. He looked into Cork's face, forcing himself to focus on his friend as he took a deep breath, trying to banish different ghosts than the one he came to fight. "Are you all right, sir?"

"There's a shed in the back of the stalls," he said softly, bowing his head and refusing to look at the children as their parents gathered them up. "Let's take it. I can't deal with this tonight."

Cork nodded, but he glanced at Fordel who gave a quick, silent nod of his own. Katashan tried not to feel guilty about assuming control, although they would probably have been pretty crowded in the main building, and getting Fordel to somewhere with less people might be better anyway. Katashan thought there must be twenty to thirty of the starlings inside from the racket they made, and that didn't count the children.

Fordel's men took care of the horses, working with some of the mountain men to move their own stock out of one section while they took the other. The mountain men seemed amiable enough, at least, and that put Katashan at ease.

Cork quickly escorted him into the small, weather-beaten shelter and helped him settle against the wall by the hay. Fordel remained by the door, acting like a guard while Katashan leaned back, content to be out of the way.

"My apologies," he told Fordel who looked at him, obviously not understanding. "I don't think I could have handled being part of that group tonight."

"This works well for both of us," Fordel said. He wrapped his cloak around his arms, looking weary. One of the guards took the spot by the door, and Fordel came to sit on the floor. Katashan realized this could not have been a good few days for him either, with his father's unexpected and spectacular death, and the work that had to be done since then. They were probably both fools to go rushing off to the pass just now.

But he felt as though something needed done and quickly. He didn't usually rush into anything important with such haste, but it seemed that ever since he had found Sherina time pressed in on him.

"Katashan?" Fordel asked. "You look as though there's something we ought to be talking about."

"I just wondered why I feel as though we need to hurry. I wonder why I keep thinking we're running out of time and that even a night's rest is taking a chance."

"You too?" He frowned and leaned against the wall. Katashan hadn't expected him to look so at ease in such an uncomfortable place. "I don't know why I insisted we head up here right now. It's bound to draw attention."

"Time," Katashan said. "There is something coming that we must beat --"

"Spring." Fordel sat up straighter, looking startled. "The spring equinox is only three days away."

"Gods." Katashan felt a stab of understanding that set his heart pounding again. "You're right. Spring is coming. The body would have been found as soon as the spring melt came, so whatever the magic was triggered to do, it would have to happen before then."

"But why wait so long?" Fordel asked.

"Because. . . ." Katashan began and stopped again. He closed his eyes for a moment, and there he saw the answer that made him shiver with the power and simplicity of it. "*Life, bond, death.* The coming of spring is part of the ritual. Winter is death, and spring is life. This goes far beyond the human realm, Fordel. I fear that whoever set this spell is attempting to bind nature as well."

"Oh hell." Fordel's face paled. In some ways the look of worry relieved Katashan. They would be working together and he appreciated that Fordel understood the depth of the problem and the dangers involved. "We should have brought Matish, at the very least. Or I could have called in the high priest from . . . no, that's not such a good idea, is it?"

"Not if you intend to remain quiet about your own abilities. And the fewer people who know about mine, the better it will be," he added. He pulled his own cloak up closer around him. "I think it wiser to have Matish where he is unless he is needed."

"Yes," Fordel said, nodding emphatically. "He'll be good back up if we don't do well."

Cork appeared at the doorway, looked the two of them over, and shook his head. "You make me worry, sirs, when you both look as though things have just taken a turn for the worse. I don't want think it."

"There may be complications," Fordel said softly.

Cork sighed, looked from one to the other, and didn't ask for explanations. He had already gone through complications enough, Katashan suspected, and likely saw no reason to worry too much about another one. That seemed wise for someone who couldn't help in the magical side of the work.

"Lord Fordel, sir," Cork said softly, and dropped down on his heels. He made sure he had a clear view of the doorway and anyone coming from that direction. A horse protested outside but the guards seemed to get it in hand. It sounded normal. "Your man Bullis says he and the other guards will camp between us and the building with the Starlings, just to keep an eye on things. They think that you should be safe here, sir, with Katashan and me as guards."

"Sounds best," he said, though he did look around with a little unease. "At least we have some hay to sleep on."

"Yes, sir," Cork said. "I'll bring the bedding in and help get things settled. The guards are seeing to food, sir. They said you wouldn't mind sharing what the Starlings offer?"

"Not at all. They're excellent cooks."

Cork nodded, looking relieved. Katashan felt sorry for his friend, thrust into this mess and relegated to guard and servant for two rather eccentric men. Katashan thought it must seem a very strange and frightening world to someone who hadn't the ability to even sense the coming of magic. Katashan found it frightening enough for someone with the power.

While Cork went about the work, Katashan rested against the wall, feeling worn from the little journey. He wanted rest, and even the idea of food didn't appeal to him tonight. He closed his eyes, despite that he thought he should speak with Fordel for a while longer to discuss magic and what they both knew and could guess about what would happen when they reached Silver Pass.

But he couldn't. He hadn't the strength.

"Sir. Kat?"

He opened his eyes a slit and frowned. Cork knelt beside him, a bowl in one hand and a cup in the other. Fordel had already begun eating. The food smelled rich and his stomach growled before he could remind himself he didn't want the food or to do the work of eating.

"Thank you," he said and took the offering. Cork still remained there, watching him. "Is there a problem?"

"I'm wondering, sir, if maybe we shouldn't spend a couple days here."

"No," Katashan said, though he felt tempted to agree. "No, we don't dare. We have just realized that time is short."

"But you took the body away. You broke that spell, right?" Cork asked softly.

"I . . . disturbed the spell," he corrected. Cork frowned. "The sacrifice had already been made, and it's obvious, from the trouble we've had with Sherina, that there's still power. I want to get up there and see what more we might do to stop whatever had been planned."

"Do you think you can?" he said and looked to Fordel to include him in the question this time.

"I don't know," Lord Fordel said with a shrug. He sat aside his already empty bowl. "I've no experience with this sort of matter or anything connected with it."

"Except for your own link with Sherina," Katashan reminded him.

Fordel frowned. Katashan wished he hadn't mentioned that part, wondering how Fordel must feel knowing his sister had died, bound to evil, likely to be a problem. . . .

Fordel ate several bites of bread, chewing carefully, staring at the wall. Katashan didn't bother him, turning his attention to his own food instead. Cork sat down near the door, watching through the opening into the area beyond. They could hear the sounds of too many people, far too close. Children sounded shrill and some of them unhappy. Katashan tried not to listen, to worry about what might happen to them if --

"I don't want to stay here," he said suddenly, startling his two companions.

"Katashan?"

"If she comes it will put all of them in danger, Cork. No more protection than the soldiers had when she came to the camp. I can't stay here. I can't risk drawing her to these poor people. I should have considered that before --"

"Calm, calm," Fordel said, leaning over to put a hand on his shoulder before he could stand. He had intended to leave, to get away but he stopped now and looked at Lord Fordel, thinking the man couldn't understand. "You said we needed to be in a building tonight so you could ward. Can you ward this entire place against the danger? Or is this too large an area?"

"Can you ward at all?" Katashan asked, uncertain of his own abilities.

"Not well. You said you warded the first night here, when you came down from the mountain. Can you do it again?"

"Yes," he said, forcing the panic to subside. "I only fear that she's gained strength and I may not be powerful enough to keep her out. However, these people would be along the path she would likely take to find me anyway, especially if we stayed anywhere near. Yes, here is the best chance for protecting us and them. Cork, I need my Ritual Blade."

Cork had held on to the blade while they were still at the fort, saying he would be a better guard of it if trouble came to Katashan. He hadn't argued. Now Cork looked worried as he reached inside his own tunic. However, it was Fordel who sat forward, shocked. That movement stopped Cork from continuing.

"Ritual Blade?" he said, putting aside his empty plate and looking surprised. "You are a heartblood wizard? Gods, man -- I had no idea!"

"Oh," Katashan said, a little embarrassed, and then worried. "Is this going to cause problems? I know that my kind were banned from your lands a century ago, but --"

"Katashan, you suddenly give me more hope for survival," Fordel admitted. He did look better. "I don't know why they destroyed your sect, Katashan. Maybe they had cause -- but I am dealing with you and not the mages of a hundred years ago, and so far I find no reason to cling to the ancient fears of my ancestors, who never trusted any cult from the north and all the more so when I know that they would condemn me for my own magic as well."

Katashan felt a wave of relief overlay the dread of the moment before. "I should set the wards then."

"Yes, you should."

"But don't put too much into it, sir," Cork told him, standing and offering a hand to help him to his feet. "You're weak already, and we have a good long journey and hard work ahead."

"Excellent warning," Katashan said, and began to rethink his work. He had been ready to throw as much power into the wards as he could, but he really only needed enough of a ward to warn him. That would take little more than a touch of blood at the gate and the wall, and a little on the building where the Starlings rested, quieter now.

He had expected Lord Fordel to follow him out to see the work done, but remaining where he wouldn't be seen seemed wiser. Katashan took his time at the work, pausing for a long moment at the gate, listening in hopes of hearing Night coming to help them.

He felt inadequate to the work, even though there didn't seem to be anything particularly wrong tonight. Rest would help, and with that in mind, he headed back to the shed, Cork as always at his side.

Cork quickly made a bed for him in the straw, and brought more warm food, which he insisted that Katashan eat. He did as he was bade, too weary to argue the point.

Then he noticed Fordel sitting up against the wall across from him, and watching with what appeared to be a look of amusement. Cork looked where Katashan did and he expected the guard to be embarrassed. Instead, he shrugged and smiled.

"I've decided that if so much depends on Katashan, then I'd do well to make certain he's at his best," Cork said and continued to make the bed while Katashan ate. Katashan did notice that he was making two spots, praise the Gods, so he hadn't left Fordel out completely. "He's gone through hell, your lordship, sir, and there's damned little time -- begging your pardon -- very little time in which he can recover."

"You need not apologize to me for the care you take of your ward, Cork," Fordel said. He shifted a little, and for the first time showed discomfort at their surroundings. "Nor for your language. I grew up around the troops and spent more time around them than any nobility expect my father, whose language was never gentile. Besides, you have a good point. And Katashan, forgive me, but you do look like hell."

"Yes, I imagine I do," Katashan said with a sigh. He knew how he felt and he didn't have to guess at how he looked.

"Rest." Fordel leaned back against the wall, pulling his own cloak around him. "We'll regret if we don't take advantage of this time."

Katashan didn't argue.

He rested, but not well.

CHAPTER SEVENTEEN

They might have made it all the way to the summit of the pass the next day except the weather turned on them. Katashan watched the storm rushing over the mountain top and down at their party, and he could do no more than summon a feeling of annoyed resignation. He should have expected this. If something could go wrong, it was bound to.

The winds hit only moments before the falling rain caught them in a frigid drenching that set Katashan shivering within a few steps. The horses balked at the sudden change and the bite of ice in the wind. Katashan caught tighter hold of the reins, grateful when Cork came closer, making certain the horse didn't bolt and get away from him.

Everyone else, including his lordship, cursed. Katashan only leaned into the cold and pulled up hood of his cloak. He'd already begun looking for a likely place to camp and decided, given the weather, that they should break early. He thought he could feel magic in the storm, but that didn't mean someone directed it. The world was filled with natural power, and it would be drawn to places like a sacrifice on the mountain top.

Katashan looked upward as rain fell in a deluge, pelting his face and making his eyes water from the cold. In moments the rain turned to ice and then to snow sending small white flakes swirling around them like a fog made solid. He could no longer see the pass.

"We need to stop!" he called out and the others agreed without any argument.

Lord Fordel's men quickly found a spot to camp to the side of the trail. The glade, though covered in ice-incrusted snow, sat slightly out of the wind and not far from the trail. Branches were downed in the area, and the others had little trouble gathering enough to make a shelter which they overlaid with evergreen branches, still heavy with needles. The makeshift covering looked like a fragrant, though drafty, refuge for the night.

Fordel and Katashan remained with the unhappy horses. The snow fell harder, promising them a long, cold night. The five guards and Cork worked quickly, cursing, and getting things in order with as much speed as they could manage.

"Do you feel half as useless as I do right now?" Fordel asked. He stomped his feet much like the horses.

"More so, I imagine. I can barely hold on to two horses and you have the rest."

Fordel laughed, shaking his head. "Thank you. I hate feeling I'm useless, you know. And I'm not used to my position yet. I don't know what I'm supposed to do."

"I suppose that this has come as a shock. I'm sorry. Have I said that?"

"Sorry?" he asked, looking confused.

"At the death of your father."

Fordel stared at him, snow falling around them and the wind biting at their faces. He said nothing for a long time.

"My lord?" Katashan finally said.

"You honestly sounded as though you meant those words -- that you were sorry."

"I am."

Fordel shook his head, and then continued. "My father intended to murder you. You knew he wanted your death because he feared what you would say about Sherina."

"Yes, I know," Katashan answered. He tried not to show the discomfort of wounds that hadn't fully healed yet. "But that doesn't mean I cannot be sorry he died and left you in this situation. Though, truth be told, it's obvious you are better suited to being the leader of this land than he ever could have been."

"Thank you. But I didn't want to be next lord. When Sherina disappeared, I spent a lot of my own funds trying to find her to make sure she was still heir. Does that shock you?"

"Not at all."

"I didn't think it would." He met Katashan's quick glance with a little nod. "So, tell me why you left the north, Katashan."

"To leave behind ghosts and emptiness. To find a place where I might make a difference, since I could not do so there."

"You sound bitter." Fordel looked surprised. "I hadn't expected it."

Katashan bowed his head, silent again. He could have told Lord Fordel many things about his past, but none that would help them now. Instead, he watched as the guards set up makeshift poles, and piled more pine boughs to make a sort of shelter for the horses as well. Good. He could cast a ward if they had even a little bit of a shelter around them tonight, and he could protect the horses from the worst of the weather.

Fordel didn't ask any more about his past.

Cork came to take the two horses, relieving him of even that much use. He carefully trudged through old snow to the shelter. It would be a close and uncomfortable night. He hoped it remained a safe one.

He crawled into the opening, wrapping his cloak tight around him, and waiting for the others to come in. He would set the ward and then sleep. Sleep, at least, would make him less aware of the cold.

But they took longer than he expected, and he tried not to

grow cross. He wanted rest --

"Sir?" Cork said, leaning down under the covering where Katashan sat, huddled and cold. "I think you had best see this."

Katashan managed not to curse, knowing it couldn't be good. His body ached and trembled as he crawled back out of their little covering again. He wasn't ready for this. Really wasn't ready for anything.

He looked towards the summit of the pass without Cork even telling him where the trouble would be. The snow blew harder. He didn't want to stand out here and even the little pine-bough shelter seemed not so bad. But as he watched, he saw a flickering of light through the storm, like land-based lighting.

"Damn," Fordel whispered close behind him. "I don't like the looks of that."

"Me either," Katashan needlessly added.

Katashan slowly lifted a hand, ignoring the ache along his arm and up through his shoulder. He could feel a hint of magic in the storm, but now he could feel the stronger surge of power from the mountain top, though he detected no real signature to the power. For all he could tell, a lightning storm had settled to ground and played among the trees.

"What do we do?" Fordel asked

"Not much unless the trouble comes closer. We'll face this soon enough when we climb up there," Katashan said.

Cork looked at him uncertainly and then nodded. "Yes, of course. Forgive me. You need rest tonight, sir."

"I need far more than just a night of rest," Katashan admitted. He put a hand on Cork's arm when the man looked worried. "I'll be fine. I'm just very weary and far less certain of what I'm supposed to do now that I see the trouble."

"That's not reassuring."

"No, it isn't."

Cork sighed and took hold of his arm and the three of them went back to the little shelter. One of the guards -- Tyos --

handed Katashan a cup of tea he'd warmed over a small, fitful fire which proved to be mostly smokeless thanks to some little magic one of them knew. Katashan wrapped his hands around the cup, grateful for that warmth.

"It'll do better inside you while it's still warm, sir," Cork said, gently nudging his arm as he sat beside him.

"I don't know. This is pretty nice."

"Drink. I can warm your cup again, foreigner," Tyos said, and then frowned. "Your pardon --"

"It's quite all right," Katashan replied. He leaned back, glad to find they'd given him a relatively soft spot. The wind blew through the little shelter, though, sending a sprinkling of snow and ice to sizzle in the fire. The temperature had begun to plummet.

"We'll have to do more than ward," Katashan finally said. He felt a little odd -- he'd never been open about using magic, even among those who knew about his abilities and would not condemn him for them. "Well need protections not only from magic but also from the cold. This is a damned mess. We'll drain power tonight and I fear we'll need far more when we reach Silver Pass."

"And that's probably why we're in this situation," Fordel said with a quick nod as he took a cup of tea as well. "Something wants to weaken us."

"Weaker," Cork said. He looked from one to the other. "It's not as though you're strong yet anyway, sir. This may not have been the time for this journey after all."

"Whatever is at play here has been wearing me down from the moment I found the body." Katashan realized the truth of those words as he said them. He leaned closer to the fire, letting it warm his fingers while he tried to think this through again. "I don't think waiting would have helped. In fact, I believe the longer we wait, the weaker I become."

"Because you found the body," Fordel said. "And you are

the one who already disturbed this magic, and it is obvious that whoever -- *whatever* -- is behind this has targeted you. Sherina follows you, but the mage hasn't killed you."

"The mage has recognized me as an enemy and knows my powers are substantial."

Fordel leaned forward, warming his fingers as well. The others had settled in around them, as comfortable as they could get on a night like this. "It may be this isn't even consciously directed. You are the one who disturbed the site. You said mage. Are you certain whatever is directing this is human?"

That question finally did make the others uncomfortable. Katashan didn't blame them; it made him uncomfortable as well.

"Someone human-like, at least, wrote the runes that bound your sister," he answered. "I can't say more until I learn more. But we need to be safe tonight."

Katashan pulled out his ritual blade and paused, considering how much power to use. Not the wrist this time. He nicked several fingers and touched them to the wood to his right. Branches crisscrossed everywhere, and he closed his eyes as he spread his spell around the edges of their little area and to the connecting area with the horses; warding against magic, but also against the worst of the wind and cold as well. The magic helped almost immediately, and he heard sighs of relief from the others.

Katashan pulled his cloak up and settled into the pine rushes, grateful for the blanket that kept most of the needles from stabbing him. He stared at the fire for a moment, and silently wished his companions well for the night. He even put a little magic in his wish. He hoped it was enough.

CHAPTER EIGHTEEN

Morning came too soon and looked no better for the light of day. Storm winds howled around them, battering at his wards perhaps even more fiercely now, as though to blow hope away. Katashan could still hear the crash of thunder, though the combination of daylight and the blowing snow obscured the flashes they had seen the night before on the pass.

The snow had piled up around them during the long night, but they and the horses had remained safe within the wards. If Sherina or anything had tried to get in, he never noticed in the fury of the storm.

Katashan slipped out of their makeshift covering and stood slowly, stretching stiff muscles and hoping his aching head would ease as soon as he had some of the tea Cork had already started making. The constant assault of untamed magic felt like an irritant, scratching at his brain like insects. He could see Fordel felt much the same way, though neither of them said anything aloud.

"Drink this, sir," Cork said, pushing a warm cup into his hand. His fingers wrapped around the cup, even if he didn't look at the contents or Cork. "And stop thinking for a few minutes, sir."

"Pardon?" Katashan said, glancing back at Cork this time.

His guard hadn't shaved in a few days, reminding Katashan

that he was in the same state -- haggard, dirty, and worn. Snow lighted on Cork's hair and shoulders, and then blew away in the next burst of wind.

"Stop trying to think it all out, sir," Cork said at last, tapping the cup to remind him to drink. "You've made it plain you don't know what to expect here. We accept that answer. You should as well."

"I don't know what I'm doing. I don't like feeling as though so much rests on what I've done and what I might do wrong."

"Or right."

"Far better chance that I'll make some mistake, especially if I don't have the facts to go on."

"Maybe so," Cork said. He looked up at the hilltop now as well. A flash of lightning brightened the snowfall for a brief moment and they could barely hear the thunder above the roar of the wind. "We'll be there soon enough, sir."

"And I should enjoy my tea and trail bread while I have the chance, eh?" Katashan said, and finally sipped.

"That's my way of thinking it, sir," Cork said. "You aren't going to find any answers standing here freezing. So don't waste the time on looking for them."

He didn't argue this time. He found the least windy spot he could and savored the warm tea, trying not to think how long it might be before he had a chance at more.

"Katashan, I think we're going to have to go in on foot from here," Fordel said, coming up beside them. Cork gave a little sigh of frustration though Katashan couldn't decide if that came from the interruption or the idea of walking.

"Probably wise," Katashan agreed. "The horses would likely bolt closer to the magic and we'd need to use magic to hold them, which would be a waste of power. It will mean less we'll need to ward as well. In fact, if just you and I --"

"No way in hell," Cork said, and the nearest two guards echoed him, though in less terse terms. "Begging your pardon, my Lord and Katashan, but there's no way we can let the two of you go up there without a guard. You have already said you don't know what you'll find. Maybe it'll all be magic and nothing I can do to help. But maybe it won't be, and you'll need guards while you do what you can to deal with the magic."

"He's right," Katashan admitted. "Best not to take any chances. It won't take us long to make the rest of the hike, even in this weather. A little magic can help to make the trail less wearing on us."

Fordel looked at him, head tilted for a moment. "Are you sure? You don't look up to a climb out of bed, let alone a climb up a mountain."

"The sleep helped, but the wild magic is giving me a headache. If we can do something about that damned storm, I think we'll both feel better for it."

Fordel grunted agreement.

Katashan drank the last of his tea and had a second cup to please Cork while the others gathered a few belongings for the hike. They traveled light, taking only cloaks, weapons, and a few flasks of liquids of varying types to help along the way.

They didn't bother to leave a guard for the horses and the supplies remaining at the camp. No one from the low land would hike up towards the summit in this chaotic weather and anyone the other side of the peak would have retreated in haste. Fordel used a little magic to settle the horses and then they headed back for the trail.

Unfortunately, the trail had a knee-deep covering of snow laid down overnight with ice formed underneath, making it exceedingly treacherous to climb. Even the magic Fordel used didn't help much.

The wind blew with such a force it made talking impossible and Katashan could do nothing more than lean into the gale and follow in the footsteps of the others as they headed upwards to the pass. Cork stayed at his back and helped him up each time he fell.

The closer they came to the top, the louder the thunder grew and the brighter the lightning. It was, he suddenly realized, unwise to go any farther. He signaled a stop and no one argued. They huddled in a small semi-circle, flinching as the storm struck the already blackened trees not far up the trail from them.

"There is no way we'll ever be able to explain this as natural," Fordel said, waving a hand towards the area above them. "Damn."

Katashan nodded. He had seen the destruction of the trees, the burnt ground, and the twisted and broken boulders that had been hit by lighting. This would add a layer of trouble to the situation for them, but only if they survived to leave this mountain. Looking at the storm, he thought survival might be questionable, though he didn't say so aloud.

"Any suggestions?" Fordel asked, looking at him.

"I must get to the altar. No matter what, Verina is strong here, or else she would never have been able to direct me to the body . . . ah."

"Ah?" Cork asked, after a moment.

"That's our protection." He lifted his hand and tested the magic in the air. He could feel her presence, even over the other magic that had been battering the area for two days. "We need to reach her statue. She'll help us."

"You're certain?" Fordel said, looking upward with a frown.

"Yes," Katashan answered and felt certain of this if nothing else. "She wants this abomination away from her holy site. That was a mistake they made, to choose this place."

"We tend to think of the old gods as gone from here," Cork said. He started to stand first, having been with Katashan long enough to know it was time to move on. "That would be a mistake, I think."

"Very much so," Katashan said. "And that might give us a clue about what happened here, you know. It could be that we're looking for someone local who thought this just a convenient site, away from everyone and with a ready-made and unused altar. I had expected it to be someone from the outside, perhaps another northerner, since magic isn't well known here -- but I don't know that a northerner would make this mistake with Verina, though she is not known as a dangerous Goddess."

"Good points," Fordel said. "You might be right. We'll never make it past that storm, friend."

"Yes we will." Katashan drew his ritual blade from beneath the layers of warm cloth and pulled back the edge of his shirt sleeve. His skin looked white with the cold.

"Kat," Cork said softly.

"I know what I'm doing."

He sliced before anyone could say more or move to stop him: A quick and deep cut this time -- already too cold to really feel much -- and he wove magic with the drops of blood and blowing snow, creating a shield as strong as he dared without leaving himself so depleted he could neither hold the power nor move. The magic glowed around them with an ice-white light, substantial and strong, though little warmer, except the wind no longer blew against them. They had to reach the pass. They didn't have time to waste.

As they moved upward, Katashan could more clearly feel the power in the blasts of lightning. The magic it took to create this storm had leached nearly all life from the area and even from the ground itself. It would be years before anything grew here again. This would be an ill-omened place for generations and he doubted anyone else would pause there to look at the sea below.

Katashan led them straight towards the pass and the Verina statue, knowing they had little time. Magic drained from the ground around them and drained from him as well, slipping away with each step.

Climbing the last hundred yards would have been

impossible for anyone but a heartblood mage whose innate magic gave him power. That power wasn't available to someone like Fordel, who had to pull most of his magic from outside himself. He could feel damned little magic left in the world -- but as they reached the final rise he could see the Verina statue, untouched by the storm and glowing with power. She welcomed him, and he could feel her power like a warm breeze in this place of ice.

Lightning struck his shield, sending ripples of golden light over them, almost blinding him in a dangerously glorious show.

"Stay with me," Katashan warned. He laid the blade against his still bleeding wrist and then lifted it and wrote runes in the air. They hung there, glittering red and adding a little more strength to the ice wall around them. "If you slip outside the shield, you'll be lost."

"You'll be dead is the plain way of saying it," Cork said, yelling above the crash of thunder. "Stay close! Your lives depend on it!"

Katashan didn't look back at his companions. He had to keep their goal in sight. He feared he would falter now with others depending on him for protection. He'd failed too often before: the men on the ship when it sank; his wife and daughters when he wasn't there --

Fordel put a hand on his shoulder, and carefully fed him strength from his own small magic hoard. He hadn't expected the help and for a moment the shield flickered with blue light and cold wind -- but Katashan steadied the power before danger found a way through.

"Sorry," Fordel said from behind him. The man sounded breathless already. "You weren't answering me and you weren't moving. We have to go on, Katashan. There's no turning back."

Katashan hadn't realized he'd stopped. He felt a lethargy trying to take hold and drag him down the path of self-recriminations and loss. This had been a subtle attack. He slapped the feeling away with a wave of his hand and accepted the help from Fordel as they moved upwards again. They would reach what he hoped -- what he *believed* -- would be sanctuary in the next few steps.

The blackened stubs of trees stood around them, with little left for the lightning to strike except the bare ground. Much of the dirt had been fused into a glass-like surface, cracked and twisted in places by the repeated strikes. He saw boulders that had been shattered . . . but the area around the Verina statue remained untouched.

If this had been summer, the entire mountain would have gone up in flames. Instead, the snow had melted; fog and smoke hung in a perpetual swirl like the ghosts of the trees that had been lost. Each step proved to be treacherous, but brought them closer and closer. . . .

He didn't know how long he fought his way across to the Verina statue. The storm grew and he could feel the cold of the wind sometimes batter its way through his shield. Another step. Closer. He lifted his hand and touched the statue.

Mistake. . . .

Verina was not a dead Goddess. She came to this place, disgusted and angered, to deal with the dark magic done on her sacred ground. She came in a very strong emanation of her power, real and intense, and not something even a powerful mage should ever interact with, and especially without any preparation.

Her power coursed through Katashan like a wave of fire, burning his body and soul. He distantly heard Fordel cry out. He sensed a surge in the storm as the enemy sensed weakness. People depended on him!

Goddess save them! Don't let the shield fall!

Fire, bright . . . and then darkness.

CHAPTER NINETEEN

K atashan thought he awoke in a different place; a strange world, devoid of color and shape, sound and touch. He could be anywhere. He could be everywhere.

His spirit was no longer a part of his body. The thought startled more than frightened him and if he hadn't remembered the others he left behind in such trouble, he might have stayed here, content to be . . . nothing.

"Goddess," he whispered, a sound without voice, words without a mouth. "Goddess, help me."

Ripples came through a void of nothing, indicating notice. He couldn't say he had really drawn Verina's attention, but he did have something's notice.

"Goddess, please aid us in our time of need."

The world destroyed if you do not win. What does it matter?

Her thoughts?

"It matters to us. It matters to me. Help us. I have done what I can in your name and your cause."

But he lied, and she knew it. She showed it to him, the lie of his soul that had turned its back on duty when he walked away from his own land.

"I am only a man. I couldn't bear any more."

And should I care?

"Should I?" Despair came when he least wanted it. She had

torn open too many wounds and he could not seal them before they bled out his anger and despair. "Should I care what happens to these people? Not mine. Not my family. Not my --"

And he saw frightened, weeping children dying in the streets of Salbay. He saw the wondrous city crashing into the sea, cliffs giving way --

"No!"

You care?

"Yes. Goddess, yes I *still care*. I slept for a while, that's all. I slept to escape my personal loss. I slept to come here and help these people. Didn't you bring me here? Isn't this your idea? Tell me why! Tell me who controls my life, who destroyed all I love, who brought me here to this --"

You. Your choices.

"No!" It could not be his fault, the death of his family or the years as a slave, bound by dark magic, unable to help the others. Waiting, waiting for a chance to escape and a chance to save some of them. How could he have saved the others and let his own family die? How could he have made such a choice? His fault -- she showed it to him. His fault for saving others and not helping those whom he had loved instead.

No.

"Goddess, please . . . absolution. Sanctuary."

I cannot give you peace. I cannot save you from your own darkness. And only you can save the others.

"Tell me what I must do!"

Be who you are; do not hide from it. Do not listen to the dark you bring with you in your soul.

He felt an answer in those words, a whisper of truth pushing into his soul, becoming a part of him, awakening something he had thought lost. . . .

"Katashan?" Cork whispered softly. His head and shoulders lifted a little as someone gently moved him. "Please drink a little of the ale. Come on, now. Fordel can't hold the ward much longer. We need your help, sir."

Katashan forced his eyes open, but only a slit at first, afraid that he'd still find the void. Instead, Katashan found himself on the cold ground, hard rock beneath his back, and the world not really changed around him.

Had he really spoken with the Goddess? Or had the exchange only been some game of his mind, looking for answers even in the dark depths of unconsciousness? Better to think that, he suspected, then to dwell on words that stung.

"Sir?"

The shield still held. He remembered wishing it to do so, and obviously he had wished strong enough to drain magic from himself to fuel the protection. The others huddled close around him and Fordel sat with a hand on the ice-cold shield, feeding power that drained him far too quickly. Fordel already looked almost as pale white as the ice shield; he wouldn't hold up much longer.

Lightning struck the shield. Katashan felt the tingle, a little fire seeping through with a promise of the destruction they faced.

Cork had hold of him and placed the flask to his lips. He sipped as he looked up past his guard. He hadn't thought to look up before, even though the lightning came from above. Something unnatural hung in the sky above them: a large dark stone, like a cloud of rock. He could tell it had been imbued with magic and turned loose here, like a guardian trained to strike when someone with like magic came too near.

He could deal with this.

"There," he said softly as he pointed upward. "Must drop the shield to destroy it."

"Sir?" Cork said, worried at the words.

"Ah. Yes. Not drop. Just -- I must go outside it."

"Not alone!" Cork grabbed tight on his arm.

"Alone." He sat up, surprising Cork and the others. In fact, it surprised him, but he felt power now that had not been there before. Had the Goddess given help? He hoped so, because they needed her help in this madness.

"Katashan," Fordel whispered, his face drenched in perspiration. "I can't --"

"A moment longer, friend."

Fordel bowed his head and placed his other hand on the shield. The surface fluctuated and moved, like the beating of the man's heart.

Katashan rose unsteadily to his feet and stepped outside their protection before Cork could stop him, a quick push through his own power and past Fordel's magic which had a different feel, tingling where his had only been warmth.

Lightning came straight for him. He had known that it would with magic drawn to magic. Right now he was a far more powerful magnet than the shield. He could see the faces of friends, watching him in horror when he reached one hand into the sky for the lightning, and put the other again on the statue. If this did not work, at least the end would be quick.

Lightning struck, but not true lighting. Magic made, and he could control magic. Even so, it felt like fire burnt through him, grounded through her statue, and then upward again. . . .

His power and his will flew on the lightning bolt and beyond the pain he could feel the power of the world in his hold: Nature, not tamed, but held for a moment, and bent to do his will, to destroy the stone above them. He played lighting against the surface searching for weakness, imperfection . . . there. A little flaw, but the lightning found the crack, traveled along the path into the heart of the stone and spread outward. . . .

"We need him to be conscious now, Cork," someone said. Katashan heard the words and wished them away. "We're running out of time."

"Yes, Your Lordship, sir. I'll do what I can."

Katashan wanted the peace and the emptiness, a little longer. It would not last. He awoke again in the cold as Cork worked at wrapping a cloak around him.

"The others --" he said, his voice harsh, but loud enough for Cork to hear.

"We're fine, sir," Cork said, though he didn't sound like he particularly meant those words. "Got hit by a bit of falling rock, but we have no more than a bruise or two. That was -- spectacular, sir."

"Was it? What's happened?"

"The stone shattered about the same time Lord Fordel lost hold of the shield. The storm died and it got very cold, sir. Can you sit up? Lord Fordel would like a word or two, I think."

He remembered they had come here with something else that needed done, not to destroy the storm. With half a moan, Kat forced himself to sit up. Fordel, who had been standing by the trail, hurried towards him. Katashan had collapsed at the feet of the Verina statue, which still glowed with latent power. Fordel looked towards the statue and away, plainly someone who didn't like to be involved in the matters of Gods.

Wise man.

"Are you coherent enough to discuss what we should do next?" Fordel asked.

"I don't know," Katashan confessed, rubbing the back of his neck. He had felt uncertain of what to do about the sacrifice on the climb up to this pass. Now he had slipped beyond such simple thoughts to confusion about life itself. This didn't help.

"I've looked over the runes." Fordel waved a hand towards an area to the left. "You said you had destroyed them?"

"Part of them."

"They're whole again."

"Well. Damn. Let me see."

No one argued. Cork helped Katashan to his feet and held him there, the cloak wrapped tight around him, though it did little against the bitter cold. The guards kept watch by the trail, as if they expected trouble to come from that direction. With the storm gone -- some time had passed since he had destroyed the boulder, he thought from the placement of the sun -- the more curious and foolhardy might rush up here. They could not allow Lord Fordel to be found at the scene of such recent magical havoc. However, the man couldn't leave until they did what they could about the runes and the spell.

Katashan felt as though every time he made a step forward, something worse moved into the path to stop him. He wanted to suggest Fordel leave quickly, but that might not be wise, even if it were safe. Katashan didn't feel nearly strong enough to deal with another magical attack and this seemed the time when one should expect one.

He also, of course, had no right to give orders to the local lord. While Fordel seemed amiable enough, the man still had been raised to hold power. Probably because he had so lately been appointed to the position, Fordel still listened to others.

Or perhaps, Katashan thought, his own background had soured him towards those in power. The Goddess had touched on that problem, though perhaps it had been his own guilt -- his own mind telling him to stop turning away from everything connected with the power he now used. He tried to push that thought away again as he limped behind Fordel, heading towards the spot where he had first found the body.

The body, he suddenly remembered, was Lord Fordel's late sister. That kept getting lost in all the rest of this madness. Fordel had not, obviously, been close to Sherina -- but he still must have felt some ties of blood and suffered some feelings of loss. Double loss, with his father also gone. And triple loss, since he had lost his mother in this insanity as well, even if it had been some time in the past.

Katashan didn't want these thoughts as the wind blew through the cloak and left him cold. He thought he would never be warm again or ever find a place where he would feel safe.

Katashan had come here to get away from his own past, only to find himself caught up in lives as twisted and troubled as his own had been. He looked towards the sea, as he had the first day he stood here, right before all hell broke loose and he found Sherina chained, dead, and magically bound. He could see only a fog on the shore today, and the sapphire sea lost behind the wall of gray. He again wondered what world he could find across that water. He wondered how soon he could catch a ship and go.

"Careful, sir," Cork said, taking hold of his arm when he started to slip on the newly formed ice and slick rock.

"I didn't come here for this," he said aloud, and regretted the words, though the others only nodded agreement. Obviously, none of them sought this trouble, but they still all stood around him, hoping for answers. He needed to stop considering this as his own personal hell. The others had been drawn in with him and none of them any happier for it.

Fordel led him back to the runes and there he found the full extent of the problem. The runes were not only whole again; they glittered. They *moved*. He watched in fascination and growing horror as he carefully knelt beside the spot.

He had never faced anything of this sort. He'd never even heard of such a thing. He didn't say so to the others, who still held some little hope in his ability. They didn't need any more discouragement. Katashan automatically held up a hand to stop Cork when he came closer. He did not want anyone unprotected to come near.

"What should we do?" Fordel asked softly.

"I don't know," Katashan admitted. Fordel frowned. "I'm sorry, but I have never worked with anything remotely like this. The runes should not have reformed after what I had done. It is possible someone came and repaired them, however. That would be a relief, in some ways, even given the amount of magic

I sense here. If a person did not come back and fix this, then the runes did it themselves, and that idea frightens me, Lord Fordel."

"Yes," Fordel said, understanding the problem. He looked at the runes and shook his head with worry again. "Can we try to destroy them again?"

"Yes, we can try. I don't give us much hope of succeeding. When I was here, the runes were dormant, as though. . . ."

"As though resting through winter," Fordel finished for him. He knelt closer as well and studied the runes without reaching towards them. Plainly, neither of them liked what they felt here. "And spring has come and they're awake now. We've already decided there is some link with the seasons. I like this less and less, Katashan."

Lord Fordel lifted a hand, testing out the feel of the magic, and it was all Katashan could do to force himself not stop him. The man understood the dangers, and what he did would help them understand the problem better. Katashan wanted to run away. It wouldn't help. Sherina would follow him, if nothing else.

"Suggestions?" Fordel asked.

"One which you will not like," Katashan replied and continued despite the narrow-eyed look the statement won. "You need to get away from here, Lord Fordel. Quickly. The storm has passed and the last thing you need is to have your people find you at such a site as this."

"They would only think I came up after the storm."

"No," Cork answered. He looked a little worried at the glance Fordel gave him, but he kept talking. "They'd have come from the fishing village down the trail opposite from the way we came and closer than anywhere we could have been waiting. They will know that to get here so soon, you had to have headed up before the storm ended and well before they started up. Otherwise they would have seen us on the trail, sir."

Lord Fordel started to argue. He stopped. "A compromise. My guards will stand posts where they can see anyone coming toward us. If they spot someone, I will head into the trees. I suggest the rest of you come with me."

"No, Your Lordship, sir. They'll see the camp heading up here. We'll only say we got caught by the weather and came up after the storm."

"And why can't I do the same?"

"Because it would be wiser if they don't think of you as involved in this," Katashan said, taking over for the nervous Cork. "Only the Starlings saw us, and they didn't know who you are. Don't chance it, Fordel. Not with trouble like this."

Fordel finally nodded, but didn't look happier for it. "In the meantime, we had better try to find something that will help here. Do you have any suggestions concerning what to do?"

Katashan turned his full attention back to the runes, not that they had been far from his thoughts anyway. Light slipped and played along each sigil, dancing with power. Life, Death, Bond and the circle of the seasons, all bound into one spell. Life had been bound to death -- to winter. As the seasons changed, both the runes and the spell had begun to change as well.

Unfortunately, he still couldn't quite see how they intertwined. Not knowing the dynamics of the spell made him uneasy at the idea of doing anything more than watch. He had already upset something which had released a malevolent spirit in the world and killed far too many others. He didn't want to make another mistake.

He had forced himself not to think how those deaths were his fault, but it came hard to him now since he was tired, worn, and unprepared for this battle.

"Sir?" Cork said suddenly, a hand on his shoulder.

His head had lowered. He must have looked defeated at that moment, before he even tried to make amends for his mistakes.

"Sir, do you need to rest?" Cork asked, his fingers tightening.

"I need not to make another mistake," Katashan said. "I need not to get other people killed."

"Other people?" Fordel asked.

"Your father and his men -- if I had not let Sherina loose from here --"

"Do you think leaving her tied to this spell, letting her fuel these runes, would have been better in the long run? Your Goddess called you here to do something, Katashan."

He wanted to snap an answer but instead gave a civil nod and reached out to test the edges of the magic. Dark, fiery, angry. He could feel all those emotions which meant the control came from something human, conscious . . . a person.

Nearby? Or was that just the echoes still of Sherina in the spell?

He tested again trying to find some path that might lead to a real enemy. Nothing went anywhere but back to the runes, however and he knew the runes were not intelligent. They could not radiate emotions.

Someone had made them. Someone had pushed the dagger into Sherina's heart. Someone wanted to create a magic that would change the world.

Katashan peered closer at the swirling movement, trying to gauge the power employed and what it did. Renewal? Yes, that definitely. And protection. He suspected, in fact, that the overlay of protection had been added since his first work here. And that, again, meant someone taking an active local interest in this place. And yet he couldn't find any link to a person --

He mumbled a curse in his own language and looked up at Fordel.

"You don't look happy," Fordel said. He wisely took a step back from the runes.

"I've been feeling for a link to whoever has been looking

over this site," he said. "Unfortunately, I limited my search parameters."

"Pardon?"

"I searched for who it might be. I should be searching for *what*."

"Oh hell," Fordel whispered.

"Probably. Peralin even tried to warn me it might not be a human, but I really didn't listen. We know from history that demons do occasionally show an interest in this world." He looked back at the runes, held his fingers barely a hand's breadth above the one for life and tried to feel -- but he couldn't draw anything more from it. "Or maybe it's something worse. You and I are not prepared to handle this, Lord Fordel, not today. I suggest we leave and get back to Salbay, contact Matish, and prepare for the battle. Now. Quickly. Whatever is behind this spell doesn't appear to be watching. Everything we've triggered has been automatic. I'm not up to facing something with reasoning behind it as well."

Fordel didn't argue this time. He looked far less assured than he had when they came up the hill. Katashan felt the same and that was hard given what little confidence he'd had to begin with.

"People coming, sir!" one of the guards said, coming at a quick jog. "You'll need to get to cover."

"Damn. We need to keep them away from here," Katashan said. He shoved cold fingers into his cloak.

"The guards can handle them," Tyos said. "Cork, I suggest you and your gentleman go with Lord Fordel. Get out of sight. Can you find the way back to Salbay through the hills?"

"I can," Cork said. "I can't say I want to, though since we left the supplies and horses in the camp below."

"I would think you might want our okay on this," Katashan said. "I don't seem to remember saying I would go to the hills."

Cork looked at him, his lips pursed, and eyes narrowed. "Sir

--"

"All right, all right," Katashan said. "How long until the others get here?"

"They're coming quickly. We didn't see them through the fog until they were most of the way up the hillside, so they've been heading this way since the storm broke. I'd be happy if you three disappeared as quickly as possible," Tyos said. He looked at Fordel, who still frowned and looked unlikely to go without a disagreement. "My lord, you and Katashan are the only two with a chance of stopping whatever is going to happen. Do you really want to get involved in a confrontation -- friendly or not -- with the local villagers right now? Do you want them to mistrust you by finding you here?"

"No. Shall we go, Katashan?"

"After you, Lord Fordel."

Fordel gave a snort of amusement. Cork had gathered food and flasks from the guards, who would be able to replenish their own supplies from the camp. Katashan kicked mud and snow over the runes and Cork, wiser, dragged some brunt and broken limbs and piled them atop it. Katashan hoped it would hide the trouble, at least long enough for the guards to convince the villagers to go away. The Verina statue didn't glow quite so brightly now, either.

Cork led Katashan and Fordel down the trail from the Verina altar and past the stands of ruined trees. Katashan wanted to stop and wait, but Cork urged the two along as though he herded recalcitrant sheep.

"Begging your pardons, sirs," Cork said, but didn't slow down even when they both looked back at him. They had reached a line of live trees: tall pines, fragrant with the scent of resin, needles and life. Katashan gasped the air here as they hurried along. "But it's damned important that the two of you get clear of here as soon as possible. I'm not going to let Katashan fall back into the hands of anyone who intends to do him harm if I can help it. And I certainly wouldn't want to see such harm come to you either, Lord Fordel."

"You are not responsible for me, Cork," Katashan said.

"I most certainly am, sir. The captain himself told me to watch out for you and I intend to do so. Nothing personal, sir -- but you haven't shown a great deal of ability in taking care of yourself so far, and I think it important you be kept as safe as possible."

Katashan felt his cheeks burn with embarrassment, even though he knew most of what had happened had not been his fault.

They went past a curve in the trail, where a slight hill and a stand of trees stood between them and the site. He could still feel the darkness back there, but he stopped and turned to Cork intending to set things straight. "I'm not helpless."

"No sir. But you aren't --"

"May I borrow your sword, Lord Fordel?" Katashan said.

"I don't know. I'm not sure I trust you with sharp things. Are you going to cut yourself with it? If so, I'd rather not hand it over."

"I will not," Katashan said with a bright grin. Lord Fordel pulled the sword and carefully handed it to him, though with the look that said he didn't trust Katashan's word very much. "Thank you."

"You're welcome. I think."

He tested the weight, balanced it on his hand for a moment, and nodded. "Good weapon. Draw your sword, Cork."

"I will not, under any circumstances --"

"Draw your sword."

Cork sighed, obviously realizing this would take longer to argue. He reluctantly pulled the weapon. Katashan brought his own sword up.

"Sir, we really shouldn't --"

"This won't take long."

He engaged, forcing Cork to do the same. For the first four parries he moved slowly, carefully, watching Cork's movements. He saw that Cork did the same, and finally realized Katashan knew swords.

Katashan moved in. Cork parried -- and again, and by then Katashan knew everything he needed to. Five heartbeats later he had Cork disarmed.

"That was damned good, sir," he said, retrieving his sword and cleaning the dirt from it. "Maybe we can talk about swords while we walk?"

Katashan laughed. He grinned at Fordel who eyed him with a little more suspicion. It hardly mattered. Kat balanced the sword in his hand and then flipped it up in the air and caught the pommel again before he gave the weapon back to Lord Fordel.

"You've had a good trainer and I don't mean for that last little trick," Fordel said. He sheathed the sword. "Why don't you carry a sword?"

"I didn't want to provoke anyone into a fight," Katashan explained as he drew his cloak back around him, chilled now after the little workout. Cork had started them moving again. "I knew I headed to a land where people might find me objectionable just because of my background. And yes, I had a very good trainer. My father and his. . ."

He stopped and said nothing, wishing he hadn't been that open.

"Your father and his Master of the Sword," Cork said after a few steps. "You can stop dancing around it, sir. It's obvious you're not exactly a commoner."

"True enough, I suppose."

"And out of curiosity, I'd like to know just who you were before you came here," Lord Fordel said.

"Do you know much about my native lands?" Katashan

asked.

"Some. I have a trade delegation at Kirin, the capital."

"Do you?"

"Yes. It's the kind of work my father and sister despised so they left it in my hands. Good money to be made in trade. And you're dancing around telling us your rank, aren't you?"

"I left who I was behind when I came to here. But never mind, I think it important that you know, with all else that is going on. I had left my rank behind along with my family ties, because I never intended to take part in magic again. My family is well known for many reasons and one being that the old blood is still strong with us. We carry magic in our veins, Lord Fordel."

"Ah, of course. Heartblood mage," he said. He took a couple steps before his eyes had widened and he almost stumbled. "As I've heard it, there's only one family in Taris who can make that claim."

"True. And I am of that family."

"Sir?" Cork said.

"I am Prince Katashan Natarius, nephew to the King of Taris."

CHAPTER TWENTY

E ven though Lord Fordel had obviously guessed at his family ties, he still hadn't realized the full extent of his rank. And Cork . . . Cork just walked in silence for a long, long ways.

Katashan checked to make certain no one followed behind them and then used a little more magic to spread fresh snow over their tracks. It would, he thought, keep them safe from any trouble at the pass, but now he realized what a long journey they would have back to the fort.

The silence, finally, began to tell on his nerves. Katashan found it odd that after so long alone this quiet bothered him. He had come to enjoy the companionship of his new friends.

"I am not anyone different than the person you knew before," he finally dared say.

Cork looked at him with surprise and Fordel glanced his way for a moment, though they continued in silence. He said nothing more.

"All right, sir. You're right." Cork stopped and turned so suddenly that Katashan nearly ran into him. "And it's not as though I haven't seen far stranger things than exiled princes. But can I ask why, sir?"

He should have expected that question but the words still caught him off guard. He fell silent for his own reasons, as he tried to get his thoughts in order and to present the tale of his life with as little emotional adornment as he could manage.

"Sir, I didn't mean --" Cork began, sounding apologetic, but he stopped when Katashan lifted his hand.

"No, it's all right. I am trying to get the story clear in my mind, to translate it as best I can. I left Kirin and the castle because the world I had loved was already gone. I went to war with my brother and I was captured. They could have ransomed me back home, but my father was out of sorts with me for having left the temple to take up the sword. So he left me in slavery for more than four years."

"You?" Fordel said. "I would have thought that you could have saved yourself from that. Magic didn't help?"

"They had taken my ritual blade," he said, trying to keep all the darker emotions from his voice. "And they used just enough magic of their own to control slaves. It took a long time for me to get free. I escaped, eventually and lived in the hills until I could get my hands on the blade again. It was no easy task. Afterwards, I used my powers to help others escape and to form into bands to help protect each other."

"Gods," Fordel whispered and looked at him again. "How did you survive?"

"I survived by wanting to go home so badly that I wouldn't let anything kill me." Emotions threatened to well up, and he took a deeper breath, because worse than the memories of his years of slavery came back now; dark memories laced with such bitterness that he hated to recall. "And I survived by starting an insurrection, Lord Fordel. I started a rebellion of slaves that I think might still be going on -- a long, bitter war and I can't say which side will win. But I left it to them once they no longer needed me. And I came home."

"But didn't stay there," Fordel said.

Katashan bowed his head, took a breath of bitter, cold air. He looked up again, and knew the desolation showed in his eyes. "I did not stay. There had been a war at home, you see.

Barbarians had broken through on the north, and devastated the countryside nearly to the capital. They . . . they destroyed my home, and killed my wife and children. I came home to find only ruins, everything gone and dead. The choices I had were limited. I thought I might lie down and die there as well, but instead I came here. I'm still not certain why."

Silence stretched on again, long and painful until Cork put a hand on his shoulder, meeting Katashan's eyes. "You came here because we needed you, sir. And that's better, in the end, then dying for nothing."

He shook his head in bitter denial, unable to speak just then. But Cork, despite all the urging he'd used to keep them moving, stood his ground and waited for Katashan to speak again.

"It -- It wasn't for *nothing*," Katashan said, finally, fighting to bring back words in their language. He had lost it for a moment, drawn back to the past and the pain. For a moment he saw his wife, his daughters in the garden, singing the way they had the day he left. He could have stood there, trapped in the memory forever, and not have regretted it. "It would not have been for nothing. *I loved them.* They were all that kept me alive."

"I'm sorry, sir," Cork said. "I had not meant to belittle them, sir, or your loss. Only once death comes between the living and what they love, there is nothing that can change it, is there? Not all the magic in the world. And to lie down and die was no answer, sir."

He started to argue, and changed his mind. "I know. I never admitted it to myself, but I knew even then. And that's why I'm here."

"And now it's time to go on, yes?" Fordel asked.

Katashan started to apologize for having brought such a morose subject to them and changed his mind. He thought they had probably needed to know, because everything that had happened to him had an effect on his actions now.

"Yes, let's go before anything else happens," Katashan agreed.

Both Cork and Fordel looked back as though they expected an army of demons to spring up at those words. Perhaps, Katashan thought, they had been foolhardy to say, inviting more trouble. Katashan found himself doing nothing but concentrating on one step in front of the next. After a while he realized the trail had been very well-traveled even through the winter.

"Where does this go?" he suddenly asked.

"A hill village," Cork said. "A place called Holding. One on the borderland between *their* mountains and *our* plains. It's more a trading post than anything."

"Where the Starlings live?" Kat asked.

"No. They come from farther inland."

"Well-used path," Kat said, waving a hand at the trail.

Cork stopped and looked down, frowning. "Yes, you're right, sir. I don't like the looks of this. It's never been this well-traveled before that I can remember."

"From one problem to another," Fordel said, shaking his head. "Forward or back to the pass? To the unknown or back to deal with the villagers?"

"Forward," Katashan said. He looked up for the first time in at least half a mile. The open cliff had given way to woods, and the path wound past a half-frozen brook glitter with ice crystals in the bright daylight. He hadn't realized it was beautiful.

And that stopped him again. He looked around, taking the full circle of where he stood, and stopped only when he saw both Cork and Fordel looking at him with worry.

"It's all right. I just only now realized how blind I've been to beauty. This is a lovely place. I should enjoy the walk in such a place."

Both Cork and Fordel glanced quickly around, both of them startled by the words, and maybe by what they had missed as well.

"I think you'd enjoy it more if you weren't half dead," Cork said.

That nearly made him laugh. "You're right. But I should accept beauty whenever I can find it. It is rare in the world these days."

"No," Fordel said. "Forgive me, but it's not rare. It's just that you've been too numbed to see it."

"Ah, perhaps you're right." He felt uncomfortable at the observation, but he pushed the feeling away. He'd bared his soul to them. They had needed to know because, like his knowledge of swords, his past might be important to what he would do. He knew Fordel now had more trust in him and not because they were both of the ruling class, but because Fordel knew he didn't purposely hide some truths. Working magic with another required that they both have full confidence in the other's abilities. Doubt, which Fordel had kept at bay so far, might have played too important a part later.

So he had done right. He knew it.

They walked on, the trail heading up into the hills and winding down again. Now and then he spied the sea back behind them, the fog lifted now and inviting them back to the warmth of the shore. Here patches of snow remained in the shadows of trees, while small rivulets of water ran down over the rocky outcroppings, heading towards the brook, and eventually the sea. This was a sign of spring and warmer weather.

Deer moved away as they climbed higher. Squirrels and rabbits darted through the shadows, and birds protested their appearance. He smiled, and wished doing so didn't feel quite so unfamiliar.

The air turned cold and thin, and even Cork finally paused and waved a hand to two large boulders. "Sit down, my Lords. We need to get our breath back. We don't want to run into any trouble if we're not ready for it."

"I'll never be ready." Katashan gratefully settled on one of the boulders and turned his face up into the sun, basking in the little bit of warmth. It felt odd, as though he had been lifted out of a deep hole and into the light. *Don't look back*, he told himself. He had to start looking ahead again.

And he did and saw -- movement.

Cork turned, drawing his sword. Fordel drew his as well, but Katashan could already tell it wouldn't do them much good. They were badly outnumbered.

"Mountain people," Cork needlessly warned him.

"Are we in trouble?" Katashan asked.

Stupid question, he thought, as he watched the mountain people rush forward, weapons drawn. They were always in trouble. . . .

CHAPTER TWENTY-ONE

Fordel and Cork moved to each side of Katashan, putting him safely between them. He didn't argue or distract them as the ten warriors closed in. The newcomers did not, praise the gods, rush straight in for the kill, even though they kept their weapons up and ready. They might be open to reason if they were not out for blood.

Their thick wool cloaks and baggy clothing covered everything but the bearded faces of the men. There were two women as well and they looked quite capable of handling their swords.

"We don't want trouble," Cork said. He sounded remarkably calm, which didn't surprise Katashan. After all, the two of them had faced far worse than swords in the last few days. "We're only passing along the trail, heading elsewhere."

"Trouble follows everywhere the lowlanders go," one man said, the accent different. He stepped closer, his sword still up. Katashan could see a cut -- new -- on the side of his face. "Go back. We will not let you travel closer to the village."

"You've had trouble with others lately?" Katashan asked. He started to step closer, but Fordel caught his arm, and Cork moved in front of him again. He tried not to show his frustration. "Others have come this way?"

"They raided the village, your people --"

"Not *mine*," Katashan and Fordel chorused.

"Go back," he said. "There is nothing on this trail for any of you, unless you seek trouble."

"We don't need to seek trouble," Katashan said. "You've already said it; trouble follows us and we are not ready to go back and face it."

The swordsman looked past the group, as though he could see the trouble coming even now. Katashan did not look, though his fingers moved, magic almost ready should he need it.

"There is danger at the Verina altar. Are you part of that trouble?" the man demanded.

"I am trying to end it," Katashan answered.

The man sneered, hand tightening on his sword. *Careful*, Katashan thought. These people had already seen trouble and they didn't look likely to take chances on more.

"Maybe we can find another way to go," Fordel suggested softly. He obviously didn't want this fight, and both he and Cork had started to look down the hillside, mapping out the way they would go.

And then Katashan saw something that made him throw all caution to the wind. A silver clasp held the man's cloak closed, the surface etched with a very old symbol. Ancient and holy . . . and Katashan understood, suddenly, a major difference between the people of the shore and the people of the mountains.

Katashan stepped forward, easily avoiding the hands of his friends this time. He reached inside his tunic and pricked his finger for just a little blood before he lifted his hand, and brought a globe of light to his fingers: bright, prismatic, like a glowing rainbow made into a ball and brought to earth. He heard some of the newcomers gasp. They looked at him and he could see hope in their eyes.

He lifted his head and said words he had not spoken since his last day at the temple. "I am of the light of the sky, the warmth of the land. I am of life and hope."

A heartbeat passed as the swordsmen's eyes went from him

to the light and then back to him again.

And then they knelt. Katashan had not expected that part.

"Welcome, Bringer of the Light," the man said, his head bowed. "We are honored to have a priest among us."

He winced at the title, glad the mountain people had bowed their heads and didn't see his reaction.

"We need to travel through your lands --"

"We shall take you safely wherever you need go," the man said and dared look up. "Will you help us?"

"I will do whatever I can," he said. He meant it. "Do please get up."

They did as he asked, which didn't exactly put Cork at ease, though he wisely put up his sword even before the mountain people did. Fordel looked slightly less upset, though he did eye Katashan as though he had just shape-shifted on him again.

"They are believers in the Old Gods," Katashan said, and brushed his finger against the symbol on the man's cloak. "The ones who reigned here before Cyrenia existed. This is a sign of the Old Gods, like Verina."

"Ah," Cork said. He dropped his voice as the mountain men stepped away. "And he thinks you are a priest because of the magic?"

"No. He thinks I am a priest because I know the ritual words."

"And you know them because. . . ? Fordel said looking at him.

"Because I am a priest."

"You never mentioned this," Cork said, shaking his head.

"I did say I had left the temple. I thought I had left it behind, as well as everything else," he said and gave a little shrug. "No matter. I see where this is important again."

Cork looked at him for a long moment, his head a little tilted. And then he unexpectedly nodded. "It's what you are. You are more assured now that you've admitted what you are to yourself and us."

He did feel more at ease. Had he really found himself again? He felt different . . . as though the memory of family, temple, and slavery had all found their rightful places within him and no longer warred to take his soul. Even though he had dealt with Verina and Peralin, it hadn't been until he said those words of ritual greeting that he had felt right about his presence here.

And having accepted, he could look into his past and welcome old rituals, half-forgotten prayers and old paths to power that went beyond a touch of blood and a quick spell.

He welcomed back the part of his soul he had buried beside the graves of his wife and children.

"This way sir," the mountain man said. He glanced at Fordel and gave just enough of an inclination of his head to indicate he recognized the man but did not recognize his authority.

Fordel, having survived without a battle, obviously didn't mind. They headed away from the trouble at the altar and they'd avoided a battle they could not win. Katashan offered a silent little prayer of thanks to the Gods for getting him and his friends out of this mess. He tried very hard not to fear they were walking into worse.

CHAPTER TWENTY-TWO

The warriors led them the last half mile to the village. As they came over the hill and down the last of the path, Katashan could see signs of battle everywhere he looked from bandages on several men to the debris scattered about the narrow path into the village.

Bodies, covered in thin shrouds, lay to the side of the trail just inside a low wall. Not just warriors; he saw the size and shape of even small children, and sometimes a parent kneeling close by, bereaved and lost.

Katashan had to look away, his heart pounding, tears almost to his eyes -- but the tears would be lies here. They would not be for *these* lost children.

"What happened here?" Fordel asked. Demanded, in fact and with anger in his eyes as he looked away from the shrouds. People stared back with their own anger barely held at check.

"Your soldiers came," a woman said. "Came and killed everyone they could reach. Most hadn't time to get to their weapons."

"Not *mine*," Fordel said. He looked so appalled that some of the anger disappeared in the faces around them, including the people gathering at the sight of strangers. "I never ordered --"

"They were your father's men, the ones whom he kept in the mountains ever since your sister disappeared. He thought we had her, at least until this man found her at the altar."

"Did you have her before?" Katashan asked.

"Not us," another woman said, stepping through the group and facing him and Lord Fordel with narrowed dark-lashed eyes and a lift of her head that said she would not bow to either. She seemed someone of power, even though she dressed no differently than the others. They paid her deference, though, in the way they moved aside when she neared and allowed her to ask questions. "Why did you bring them here, Namsok?"

"He is a priest, Lady," Namsok said. She shook her head in denial and disgust. "No, truly he is. He knew the words and. . ."

Namsok touched the clasp on his cloak and looked back at Katashan, obviously hoping for some aid.

"I am from the north," Katashan said, as though she could have missed that part.

"And you know some words."

"I know a good many," he said. For some reason her irreverence pleased him. "And more than words, too."

He scraped one fingernail over the little cut on the tip of his finger, lifted his hand as he called the light again. She blinked and for a moment he saw hope in her eyes, but when she looked back at his face, she hid that feeling away once more. Another who had reason not to dare hope for better? Another who would not accept too easily? He understood, at least.

"Why were you not here when we needed you?" she said, and waved a hand towards the dead.

Gods.

It was not the words she said that struck at his heart so much as the way she said them with a whisper of his wife's voice, he thought, a ghost in her face. Dead children lay behind him. And he should have been there to protect them. He should have helped them, who were followers of the old Gods. He should have --

"Priest?" she said softly, a different look in her eyes.

"I wish I had been there. *Here*. I wish I could have saved them."

She stepped closer and unexpectedly put a hand on his arm, a gentle touch. His breath caught and he almost pulled away in shock and fear of . . . he didn't know what. Cork came to his side and put a hand on his shoulder.

"Careful, Katashan," Cork said. "Lady, I beg that you allow Prince Katashan to rest. This journey has been very hard on him."

"Priest, Prince? What more?" she said, but without any bitterness in her voice.

"Do I need more?" he asked.

"Ah, no. You're right. And we are usually better hosts for those whom we are glad to see. Lord Fordel, will I be glad to see you?"

"Yes. I will do my best to stop my father's men. I will put my own men on them if I have to."

"Will you really?" she said.

"Yes."

She looked at him and then bowed her head, apologetic this time. "Thank you, Lord Fordel. And be welcome in the village of Holding. Please come with me. I think we can do better than to stand out here in the cold."

Katashan bowed his head in acceptance and trusted Lord Fordel wouldn't mind either. Cork switched his hold from shoulder to arm and led him forward, as though he feared Katashan would get lost in the small village.

They walked away from the dead. He started to look back, but Cork purposely put himself between him and the view. He thought the others noticed, but they said nothing.

The village showed less sign of trouble after they went past the waist high wall and the first few buildings, all made of rough-hewn wood. The villagers had chosen an uneven spur of land that fell away on two sides, close in to the trees at the back.

It would have been a lovely place to visit at a better time, he thought. But now he could hear the sobs of wives, husbands, mothers, children. . . .

The woman walked ahead of them, tall and thin, her dark hair pulled back and a bandage around her right arm. She led past most of the rest of the village until they reached a building where wood and stone blended into a shape that looked as though it had grown from the hillside. Pure white snow brushed the roof and eaves.

The woman took the four steps up to the door at a steady pace, but then turned back and lifted her hands. "I am Onshara, guardian of this place. Come in peace into this building and be welcomed among us."

She turned and pushed open the door, slipping into the darkness within. Cork, with a hand back on his shoulder, tried to pull Katashan back and go first, but he wouldn't allow it this time. He walked in behind Onshara without fear of trouble.

Pleasant warmth, tinged with the scent of burning wood, greeted him. A short hall shown bright with light from candle tapers, carefully shielded in glass. Beeswax candles -- not tallow -- and with a sweet scent that reminded him of spring.

They went from the hall into a much larger room, filled with more candles, and lined with benches covered in fine cloth. A small stage stood at the far end and two fire places flanked the walls, both of them with flames warming the interior. Looking at the room, Katashan couldn't decide if it was a holy or a secular place. Perhaps both, since a village this small probably couldn't afford superfluous buildings, especially as ornate as this one.

"Come and sit." Onshara led them to benches near the stage. Places of honor, he realized. Fordel, Katashan and a very uncomfortable Cork, settled on a bench covered in pillows so soft Katashan wished he could have slept here instead. Onshara stood before them, her back to the upraised stage, the platform reaching the back of her knees. She looked comfortable here, he thought.

She gave a little nod when they settled. "Here we will find peace for a little while."

"What is this place?" Lord Fordel asked. Katashan was grateful since he feared to ask anything and ruin his image among these people.

"It is the Place of Deliberation," she said. "Here we talk with each other and with our gods. We rarely bring strangers into this place."

"I am honored," Fordel said, bowing his head.

"You are not much like your father," Onshara said, looking at Fordel.

"Thank you."

The answer won a look of surprise and then a nod of acceptance. "Nor are you like your sister, may her cursed spirit leave the world soon and never return to plague it."

"Her being here is my fault," Katashan said, admitting it aloud as he looked at Onshara. She deserved the truth. Unfortunately, he sounded weary when he spoke the words and she frowned, shaking her head. He started to apologize, but she lifted a hand and silenced him.

"You are the one who upset the runes before the spell reached completion. That's good," Onshara said before he could comment. "We know a little about magic here and we understand how it works. Think how much worse it would be, if on the Spring Equinox, the spell had come into the world, whole and with all its power."

"What do you know about the spell?" he asked, leaning forward, anxious for answers even at the cost of his reputation. They didn't have time for any kind of games where he might tease the answers out of her. "Do you know who set it?"

She frowned, looking at him as though she suspected some lie on his part, but once again he realized that he dared not hold back. "We have so little time," he said. "And I am ignorant of far too much to play guessing games. We must do our best to stop Sherina and the evil she has been tied to. Who took her to be sacrificed at the altar? Do you know?"

"Took her? Why do you think someone had to *take* her?"

Katashan caught his breath and looked at Fordel, who didn't seem at all startled by this idea. Even Cork nodded as though it suddenly made sense.

"You're certain?" Katashan asked.

"We watch the trails," Sherina said. "We saw her going to the altar, though she went alone, but she already had the knife with her. We did not see whom she met, though. We could not get close because of the magic."

"I should have considered the possibility before now," Fordel said. "This is something of power. She has gained it, even in the state she's in. Sherina wanted power more than anything else in life."

"She would willingly let herself be killed and sealed in this spell?" Katashan asked, appalled at the idea.

"It would depend on what she thought she would get out of it. I assume she was to get considerable power, Katashan," Fordel said. He shrugged. "Yes, she would do it."

"Life, death," Katashan said. "Winter, spring -- bond. Not just the seasons, but herself. She went into this looking for immortality."

"And you stopped her," Fordel said. "She's angry she didn't get what she wanted and she's throwing a temper tantrum. Typical."

Cork laughed, and then bowed his head in apology. "Sorry," he said.

"There is no harm in true laughter," Onshara said. She seemed to take pity on him. "Even here and now. Lord Fordel's assessment of his sister is very true. Be at ease here, friend. As long as you do us no harm, you shall be welcome. But if I may make a suggestion? Be rid of that uniform if you stay here long. It is bound to bring anger, which I should hate to see misdirected at you."

"Is there a chance that we will stay here long?" Fordel asked.

"Would you wish to?"

"I would wish for a little peace," Katashan said softly. "For a place where we can rest, and learn some answers. But we are not safe guests, Onshara. And I still have no idea of how to deal with her," Katashan admitted. "I'm sorry that I have no answers --"

"But you seek them. I have no doubt you are dangerous guests but there is danger without you as well. And, Priest, if the danger comes again, can we expect help from you?"

"I will do whatever I can to protect this place, both while I am here and away," he said.

She blinked in surprise and then shook her head a little, as though to deny his gift. "Be moderate, Priest. Be calm. Do what you can to end this evil for everyone involved but do not commit yourself to more than you can do."

"Why are my father's men attacking your village?" Fordel asked. "Is it related to the other matter?"

"Magic is involved in both. I can show you what they want from us." She signaled them to stay as she crossed the room to a very large, ornate cupboard.

Onshara brought out a huge, heavy book and carried it back to put into Katashan's lap. He noted two things: The tome was ancient and it held a little magic, old and sublime. He found himself brushing his hand against the cover as one might pet a very old cat. And he was not at all surprised to find it responded to the touch, a little whisper of magic brushing against him.

Onshara knelt before him and put her own hands on the book. Then she looked up and nodded. "The book remains cold in the hands of anyone without magic. It answers to you. The soldiers want the book because they think it will give them powers, but it won't. If there are spells, they are not in words any of them would understand. We can no longer read the original words, but there are occasional translations slipped in."

He pulled his hands back and glanced at Cork and Fordel. They both almost dared show a little hope, but he didn't allow himself that emotion yet. The book hinted at more help than he had expected, but that didn't mean it actually held answers.

Onshara opened the tome; old pages turned under her fingers, yellowed with age, the ink fading or worn away in some places. She didn't pause until she reached a spot, about a third of the way through the book, and a page with several sheets of yellowing parchment folded in place.

"This is the translation," she said, lightly touching the paper. It looked very old and dry, and he feared that any rough handling would send the translations crumbling into pieces. He saw a few large, ornate letters at the fold, and he thought there couldn't be more than 100 words on the two sheets.

"Here," he said. His finger still bled a little. He touched each of the pages in turn and whispered a little power into them. They would now last . . . longer than him, he suspected.

"Ah." She ran a hand over the parchment this time as she unfolded the sheets. "Thank you. That helps. Can you read it?"

"A few words," he said, and looked at the page of the tome as well. "And a few more words here. I think with time and magic I might do better, but I fear that we have neither to waste."

"True enough. I can read it for you."

"I would be grateful for your help." He ran his fingers over a page and frowned. "Where did the book come from?"

"It was given over into our care in some ancient age," she said softly. "The duty of the Nisbe Clan has always been to keep the book safe."

"By whose order?"

"We say it is a word of the Gods, but I wasn't there," she said and smiled, though that look quickly passed. She glanced towards the door and he could almost see the ghosts in her eyes, recognizing the look he knew too well from himself. "There are other pages with a few translations as well, but this one . . . Let me read these words:

"I am Aster, who will not die. That tale I've told. The years grow long, and the faces around me change. I would wish, very much, for a companion who shares more than an hour, a day, a year. I want one with whom I might share my life and existence. Not just today, but forever.

"There is a spell, but I dare not use it, except for the perfect mate. And how can I find such a woman, willing to spend eternity in the company of a man half blessed and half cursed? For it is a curse to watch everything wither and die around you, and know you cannot save anything. Everything you love, everything you touch . . . gone.

"I must search through the ages for her. And then the spell, which I have so meticulously researched, must be carefully created, nurtured, and set in motion. Winter, spring, life and death -- magic as was used to make me what I am. The choices will be difficult. And the power I use will render me weak for a long time. I cannot say how long.

"I will search hard and long. I will find the right one."

Onshara carefully placed the paper back on the pages and looked up at Katashan. He sighed and ran his hand over the old verse, written in Aster's own hand, thinking what a fool this man had been if he thought Sherina would be the one to share his world forever with him.

The words brought other things into focus for him, though.

"So, I have annoyed Sherina because I denied her immortality and I have angered this immortal mage because I denied him a mate. Is there anyone else I've made an enemy in this matter?"

"None that I can name," she said. "But you're not done yet."

Those words unexpectedly made him laugh. She smiled

with a brief but true look of amusement. Her hand reached for the heavy book, but he stopped her and carefully turned some of the other pages, going back to the opening. He wanted to see if he could read how this started. He wanted to understand the enemy.

But the words on the first page proved to be more ornate than the others, and he could only make out a few letters and no more than three words. What did draw his attention was a sketch on the inside cover. It showed a young man with long hair, a short beard and mustache, and wild eyes. He had no doubt he looked at Aster. He wondered who had drawn it for him and how long dead they might be.

Staring at the yellowed page, Katashan had an odd feeling he knew this person, though he couldn't say why or where. Perhaps the feeling only came as a sort of kinship, finding a link to someone else with magic. It might even be a fond whisper from the book, a memory of the one who created it and gave the pages enough magic to keep it safe for a long time.

He shut the book and handed it back to Onshara and she carried it back to the cabinet and placed it carefully inside. She closed the door and stood there a moment. He thought she might be saying a prayer.

He wondered if he had really found any answers after all. Another piece of the puzzle, yes, but not anything that would help. He had been convinced at the site that this was not a human involved in the sacrifice of Sherina. Now he thought he must be wrong again, and that made him mistrust everything else he thought of this matter.

"Come," she said as she turned back to them. "I will find you quarters for the night, and food. I am afraid we cannot feast, not on such a day as this."

"No, you cannot," Katashan said as he stood. "At midnight I will say prayers for the dead, if you like."

She looked at him, her blue-green eyes widening this time,

and her hand lifting a little. "We have not had a priest in more than a lifetime," she said softly. "It would help; it truly would, if we didn't feel abandoned by the gods."

"I'll say the prayers," he promised, and for a moment he felt as though he had found a place as well --

And then a din of bells filled the air, and people began to shout. Even before Onshara turned back, her face white, he knew what it meant.

"We're under attack again!"

CHAPTER TWENTY-THREE

As they left the building a group of well-armed women herded a dozen frightened children up into the trees beyond the village. Some even carried babies. Katashan watched them go, wishing them well and whispering magic to keep them safe, though he couldn't be certain it would work. Then he turned towards the battle. He couldn't see through the twist of the main path and past the buildings, but he could hear the clash of swords, and the cries, oaths and prayers of those fighting.

He grabbed Onshara by the arm. "I need a sword."

Both she and Cork shook their heads, though Cork had the foresight to snare Lord Fordel as he started by, the man intent on throwing himself into the battle.

"I want you safe, not in a fight!" Onshara said, trying to push him back.

"I will be safest with a sword to protect myself!"

She shook her head again but Cork finally came to his aid. "Find him a sword, Lady Onshara. He's right -- better to be protected than not."

She shouted at someone to bring two swords, and then looked at Lord Fordel, who tried to pull free of Cork's hold and looked annoyed that he would not look go. Katashan put a hand on the young lord's shoulder, relieving Cork of that duty.

"I must get down to the battle," Fordel said to him. His

eyes flashed, and Katashan felt a little whisper of magic growing with his rage. "Those are my people attacking. I might be able to order them off."

"But even you don't think you can," Onshara said.

"That doesn't mean I shouldn't go down and try! And if that doesn't work, I will fight them." He looked up at Katashan, "With whatever means I can."

"As will we both," Katashan answered.

"Priest --" Onshara said, but she stopped when someone hastily brought the swords. She took one and held the other out to Katashan, reluctant though she was to hand it over. "Take care, priest. We still have need of you."

They rushed down to the battle. Katashan nearly tripped on the downhill slope before he made himself slow. He didn't need to go breathless and crazed into this fight. He would protect the people best if he kept his head. He must protect the people and the book which might hold more secrets. This place gave him a little hope again.

Cork, Fordel and Onshara stayed with him as they reached the line of battle at the first row of buildings. The dead from the last attack had not yet been taken away and he already saw three more added to that number and not yet covered in shrouds. None were children this time but it did not make the loss any less in his mind.

He'd never liked to fight in battle, even now against enemies he knew were evil. He parried and parried the first man who came up against him, and saw the changes in the stranger's face as he realized he had engaged someone who knew swords far better than he did.

Katashan would have let the man go if he'd chosen to back away and to leave the field of battle. Instead, the stranger stepped away and looked around, trying to find an easier target.

"Go, you fool," Katashan told him with his sword coming up again. The enemy snarled something, lost in the din of battle and tried to attack a young man who already had one soldier on him. The soldier didn't, for some reason, expect Katashan to come after him.

Katashan stepped in and made the kill as clean as he could.

And he dared not stop to think about it as another came for him; a larger man this time and though this one didn't have skill, he did have strength and power.

Katashan heard, through the clash of swords, Lord Fordel ordering the men to put down their weapons. His voice soon became frantic and then angry. The men paid the words no heed, though Katashan realized they wanted to reach their new lord for different reasons. Killing Lord Fordel would leave this area without leadership, opening it up for anarchy which would be a gift for men like this.

Katashan had no trouble fighting the new man back and finally gave the killing blow. He'd taken a little cut on his arm, the blood flowing with fire and magic. He thought he should seal the wound and save that power but he hadn't the time.

Cork fought like a madman as he tried to protect both Lord Fordel and Katashan. He took dangerous risks: Katashan saw Cork swing at one man heading his way, and then charge one of the three advancing on Fordel. Katashan moved closer to Fordel to keep Cork taking too many chances as he also tried to protect Fordel, who continued to draw too much attention. Fordel, having spent considerable time with his late father's troops, at least knew weapons.

Swords and axes clanged in a dull cacophony of sound, blunted by the curses of some and the cries of others. The sounds blended into a murderous magic of its own, deadly and alluring, in the dark way of all battles.

Men tired on both sides, drew back. . . .

"They want Lord Fordel dead," Cork said, breathless as he stepped back by Katashan in a moment of near calm.

Katashan nodded and parried away two blows before he

killed another man with an easy move . . . and he regretted that moment, when he took advantage of his skill over someone who was no match.

"They know he's the rightful lord and he's ordered them back. They disobeyed, and they can expect no mercy from him now," Cork said, summing up the situation that looked increasingly desperate. "He does still have an army to come after them. If he tells this tale, no lord will hire them, and they'll be hunted in every land."

"Their only safety now is have him dead," Katashan said. Even Onshara had come to help protect Fordel. "I wonder why they have kept at it, though. Dangerous for them."

"They probably thought I was an easy target," Fordel replied. "By the time they realized I was not going to be taken out so easily, they had already gone too far."

They battle fell on them again.

Katashan couldn't tell how many soldiers had come to the attack. At first Kat thought he saw only a few dozen, but the number seemed to grow, as though for every one they killed, three more took his place. He fought them back, and back again.

"Get me a horse!" Lord Fordel suddenly yelled. "I can lead them away!"

"No!" Katashan, breathless, hadn't time to say more as he swung, sword-against-sword. The enemy would wear him down by sheer numbers as he fought them back again, with Cork and Fordel at his side.

"Damn! A horse!" Fordel shouted again, frantic. "Cork -- I am your lord! Get me a damned horse!"

Katashan saw Cork turn back at Fordel, white-faced. He even missed the sword swung at him, but Katashan caught the weapon in time. Cork looked around frantically. When he started for a horse the enemy had abandoned, Onshara stopped him.

"No," she said. "We shall not allow Lord Fordel to ride away and sacrifice himself."

"They'll follow me!" Fordel yelled, frantic, angry and careless. He very nearly got a sword through his side, if Katashan hadn't moved quickly to protect him as well. "I can get them away --"

"Some will follow -- until they kill you and come back," Onshara said. She shook her head. "No. Better to have you here and fighting with us, rather than dying alone! Here you can still protect my village and help my people. Alone, your death would mean nothing!"

Fordel glanced around, wide-eyed, afraid and angry at the same time. "It's not right!"

"No, it isn't," Onshara said. She had to fight back another as well and Fordel leapt to her aid, quickly killing the man.

And in that moment they found another small lull in battle, both sides pulling aside, winded and wounded. Katashan could see the soldiers already preparing to charge again. He needed more time to rest.

"Give me your word you will not try to run, Lord Fordel," Onshara demanded. She even caught hold of his arm. "Do this or otherwise I will put my people to watch over you, even though they could be better used to help protect the village."

"I am not your responsibility!"

"You are. You are a guest in my village. You are fighting for my village against your own people. You are, by some laws, even my lord. I will do my best to keep you safe, because it is far better to have you alive as a friend then dead as a martyr. Give me your word, Lord Fordel." She looked at the enemy who started to gather again, obviously intending a new attack. "We haven't time to waste."

Katashan saw the way Fordel looked at the line of men on the trail below the village, their swords ready and the bows brought out.

"Damn them." Fordel looked at the others and bowed his head in capitulation. "You have my word that I will not try to lead them away, Onshara. I shall stay and fight with you, to whatever end we meet."

She nodded her head in thanks and then began ordering her own people to their places. Katashan, Cork and Fordel retreated with the rest of the villagers to the first line of buildings, where they had better coverage from the bows. They'd not used them before while their own men were in close combat. Onshara's people didn't give them any easy targets.

"They're going to try and go up over the rocks and get behind the village," Onshara said, pointing out where some of the soldiers had begun to slip around to the side of the building. Fordel started that way, but she caught his arm and spoke softly. "They're in for a surprise. Those areas are trapped for more than a quarter mile on all sides. It's an easy way to be rid of some of these animals."

She sounded blood-thirsty but Katashan saw something different in her eyes. She desperately wanted to protect her people. Kindness had made her stop Lord Fordel from throwing his life away: kindness and honor.

"Why didn't they stop when Fordel ordered them?" Cork asked. "They know Lord Fordel is now their commander."

"I suspect --" Katashan lifted a hand, letting a little of the blood from his arm give him power. "Yes. There is magic. Subtle. They will not even know it, but the power directs them here."

Onshara put people back to guard the building and the book -- and then looked at Katashan again, as though wondering if she could order him back as well. He lifted his head to meet the argument and she gave up without a word.

A deep breath. Another.

And the enemy charged again.

They fought a long, disjointed battle through the last hours of daylight. The soldiers, though persistent and well-armed, could not get past the villagers, who were determined to hold their own, and who had the better cover.

Even so, the soldiers didn't give up. Katashan finally resorted to magic to stop a group who nearly breached the wall; a dangerous ploy since he already felt weary. He drove them back and the villagers even regained some lost ground. It would keep them safe for a little while longer.

Katashan stood with his back to the wall of a building and gasped for air, trying to focus on the world again. Where were Cork and Fordel? For a moment fear of finding them dead stopped him from even looking, but they slipped into his view, moving towards him and looking relieved.

"That was far too close," Fordel said. He leaned back as well. A cut in his shoulder had been bandaged and didn't look too serious. Katashan had started to reach out and see if he could help heal the wound, but he stopped. None of them might survive if he didn't get control. His magic might be the deciding factor and he had to be careful of how he used it.

"Sunset is coming," Cork said, weariness sounding even in his voice. He shook his head, damp hair falling into his eyes. "Damn them. Why don't they pull out? We've killed at least half already, and I don't know how many fell to the traps."

"They know when the sun goes down we will be in a worse position," Fordel said, looking around with a desperate shake of his head. "Once it's dark, we'll never be able to see into the trees, or guard all the walls."

"We may surprise them," Katashan said. He looked around and found Onshara. She stood by the dead, her head bowed. He didn't want to go there -- but he did, with the other two trailing along.

"We've not much time," he said. "Darkness is falling and --"

"And there's not much we can do," she said, sounding defeated already.

"No. I need help. It will not get dark."

"You can stop the sun?" she said and scoffed.

"No, but I can create a small one."

She started to speak, blinked, and looked as though she almost dared to hope, but she buried the emotion away in the next breath. It was not a time for hope, he supposed. "Do you have the power?"

"I can do it for a while." He bit at his lip and looked at his hands, knowing what this work would take from him. He could see no other way they would survive, though. "You should be ready to take advantage of the light which will likely startle the soldiers. I can't say how long I will hold it."

"Will you survive?" Fordel asked.

"I hope so," he answered truthfully. "But I won't guarantee so. However, if we don't do something daring then none of us are likely to survive. Don't argue with me."

Fordel looked back at him, eyes narrowed. They were both tired and worried and they both knew the chances of survival were slim. However, before Fordel could begin to argue Katashan felt something and turned --

"She's here, isn't she?" Fordel said softly. He rubbed at his arm, as though he, too, felt the cold.

"Yes," Katashan said. He looked out into the graying night hunting for the movement he knew too well. He saw nothing yet, but he could feel her, the cold touch of death on the air. "Yes, Sherina is here and far too close. That's another danger. However, she likes the dark, and my light will surprise her as well. Whatever you do, stay out of her path. She can kill with a touch."

No one argued. They passed around a little food, a flask of water, and dealt with both the injured and the dead. Katashan kept his place near the wall and watched, trying to find some weakness in the enemy and trying to find a miracle he that would save these people.

Was he a fool to stay here? Shouldn't he try to escape, because the bigger war needed him still?

He couldn't do it. He could not walk away when this time he truly might help.

As darkness came closer, the enemy again began to gather into a mass. They looked weary but no more so than the villagers who stood around him. Both sides could not stand through the night in this battle, and he couldn't guess which one would fall, at least if he could bring the light.

Katashan put a hand on Onshara's arm, stopping her before she stepped away to talk to villagers. "Spread the word that there will be magic light, but I cannot say quite when or for how long. Just tell them to be prepared and not to despair."

She agreed with a nod of her head, but he could see the despair in her eyes, and light alone would not dispel it. Onshara slipped away without another word.

Katashan, glanced at the shrouded bodies and quickly moved away from the dead. Cork and Fordel kept close beside him, stopping when he did to stare out at the line of dark shapes and the occasional glint of a weapon. The sun had nearly gone down and shadows crept out the woods like pieces of death come to claim the world.

Death . . . yes. He found Sherina at the edge of the soldiers, a white filament of movement, like a cloud tethered to the ground. The soldiers moved away from her though they plainly only worried and didn't fear her. They had made some kind of pact though he doubted the soldiers were as safe as they might think.

"She'll come for me," Katashan said with a wave of his arm towards the ghost. He looked at Cork and Fordel and shook his head before they started to speak. "Don't get in her way. I have a better chance of stopping her if I don't get distracted trying to save others."

Neither argued, though whether they would really stay

back, he couldn't say.

"Not much longer." Fordel wearily pulled his sword back up as the soldiers formed a line.

The night drifted to a cold, empty silence filled only with expectations. They stood their sides in a last moment of peace before Katashan heard orders shouted. He wanted to step out into the forefront and meet the enemy head on. He had powers he could call upon still . . . but so did she. He looked out towards the trees and couldn't find Sherina, and that worried him. He dared not move too hastily or forget he faced more than men in this hellish battle. Did her immortal mage lover wait nearby as well? Katashan still didn't have all his enemies in sight and the ones he could see clearly were the least dangerous, no matter how often they attacked.

Twilight passed into night and the enemy attacked. Katashan held back a little longer as the villagers moved in before him and stood firm. Fordel stayed with Onshara and even Cork joined the villagers in the lines, though he remained close to Katashan.

The soldiers came on, shouting ragged cries, weary . . . but Katashan waited still. The villagers would tire quickly and his light would help them best after they began to fail, to give them strength once more with a little magic shed upon his companions.

He wondered when she would come for him.

He leaned against a cottage wall, the Ritual Blade in his hand, ready. He would not let her take this village the way she had the soldier's camp and suck the life out of everyone here. He would not leave more dead children behind. No.

When she finally came for him, a screaming apparition in the night, he raised a bleeding hand and sent her back as much by will as by magical power. She howled and came on again. He could hear cries of dismay from the villagers and saw the line start to falter when she neared it, so he finally sent a globe of light flying out to fill the sky and banish the shadows. She shrieked as she became transparent and fled back to the shadows. He had expected as much, given her penchant for showing up at night.

The light pulsed with his laboring heartbeat. He could hear the battle, but he dared not look, focusing on the magic and the power he fed into the light, parceling out his life, hoping he could hold on and give them the ability to win.

Drop of blood by drop of blood . . . midnight passed. He whispered prayers for the dead as best he could and hoped the Gods took them kindly into their fold.

On his knees. He hadn't realized he'd gone down, but he held to the light. He heard shouts all around him. Please Gods, let them finally win --

But he knew from the sound the villagers made that they did not shout in victory. Weary, hardly able to move, he lifted his head and blinked, watching as more soldiers arrived on horseback. Another two hundred? Perhaps more. They could not fight more men, fresh to the battle --

"Gods," Onshara whispered, her voice shaky. She dropped to her knees beside him. "Priest, if you can go --"

"No, no," he said. Fear gave him power again and the light brightened. Probably a waste, but it was done and the others seemed better for it. "Where was I when you needed me?"

"*Don't,*" she said and gently touched his arm. The light faltered and dimmed. "You have done more than we could have asked from anyone. You, Lord Fordel and Cork. Don't --"

Sherina swept down at him. He saw the movement and barely shoved Onshara aside in time. Sherina's face, baleful and filled with glee, leaned closer as though she meant to kiss him. He threw fire and blood into her and she slipped back, snarling, though she didn't go far this time. Grabbing the ritual blade, Katashan cut deep into the palm of his hand, and sent blood spattering across her face. She screamed in whatever pain something incorporeal could feel, and retreated to the woods in a howl of wind that sent dust and leaves scattering around them.

"Damn, damn," Onshara whispered. "We need help. And there is none to be had."

The sound of wild hoof beats . . . coming from the night and the dark. He stood, and when Onshara gave a cry of fear he put a hand on her arm.

He knew the sound of that horse. He felt a surge of hope at last, something that overlaid his own despair. Sherina retreated and disappeared into the trees, her anger sending branches breaking.

Onshara cried out in dismay again and brought up her sword.

"He has come to our aid," Katashan said. He swayed on his feet, lost the link to his magic, and his light started to die --

And then came back, brighter than before, but not by his power. Cork rushed back to Katashan, knowing what the sound meant as well. Fordel came with him, limping badly, his leg gashed and bleeding. Cork grabbed hold of Fordel just as rider and horse emerged from the dark and raced through the line of soldiers.

Some died in that rush of Godling and immortal horse through the enemy. Men shouted in fear and ran, panicked from the field.

Katashan thought they were saved, until he saw the frantic look that Peralin gave him.

The villagers began to kneel before Peralin, his name whispered through the lines. Lord Fordel knelt as well, his face white with pain. However, Katashan and Cork headed for the Godling, which got shocked looks from nearly everyone.

"Drink this!" Peralin ordered handing down a goblet to Katashan. "Drink it all, quickly!"

He did so, even knowing what it would do to him. The liquid tasted of fire, warmth, power, but it made him so giddy

Cork had to grab hold of him before he melted into the ground.

The world came into sharp focus and he could too clearly see the dead and the wounded. He wanted to help them all, and turned to start the work, and stopped when Peralin caught his shoulder.

"We must ride, Katashan. You need the strength to ride with me. And only you have the magic to survive such a journey!"

"Ride?" Katashan echoed, knowing he didn't at all want to be on a horse right now, especially *that* one.

"Back to the fortress. The dawn is coming too soon and I cannot stay! Come!"

He reached down and caught Katashan by the arm and lifted so easily Katashan felt as though he flew into the saddle. Peralin somehow maneuvered him to the front of the horse. Katashan started to slide down; not his idea, he just had little control of his body right now, between exhaustion and the wine.

"No, stay here," Peralin said and touched Katashan's shoulder with a wish for him to remain. After that he wondered if he would ever be able to leave the horse again. Peralin leaned down in the saddle and put a hand on Cork's shoulder as well. He looked up, stunned by the touch. "I will take as good care of him as I can, Cork. And I'll send him back with the troops as fast as I can. This is the only way. Hold out until they arrive. I will open a path for the soldiers to return here and they will be here by the dawn."

"Sherina -- we can't hold her off," Cork protested.

"The dawn is nearly here," Peralin said. He waved a hand and the air filled with a sprinkle of stars for a moment. "She will follow Katashan, but she cannot take the path I take. I left some protection for you which will fade with the light, but so will she."

"Can't you order the soldiers away?" Cork asked, looking back at the army that had not retreated far enough.

"They're madmen. Gone beyond reason and in the control of something already dead," Peralin explained. "She controls them and many more like them, and she has links to things I cannot control. Someone likely put them in her hands, but we can't see who it might be. Verina holds the line between here and elsewhere and I must take Katashan and run the gauntlet between them and open a way back for the soldiers. Humans against humans. It's the best way. You do not want the Gods to fight a battle *here*. I take Katashan with me because he has the magic to follow the path back and bring the others with him."

"Then we must go," Katashan said beginning to understand the problem far too clearly. "Lord Fordel --"

"I'll keep the light strong," he said.

"Here," Peralin said and handed down another goblet into Cork's hands. "Take this. Each of you who fight here need to drink only a small sip. This will give you strength."

Cork took the goblet and bowed his head in thanks.

"You have my blessing, all of you. It may be of help," he said, his voice filling the village. "Be strong. Help will return."

He spun the horse and in the next moment they flew back through the ranks of the enemy. Katashan closed his eyes, unwilling to see them killed, even now. They were her thralls and even if they went willingly to her -- as some fools would -- he couldn't feel pleasure at their deaths.

In a dozen fast heartbeats they had pushed through the enemy lines and reached the wild woods. He finally dared open his eyes as the horse slowed. He even looked back.

"Yes, she follows us. You need not worry about that part. But I have something else to show you, Katashan. Look ahead. *Watch*."

Katashan turned. Light and dark merged, moved, and the view changed. He suddenly felt as though he could see forever; neither the darkness of night nor great distance impeded the view. He saw a path that stretched from where he stood on the mountain all the way down past a spring fed stream, and through a draw, out into the forest again, and then down to the trail to within yards from the fortress. He could see it all, from the stands of trees to the owl sitting on a branch.

"Do you see it?" Peralin asked.

"Yes."

"Mark this path in your mind. Hold to it. I have opened this way through the world for you, and you'll be able to return here in hours, rather than days. It will remain open for all the daylight hours, and disappear again in the next sunset. Do you have it?"

"Yes," Katashan said, marking the way in his mind so well that he knew he would remember the unnatural trail forever.

"Good. We travel a different way, filled with wonders and dangers, Katashan. This is the only way we will get there in time before I must go back to my place."

"Then we must go," he said.

Peralin urged Night forward and they rode to . . . somewhere else.

CHAPTER TWENTY-FOUR

Night moved forward and the world Katashan knew went away. In its place came a swirl of color, a hum of sound, and a scent like everything wild in the world brought together. He could not breathe for a moment, inhaling so much life. Too much: too rich for a mortal to breathe, see and hear.

They rushed through this place; man, Godling, and immortal horse. He had no sense of direction or distance. Only that they went, traveling through wonders that he could not name and could barely perceive.

"They've spotted us," Peralin said softly.

"They?" he whispered, surprised that any words had meaning here.

"We're treading in a place where only those who are invited should go. They ignored my requests since they have no interest in a war between humans. They stay apart. It is their way."

Katashan nodded, as though he understood any of what Peralin was trying to tell him.

And then *something* moved in around the horse, startling even the stoic Night. Katashan sensed a presence that had nothing remotely human in it. He felt as though light and dark, sound and silence were all the same to them. Katashan, who had faced many things strange and horrible, found himself panicking as he confronted something with which he could have no

common ground. How could he deal with them? How could he
--

Peralin put a hand to his shoulder, saying nothing but
plainly suggesting calm. Katashan tried to take a deep breath,
but the place still held too much life and he felt as though he
drowned in the very air. He had to trust Peralin, who seemed
more akin to him than he did to whatever lived -- *existed* -- in
this place. They rode on. Katashan held tight to the belief that if
he could not deal with them, then they could not touch him
either.

That proved untrue.

Something grabbed, possessed -- held him -- *theirs, their
place, their find, their being.*

Eddies swirled. Light and sound, darkness, shouts, silence -
- pain so intense his body felt like a living flame, burning so
bright and loud --

Peralin did not let go of him, and held against the wants of
things that had never touched such a life and wanted another
taste, *wanted to have, their find, their place, their being now.*

Katashan, with whatever little sanity he had left, reached
beyond pain and confusion, and knew this wasn't where he
wanted to stay. He grabbed hold of the Godling's hand and held
so tightly he thought even Peralin might be surprised.

The horse moved unsteadily forward. Peralin pushed aside
the things that came too close, even though it took his energy.
Katashan realized his companion had less power here than he
did in the mortal world, probably because this place was so
different.

How far did they have to go? How far had they gone? He
had no sense of distance or time now.

"Almost," Peralin whispered. His voice sounded harsh, and
he trembled, weakened by what he'd done. And yet he pushed
them away again and would not let these creatures take
Katashan. Katashan held his breath though he wasn't certain

now if he had really breathed in this place after all. They moved on. Nor how long. A moment? An hour? Surely years had gone by. . . .

Another of the beings grabbed him, a physical sensation as it tried to yank Katashan from the horse, but Katashan knew he did not want to be parted from his companion. He saw only a hint of movement, a ripple in the colors around them, but the creature held tight and drew blood along his leg.

Which unexpectedly helped. Katashan swept out with magic and he thought he surprised the creature more than hurt it. In that moment Katashan felt as though his entire existence grew alight with his magic, bright and fiery. Painful, and beautiful. Too much.

But Peralin kept hold of him.

They slipped out into the real world again. He tasted it on the wind, the magic that belonged here, along with the life. The call of birds --

"Barely in time," Peralin whispered, gasping. Katashan clung to consciousness as the horse continued to move, stumbling through the brush. "Dawn is too close!"

They broke through a line of dogwood brush and down to the familiar trail. There ahead stood the fort, rising out of the fog, illuminated by torches at the towers and gates. Katashan heard men call out the alarm, surprised to find a horse and rider so close in with no sign before.

"Hold on, friend," Peralin said. "No time now for subtlety."

Katashan had barely enough wits left to worry over those words. He looked up to see the closed gates of the fort before them, and the guards shouting out a warning to stop and identify themselves.

They did not stop: They went through the closed gate.

Well, that was bound to get some notice.

Soldiers scattered in the courtyard before them, and cries of alarm went up everywhere. He heard Peralin's name shouted along with his; a strange combination he feared would be linked in legend for a long time to come.

Peralin swept off the horse and left Night standing, stone still in the midst of chaos. He pulled Katashan into his arms, and started up the stairs and into the buildings while everyone scattered. They might have gone through more closed doors, but it hardly mattered to Katashan now.

Peralin took him straight up to Serrano's rooms, where the captain had just pulled on his tunic, and looked in shocked dismay as the door swung open and the Godling walked in.

"I leave him in your care, Captain," Peralin said. He placed Katashan in a chair and looked around, worried. "I can neither stay nor lead you back to the village. But here, have him sip this, and it will see him through. Ride hard and fast. They will not survive without your help."

He put a goblet in Serrano's shaking hands.

"What shall I do?" Serrano asked softly.

"Save the others. Katashan knows the way back -- a special way I have prepared for you, and with his magic he can find the path again. But if I don't return to my place before the sun rises, I shall never be able to help again. And I think my work is not quite done here. Take care of him."

The Godling turned to leave, but Katashan caught his arm, surprising Serrano, who whispered a sound of warning or maybe a prayer. "Thank you," Katashan whispered.

Peralin nodded. And then he left; a movement so swift that the bedclothes rustled. Almost immediately shouts came again in the courtyard, and he heard the sound of horse hooves.

"Gods grant that he makes it back to his place in time," Katashan whispered.

Serrano stared at him, silent and still. His face had gone pale white, and Katashan could see his chest move, as though he fought for a breath. Then Serrano shook his head and shivered. "What are we doing?"

"There is a village in the hills called Holding and it is under siege. Lord Fordel is there, if you want a good excuse to mount a force to relieve them. The attackers are the old lord's mercenaries, whom he had set on the mountain people before he died. They refuse to come under Fordel's command partly, at least, because Sherina has her hand on them. We must ride now."

"Ride now," Serrano repeated. He looked towards the window. Morning birds called out the songs of dawn. "He was here."

"Yes. To bring me to you," Katashan said. He tried to stand and failed. "Give me the goblet. Then we ride. This is something important enough for Peralin to risk his presence in the world. We must go now."

Serrano finally understood the importance of the situation. He crossed to him and held out the goblet. Katashan took a little sip. Another. He dared not drink more, remembering how it had hit him back at the village.

By then the Captain had gotten enough of his senses back to order the soldiers to arms and prepare for a march. Katashan rested a little longer, but he could hear the frantic haste of others all around the building and the courtyard. He could also feel every cut and pain in his body, and even the elixir could not help him as well this time.

"Katashan," Serrano said, standing over him. He hadn't realized he'd closed his eyes until then. "Can you ride?"

"Not well. But I will. We must go now." He put aside the goblet and started to stand. Only Serrano's strength kept him there. When he looked into the Captain's face, he saw worry and fear. "Tonight I have been to some other realm where humans do not tread, Captain. I have ridden on a horse of legend with a God to protect my back. It will not have been for nothing."

"You'll ride with me this time," Serrano said.

"And grateful for it," Katashan answered. He put his aching

and bleeding arm across the man's shoulder and with Captain Serrano's aide, he limped out of the room. It had been easier with the Godling carrying him up. It was a damn long ways down to the courtyard again.

But they reached the horses and soldiers in good time. The courtyard held wisps of fog, everything illuminated by the first hint of grey dawn. Troops gathered, nervously glancing at him. Oh yes, it would be a long time before he outlived that bit of legend when he and Peralin arrived.

Katashan hoped Peralin had made reached his appointed place in time, but not just because they might need him again. Katashan realized he wanted to talk with the Godling when this madness was past. He wanted to understand the ways of the Gods better than he had, even if he never had reason to deal so intimately with them again.

Besides, he liked Peralin.

The others were ready to go. The men on foot glanced around, asking each other if they'd seen Peralin, and wondering what work they were going to do for him. Serrano somehow got Katashan onto the horse and slipped up behind him. The gate opened and they rode.

Katashan didn't like this journey any better, but he held on and led them back up the mountain and through the path Peralin had prepared for them. He headed to the battle and the war -- and Sherina, who would find him again, if he survived to see another night.

CHAPTER TWENTY-FIVE

The soldiers never tired on the trail Peralin had laid for them. They climbed upward at a run, startled by the power and quick and sure in their movements, no matter what the terrain. They darted over rocks and ice, across brooks and streams with the same ease as walking a flat land. Serrano and Katashan, riding the only horse, never had to slow for the others.

Up and up . . . they passed a startled owl and then they reached the trees Katashan remembered, and even from here they could see the smoke of the village and hear the faint yells of battle. That the villagers still fought gave Katashan hope as they crested the last hill and came in view of the battlefield.

Serrano's soldiers came up behind the others, and with the understanding that these men were rebels against their true lord, they had no problem at all falling upon them.

Katashan stayed well back from the battle, leaning against a tree and waiting for it to end . . . and for the world to settle around him. Even the tree didn't feel as solid as it should be, and the morning light swirled in shades of yellow and orange which could not be real, at least to this realm. He closed his eyes and stayed very still.

Serrano left a guard with him, who seemed very glad not to be joining the fray. Serrano's soldiers, even after their magical race to reach Holding, hadn't tired, while the rebels had been fighting all night. They also had surprised the enemy by coming from behind and from an area without a trail.

In the end, none of the enemy survived, but only because they wouldn't give up the battle. Serrano's men had no choice but to kill them all. In those last few moments they made fast work of the job while Katashan kept his head bowed and stared at the ground, which had an unfortunate habit of seeming to move beneath his feet.

"Sir," Cork said, suddenly by his side.

"Praise the Gods you're all right," Katashan said, lifting his head, and nearly losing his balance.

Cork caught hold of him. "Wish I could say the same for you, sir! Here, sit down. I've got you."

He let Cork lower him to the ground. He had a hard time keeping his head up now, but he looked at Cork, who knelt beside him, his face pale and his arm bleeding.

"Fordel? Onshara?" Katashan asked, fearing the answers.

"Both alive. Lord Fordel took another bad cut, but he should be fine. Onshara is seeing to her people."

"I should --" he started to stand, but Cork pushed him back down.

"No, sir. You need to stay right there for a while. You're pale as a ghost --"

"Ghost. Sherina?"

"She disappeared shortly after you did. She lost track of you, and she lost interest in anything else here. But I'll keep my eyes open, sir. I'll let you know if she comes back, but I doubt we'll see her before nightfall. And if that's so, you should rest and be prepared to deal with her then."

"Yes. True."

"Lean against the tree and rest. The Gods know when we might need your help again, and you don't look well enough to give it right now."

He leaned back and closed his eyes. They were moving the

bodies, clearing the battlefield. He wanted nothing more to do with it.

Later, he became aware of people around him. His eyes fluttered open to a day filled with bright light and shadows. Cork still sat beside him, Fordel nearby with Serrano and Onshara. They had food, and a flask of something they passed around.

"Would you like a sip, sir? This is very good wine. Onshara brought it out for us."

"Just a sip," he said. His voice sounded ragged and his lips felt so dry they hurt to move when he spoke. He tried to lift his hand to take the flask, but Cork shook his head and brought it to his lips for him. Katashan could not have held it there.

The wine tasted cool and sweet. Human wine and very unlike the last sip of anything he'd had, that drink from one of Peralin's goblets. The sip helped. He nodded his thanks to Cork and blinked the others back into focus. "Gods, I'm tired," he said.

The others nodded understanding. Even Serrano looked worn even though he'd slept the night before.

"You left in the company of a God," Onshara said.

"Ah." He had forgotten, for a moment, how that part would affect the others. "It is not such a big thing --"

"You really don't believe that," Fordel said with a shake of his head.

"I want to."

Onshara gave a little smile. He saw dark circles under her eyes from lack of sleep and those eyes still looked red from tears. He wondered how many villagers she had lost. He didn't ask.

"We have decisions to make," Fordel said, though softly. "And we hoped you would be well enough to help us work this out, Katashan."

"Decisions?" Why would they wait on him for decisions?

This was not his place, and he wished . . . but he couldn't even let that thought fully form. He looked up and nodded.

"My people aren't safe here," Onshara said. "Fordel has offered to leave troops to our defense, but. . ."

"But does he have the troops to spare, given the trouble we are facing?" Katashan asked. "And would your people feel safe with them?"

"Those are the problems," she agreed and frowned.

"Would you and your people come and stay in the safety of the fort?" Serrano asked. "At least long enough to see how this problem might be settled?"

Fordel nodded at the suggestion and looked hopeful. Onshara didn't look as certain, but that was only -- Katashan suspected -- because the mountain people and those who lived on the shore had rarely found themselves on the same sides of a battle.

"This is a bigger war than anything from the past." Katashan painfully leaned forward and put a hand on her knee. "Take your people to safety, Onshara. We don't have time for old disagreements and distrust."

"Yes," she said and nodded more emphatically as though she took the answer to heart once she spoke the word aloud. "Yes, we'll go to the fort until this bigger question is settled. I'll begin gathering my people for the journey. It will not take long."

He almost told her not to forget the book, but that was a useless thing to say. The entire village revolved around keeping that book safe and generations had grown up doing so. He did not imagine they would forget it now.

"I'll send scouts ahead to prepare for the incoming villagers," Serrano said. "Katashan, do you think your passage will be open for us to go back again?"

"As long as we are back before nightfall," he said and shivered at the thought of taking that journey again -- ah, but far better than going the long way. "We had better hurry."

Onshara stood. "Yes, hurry. We will pack what we can carry."

Katashan didn't really want to hurry again, but he nodded. Cork handed him some cheese. He was very nearly too tired to eat it.

And then he slept again for a while.

When they prepared to leave, he rode with Cork on a horse that had probably belonged to the enemy. He didn't care. He didn't look back to see what they had done with the dead. Katashan only noted that Onshara carried the book and she had adequate protection around her. He noted she also carried a goblet Peralin had left behind when he and Katashan rode away. Oh yes, it would be carefully guarded as well, until the owner might claim it again. It seemed the people of Holding were apt to collect odd relics.

The horse had a gentle gait as they started down the hill. Despite being worried, Katashan was eager to leave. He wanted back to Salbay and the relative safety of the walls there.

And he tried not to think that nothing they'd set out to do had been accomplished, and that matters had gotten worse instead of better.

"We'll get you back to the fortress soon enough, sir."

"Too soon," Katashan mumbled. "This is the most peace I've had in days."

Katashan didn't dare sleep while he held on to the path for the others to follow. As they rode he felt bits of it slipping away in the growing shadows, but he thought they would reach the lowlands soon enough. Even so, he had a strange waking-dream, troubling at some levels, but not unpleasant. He imagined he had met the Immortal Mage, Aster, and he'd even talked with the man, and had a pleasant discussion with him, though he didn't actually know what they said.

He shook himself back to reality, feeling uneasy and uncertain. He didn't want to feel akin to this man who created a monster like Sherina.

When he lifted his head, he found they had nearly reached the gate of the fortress. The townspeople watched them pass through the outer village, curious but not hostile. The sun had settled low on the ocean, a beautiful sunset of golds and blues.

They reached the fortress. There would be safety, and rest, within those walls. The sight of it gave him a little strength, but when he started to sit up straighter, every bone and muscle ached. He moaned.

"Ah, back again, sir?" Cork asked from behind him.

"I'd rather not be."

"Yes, sir. I know the feeling. But we're nearly there. A bath and bed, maybe some nice broth between --"

"I could stand that," Katashan said, rousing a little more at the thought of a bath.

"Good, sir."

"Kat."

"Kat, yes. Sorry. Damned tired, sir."

"Ah, of course." He had, in fact, forgotten that others might be very tired by now -- battle-weary, as well as having missed sleep. "It will be good to sleep again."

"Yes, Kat, it will."

They reached the gate behind Serrano who ordered it open. Katashan remembered going through it the last time, although he couldn't quite get his thoughts to focus around that time. Just as well. If he thought too hard, it might keep him awake.

The gate slowly opened. Too many people began to gather in the courtyard, and for a moment the sight worried him until he realized they had brought out tables with food for their unexpected guests. Others looked prepared to treat the wounded. Onshara's people would get a good welcome here.

The horse came to an uncertain stop inside the gate and Cork could not get him to move in any direction.

"Damned animal," he said. "If I get down and lead it, can

you stay in the saddle that long, Kat?"

"I doubt it," he answered. "I could lie down right here and sleep."

"Not for long in the path of everyone else."

"I wouldn't notice."

"Ah, probably true. Race! Come lead this damned horse out of the way, will you?"

A young, dark-haired stable boy rushed forward and took hold of the harness, coaxing the animal off to the side where Cork directed. They passed the tables and with each step into the courtyard, Katashan felt as though peace enveloped them within the high, thick walls.

"Here, I've got him, Cork," Serrano said. Katashan looked down to find the Captain beside the horse, reaching upwards. "Come down, Katashan. We'll get you inside."

Katashan looked around, noting everyone finding their own places here. They did not, praise all the gods, need his help right now. They moved, colors and shadows, and he couldn't quite focus. He watched as Fordel slipped from his horse and stood, supported by Onshara. Her people looked grateful for the refuge and the help.

Safe.

Katashan tried to get his leg up over the pommel, but it would not cooperate. Cork finally pushed him from the saddle and into the hands of Serrano and another soldiers.

"Your pardon," he said, and then realized he spoke in a language they didn't understand. "I'm sorry," he said. He wasn't sure for which, though -- the language or the fall.

"You're fine. Let's get you inside. We need to discuss what to do next," Serrano said.

He moaned. He desperately wanted rest. Sleep. Tonight, tomorrow. For a long time. *Let the world be in someone else's care.*

He heard a dreadful sound and looked back to see Sherina screaming out of the darkening sky towards him and he almost didn't have the strength left to care. Fordel must have seen. He moved towards Katashan and tried to throw a block of a shield in her direction. However, the magic only angered Sherina, and she swung down towards the pale, and still bleeding, Fordel with a yowl of anger.

Katashan moved to help, where his own safety would not have won much of a response. He pulled free of Serrano and the soldier, pushed Cork aside and grabbed at his ritual knife. No time for subtlety. He cut straight into the wrist and brought enough blood to his fingertips to splatter her with fire and light.

The ploy worked. She screamed and fled before his power.

Cork grabbed hold of him as he fell and even breathing became nearly impossible now. People spoke, but he couldn't understand them. He only knew he had to make them safe from his enemy.

Katashan reached over and laid his hand against the wall, urging the power of a ward up through the stones. More and more until he felt he was almost a part of the fort, the stones melding into his soul, the place forever apart of him.

"Make certain everyone is inside tonight," he said softly, each word more difficult than the last. "Inside the ward."

Fordel nodded.

And then Katashan felt the world go out from under him. No meeting tonight. No food and no bath either. Just blessedly empty darkness.

CHAPTER TWENTY-SIX

Katashan awoke and turned his head though even that much movement proved difficult. He found a candle beside the bed fluttering and nearly gutted in the liquid wax left behind. Nearly dawn, he thought. Cork slept on a cot beside the bed.

Someone else stood in the room as well.

Katashan sat up with a start his hand moving. He found they'd wrapped his wrists in cloth and he grabbed at the knife --

"Calm, friend." Pater Matish crossed to the side of the bed and within the little circle of light. "I had hoped not to awaken you."

Cork sat up, blurry-eyed, his hand on a sword beside the cot. "What?" he asked, uncertain of the danger.

"I'm reinforcing the wards," the priest said softly. "You're safe. Go back to sleep."

Katashan fell back among the pillows and blankets, suspecting Pater Matish had reinforced the suggestion of sleep with a little magic. For a moment Katashan thought about fighting the compulsion. Then he decided he wanted to sleep instead.

However, this time the sleep proved less restful. Almost immediately images began to shift their way into his consciousness. He relieved the journey with Peralin and tasted the air of a place that was not part of this world. He saw the unworldly colors and felt Night beneath him. He also remembered the pain so acutely he knew he cried out. Cork quieted him, and he slipped back again. . . .

To another dream memory: This time he held the ancient book. He stared at old words swirling with powers he couldn't touch or understand. He tried to absorb them into his mind, but they slipped away and he saw nothing except the drawing of the man. And then the picture *looked* at him. He felt as though he should know this man . . . that he *needed* to know this man.

He came awake. Cork sat by the bed, cleaning his sword.

"I need to see the book."

Cork leapt from his cot, sword in hand, and his eyes wide. Then he sagged, almost leaning on the sword while he caught his breath.

"Well, we don't have to move quite that fast," Katashan said and moved slowly to sit up.

"You were dead asleep a moment I ago. I checked myself. Closer to dead than asleep, in fact."

"My apologies for coming back to life." Cork took several deep breaths, obviously still recovering from the start though he looked pleased. "How long have I been asleep or half-dead this time?"

"All of one entire day, sir. Kat." He finally moved back to the chair and settled there, putting the sword aside. A bruise covered the back of his right hand, and another showed at the side of his neck, where a bandaged also covered a wound -- damned close, that one. "It's sunset of the day after we arrived. The others have been worried about you."

"I'm better."

"But not well."

"Better is as good as I can manage just now and nothing to complain about, considering all that happened. The others?"

"Doing well, sir. Lord Fordel was down for most of the day and had taken a bit of a fever from the wound, but Pater Matish cleared that up. There's been some talk about Lord Fordel and magic. That's likely to lead to trouble later but for now the people are mostly glad to know they have some protection, having seen what they're up against. Sherina came to the walls last night. She couldn't get in."

"That's good. I hope this goes well for him." Katashan slowly shifted his legs off the edge of the bed, trying to ignore every ache and pain. He felt almost ill at first and took everything slowly. Cork watched him with a growing frown. "You aren't going to try to argue with me about this, are you? Do you really think we have time?"

"No sir, I won't. You're right." He leaned back in the chair, plainly not in any hurry to get up either. "It's the book, is it? I believe Onshara still has it in her possession. She and Lord Fordel have gone over the pages a few times already but not found anything as far as I can tell."

"Which will probably be the same for me but I must go look."

Cork nodded and stood. "I've got clean clothes, if you like."

"A shirt at least. And can you arrange for that bath when I get back?"

"Yes sir. I can do that," Cork said. "We have a guard at the door, by the way. Captain Serrano feared I was too worn to do the work properly."

"I'm grateful."

Cork went to the door giving quick orders before he came back and began fishing through some clothing for a shirt. "This one, I think, sir. And let me help. "

Katashan almost told the man that he could dress himself, but he wasn't entirely certain it was true. With Cork's help they took half the time it would have if he'd tried to do it alone. Cork even pulled his hair back into a tie. He wished there had been time for a bath, but not with the darkness and Sherina both no doubt very close. He stood, took a couple steps getting the feel for ground under his feet again. His legs ached but walking would probably help.

"I'm ready," Katashan finally said. Cork watched him for a moment more and finally nodded agreement.

The guard outside the room saluted as they left the room, which amused Katashan, who wasn't certain what sort of rank he supposedly held here these days. Companion to Peralin probably rated at least a salute, though, and far better than a bow.

The building seemed busy with servants everywhere in the halls, obviously caring for a number of people. They smiled and greeted both him and Cork. Those with food tried to press tidbits on Katashan and he finally ended up with a sweet cake and an apple. Cork smiled brightly. Kastashan realized the gifts meant he had found acceptance here, at least among the servants. He wondered why.

They found Onshara in the Great Hall, sitting on the stones by the hearth and looking over the book. She smiled brightly at the two and immediately made room for Katashan beside her. Cork pulled a chair over from the table and settled, forgoing any sort of formality.

"You look better, Katashan."

"I assume so since I have been given to believe that I looked dead prior to this."

She laughed and put a hand on the back of his hand. He almost shied away from the touch and she must have seen the reaction, but she didn't pull back. "I am grateful for all you did at my village, Katashan. We would not have survived without your help."

"I did what I should," he replied. The hearth felt warm, but the stones hard and he wished he could be back in bed right now. But no time . . . no time at all. "And I'll help you get your homes back as well, if this is in my power. Right now, though, I came to look at the book."

"Ah yes. We have all had our chance to look at the book. This has become a very popular tome. I cannot think of the last time the pages have been turned so often."

She carefully placed the heavy book in his lap and slid closer to him. He became too aware that she'd had a bath and smelled of sweet soap and oils . . . and he had not. However, he knew more than her cleanliness unsettled him, as though just her closeness touched on raw nerves. He fought the feeling away and turned his attention to the book.

The pages immediately took his attention. She'd had the book open to a page of plant drawings and he turned a few more, marveling at the work. The man had been a fairly good artist, and Katashan easily recognized some of the plants, and could even guess at what the notes meant. That might give him some chance to figure out the language. Eventually.

They didn't have that much time.

He carefully folded the pages back to the front piece and the drawing of the man. He stared, wondering if this image had been drawn looking in a mirror. He tried to imagine the picture flipped . . . and then he realized Cork frowned as he looked at the picture.

"Cork?"

"I know that face, sir. I feel like I know him."

"Then it's not just me," Katashan said, startled.

"This is the first time I've really looked. I wish I could tell why I think I know him, though."

"That's my problem," Katashan said and leaned back. He smiled when he saw Serrano, Fordel and Pater Matish coming into the room.

And then he looked back down at the book.

"Oh hell," Cork said.

"I thought you would realize soon," Pater Matish said with a little wave of his hand. He came and looked down at the book, a slight smile on his lips. Fordel and Serrano both turned to stare at him. "Yes, I am the one who wrote the book."

"You?" Serrano said. He sounded as though he thought the man could not know what he was saying. "You can't be."

"I am." He looked around at the others, and in the turn of the head, Katashan could clearly see the resemblance. "My name is Aster. I was born . . . oh, long before the wars. And yes, Lord Fordel, I was the one who taught your sister her first real magic. She could be quite charming, you know, when she wanted something. Only when I started telling her *not yet* or daring to tell her *no* outright, that I learned her true nature. I quickly changed my mind about teaching her more. I *did not* do the ritual at the Verina altar."

"Who then?" Katashan asked. Oddly, he didn't feel shocked. He had finally found someone with answers.

"Not who. *What.* She learned too well from me, and I quickly saw her ambitions knew no bounds. I tried to dissuade her."

"Sherina always got what she wanted," Fordel replied. He still looked surprised as he and Serrano sat on the hearth. Only Pater Matish remained standing, looking with uncertainty at the four as though he faced some court.

"Yes, she did have a will of iron, your sister. And that's what fuels her still." He focused on Katashan, as though to forget the rest of the people around them. "I confessed to her about my own life and my immortality. She went in search of the answer when I said I wouldn't do the ritual, and she awakened many ancient beings in her attempts to get one to give her my . . . gift. Peralin isn't the only one wandering in the world now."

"Why didn't you stop her?" Katashan asked.

"I couldn't." He sounded, in that moment, as much embarrassed as annoyed. "By the time I realized her plans, she had drawn the interest of someone -- *something* -- powerful. Look to Emista. He created my immortality. She told me once she thought she could get at least that from him. We laughed. I should have realized she meant those words."

"Emista?" Fordel asked. "I don't know this name."

"One of the very old gods from the north, long gone from here, even before the rest had been expelled," Katashan said. "He's the God of Ice, and in legend he is always looking for a human woman to warm his heart. In ancient times they sacrificed a young woman to him to bring back the spring."

"And she went to him for immortality," Matish said with a shake of his head. "I fear Sherina never really thought through all the logical steps."

"So what did she get?" Katashan asked. "Neither life nor death and she is still a slave to the dark god. Are you?"

"No. Emista found me too dangerous." He gave a sudden, bright grin. "He hadn't had much contact with humans for a long time before we fell in together. He learned a great deal about how tenacious and troublesome we can be in the century that I served him. He finally cut me loose."

"Can you undo the magic that has tied her to this form?" Fordel asked.

"I would undo myself as well," he said, looking at Lord Fordel. "I like life, even still."

"What did you learn from Emista?" Katashan asked, sitting forward, aches nearly forgotten in that moment. "What can we use?"

"I fear I don't know nearly enough," he confessed. "But I did write many things down in the book, between pictures of plants and rather poor poetry. We'll find some answers there, even if I have forgotten them. That's one thing I learned, Katashan. The mind can only hold so much information."

"We can't read it," Katashan said, running his finger over the print.

"But I can. I wrote it," Aster looked at Onshara, whom Katashan only now noticed sat almost stone still. Why not? Her people had watched over this book *forever*. She could not have expected to find the author come back. "I put the book in the care of people I trusted. I'm grateful for the care you have shown it. You may have saved us all by being so diligent."

"Thank you, my lord," she whispered. She blushed. "What can we do?"

"I have to read the book," he said. "It will take me a little while to remember some of the words but I should have it by morning."

Matish -- Aster -- held out his hands. Katashan felt a moment of trepidation before he handed the book over. Aster put his hand on the cover, smiling softly, as though he found some old friend whom he hadn't seen in a long time. How much of his past could he hold on to? How long had he lived?

"I want a bath now," Katashan said.

Cork laughed as the stood, stretching slowly before he reached a hand to help Kat up. "I've ordered it ready, sir. And there will be food as well when you're done. Is there anything else needs done down here?"

Katashan stood slowly. He wanted a warm bath and he might even use some of the scented oils he had brought from home. He craved a little luxury tonight.

Serrano looked up at him, frowning before he glanced back at Aster. The Captain obviously couldn't quite come to grips with what he'd learned. Katashan leaned down and put a hand on Serrano's shoulder, drawing the look back to himself again. "Rest easy, friend. We need his help, and you have known him a long time, even if not by the proper name."

Serrano looked at Aster once more. "Trust."

"Well, you are more than welcome to sit here and keep me company, Captain and Onshara. And you too, Lord Fordel, of course. I would think all of you could keep your eyes on me well enough, and Lord Fordel knows magic enough to keep you all safe from me."

Katashan left them to discuss the matter. He and Cork had a long walk back up to the room, but by the Gods, the bath waited for him when he got there.

He slept in the water for a while, and finally got out to a warm robe, good soup, and then a wonderful warm bed again. He slipped back to sleep and this time he didn't even dream, having put the problems in the hands of the others, at least for a while.

CHAPTER TWENTY-SEVEN

atashan awoke to the sound of a fierce storm and the gray light of another day. Someone stood at the door talking to Cork. He saw a halo of hair, light shimmering around her as Cork glanced towards the bed.

"Yes, he's awake now. We'll be down in a few minutes, love. "

Maylee. He calmed the sudden pounding fear that had chased all whisper of sleep from his mind. Katashan was sorry to see her scurry away. Thunder shook the building, and wind pounded hard against the shutters. Not a good day.

"We've problems sir," Cork said and was already at work setting out clean clothing. "The storms are rolling in. There's been trouble elsewhere with them. Floods and downed trees and such."

"And the storms aren't natural," Katashan said, sitting up and lifting a hand towards the window where wind and magic leaked in around the shutters along with a fine spray of rain.

"Seems not. Aster says they are part of the spell Sherina used and the weather is not quite aligned properly now."

"Yes, that makes sense."

"Does it? Good then. Sounds insane to me."

"It is insane but it's a logical insanity."

"I'm sure that's fine, then."

Katashan slipped his legs over the side of his bed and

experienced a moment of déjà vu from the day before. It took him a few breaths before he dared stand and prepare to face the others.

Katashan guessed the time must be late afternoon, though he could hardly tell by the faint light coming through the shuttered windows. It seemed that lately he slept and rose to do battle, with little else between. As he pulled on his tunic, he could hear harder strikes of hail against the wooden shutter. Not good.

By the time they made it down the stairs, rain and hail pounded the building, tearing open shutters along the way. A quick glance showed the fort grounds awash with water. At another window, the sea beyond looked wild as waves crashed against the shore and sent salty foam high into the air.

"What about the fishing village?" Katashan asked as he and Cork fought the shutters closed again.

"They evacuated earlier today at Aster's suggestion. They'll lose their homes, but that's nothing new," he said with a sigh. "The worst problem will be the ships at harbor. They're taking quite a beating, and they're far harder to replace."

Katashan nodded, brushing water from his clothing. He hadn't been dry for very long.

Cork greeted a few frantic and worried servants as they headed through the maze of halls. When they stepped into the Great Hall, Katashan could see a group of people stood gathered at a table near the hearth, and no one looked happy. The servants had brought food but Katashan could tell it had only been nibbled.

"We have problems," Lord Fordel said as they approached. He signaled Katashan and Cork to sit beside him. "The weather has taken a turn for the worse and it's not a natural turn, either. Can you feel it?"

"Some," he said. "I didn't try for more. What can we do?"

Fordel shook his head, looking glum. "I don't know. The

magic is too transfused to pin down. Whatever is happening at the pass with those runes is finally reaching beyond the mountain top. I've had word of flooding in nearby villages, along with mudslides in the hills. I suspect things will be worse in the capital."

Katashan nodded and sat down, feeling worn, even after nearly another day of sleep.

"We have a more immediate problem," Serrano said, pushing aside a plate of food that didn't look touched at all. A shame; the roast smelled wonderful. "The rain is cutting into the city, and parts of the walls are starting to erode, despite the magic. Fordel says that the magic in the rain is actually countering the magic in the walls, which is already old and weak."

"We need to get down there and reinforce it." Katashan stood, food forgotten. Fordel rose as well as he grabbed a cane. Katashan had thought to leave him behind, but Salbay was his city more than Katashan's. Cork obviously intended to go along as well, of course. "The rest of you need not go with us. We'll bring back enough rain to share, I'm sure."

Onshara laughed. Serrano looked less certain, but finally nodded.

"You should take guards," Serrano said, and started to signal for them.

"Please, no," Fordel said, with a wave of his hand. "I don't want to make the people think I don't trust them or need to protect myself from them, just because they know about my magic."

Serrano gave an uneasy nod of understanding, even though he plainly wanted to argue. Katashan could hardly blame him, but they had to weigh all pieces in this trouble, and right now Fordel and Katashan would do better without soldiers. Neither had said the one obvious truth: with magic in such a flux right now, things could go spectacularly wrong, and having fewer people around would be safer.

Best not to worry them about that possibility when there was so much else going wrong already. If they couldn't handle this trouble, the Captain still had Aster, who as not present, though the book sat on the end of the table like an honored guest in the spot of honor.

"We'll go through the back way, and avoid a lot of the rain," Cork said. "This way, sirs."

The trip down through the halls proved quicker this time since they didn't have to backtrack to avoid any patrols. Fordel, despite limping, looked amused and pleased as Cork led them unerringly through the labyrinth building and they stayed dry until they reached the herb garden. Servants had brought inside as many of the potted plants as they could, and they had to thread their way past them. Chickens huddled in corners of the steps, none of them looking happy. Cork gave them bread as they passed, and Katashan wished he'd thought to bring some as well.

Fordel stopped to move some of the plants up a few more steps from a pool of water seeping in under the door and almost up to the first step. Katashan braced himself as he stepped down and hissed at the icy cold that swept up over his boots and soaked his feet. He knew they would face far worse when they opened the door and went out. Cork even had trouble getting the door open, and all too soon the three of them stepped into the tempest.

This was cold, wet, miserable and *dangerous*. They fought their way to the gate and out, the bell already ringing wildly in the wind. A single guard, drenched and unhappy signaled them as they left.

"He has a way to warn someone up top if there's trouble down here?" Fordel asked.

"Yes sir. There's a chain he pulls and it rings a series of bells all through the fort, it does. The chain is worked into a channel that runs through the stone itself, and the Captain has it rung once a month or so as a test. It makes enough noise to wake the dead, sir." He stopped and winced. "Though I dare say that's not really what we want these days. We only put a guard there when there's some sort of trouble."

Fordel nodded and stepped past the gate and into the city. Unfortunately, with his wounded leg, he looked likely to go sliding down the path and straight into the sea. Katashan nudged Cork in his direction. He nodded, and went to help the local lord. Fordel almost argued until he saw Katashan's face.

"All right. Fine."

"Where do we go from here?" Cork asked, looking around.

Everyone had deserted the open streets, and rivulets of water rushed over the chiseled edifices and made swift moving streams searching for a breach in the city walls through which it could rush to the sea. Katashan could see there were a few such culverts, but they were overwhelmed with the amount of water and debris already in them.

Katashan stepped out into the path and lifted his hand, feeling out the lines of magic within the stone. Much of the ancient magic had weakened and begun to fade through age and this storm drained more of it away with the water.

And he remembered, with a new shiver, that vision Verina had shown him of the city collapsing and falling into the sea. The fear of the vision being real gave him purpose and strength to do this work. He found the closest weak spots and they began the arduous job of working their way through the drenched city and finding the best places where he and Fordel could feed magic into failing lines. Though neither said so, if the storm did not pass soon, they wouldn't have the power to keep the city from crumbling away.

Now and then Katashan could see pale faces looking out from the doors and scalloped windows. Looks of worry followed them everywhere but he thought he saw signs of hope as well. The people might realize how lucky they were to have a lord versed in magic at a time like this. They lived in a city only made possible by magic and Katashan thought it probably helped them accept more than any other group might. He hoped so. Lord Fordel was putting as much power into saving their city as he could and he deserved their support.

They worked their way up past the baths and Katashan thought longingly about a nice rest in a warm pool. Then he happened to see a familiar face. He stared for a long moment at the woman standing in the shadows across the road. Only when she smiled did he realize. . . .

"Gods," Fordel whispered.

"Tell me you have *another* sister," Katashan whispered, already inching his way along the wall and looking for a way past her. "Because if you don't, she has somehow gained the power to become corporal again and even in the daylight, and that's more damned power than I want to face right now."

"It's Sherina," Fordel replied and somehow made a curse of his sister's name. She stepped forward, straight into the light. Whole. "How in the name of the gods can she do that?"

"We don't know what she's been doing the last few days," Cork said softly. "Though she had the mercenaries -- and I suspect they've served their last purpose for her now. We'll never get past her back to the fortress, sirs. Not unless you can come up with magic to stop her this time."

"She might be more vulnerable in a human form," Fordel suggested, and then he shook his head in denial. "No, she wouldn't do that to herself. Back up. We're near the temple. That's our best hope for any kind of sanctuary."

"Do you think it will stop her, then?" Cork asked, glancing dubiously towards the distant building.

"Perhaps not the building but Aster is there," Fordel said. He took a step backwards while still watching his sister with trepidation.

Katashan suspected the temple would prove as good a choice as they were going to find. He started that way, a few steps backwards at first, keeping his eyes firmly on her. When he nearly fell on a step, Cork took over the job of leading them to the temple, allowing the two mages to watch the enemy.

"She's not going to let us get that far," Fordel said, carefully watching Sherina who appeared amused.

"Unless there's no reason for her to fear us finding shelter at the temple," Katashan suggested.

"Not exactly what I wanted to hear, sir," Cork said.

"My apologies. I always err on the side of truthfulness."

"Huh." Cork gave a little laugh and paused, hands on both their arms still, and steadying them on the slick stone walkway. "The way's clear between us and the steps, but this is going to be a hard run. There are two streams, about knee-deep, converging right below the stairs, and it looks like a maelstrom of eddies. And then we have to climb the stairs, which are no easy job and worse with the rain water rushing down over the roof. I'll stay by you, Lord Fordel."

"I. . ." Fordel started to argue and then shook his head. "Thank you."

Katashan watched Sherina as she moved closer with a steady step and a look of haughty indifference at the storm since neither the wind nor the rain touched her. She moved as though the world would bow to her command and nothing mundane would affect her again.

Katashan glanced towards the sea, barely glimpsed through the windows of the building across from them. The gray began to turn to a tint of red; fire and blood.

"Sunset. I suspect she'll only get stronger in the darkness. She always has," Katashan said. Shadows already fell across the path where she stood but she glowed with a light of her own. She would have been beautiful had she not been so evil.

"We were fools," Fordel said. He drew his belt knife,

though Katashan couldn't be certain it would be any help, even if she did look solid now. "The draining of the magic through this storm was probably her work, knowing we would come to see what we could save."

"True," Katashan agreed. "But even if we had known she walked here, we still would have come out to do the work. This is what makes us different from her, Lord Fordel. We will always do what we can to help."

"And damn the odds, eh?" Fordel said.

"The odds?" Cork said, still navigating them back toward the temple. "She's only one mostly dead woman, right, sirs?"

The words won a little laughter from both of them. Katashan thought she looked startled by the sound. If nothing else, at least they could confuse her.

"We're as close as I can get you safely, without you watching your own step, sirs," Cork warned at last. His hand tightened on Katashan's arm, and then let go as he moved to help Lord Fordel.

"When you're ready, Cork," Katashan said.

"Now, then," he said.

Katashan took two more steps backwards, and then spun and rushed forward. He nearly went down when he found himself knee deep in water. Already drenched, he couldn't feel any colder, except for the mental chill that came when he glanced back and found Sherina moving towards them, gliding over the ground with no trouble at all.

"I'm clearing the way for us," Fordel said, breathless already. "Watch her!"

Katashan didn't argue. His wrist already bled from a little cut he used to form magic that helped stabilize the walls. He brought a spell to mind that he hoped would help if they needed it. He suspected they would face a long night, though, unless Aster had better answers.

He heard Fordel whisper magic of his own. Sherina's head

came up and she started forward far faster, her own hands lifted and light playing between her fingers.

The ground beneath his feet dried. He lifted his hands as well and waited a moment longer before he cast a fireball that lit up the sky like a miniature sun come into the world. The fire changed rain into fog and brightened the world all around them.

Sherina howled and retreated, ghost pale in that light though he couldn't tell if he robbed her of power or just surprised her. In the moment she fled, he turned and ran with Fordel and Cork up the stairs. Water still poured over the roof and raced down past them, cold and slick in spots. He fell to one knee but got back to his feet before Cork could help him.

They hurried past the statue, which made him shiver for another reason, to think his *friend* sat trapped there, waiting for the night. Did he see? Katashan brushed his hand against the horse's flank as he went by and thought the surface felt a little warm to the touch.

Up to the door --

Which did not open at Cork's shove or his insistent pounding. Katashan saw Sherina had gotten her nerve again and looked very angry, which wasn't a good combination.

"I can't get it open," Cork said.

Fordel was already attempting magic to force the door open, but they quickly realized it had been warded by Aster himself, and the man was far more of a master mage than either of them would be in their short lifetimes.

"Damn. Why would he ward to keep the door closed?" Fordel demanded.

"I suspect to keep her out," Katashan said, waving a hand towards Sherina. "She's likely been in there before if he had been teaching her magic. He would need extra protections."

Sherina laughed with a sound like ice in the wind. Katashan put his back firmly against the temple wall and prepared to face her. He couldn't think of anything he hadn't already tried. The only thing that might work would be to throw the knife again, and hope that in her more solid form it did greater damage this time. However, she would be ready for such a ploy, and he dared not lose the ritual blade in the midst of a battle like this.

He had only one other hope of help. As much as he hated to waste the power, he decided to try one more trick. He laid his hand against the wall, a brush of blood on the stone, and used his senses to feel his way past the ward and find Aster, who surely had to be on the inside. This wasn't easy since the ward had been made to repel magic and solid forms. He wondered how Aster could have missed them at the door and the thought lit a small fear that the man was not really a friend after all.

He found Aster in a trance, and hadn't the power to awaken him. He thought perhaps the man felt distantly aware of the trouble, but that he had been so far away himself that he couldn't slip back to this world so easily.

No help there.

When he opened his eyes, only heartbeats later, she had swept much closer, a glowing harbinger of disaster. Her laughter came in the wind again with a promise of winter cold in the warmth of a spring rain.

"Ward is all we can do," Fordel said with a worried shake of his head. "Did you find Aster?"

"Trance," Katashan replied, taking quick, deep breaths. "I think he's trying to return. Ready?"

Cork had put himself back against the door, his sword in hand, which might do some good if she got through to them. Better to keep her away and hope Aster came to their aid before their own powers gave out.

With the ritual blade in hand again, he began a spell, feeding his and Fordel's power into the ward which glowed around them, bright enough to banish shadows on all sides.

She lifted her head and slowed, but kept moving towards them.

"She thinks the ward won't stop her," Fordel said, who must know her mannerisms well. "I don't think I like that."

"She's gained some tricks," Katashan agreed, trying desperately to balance their powers and still keep track of what happened around them. Fordel had a strong reserve of power and he hoped the two of them could hold out against her.

The rain had eased and with the change he saw something that worried him for a new reason. People headed their way, probably to reach the temple. Surely they saw her, but they had probably heard about a phantom, a creature of the dark and night and Sherina had moved closer to the living again, and hovered only a hand's breadth above the ground. They had not noticed.

"I'm stepping out to warn them away," Katashan said. Cork and Fordel both grabbed at him. "Don't argue! Just hold the ward steady, Lord Fordel, because I intend to leap back in before she can get me."

"She's damned close," Cork said. "Sir."

"I have my knife. She'll be wary still." He used the ritual blade to cut a little deeper in the already scared skin at his wrist and pulled more blood magic. Fordel winced at the sight, and Katashan wondered when he had gotten so used to the blood and pain that he didn't even pause in the work anymore.

Katashan touched the side of the ward, felt the power fracture under his will, and pushed out into the cold wind and rain. "Go back!" he shouted at the people, and even added a little compulsion into the words.

Sherina had started towards them strangers, but finding Katashan free proved an irresistible lure, just as he hoped. They were tied still. He tried, again, to find what drew her to him, but the ties were lost in the magic surrounding them both, and he couldn't sort it out.

She drifted towards him, eyes bright, and a smile curling back on teeth that looked ready to bite away his soul. He held his place and tested his magic. When he lifted the blade, she stopped at last almost to the stairs.

"Be gone, Sherina. Go to hell or your master, or wherever the dead like you are given sanctuary. This world is no longer yours."

"Mine," she said quite clearly, her voice shrill. He wondered if she had sounded that way when alive. "All mine now. He has promised."

"He lied."

Her eyes flared with a little red in the depths. Did he want to make her any angrier? And did he want to talk with this thing, to try and reason with it? Even if she had been human once, she wasn't now. And by all accounts, she had never been reasonable anyway.

"Go, Sherina," he said again.

She laughed this time. "You do not have power over me."

"Oh, but I do," he said and smiled, though no friendlier than her look. "I could leave this place. I could go to an island at the end of the world, and put up a shield around me even you could not breach. And you would be trapped there with me, wouldn't you? Shall we see?"

Her eyes widened. She pulled back, afraid --

This was the break he needed. He turned and started to push back into the ward. She swept up at him, far faster than he had expected as her claw-like hands grabbed at his back. She nearly pulled him away but made a mistake and drew blood. He used that against her, sending a surge of power up through his body.

When he staggered into the safety of the little ward, he looked back to see her screaming in rage as her fingers smoked where his blood burnt her. But she was not, as far as he could tell, any weaker for it.

"She's going to focus on you now, isn't she sir?" Cork said. "That's why you told her what you did, about making her go away with you."

"Yes. Keep her focused on me." He gasped as he knelt within the ward, too weak to stand at the moment. His back felt half on fire but he waved away the help Fordel started to give. "No. Save the magic because I fear we will need it to stop her."

Fordel only drew back when Katashan used his own magic to slow the bleeding across his back. He didn't want to lose power anyway.

Sherina hovered nearby, her face livid with rage. Her pale, ice-covered hair blew back, her dress floating and twisting like something alive that wrapped around her. Was Aster any closer? Was there any hope?

The storm rose with her rage. Lightning rent the sky . . . and then came to her up-reached hand. She caught fiery light and glowed with the power, her face a baleful visage of destruction.

"Well now, that's not good," Cork decided.

And she threw the lightning at them.

Katashan shoved his hands up against the shield, willing power into it as the lightning flared, hot to the touch, blindingly bright. He blinked and when he could see again, she came close enough to put her hands on the shield just opposite his own.

He could feel her: anger, evil, pain. And power. She pushed, and even with all his power and Fordel helping, she still pressed forward with her icy fingers nearly touching his. In a moment she would reach through the shield and have him. He wasn't certain what he could do then --

Lightning came to her again, and the fire surged through him, so painful he thought he would burn up in it this time. The shield crackled, and he heard Cork gasp. He didn't look. He could feel one of her fingers on the palm of his hand, ice and fire taking his breath away.

Stop her. Stop her somehow --

She lifted her head and smiled.

And then he saw movement close by.

Nightfall!

A double image for a moment: God and horse, statue and real. Then the essence of Peralin moved away from the statue prison. Peralin reached down from his mount and grabbed Sherina by the scruff of the neck and shook her.

"No, little demonling. No, you will not have them on the steps of *my* temple. Be gone back to your master."

He threw her out towards the sky and the sea, and she disappeared into the dark so quickly Katashan suspected she had left this world. Katashan blinked and lowered his hands, unsteady as the shield disappeared. Peralin slid from the horse and caught him before he sat down on the stairs.

"It's wet out here. Let us go inside."

He was getting too used to dealing with this Godling. Katashan nodded, accepted a goblet to sip, and went with him into the building. The ward did not even slow Peralin.

They stepped into the building; a series of halls to the right and left, a large room ahead and an altar at the end. Candles flared to life all around them at the presence of the Godling in his own temple. Warmth came a heartbeat later.

Aster stumbled through the long inner hall to the right, his face white. "My apologies. I tried to draw on other powers and I couldn't break free of them. It hadn't occurred to me that the ward would be a problem. I just dared not be interrupted, or powers that should not be lose in this world --"

Katashan lifted a hand and he fell silent. "We survived. I doubt even if we had gotten inside the temple, it would have done much more good. In fact, I am rather glad we were so close to Peralin."

The Godling nodded and didn't smile this time. He signaled the others to sit at the first benches they reached. Even Cork, who had used no magic at all, looked drained. Kat wondered if he had come too close to Sherina again, who drained life. He didn't ask.

Peralin paced before them which was not a sight to calm poor humans. He ran a hand over his face, once, and then finally turned to the four.

"You do not have much time left," Peralin said. The ominous words drew all their attention. "The vernal equinox will fall at sunset tomorrow night. If the runes aren't destroyed and she is allowed to finish the spell, then the world will be changed beyond what can be fixed. You are seeing the first power of such changes in the storms. Rain, winds and even magic will sweep through the world without any control. If this trouble is not stopped, I suspect that nothing will remain standing by this time next year."

Katashan looked at him, not surprised. "We must go back to the mountain top."

Peralin nodded. "But this will not be easy."

"It never is," Cork said with a sigh.

"So true, friend," Peralin replied. He looked at Katashan, obviously expecting answers from him. "It's all about timing."

And the answer came to him, finally. "Of course. The runes and Sherina are only vulnerable in the moment the spell comes to fruition," Katashan said. "Like many spells, the weakest moment is when it transfers power from potential to reality."

Peralin bowed his head in agreement. "This is what Verina has told me. In a spell of this type, you can hinder beforehand, but you cannot destroy the core until the proper moment. Anything else only creates more havoc."

"What if we don't destroy the spell, but whatever is behind this cannot complete it either?" Fordel asked.

"Then the magic loosed runs wild, as it is now. The storms will feed each other."

"We better get back to the fortress and prepare to travel," Cork said, practical as ever. "We barely have time to get back to Silver Pass, unless you can get us there faster, sir?"

The Godling gave a little shrug. "I'll open a path, but by tomorrow the weather will be worse. You might be wise to get there as quickly as possible and be prepared."

"Then we go now," Katashan said and stood.

No one argued.

CHAPTER TWENTY-EIGHT

A s he stood at the high point of Silver Pass, Katashan thought the day felt as bitter cold as any northern winter. Storm clouds towered on both sides of the peak, some over the mountains and another set out over the sea. Katashan could feel them growing in power, ready to sweep in as soon as the spell finished the transformation.

Devastation already stood all around him. Trees had been burnt to stumps by the massive storm that had raged here the last time he had come to deal with these damned runes. And the runes, alas, looked no worse for all his trouble. He could feel their power whenever he passed within a yard of them, dark and malevolent, they drew life from an ever widening circle of ground. The snow had melted all around the area, but nothing green had grown. He suspected nothing would grow here for a long time.

The Verina statue still stood untouched, which he took to be a good sign. They needed one.

The ominous clouds began to roil across the sky like two armies poised to do battle. However, in the pass -- for the moment at least -- all remained calm. The group of mages had gained some control of the space around them in the long hours they'd spent here. Katashan had reluctantly left most of the work to Fordel and Aster. He'd rested at their insistence and ate when Cork ordered him to, knowing the battle at sunset would take every bit of power he could manage. While the others must help if they had any hope of winning, Katashan knew the fight would mostly fall to him. He had been called here by Verina, he had been the one to upset the spell, and he had the link to Sherina. He had to be ready to face her.

Unfortunately, nothing he had done so far had more than annoyed and slowed the woman. Katashan tried desperately not to doubt he would do better because he knew the feeling could cripple him. However, he couldn't help but worry. He had no new tricks and none of the old ones had worked very well so far.

They had studied the book, but Aster couldn't be certain if the magic used to help create Sherina could be safely undone now, whether he forfeited his own life or not. Katashan knew destroying her would not end the larger battle, anyway. She had become only one lose end -- a troublesome, and dangerous one -- but the larger war would be between her master and everyone who stood to protect this world.

They were pitifully few on his side.

The sun dipped lower, bleeding dull crimson light into the turbulent clouds and tinting the sea with red. His wrist hurt to see it, a reminder of what he must soon do.

Katashan lifted his hand to feel out the magic, drawing startled looks from all around. He crossed towards the runes, but he only glanced at the glowing, swirling things before he moved on to the Verina altar.

He laid his hands on the statue, and felt her warmth beneath his fingers, just as the statue of Peralin and Night had been warm to this touch last night. Did that mean she stood close to this world? He hoped so.

"Please, Lady, keep us safe here," he said in his own language. He tried to quell the fear sweeping through him along with the longing to run away . . . but he'd done that once already, and it had only brought him here. "I do not regret you have chosen me to do this work, but only make me worthy of the job. Don't let me fail again."

Katashan pulled back his hands, bowed his head and brought out the ritual blade, cutting just the tip of his finger. He put a drop of blood into her outstretched hands. He dared not sacrifice more with the battle to come and he hoped she understood.

The spot of blood disappeared into the stone. A good sign, at last.

The sun slipped lower still, rays spraying out beneath the clouds, golden and beautiful. The wind howled nearby, but here they had peace for a moment longer.

"The wards are ready to be set," Aster said, stepping up beside him. Katashan looked from one set of clouds to another. A war was about to be fought the likes of which he didn't think any human had ever witnessed before. "We've not much time now. I'm just as glad. I was never good at waiting."

"Must be hard for someone who has lived as long as you have," Katashan said.

"So true. Ready?"

He nodded. They went to the runes together. The others retreated, save for Fordel. Cork looked back at them, worried but not afraid as he moved to where Onshara and Serrano stood. With them had come a hundred troops and as many villagers because Peralin had said he couldn't tell what might come to this battle. Fordel's guards, with their own little magics, had turned up late in the afternoon and now were with the troops. They would be some little help, Katashan hoped, in protecting those without magic.

A single arc of light rested above the sea, lessening even as Katashan watched. No more time for prayers, warnings and hopes. Fordel began to set his ward, weaving the first layer of magic. Aster joined in and the ward rose around them like fine crystal and sparkling with power.

Katashan knelt over those damned runes, his ritual blade in hand and ready.

The world went a little darker. He had to begin now, even though he didn't want to draw the trouble to them and give up this seductive peace.

He slit the tender skin of his wrist and winced at the pain this time. In some ways he found that reassuring. It made him feel more human again.

"She'll come now," he warned the others.

He dropped red blood onto the runes and used his blood stained knife to cut at the magic, breaking the runes up again, even though they immediately tried to reform. He kept at the work, hacking into the symbols that tied life and death, spring and winter.

"There she is," Fordel warned. "And not alone."

He dared to look because he needed some idea of what he dealt with this time. Sherina came out of the growing darkness over the sea, a bright wraith again, and far angrier than the last time he'd seen her. The allies at her side were dark shadows with red eyes. He had heard of such things, but never seen them before. These were lesser demons from her master's world that had come to earth where they should never have had the power to reach. And behind her came a train of ghosts, willowy and howling in the wind.

The first wave of demons reached the soldiers and they fell into battle though the ghosts remained caught in the maelstrom of the storm, still powerless in the winds. They would come later, he thought. For now the soldiers and villagers faced the demons, and these things could at least die. He saw swords cut through them, and their bodies wither and shrivel to black husks. They came on, wave after wave, while his allies held their ground.

He cut at the runes again, but they reformed more quickly. He had known he couldn't destroy them -- not quite yet. He gave up the battle and stood. Fordel moved to his right, Aster to his left. They had both known her in life, and he suspected they both felt responsible for this trouble. Katashan knew the folly of such beliefs, though. Some things happened. Not their fault. Just as it had not been his fault for . . . other things that were best left forgotten at a time like this.

I will not fail again.

Sherina raced forward, alone. That was her weakness, he thought. She had a single-minded hatred he suspected had been an innate part of her personality even when alive. He used the weakness against her now.

They had made the ward as strong as they dared without draining all their own power, but he also knew the protection wouldn't hold her off for long.

"This finished at last," she said, her voice clear and sharp. The battle raged between the soldiers and her demons, but she didn't look back to see how her army fared. Katashan dared not look either. He worried about those who fought but he could not help them. If he and the two other mages didn't win against her, then no one here would survive.

She put her hands on the ward, smiling. Streaks of red power sparked at her fingertips and flickered across the surface. She wouldn't take long now. . . .

Katashan put his hand up as well, blocking her entrance for a moment longer. He looked at Aster. "She has brought her allies, but not her master."

"He wouldn't come here," Aster said.

"He wanted to make you a slave," Katashan said, knowing she heard, and no doubt her master as well. They wouldn't understand the implications. "He made you immortal, Aster, because he wanted a link to this world, a vessel through which to use his power. Sherina must have been exactly what he was looking for; a totally amoral human. He made his link to this world."

Aster nodded. Ready.

Katashan reached out of the ward and grabbed her wrist. She screamed and raged and twisted -- but he held on and found a link to something else. He tried to sever the tie, but the being at the other end grabbed tighter hold.

So he caught hold of it in turn and pulled.

He wondered if this was wise, to compel such a being to come to his reality, but he did so anyway. Under most circumstances, he wouldn't have had the power to command anything of such power whether Godling or demonling, whatever Emista might truly be. However, this one had created its own weakness by tying himself so tightly to the frail human shell of Sherina. Emista had tasted lives from this reality long ago when they still sacrificed to him and before he lost his hold. He hungered for the power it would have here because. . . .

Aster put a hand on his shoulder, linked as well, understanding the need to pull Emista to them from that place where --

Understanding came through Aster who had dealt with such beings during his long, long life.

"Hell," Aster said. "Minor being, almost powerless in his own realm."

"And as ambitious and amoral as Sherina," Katashan said, breathless, but holding on.

"Not evil on purpose. It just doesn't care. There, Katashan -- careful --"

Some *thing* cold, dark and shadowed came to his call, forming by Sherina, swirling into a human shape, though faceless.

"And now that I am here, what will you do?" Emista demanded with a voice full of echoes from somewhere else. "You cannot hope to win against me."

"Your power is limited on this world," Katashan said.

"True." The face took on a little shape. "But limited does

mean different things to different beings."

He reached forward and brushed aside the ward.

And she swept in at them.

Katashan stepped aside and Aster grabbed her arm and pulled her straight to him as he threw a ward around them. He trapped her inside the shell; an avenging ghost with an immortal mage who might just stand up to her ability to draw life from him.

Katashan turned a spell towards the second target, though the power was little more than a flare against the creature. However, Emista had never stood in human form before and the attack stunned him.

They would not have another chance.

Fordel put a hand to Katashan's shoulder, opening a conduit and allowing Katashan to take all the magic he could and shape the power in whatever way suited him.

The sun sent a final flare of fire against the sea and dropped, leaving behind the last, latent hint of day. He felt the runes swell with power and the world tremble as the air screamed with winds buffeting them on every side. Katashan sent every bit of power he could into the runes, blasting them aside from the ground, and filling in the space with enough magic that he nearly went to his knees.

But he held the runes at bay.

Emista surged towards him, running out of time if he wanted his spell to take hold. Katashan, still gasping from the last magic, brought up his knife and slashed at the creature. The move had been instinctive and wise, because it sent Emista back with a cry of pain -- and unwise because the cut both angered Emista and taught him about pain.

As Emista pulled back, Katashan saw the battle. Dead black carcasses littered the ground, but so did far too many bodies of soldiers and villagers. Serrano lay so still Katashan knew him dead. Onshara knelt beside Cork.

Gods, please. . . .

Emista swept back at him, not weakened by Katashan's attack. How could they win? Why should he fight and lose again. Better to finish this eternal struggle and give up forever. Better to be gone from this world than to suffer through the deaths of more people. He could not take this suffering into his heart again.

"No, Katashan," Fordel whispered at his ear. "Don't. Those are his thoughts, not yours."

He wasn't so certain. He looked towards Onshara and Cork, and he saw the way she slowly stood and turned to him, her face bleak and lit by the lambent magic in the air. No, he didn't want to face the loss of friends again.

"Katashan," Onshara said. He reluctantly looked into her face. "Don't fail us this time."

The words struck with a rush of agony and power. He remembered his wife, his children, all those he had failed before. He cried out and threw such magic at Emista that he looked surprised. No! *He would not fail them.*

But he was only human, and Katashan knew he was no match for a being of this power. Peralin could, perhaps, help them, but he doubted they would survive long enough for darkness to fall and bring him here.

Onshara fought once more, her sword swinging against demon creatures as tried to surround her. He had the blade in hand, but his wrist already bled and he could only bleed out so much magic from his veins. Fordel faltered, nearly losing his hold on Katashan's shoulder. Aster could not hold Sherina forever.

Help. Gods, he needed help.

Gods. . . .

Yes.

He stepped aside, losing Fordel who fell senseless to the ground. No matter. Either this worked or he failed, but not because he had given up. Another step and he put his hand on the Verina altar. The blood flowed down his hand, so much that he felt weak, and his head pounded with each heartbeat.

"Help us now, Goddess. Help us or we are all lost."

He dropped to his knees beside the kneeling Goddess, and Emista laughed as he rushed forward. Katashan had no more power to hold him back.

Light spread around him, radiant and warm. Unearthly. He hadn't expected the Goddess to come in person, but he knew she stood beside him. Her hand brushed against his head and he felt strength again.

"Goddess," he whispered, and bowed his head to her.

"You have served me well, Katashan. I never doubted the battle you fought was for good, even when you doubted you could win." Her voice sounded like a song, and birds sang around them.

Emista's faceless head swung from side-to-side, either in denial or confusion. Peralin came as well, there on Night, even in this brightness. He looked fierce this time as he faced Emista, ready for the battle.

But Katashan looked up at Verina, who brushed a hand so gentle against the side of his face like the touch of a spring breeze, filled with life and love, and everything he had thought he'd lost. "I have brought you here for a reason, Katashan. You alone could keep this trouble in check and keep them weak until now; and I can only answer to the call of a wanderer, lost in the world. I could only come in the time of true need."

"You are no more powerful here than me," Emista said, daring to move closer.

"Am I not?" she said. Katashan looked up to see her smile, and the sight warmed his heart and gave him power. "You don't understand. You never have. It's not the *control* of humans that gives power. It is their *belief* in us. They're prayers. Their wishes. And the people here very much wish for you to be gone,

Emista."

She swept her hand towards Emista and he fell back, stunned. The skies filled with lightning, and when Katashan looked up, he could see a thousand beings in the skies, swirling, moving and preparing to do battle.

Verina crossed to Emista. He tried to scramble away, but this time she caught him by the leg and flung him into the sky as easily as a child might fling a stick. Something caught hold of Emista and dragged him away while he screamed in protest. Lightning flashed and winds roared, winter and spring at battle with each other just as the others fought.

"This is my battle," Verina said. She looked around. "I wish you all well."

She leapt upward toward the clouds, like a star flying into the sky. Peralin went past Katashan, leaning down in his saddle. He reached within Aster's ward and grabbed Sherina by the hair, and galloped off into the sky, dragging her with him.

The sky screamed with the powers. Lightning too bright to watch darted through the clouds. Winds as cold as winter alternated with warm spring rains. Katashan covered his eyes, and prayed -- truly *prayed* -- for his Goddess, and hoped the others had the sense to do the same. He put his hand on the statue, but felt only stone now, cold and still.

"Give her strength," he said. "Give her mine, if it will help. Don't let her fail in this battle."

The ground shook. What few trees still stood cracked and fell and he feared they would all be swept away. How long? How --

Silence.

Still.

He feared to take his hand away from his eyes. What if they had lost? What if he had failed?

"Katashan?"

He dared to look up. Onshara stood over him, dazed and

bleeding, but real. He let his hand reach out to hers, believing . . . they had survived. The sky had nearly cleared in those few last heartbeats, the last of the clouds dissipating and the stars bright in an inky sky.

"Did we win?" Onshara asked. She looked around and shook her head. Katashan couldn't quite focus on the others, but he knew that many had died. Aster sat, stunned, on the ground nearby. Lord Fordel moved a little and went still again.

Cork sat up, alive. Praise the gods for that.

But did they win? The night felt dark and still. Cold.

"I don't know," he admitted. "I don't know who won."

She looked worried at those words and watched the sky for a sign. There were no answers there. Katashan stood slowly. He ached. He wondered if that would ever end. What could they expect? The runes were gone, at least but then they would have been even if they completed their work rather than were destroyed.

They needed to know. He hated to doubt.

He went to the statue. Cold stone again. He had hoped. . . .

"Goddess, give us a sign," he whispered. And he carefully cut his wrist, letting the blood flow down into her hands again. "Forgive us our doubts, but give us a sign."

A little whisper of warmth spread over him. The cut on his wrist healed without him doing the work and for a moment a light flashed in the sky. Birds sang around them. And the blood in her palms disappeared.

Onshara laughed.

The battle was done.

CHAPTER TWENTY-NINE

E veryone felt the loss Captain Serrano, especially at the fort. Even knowing he had sacrificed his life so that the world could be saved from evil could not mask their sadness. Katashan understood too well. He said a prayer for the dead their first night back and he hoped the soldiers and villagers who had died in the battle found a good afterlife.

Katashan had come down from Silver Pass feeling like he had stepped into the world again for the first time in many long, painful years. He had finally forgiven himself for not saving those he loved and even forgiven the Gods for not doing it for him. He accepted life again.

Lord Fordel took up residence at Salbay and the fort, partly to help with the work, but also because it was safer for him to be with the troops who trusted him. The soldiers and the townspeople had voted to stand by their unusual lord, even in the face of the King's army if he chose to send one to deal with his magic-knowing noble. It seemed unlikely there would be trouble, though. The High Priests in several cities had already sent word that they'd had ominous signs of what had happened at Silver Pass and they knew magic had saved the world.

So they lived in an uneasy truce. No one could be certain that the battle was truly done so the king would not waste a weapon like Fordel.

Peralin and Night had not returned since the battle and even that statue of the two had disappeared. Katashan suffered from that loss far more keenly than he had expected. Peralin had been an unexpected friend, as human and real as Serrano, and as much missed. He hoped -- *prayed* -- the Godling had survived the battle in the skies. He hoped that he might see him again.

Aster, still called Matish, remained as the priest of the temple. His part in the trouble had not been known by many, and even the soldiers didn't realize the full extent of his battle with Sherina. He remained a priest to them, and Onshara and her people still had the duty of guarding the book. The pages had taken on a new meaning for her as she prepared to take it back to Holding. Oh yes, and the goblet as well, of course. The villagers would protect both.

Cork, recovering from his wounds, had admitted he told Onshara to say the words that sparked Katashan to his final rush of strength. He apologized for such a ploy, but Katashan knew he'd done the right thing to play on those feelings of guilt that he'd brought with him to this new land. The words had shocked him out of his acceptance of another failure.

Fordel had hinted that Cork would be the next Captain and in charge of the Salbay Fort, which Katashan thought a good choice. He was a good man, and both respected and liked as Serrano had been.

Everyone, it seemed, had begun to find their places to settle.

Except for Katashan.

On the late afternoon, five days after the battle, he stood on the shore and let soft waves brush against his bare feet. The warmth of spring spread over him and he looked out to where the blue sea went on forever. Gulls skimmed along the water, and pelicans dove into the waves, coming away with their catches still wiggling in the huge pouches beneath their beaks. He had seen dolphins playing in the waves and he thought perhaps he'd seen a sea person as well, dancing with them.

The fishing village had begun recovering from the storms and the locals were stoic in their work of rebuilding. Ships had lost masts, but this was an excellent port to be stranded in, with good, stout trees so close at hand and workers who knew how to cut, trim and prepare the trunks. He'd also seen some of the sailors, even those from far lands, helping with the work in the village. Good people, all of them. Where would they sail, when the time came? Where would they go across that blue ocean to places so far away that he couldn't name or imagine them?

"I thought I would find you here, sir."

He hadn't heard Cork coming down the path to the ocean, even though the soldier walked with a cane while a serious leg wound healed. Cork looked battered but content. Everyone should be content, Katashan thought. They had saved the world. The future could have been much different.

"Sir?"

"Just . . . thinking."

Cork nodded. He stared out at the ocean in silence for a long moment before he looked back to Katashan again. "I am a fisherman's son, you know. I took to the sea a few times. It's a wild place, but sometimes filled with such perfect peace I couldn't imagine a better life. But, alas, one cannot stay on the ocean forever."

"Would you want to?"

"Sometimes," Cork admitted. "There's trouble on land, always trouble, isn't there?"

"No matter where I go," Katashan admitted. He watched the waves, the gulls and the pelicans. Was that the only place of peace?

"Will you be leaving us now, sir?"

And go . . . where? To what new trouble? Surely there was some place out there where he could find peace again.

Or not, because the world didn't lack peace, he did. He

knew the truth. Nonetheless, the ocean called to him, just the same. The peace Cork had found on the waves whispered to him with each brush of a wave over his feet and each cry of a gull.

So maybe he would sail to another land. What would it be like? He had heard of places where it never snowed, where people lived in perpetual sunshine, and danced upon the shore each night.

Could he fit among those people?

Cork stood beside him, silent and waiting patiently, as he had so often since Katashan arrived at Salbay.

"The ocean is wide," Katashan said at last. He kicked at the wave that brushed at his foot, like he had so long ago as a child standing on the shore of a different ocean. "I'm not ready for the journey yet, Cork. I'll stay for a while longer."

"Ah, good." Cork smiled so brightly that Katashan felt the joy, infectious and bright along with his own relief. He had found acceptance here and need not go as a stranger to some other land. Not yet. He hadn't thought the feelings of others mattered, but it did. "I'm glad you're staying, sir. And what will you do now?"

There was a question he hadn't even considered.

"I'm not certain yet," he admitted.

"Well, it may be I can help you there, sir," Cork said. "I've just come from the tavern, you see. The one that Maylee's uncle owns. He might be willing to rent you a space for that business of yours. He thinks oils and such for the baths might draw a few people in, and being so close to the baths would be good for you, too."

Katashan stared at him in shock. How could they talk about such things? Business? Trade and. . . .

And life the way it should be. Cork waited, his head tilted to the side as though judging how Katashan dealt with this offer. He had come here looking just for the opportunity Cork had given him, and now he wanted to run as though he feared to fail in business far more than he had feared failing to save the world. The people here were giving him the life he had wanted: A gift for the work he had done.

"I will need to know more about the taxes," he said. Cork grinned. "And it might be nice to know anything at all about the local coinage. Housing, too. When will Tyren be through again, do you know? I need to send an order back with him."

"Spoken like a true tradesman if you don't mind me saying so, sir," Cork said and laughed. "Shall we go talk to Maylee's uncle now? And then I'll get you back to the fortress in time for the feast."

"You are no longer charged with looking after me, you know," Katashan said, though glad for the reminder of the celebration.

"Am I not, sir? No one has told me so. That was the Captain's order, sir. And I intend to keep it."

"It may not be safe, you know," Katashan said. "There are people who might not approve of me, even still."

Cork laughed. "Gods, man -- do you think I'm going to worry about what *people* think after all we've been through? Come on now, sir. We've a long walk back."

He couldn't argue the point. He started out with Cork, each of them limping. They climbed the long stairway path to Salbay's city in the cliffs, a slow walk that Katashan found reassuring somehow. Peaceful, and pleasant: No need, finally, to rush anywhere. When they reached the top landing, he stopped and looked back at the sea just as the sun set. He didn't think he'd seen anything so beautiful with the rays of red and gold blending into the darkening sky and sea. Sea birds flew and yelled, finding their places in the rooks along the cliffs and on the stone carved buildings. Cork didn't hurry him and Katashan turned at last and stepped through the corridor between the fish and salt markets and into the city.

"Katashan, Cork."

Onshara had been on the path passing through the city, a few of her people with her. They all looked worn still, but it was a wonder to see the villagers walking through the city, at peace with the others. They had probably been to the Peralin Temple. He still couldn't bring himself to go there.

Katashan nodded his greeting and then, in the fall of dark as people lit torches at the shops, he heard the familiar sound of horse hooves, which were *never* heard here in the city. Katashan laughed and looked up as Peralin and Night came into view.

"I'm glad to see you!" Katashan said, slapping the Godling on the shoulder as he swept off of Night.

Peralin laughed. People who had started to back away in shock stayed their ground. Smiles came here and there.

"Peralin, sir, if you're back, does that mean we are in danger again?" Cork asked, casting worried glances all around.

"Rest easy, Cork. Verina has given me leave to come and go as I like from this place, as long as there are believers here. There will be trouble again, of course. Doors opened recently that are not so easily shut, but I will be here to help if anything gets out of hand. Besides Salbay, with its fine port, is a good place for the Goddess of travelers, don't you think?"

"Oh yes, sir," Cork said grinning as well. "Yes, I think we can carve her a fine temple here, along the walls. Seems the least we can do."

"And good that you already have a priest on hand, isn't it?" Peralin asked with a brighter smile.

"I want to be a merchant," Katashan protested.

Everyone laughed, but then Peralin looked a little more serious, and laid a hand on Katashan's shoulder.

"For you, though, she sends a special gift. You may ask for anything, Katashan. Ask for anything you wish returned to you. But do so carefully, my friend. Some things would change the very fabric of the world."

Katashan stared at him, fears and longing growing in his heart. He could not speak at first for fear of doing something stupid.

"If . . . If I ask for my wife and children returned, things would change, wouldn't they?" he asked softly.

"Yes. You would be removed from the events here. You would come home from slavery to find them waiting for you. You would have a very happy life with them."

"But here . . . I would not be *here*."

"No, you wouldn't. The battle would go differently. Aster might hold back the enemy for a while, but he and Fordel would lose if they didn't find other help. It is possible they would because Veriana would send another of the northern priests. Such a man would not fit in as well as you did since they all still hold anger at the old war. But you . . . you would not know about such things, my friend. These events would not touch you in your lifetime, except perhaps to hear that there was trouble in Cyrenia."

"But it would come, eventually, to my children. The world would be lost."

"It might. But *you* would never know."

He feared he knew the future that would happen if he were not here. He had seen it in a vision from the Goddess. The city fell into the sea and that meant much else gone wrong.

For one, brief moment he thought me might hold his wife and children again, but he bowed his head and said farewell to them in truth, now.

"I can't. I can't throw the world away for a few years of personal peace."

"No, we didn't think you could. So what would you have instead, Katashan?"

He didn't take long to decide.

"I would like the return of our allies lost in the battle at Silver Pass if that won't change things."

Peralin nodded. "Litte time has passed. No real disruption there. . . ."

He stepped backwards and his cloak billowed out -- wide and far with a gentle darkness that came and went. People appeared in the shadows as the cloak swept back around him. Many people stood there where they hadn't been a moment before. And a dozen children. There had been no children at the pass --

"They died at the village," Onshara whispered, sweeping two of the youngest into her arms, and holding them tightly.

"Did they?" Peralin said. "My. I guess I spread my cloak a little too far, didn't I? Well, no harm done."

No harm and great good. Katashan put a hand on the Godling's arm and nodded his thanks, thinking of other families that would be whole tonight.

Serrano stepped from the darkness of the cape and looked around, frowning and shaking his head. "I was somewhere else." He shook his head and focused on them. "I think . . . I think I need a drink," he said.

"That sounds like a damned good idea," Katashan agreed. He patted the grinning Cork on his shoulder. Then he looked at Peralin and smiled. "Thank you. Care to join us?"

"I would be honored," he said and bowed his head.

Onshara, one of the children still in her arms, stepped forward and wrapped her free arm around Katashan. "Bless you, my friend. May the Gods bless you."

And in an odd way, he thought maybe they already had.

The End

###

About the Author:

Hello!

I am an eclectic and prolific author whose has published in a number of genres, including Young Adult Mystery, Urban Fantasy, Epic Fantasy, Science Fiction and numerous works on writing. While I started on the outer edges of traditional publication with sales to small press and magazines publishers, I have since moved most of my work to the Indie world and I am madly in love with the new world of publishing and the direct contact with readers.

I live in Nebraska with my husband, my cats and a small but entirely useless dog.

I also own Forward Motion for Writers and the ezine, Vision: A Resource for Writers.

Web Site: http://lazette.net

Twitter: http://twitter.com/lazetteg

Facebook: http://www.facebook.com/lazette.gifford

Joyously Prolific Blog: http://zette.blogspot.com/

Smashwords:

http://www.smashwords.com/profile/view/LazetteG

I hope you enjoy this preview of The Servant Girl, which will soon be released in print format.

Preview: The Servant Girl

Chapter One

The fever spread from west to east, not deterred by deserts, mountain ranges, or rivers. The sickness worked its way from village to village and on to town and city . . . and left behind dead in such numbers that some areas fell into ruin with no one left to care for homes, fields or flocks.

The fever took no notice of age or wealth. Young and old died; rich and poor; peasant and noble . . . King *and* Queen.

Of the royal family of Ranas, only Princess Sondra remained and she a child of six years. The surviving members of the Council hurriedly placed both the government and the princess in the care of her mother's cousin who became Prince Regent Petrin. Petrin, a military man who never married, had no idea of how to deal with a child who wept for her lost parents.

Dark times came upon the land. The living buried the dead in mass graves and the priests locked themselves in their temples and prayed . . . and died there, alone and abandoned by man and gods. Religion ebbed with few priests and priestesses left to help the living or train the next generation.

Frightened people, searching for an answer to why the country fell under such ill-times, believed enemies struck at the ancient kingdom of Ranas with foul magic and a horrible curse.

Mages became the scapegoats of the calamity, and those few who survived the mobs left for safer havens. Though rumors persisted about magic lingering in the borderlands of the country, the art all but disappeared from the coast and the capital of Teloris, where the mages had been strongest before the plague.

The land survived the calamity. Prince Regent Petrin worked with the Council and together they kept Ranas in what order they could. He had better luck in Council Chambers than he did with the child who cried herself to sleep each night. No nurse or toy could solace her for long and the prince began to fear the last heir would not live to see the new year.

Several weeks later, and quite by accident, Petrin found the princess a companion and playmate. Returning one day from some nearby farmlands, he spotted a small girl child with a sweet face and a mop of red hair. She sat on a street corner, clutching a blanket and was obviously abandoned. The rest of Petrin's party had not caught up with him. Petrin remained more military-minded than nobility, and he had a habit of riding off without them, not being yet used to having a royal guard.

He spotted a man an old man hobbling along the street, bread tied in a rag and slung across his shoulder. He'd plainly been to the castle to get the dole. Many people continued to move in from the country, swelling the city's population again. They'd have a hard time supporting them.

"Who is this child?" he asked.

"Don't know her name," the old man replied and spat. "The mother died of the fever. She been a witch, though, so none will have her child. She's been there two days now."

The Palace Guard caught up with Prince Petrin, startling the old man who hobbled away. Petrin didn't think they'd heard what the man said about the child's mother. Superstitious old fool. The country was full of them, fearful of the magic when the power might have helped them.

The girl stared at him. He saw a good face, devoid of fear, and though she had been crying, she didn't now. Maybe . . . Maybe she could teach Princess Sondra how not to cry. The idea sounded insane and desperate in his mind, but he'd reached such a stage where he could look at a child of six or so and hope for salvation.

He slipped from the horse and walked to the girl. She stood, and for a moment he feared she might run. Instead, she gave him a very proper little bow. Well-trained child.

"Where's your family, child?" he asked.

"D-Dead," she whispered as tears formed in her eyes, though she brushed them away and sniffed.

"What's your name?"

"Elizabeth."

"Come with me, Elizabeth." He offered his hand, much as he had to Sondra the first day he'd come to care for her. "I know a place where you can stay."

She blinked and frowned. Then she gathered her blanket from the ground. "I don't want to sleep here anymore."

A good, wise child, he thought. So he took her home and introduced her to Sondra.

For the next twelve years the girls remained inseparable.

And then the world changed again.

CHAPTER TWO

"Can you see them?" Sondra asked, leaning close over the silver plate where a thin layer of water sparkled in ways which had nothing to do with the light. Blues and greens moved, coalesced and spread outward in a pattern of chaos mirroring Eliza's mood.

The image resolved this time, despite a tendril of odd magic in the air. Eliza wondered what other person, hiding magic from the rest of the city, tried to learn more about the dangers coming their way.

Eliza pulled the image up, though the vision remained thin and pale in the late afternoon light. She could see a line of men moving through the streets, weapons catching the glint of the last light of day and flashing like forbidden magic. She did not see Lord Melton, but she recognized the dreaded Onpe warriors in their black leather armor with helmets tight to their heads and faces painted in barbaric designs. Some said the Onpe, who lived in the mountains to the northeast, were not entirely human. Eliza believed the tale as she watched the invaders move through the streets of Teloris. She could see them marching in step and hear the faint whisper of the grunt they made at every fifth step, the trademark sound of their approach.

"I don't want my people to fight them," Sondra whispered, her voice unsteady.

"Do you want to give the rule over to Lord Melton?" Eliza asked, her finger trembling as the held to the vision. Gods help them if anyone realized what she did now. "You can give the rule over, you know."

"Not for another ten days. I'm not of age yet."

"A technicality." Eliza drew the vision away from the Onpe until she could see the wisps of smoke and darker smudges on the horizon which were the sign of fires in the suburbs of Teloris. Lord Melton's people moved forward, intent on reaching the castle. He wanted hold of Princess Sondra before her birthday in ten days when she would be crowned queen and the regency officially came to an end. "If you stepped aside for Lord Melton, do you think anyone would question the decision?"

"I don't like Melton," Sondra answered with a shake of her head and a glare that could quell most servants, though not Eliza. "I don't like what he's done, turning my people against each other, making us choose sides. But if they had no side to choose --"

"This isn't about sides in a game of who is more popular. This is about who will do best for Ranas," Eliza replied, though she knew Sondra knew the truth of those words. Sometimes she needed to hear them aloud though. Eliza lost the image. No matter. "Will Melton make a good king?"

"No," Sondra whispered softly, but with conviction. "We better be ready to leave."

Eliza stood and poured the water out the window, where the magic would disappear along the stonework trail of the castle's wall. They'd been careful; she, Sondra and Prince Petrin who first realized she held some ability and brought in what mages he could find to secretly train her. If the people learned of her little power they would demand her death, and everyone would believe Princess Sondra tainted as well. No one would trust either of them.

Eliza could see the hint of smoke out along the edge of the city and caught the scent of burning wood on the breeze. Below in the courtyard the palace guard prepared to take to the walls, their beige and green uniforms marking them as the elite and most trusted force in Ranas. They marched with pikes and crossbows held upward like a moving forest of men.

She pulled the shutters closed, as though the flimsy wood could somehow keep the world out, and went to the bed to gather the two satchels she'd packed. She had seen Lord Melton a few times at court: a loud, boorish man who complained of the weakness of the court and who had insulted Prince Petrin at every turn until the good man's death two years ago. Melton proclaimed his displeasure when the Council took over the Regency, especially since he wanted the position.

The Council of Lords had dispersed a few weeks ago, heading to their estates to raise an army for the battle they expected in the spring. Melton surprised them. He raised an army late in the year and swept in from the north to take the city of Teloris and the throne. He'd found allies and they now pushed through with unexpected speed and unprecedented destruction. Those tasked with watching Melton never realized he'd drawn the Onpe into the fight until the armies pressed down from the north.

Princess Sondra and Eliza would leave Teloris, though they dared not travel inland. The scouts who went beyond the city reported no safe path through the land where Lord Morten's mongrel army spread, bringing fear as they pillaged villages and encircled the royal city. The two would take ship to Farin and hope the foreign land remained faithful allies.

"Do you believe the tales about Melton?" Sondra asked softly.

"Yes."

Sondra turned to her, startled by the answer. "You do? You believe he's killed people out of hand and that he's unusually cruel --"

"Yes, all of it. The servants dealt with him before, you know. I mentioned to you how they always complained of him. He liked to slap the women and humiliate the men. His own servants disliked him. I believed what they said. We have to go, Sondra -- or else stay and fall under siege hoping others can save us. I think we would be wise to try to save ourselves."

Sondra began to answer but she spun at the sound of a shout from the courtyard. Within heartbeats they could hear the clash of sword-against-sword beyond the shuttered window. Eliza hadn't expected the trouble to reach them so quickly. The soldiers fought the battle out in the suburbs. The vision couldn't lie!

"They can't be here!" Eliza frantically grabbed the last of the clothing and shoved a dress into Sondra's satchel. She felt unexpected panic at leaving this set of rooms, which she had shared with Princess Sondra for most of her life. "They can't be here!"

Metal clanged and the shouts grew louder. Eliza shivered and reached for the satchels, but Sondra took her own this time.

Someone pounded on the door. "Quickly, Princess Sondra! We must get you away!"

Eliza grabbed her cloak and satchel and followed Sondra to the door. She stepped in front and opened it, ready for trouble. Emery and Andris, two of the personal guards who always served the princess, stood outside. Any other time, the princess wouldn't leave her suite without a half dozen guards and never traveled from the castle with less than twenty.

They'd spoken with Emery and Andris earlier, deciding to flee with as little notice as possible. They didn't delay now. The hall seemed strangely empty; other doors stood open, showing scattered debris. Eliza suspected she and Sondra should have gone before now but everyone had hoped the Ranas troops would hold back Melton and his army and still provide them with time to leave if necessary.

"What's happened?" Sondra asked as they paused to rest by a set of stairs. Andris descended to the next landing and signaled them to follow.

"Melton slipped soldiers through the crowd in the guise of locals gathering at the barbican. A group of palace guards headed out to secure the market area and they didn't realize the danger until the enemy pulled swords from beneath their cloaks and attacked. No one could get the inner gate closed fast enough." Emery shook his head in disgust. "A stupid mistake."

"I think the inner gate might have been left open on purpose," Andris replied with his voice a near growl. His eyes narrowed in anger and he moved with his hand on his sword, ready for trouble as they reached the bottom of the stairs. "I think some of the men at the gate were his, not ours. Gods grant there aren't very many more."

"Where is Melton?" Sondra asked.

"We believe he might already be within the grounds," Emery answered. A moment of panic showed in his face. "We've sent the other palace guards to deal with him and his people. We have to go, Princess Sondra. The guards are fighting to keep a path out the Seaward Gate and to keep the docks clear, but they won't be able to hold for long. The army is barely holding the Onpe at bay. If they break through there will be no chance of escape at all."

At least that explained why Eliza hadn't seen him with the Onpe troops.

They found panicked servants in the lower halls though the people made way for the four. Eliza watched familiar faces as they went past, fearing some might already side with Melton. She changed her mind realizing it was not likely since he always treated the servants like animals, and lazy stupid ones at that. No one here would welcome him.

But somewhere nearby she could hear Melton's name

shouted in greeting. Damn them, she thought.

Emery and Andris didn't slow as they led the two through the servants' halls, first at a fast walk and then a run as the sounds of battle rose somewhere behind them. Eliza gasped more from the overload of emotions than from the exertion. They stopped only to pause at the doorway to the Guard's Quarters.

"The rest of you stop anyone from coming this way," Emery ordered. No one argued despite Emery's lack of rank. The half dozen guards prepared to do their duty, even knowing the enemy already held power inside the walls.

Eliza heard the bellowing, coarse shouts of Lord Melton himself as he demanded the presence of the princess. Chaotic sounds came closer and Eliza feared they would not get away in time.

She could help.

"Take her. Go! I'll meet you in the kitchens!" Eliza pushed Sondra into the hold of the two guards. Sondra cried out with worry as Eliza rushed back through the hall.

She intended to lead Melton away. With the cloak over her head and a quick whisper of magic, Eliza could make him believe she was Sondra. She rushed through the halls, servants darting out of her way, and crossed over to the south wing, and to the galley overlooking the main hall. Men swarmed below her, soldiers shaking their weapons as though they intended to fight the figures in the paintings. In fact, she watched as they tore down some of the ancient art and trampled the portraits beneath their feet. Animals, all of them.

She found Melton there in the midst of them, shouting and cursing. Stupid man.

Eliza took several deep breaths and bowed her head. She had learned magic aimed at protecting Princess Sondra. Prince Petrin had done the best he could for her since he didn't believe in the superstitious mumbo jumbo of the ignorant. Gods, she wished he still lived to be with them today. They so badly needed the advice of someone they could trust!

She would not fail either him or Sondra. Eliza knew how to create Sondra's image to distract any would-be assassins. She sometimes tested the spell over the shape of a manikin where she could see the results and learn to improve the illusion.

This time she cast the shell over herself. She concentrated and moved her hands in a vague shaping motion as the magic swept over her, a frail shell glittering a little before her eyes but enough like the princess to fool those men below. She took a breath and stepped out to the edge of the light. People spotted her almost immediately, and some headed straight for the stairs. She didn't have much time.

"You shall never have my lands, Melton! You'll hang as a traitor before you rule Ranas!"

Her voice rang out, amplified by the high roof and louder than their shouts, silencing them all for a moment. Melton cursed but his voice was soon lost in the swell of sound as she ran away, though not towards the kitchens.

The use of magic left her breathless. For the first few steps, she kept a hand to the wall. However, fear of capture gave her strength and she soon darted out of sight. She shed the cloak, shoving it behind an open door, so if they did catch her, they would not immediately think she had pretended to be the princess.

Eliza darted through the myriad passageways; she knew the castle better than Melton or his men and she left them chasing magical shadows in the east wing before she headed to the kitchen.

The two guards raised their swords as she came to a running stop, so breathless Sondra took hold of her and kept Eliza to her feet as they moved.

"You should *never* have --" Sondra held tight to her arm, near to tears. "He would have killed you if he caught you, Eliza."

"I'm safe." She couldn't mention the magic with Emery and Andris close by. "I led him off in another direction. We have to get out of here. I fear I've rather annoyed Melton."

"You frightened me. I don't want to leave here alone!"

"You have Emery and Andris." Eliza pushed away one young servant boy while the guards ordered everyone else out of the kitchens. "Stay back!"

The servants were worried and anxious at finding the princess in their midst. Melton's men would notice their behavior, though his men might have trouble getting through the crowd. Jane, an older woman with a bun of gray hair neatly wrapped at the back of her head, took up the work of keeping the others away. They were used to listening to her, at least.

"They're frightened." Sondra reached out and patted the arm of an old woman who baked bread in the mornings. Melina wept at the touch.

"Careful, Princess," Emery warned. "We don't know who might be with Melton."

"I won't run frightened and afraid of everyone. What good would that do, Emery?" She reached out and touched the arm of another servant. "Be calm, my friends. Be brave. I have to leave, but I intend to return as soon as I can. I have allies elsewhere."

"What do you want us to do?" Melina asked softly.

"Leave the castle if you can. If not, work for him and give him no reason to mistrust and misuse you. I want you to be safe. I'm sorry I can't protect you."

"Go," one of the stable boys urged. Shouts rose somewhere too close by and Eliza caught hold of her friend's arm. "Go now, Princess Sondra. We'll wait for your return!"

The two guards herded Sandra to the kitchen door. Eliza caught the scent of food which almost made her ill. As they started into the room someone tried to take hold of Sondra's arm. Eliza didn't know him, and the servants grabbed the man and began to drag him away amid shouts of anger.

"Take him away and turn him loose!" Sondra ordered, stilling everyone's movement. Anger turned to confusion as they glanced at her. "We don't know if he is Melton's man or not. He did me no harm. Release him after I'm gone. I'd rather free an enemy than hurt a follower."

People gave reluctant nods and snarls of agreement. They would obey her. Emery nudged the princess into the kitchen. Eliza followed and Andris shut and bolted the door from the inside.

The room, normally neat enough if not always clean, looked as though a battle had been fought in the narrow area around the huge table. Crockery lay smashed and food strewn everywhere. Eliza saw blood on the wall and table, and she feared it came from humans.

The door leading to the garden stood broken on the hinges.

"They came through here," she said, shocked.

"I think so," Andris agreed. He kicked some of the debris away and crossed to the other door. He peered out, keeping his sword in hand. "They aren't here now. We can take moment to rest but no more."

Eliza leaned against the table where a half cut carrot waited with other abandoned signs of the meal which would have been theirs. She could hear shouts too close, and the clash of swords. They wouldn't be here for long

"We should take some food," Eliza suggested, wanting something to do to keep her moving and not thinking about what might happen. She glanced into the crocks and then searched the cabinets. Bread. Cheese. Things they could carry in the satchels. She feared the journey might not be as simple as they planned.

"Yes, food," Andris agreed. "Get what you can. There's no telling how far we might have to go."

"Does he already hold the docks?" Sondra asked while

packing away what Eliza handed to her.

"Not as far as we know," Emery replied. He stood by the door to the hall, plainly listening for trouble. "We have three squads of Palace Guard between him and the ships. If they are loyal men, we should reach the ship without trouble. But we've reason to worry about loyalty already tonight, Princess Sondra. Nothing is guaranteed safe and no one above suspicion."

"Except the three of you," Sondra replied. "And I am grateful."

"We'll see you out of this, Princess Sondra. We'll see you to safety," Andris promised. Eliza saw the way his fingers tightened on the sword.

"This might help." Eliza reached into a long, tall closet and pulled out grey dresses, the coarse weave making her wonder how anyone could stand to wear them. She also found tunics of beige, pants of black, all of them staff clothing, stored here for quick change since working the kitchen was such a messy job and Jane insisted on clean workers. Gods keep her safe! "If we look like four more servants, I think we'll have a better chance."

"You two, yes, but not us. Being soldiers might keep the others away," Emery said.

"But being soldiers protecting two servant girls will make the disguises rather superfluous," Sondra replied. "Either we all change or none."

"Tunics," Andris decided. "Tunics over our uniform will be enough in this light, and we can tear them off if we have to. You two get changed!"

Sondra blushed at the order, but she grabbed one of the dresses Eliza held out. Emery turned and watched the door rather than the two of them and Andris did the same. Gentlemen, both of them.

"Let me help." Eliza quickly unlaced the dress, a part of her normal job. She worked quickly, pulling the dress down along with two petticoats. Fine lace tore and she winced but kept at the work. Sondra kicked the dress away before Eliza pulled the grey dress over her head and into place. Sondra frowned as she rubbed at her arm.

"This material is awful. Remind me to replace them all. No one should have to wear clothing like this."

Eliza grabbed the discarded dress and petticoats and handed them to Andris. "Hide them," she said.

He pulled a tunic on over his green and beige uniform and then shoved the clothing Eliza gave him into a cabinet and behind some bowls. They could hear shouts in the hall and the sounds of both worry and anger as trouble grew closer.

"I don't have time to change. Give me the old cloak there. It'll do until I can change somewhere else!" Eliza ordered.

Andris tossed the cloak to Eliza as she shoved the second grey dress into her bag. She reached under her skirt -- unladylike -- and yanked down her own petticoats so her dress hung limply under the cloak. Andris took the petticoats and shoved them into another cabinet.

"We must go," Emery warned from the door. "No more time!"

Eliza pulled her cloak over her dress to hide the fine, green weave as well as over her striking red hair. They slipped out into the courtyard and kept to the shadows. Smoke filled the area and she wondered what burned so close to the castle.

Frantic chickens and geese rushed through the trampled garden, which seemed a sign to Eliza of what had happened; barbarians (no matter if they were a part of the Ranas kingdom), had come to muddy the halls and trample the herbs.

She saw the first of the dead in the corner of the garden. Eliza felt her breath catch at the sight of three men and a woman, all in dull servant clothing, lying by the chicken coop as though they died trying to defend the birds against intruders. Those deaths made everything real. The sounds of swords became not the sound of war, but the sound of death following close behind them coming for Princess Sondra and anyone who stood with her.

"I should have ordered the servants away!" Sondra said, breathless as they rushed towards the wall and the shadows. "I should have done so as soon as we realized Melton was in the castle!"

"No," Emery replied, coughing a little as they hurried on. "Many of them have nowhere to go and they were safer in the castle rather than on the streets during the battle. You can't protect them all, Princess."

Sondra glanced towards the wall and more fallen bodies. "I know." Her step faltered and slowed. "I shouldn't go. I shouldn't abandon my people!"

"Staying will win you nothing. Melton will kill you out of hand." Emery took her arm, completely beyond protocol. Princess Sondra protested but he didn't let go as they kept moving. "No, Princess. We are going to do our best to get you to the safety of the Farin ship in port. If we can get you out to sea, Melton can't win. None of us who are loyal to you want him to be able to claim the throne. If you stay, then those who fought and died for you, died for nothing."

The words sounded harsh but Eliza thought Sondra needed to hear them. She could see the reaction in the princess's face. Emery didn't let go.

Andris took the point and led them across the yard, past the second stables where horses made anxious sounds. Here they found a narrow slip of an opening between building and wall where the walkway overhead leaned out and the building leaned in. A piece of broken wood caught at Eliza's cloak, and she frantically jerked it free, scraping her elbow on the rough stone wall. She feared slowing the others. The crass, loud sounds of the battle became muted, but no less frightening, as they skimmed along between wooden and stone walls.

The narrow path led them to a small postern gate hidden by

stable walls. Andris grabbed the bolt of the gate and pulled upward.

"This way," Emery whispered. They went into darkness and Emery closed and bolted the door behind them.

Eliza could hear the sound of battle as an eerie echo through the passage as they went farther into the dark, pressing against the damp walls. The men remained silent, and Eliza found Sondra's hand and held tightly, feeling both childish and grateful. The darkness gave way, finally, to a small slit of light. She could already hear more people yelling. Eliza didn't want to go out where they would find more war and death -- but they couldn't stay here. Melton's men would come, hunting for strays. *Hunting for them.*

They hadn't far to go. The passage ended in another door, sealed shut from within, which would open to the side of the Seward Gate. No barbican protected this gate, though there used to be high defensive walls all the way to the docks. They'd long since been razed. She and her companions would be out of the security of the castle in a few steps.

They had no protection inside, though, with Lord Melton already holding the castle.

"If you can't get to the port, head for the Westgate," Emery said. He sounded worried as he stared out the slit in the wall. "My uncle holds the gate and he'll watch for Princess Sondra. Staying in the city would not be wise."

A stray curl of Sondra's hair came free and Eliza started to reach fix it . . . but no. The slightly messy hair helped disguise Sondra in the role of a servant. The gray dress made her look drab, the girl who always dressed in bright colors and jewels. Eliza didn't think this right, to see Princess Sondra leave the castle like a pauper.

Better than to see her dead.

Andris and Emery fought the door open. A dead man rolled away, his eyes white and his face ashen grey. Blood covered his uniform and severed his arm fell away from the body. Eliza turned away, sick at the sight. She had talked to Brighton yesterday.

They discovered more bodies of soldiers outside the wall, and soon found the battle as well. Dozens of men fought amid cries of pain and fear. The princess's palace guard wore green and beige but Melton's men dressed in motley colors making it impossible to tell the enemy from the townspeople until they attacked.

"Treacherous cowards!" Eliza said with a hiss of anger. "Just like their master."

Andris and Emery moved them along the edge of the battle, frantic to get her away. "We put the guard here to escort you to the port, Princess. They aren't going to be able to help."

"We have to get clear." Emery waved his sword to the right. "Now, while they're still engaged."

Andris agreed and neither gave Princess Sondra a choice. While Andris took the lead, Emery came behind and twice fought Melton's men. The rest of the palace guard, seeing the four, redoubled their attack, and in the chaos they rushed past, along with other servants who took advantage of the path cleared to get away.

Emery and Andris stayed close to the princess, but the borrowed tunics helped and they didn't draw the enemy to them. Eliza could see the port past warehouses, taverns and wharfs. One ship already headed out to sea, the wise Captain clearing out with the battle so close. She could see the masts of four others and wondered which one offered sanctuary, already bought and paid for and with guards aboard to make certain of the safety. They need only reach the ship.

She held tight to Princess Sondra's hand as they rushed past doors broken, dead and wounded strewn about the streets. She could hear screams and taste smoke. Red flames erupted somewhere to the left; she measured the distance, placing the fire in the market square.

Sondra remained silent, though tears tracked through the dust of her usually immaculate face. Eliza realized she wept as well without noticing. She wept for a world changed and life gone that she feared would never return.

They found themselves in the press of a crowd a few yards beyond the castle. She didn't trust them since any of these strangers might be Melton's people. No one could tell the difference.

People looted the buildings near the wharfs. Emery and Andris both cursed -- something she doubted either had ever done in the presence of the princess before. A fire burned in a building along their path and the soldiers changed direction, herding the two off to the right instead of straight in. Eliza wanted to protest because the fire hadn't been close.

They weren't retreating from the fire. A line of thirty or more Onpe stood watch at the edge of the docks.

"They got here ahead of us!" Emery gasped for breath, leaning against a wall and keeping himself between panicked people and the princess. "I feared as much. And we haven't the palace guard to engage them. I don't think Andris and I can fight our way through, Princess. We'll have to go for the gate instead."

They had stopped for the first time since they left the safety of the castle walls. Sondra gasped for breath and coughed. Andris leaned down with hands on his knees, coughing and gasping. Emery kept the watch with a frantic turn of his head at any sound. Eliza stared towards the ships and the best safety they would find. Going through the city would be far too dangerous!

Nowhere was safe.

Unexpected help came. A band of the palace guard rushed past them and attacked the Onpe. The first line stopped, lifted crossbows and fired, downing several of the barbarians. The rest of the guard raced forward, shouting and with their swords swinging.

"Go!" Emery shouted. Eliza caught her friend's arm as they ran straight towards the battle. This couldn't be safe!

They kept close to the buildings at first, darting past people who were trying to flee the other direction, knowing the ships provided no refuge for them. She feared someone would recognize the princess and call out to her, either in hope or betrayal. The smoke here, though, stung everyone's eyes and she doubted the people running took notice of anything but the need to escape.

Eliza saw more men killed, her heart pounding at every deadly swing of a sword. Melton had come like a new plague visited on Ranas, willingly decimating the land. His evil brought death everywhere he passed and the people would suffer for his pride and greed.

The Palace Guard fought hard, pushing the Onpe back but a shout of dismay rose before the princess had reached the edge of warehouses. More of Melton's Onpe arrived at a run, their swords ready and their grunts sounding like muted thunder. The Palace Guard, already having fought one battle by the walls, had lost too many of their men. Eliza knew they couldn't hold out.

Sondra grabbed hold of Andris, pulling him back. "We'll never get through! We must try the other way!"

People clogged the passage behind them and she feared more Onpe were in that direction. When the Palace Guard raced to the docks, the Onpe knew the princess couldn't be far away. The attack might not have been wise, but they were brave, and gave the princess her best hope of escape. Eliza knew her friend wouldn't get clear of the port area unless something drastic changed the situation.

She knew what needed done.

Sondra would never agree. Eliza, frantic with worry, tried to find a way to say the things she should have said years ago. Eliza knew the gods had blessed her when Prince Regent Petrin took her from the streets instead of taking in one of the many noble children orphaned by the fever. She had lived the life of a noble, the companion to a princess when some Lord's daughter might have displaced her. Nobles made the suggestion often enough saying Eliza's lack of high birth diminished Sondra in some way.

But Sondra would not give her up.

And would not now.

Eliza pulled her into a hug, holding her tight. "You must be brave," she whispered. Her voice trembled. "You must do what is best for the land. Melton is an evil man. We can't let him win."

"I don't know what I can do," Sondra whispered, so softly Andris and Emery would not have heard. "I don't know how --"

"You know what you need to do. You must leave here." Eliza pulled away and looked into Sondra's face. "You must be strong."

"Eliza --"

Eliza pushed the princess into the arms of the guards, startling Andris as he caught Sondra before she fell. Eliza stripped off her cloak, tossing it to the ground. She still wore her fancier court dress, though torn and filthy now. She hooked the satchel with the Royal Emblem on her arm.

Sondra tried to reach for her. She took another step away.

And then she did something she once promised Prince Petrin she would never do except in dire need: Eliza called upon her magic out in the open and where anyone might see. She hoped no one but her companions would notice, though. She trusted Andris and Emery.

She bowed her head and lifted her hands. She'd already called on her powers twice today. Eliza feared she would pass out from the attempt as she moved her hands and cast the image of Sondra over herself.

Both the guards gasped in surprise.

"Eliza," Emery whispered.

"I'll lead them away. Get her to the ship." She tried not to gasp and sway, feeling as though she hadn't the strength left to breathe. She saw Sondra through the slight haze of magic, her friend's face white with fear. "Be safe. I'll meet you when -- and where -- I can."

"No!" Sondra cried as Eliza spun and ran, heading along the edge of the building and away from the Onpe and the crowd, though not towards anywhere safer. She stayed in sight, and she thought perhaps some of others already spotted her as yells rose in different places. She didn't slow, holding tight to the magic. She gasped as she moved, tripping over an outstretched arm, blood dark on the stones. If she'd been a weaker person the sight would have sent her fleeing to Princess Sondra and the only safety she'd always known.

Eliza heard someone behind her and whirled to find Emery following close as he tore off his borrowed tunic.

"She needs you!" Eliza protested but still turned and rushed onward. "She needs protection!"

"She needs to reach the ship," Emery corrected. He put a hand on his sword. "If you are going to play at being her, a guard makes the ploy look realistic. It's decided. You can't order me. Let's go."

Eliza didn't argue. She felt safer with Emery at her side, though she feared neither of them would survive. Eliza shivered at the thought, but kept control. She put her hand to her chest where it felt as though her heart would burst. She tried to remember the words of Old Ustlin, a mage who taught her for several years, but died before she turned fourteen.

Breathe slowly. Breathe carefully. Hold the spell in your mind. Don't let the world outside intrude.

Damned hard to do with the battle around her, but his words helped. She used them to try and block out all the other sounds and to concentrate on both moving and keeping the spell in place. She didn't stop. She rushed past others, and she thought Emery shouted and got many of them to move. She found a path leading from palace to port. There, in a little space of calm in the midst of chaos, she stopped, caught her breath, and prepared to move on.

She gave Emery a glance. He drew his sword and gave her a daring, wild smile, which seemed odd for the guard who usually walked the princess about the gardens or stood in his place of honor beside the throne.

They ran *towards* the battle, pretending they hoped to reach the ships. Eliza shouted to let them through, mimicking Sondra's tones as best she could. Emery shouted as well, his voice louder, and the green and beige of the palace guard uniform did more than her feeble words.

They drew attention. Melton's people tried to capture her but some of the Palace Guard raced forward to keep her safe. Eliza felt guilty to put them in such danger for *her*. Then, at the far edge of her sight, she saw Andris pulling the princess towards the wharf with a number of other people moving in around them. The plan, thank the gods, might work.

She stopped, finally, with the Onpe no more than a dozen yards away and the battle in full force. Someone reached for her, but she kicked hard and someone else took hold of the man. She wanted a knife at least since she knew how to protect herself and Princess Sondra.

The battle grew fiercer. She almost lost the magic once more. She wouldn't be able to do this for much longer, so they needed to get clear of this area before she lost control.

"We can't get through to the ship!" Eliza shouted, as loud as she could, her voice trembling. "We can't get through! To the city!"

She spun, Emery at her back, and ran towards the castle once more.

There, in the paths between the buildings, she lost the

magic and fell to her knees. Emery grabbed her by the arm and pulled her to her feet, keeping her moving. Everything went black around the edges of her sight, and she feared she couldn't breathe.

The battle moved with her, soldiers of both sides surging around the edge of the warehouses, swords and daggers slashing everywhere. She thought the Palace Guard realized the ruse but they fought no less fiercely.

The rows of buildings narrowed the field of battle and people inadvertently blocked the way. She thought they would fail when Melton's men shouted and she saw more soldiers joining them. Two broke through, and Emery killed one, but the other came close enough to cut her arm before another of the guard killed him.

"Don't slow, Eliza," the second guard warned, confirming they knew her true identity. "Go. We need to lead them away from the port before Melton gives any orders to stay!"

She held her bleeding arm, the satchel tight in cold fingers as warm blood dripped across them. Emery chose the path and she followed. He pushed past people and brought her into the open which she thought would not be good.

"Go!" Emery shouted and caught her by the arm, moving so she hadn't time to catch her breath.

She saw the rest of the Palace Guard holding the narrow defile between buildings so the Onpe couldn't break through. She suspected they'd lured the enemy into such a position on purpose.

She couldn't see the ships and didn't know if Sondra reached safety or not. Eliza needed to convince Melton and his men that the princess fled through the city. She almost drew on her magic to be Princess Sondra, but she needed to save what little power she had left for the best time and the best audience.

Smoke hung like a foul fog over the streets, so she could hardly see or breathe. She and Emery ran towards the market, but chaos ruled here, and people ran in every direction. She saw more of Melton's soldiers, this time in their brown and grey uniforms. Emery lead her into an alley, a little mment of rest.

"Go to Sondra," she whispered. "She needs you!"

"I'd only draw attention if I headed to the ship. And this is a good ploy, Eliza. I think you and your magic saved her." He frowned but she didn't think because of the magic. "I'll go with you. We need to reach the gate and make Melton think Sondra has taken to the country, rather than the ship. He has a long reach, Lord Melton. Let him concentrate on inland Ranas and not elsewhere."

He took the satchel from her hand and started on. They found another fire in the next block and she cringed from the sight of burnt bodies and a crying woman, her hands blistered and red. She could do nothing. Emery kept her going when she thought she would be ill.

He shouted and people moved out of the way in haste. She kept her head bowed, and with the smoke and soot, they might mistake her for Princess Sondra, even without the magic, as long as Emery in his Palace Guard uniform stayed close. She didn't look into their faces and told herself it was only because of the charade.

Despite having walked these streets, she didn't know this place. In the course of a day, everything had changed. She'd heard others talk of war and civil war, and how such fights changed a land but they'd only been words until now. Eliza never realized they meant things irrevocably lost until she saw the bodies and heard the cries of children --

"Eliza," Emery whispered and put an arm around her shoulder, trying to comfort her. "Come on now. We can't stay here."

"It's all gone," she said and waved to the world around them. "It's all gone and we'll never have it back."

He glanced around. She expected platitudes, but instead she

saw the bleakness in his eyes. She wondered about his family and if he feared for them.

"We can't have it back," he agreed. The words cut like a knife but she accepted the truth. "Even so, we can't let him win. Everything will get worse if he wins."

"She'll be on the ship by now," Eliza whispered. She couldn't see the port from here.

"Probably," he agreed. "Andris couldn't just rush her to the ship and shove her aboard. Someone would have noticed. We kept a row boat ready, undercover by the quay. They could slip undetected alongside the larger ships with the help of the crews and the soldiers on the shore. However the ship can't sail immediately and it would better if no one suspects she's aboard. Ships are vulnerable."

"She'll be safe with the Farin, won't she?" Eliza asked, moving though her legs felt wooden.

"Safer than here."

She pressed forward through the panicked people. Seeing a fine, blue wool shawl discarded on the ground drew tears. She grabbed the cloth, and covered her head and red hair.

Emery nodded, as though she did something wise. They would not fail the princess.

The Servant Girl will be available in a trade paperback print edition in autumn of 2015. Thank you for reading!

If you have any questions or comments you can reach me at zette@lazette.net